# LOYALTIES

# LOYALTIES

RAYMOND WILLIAMS

Chatto & Windus

LONDON

Published in 1985 by
Chatto & Windus Ltd
40 William IV Street
London WC2N 4DF

British Library Cataloguing in Publication Data

Williams, Raymond
    Loyalties.
    I. Title
    823'.914[F]    PR6073.I432/

    ISBN 0-7011-2843-7

Typeset by Rowland Phototypesetting Ltd
Bury St Edmunds, Suffolk
Printed in Great Britain by
Redwood Burn Ltd
Trowbridge, Wiltshire

# CONTENTS

❧ ✿❀❀ ❧

## LAST

The characters of *Loyalties* are fictional and are not based on any particular individuals. Any coincidence of name or situation is unintended.

Acknowledgements are made for historical information to *The Fed* by Hywel Francis and David Smith, Lawrence and Wishart, London 1980; *English Captain* by Tom Wintringham, Faber and Faber, London 1939; *Crusade in Spain* by Jason Gurney, Faber and Faber, London 1974. Development and interpretation of this information is by the present author.

# FIRST

'Merritt, did they say? Any relation to Alec Merritt?'

'He's my father. I don't see him. They split when I was a child.'

Allicon looked again at Jon Merritt, who had found his way, rather late, through the labyrinth of the television centre. There had been no apology. The voice was assured but unchallenging, the expression neutral. A fall of pale, dry hair partly covered the gold upper rims of the large spectacles.

'Yet I had a clear impression you were something to do with Phil Whitlow.'

'He married my mother.'

Allicon frowned. His large, thick-fingered left hand moved restlessly downwards over his fringe of thinning grey hair. The eyebrows beneath it were still a thick dark brown.

'That explains it,' he said, raising his voice. 'You're a prodigy as we spell it in this place: *protégé*. But still wholly on merit.'

Jon waited. It is possible to ignore brittleness, when it has become conventional. In fourteen months, first of training and then in his early assignments as a researcher, he had learned the manner of the place: a self-conscious, competitive, metropolitan exchange. He had even been prepared for Allicon by the man who had been in charge of his training: 'Jock Allicon? Yes. One of our most eminent directors. An avant-garde figure. A latter-day avant-garde figure.'

3

'You don't object to puns on your name?' Allicon asked, steadily.

'Only when it's assumed they're original.'

Allicon scratched his stomach, where his shirt had parted just above the waistband. The marks of the scratching showed on the folds of pallid flesh.

'Right. Then may I call you Jon? Actually I worked a lot with your father. Back in the old days, when we were all young and outspoken.'

'I remember watching some of it.'

'I'd be glad, for that matter, to use him again.'

'I expect you still could.'

Allicon laughed. He looked across the crowded office to the woman working at the side desk. She had been taking no notice of them. Her dark head was bent over a spread of still photographs and transparencies which she was examining and sorting into three large wire trays.

'Petra,' Allicon said, with a sharp jerk of his head.

She looked up, startled. Her sallow face, with large, dark-brown eyes, was blank as she stared at them.

'Our new researcher, Jon Merritt,' Allicon said, insistently.

'Hullo,' she said to Jon, and went back to her work.

Allicon spread his large hands, palms down, on his desk. He pressed down, experimentally, as if testing his resilience. Then he got up, taking charge.

'Jon, then, comrade-in-arms, do you really want to work with me?'

'Sure.'

'Meaning you go wherever the wee buggers send you?'

'I'll work.'

'Though we still can't get past the fact of Phil Whitlow. To be a controller is exactly what it says.'

'He's a controller of *programmes*.'

'Yes. Do you see much of him?'

'Very little, in fact. My mother comes to see me when she's left on her own.'

'Not exactly a second father, then?'

'Not a father at all.'

Allicon smiled and came round the desk. He put his hand on

Jon's arm. He was a head shorter than the tall, fresh-faced younger man.

'*Grains*,' he said. 'Petra will fill you in.'

He walked to the door, opened it quietly and went out.

Jon waited. Petra went on with her work. He watched as she held a transparency up to the light. He waited until she had decided on a tray.

'Shall I come back later perhaps?'

'Oh! I'm sorry. I just think I shall never get through these.'

'What are they?'

'They're possible visuals for *Grain Two*.'

'It's odd to hear a programme described like that.'

She looked at him, worried.

'It's the sort of shorthand we get into.'

'But I thought the general title was *Against the Grain*.'

'It is. I expect you've seen all the paperwork.'

'They gave me, they said, what bits there were.'

'It's because they don't understand creative people. They've no idea of the real work.'

Jon sat on the edge of the desk. When Petra glanced at him, nervously, he smiled.

'Have you done other jobs as a researcher?' she asked.

'Only fill-ins really. I was surprised to be selected for this.'

'Well, Jock was determined to get you.'

'I can't think why.'

'He always knows what he's doing. People complain about him, but that's because he knows exactly what he wants. He sees things, deep things, that nobody else would have thought of. And then just because he's always having to fight the controller—'

'On this project too?'

'At the beginning, yes. But in the end it got through. You saw the papers: three programmes, with the series title *Against the Grain*. The first in effect done: just some dubbing. The second fairly well on, though still these last visuals. The third, well, that's what you've been brought in for.'

'At a research stage still?'

'No, not the main part. But there's this one new thing.'

Jon waited, but Petra was unwilling to go further. He saw her glance across at a box file on Allicon's desk.

'The general idea's still the same, I suppose. Three programmes, on different kinds of British dissidents?'

'Yes,' Petra said, and seemed suddenly relieved. 'What Jock calls quirky individuals.'

'I keep hearing that phrase.'

'Do you? It could mean a lot of things but with Jock it's very clear. In fact I think only he could do it as it needs to be done.'

'Yes, I know his reputation.'

'It's well deserved.'

'My only doubt . . .'

'Yes?' Petra's question was more challenging than inviting.

'Well, I know I'm new to this kind of work,' Jon said, 'but there's still an essential difference between dissidents and quirky individuals.'

'Right. Though in practice they are usually both.'

'It isn't that. It's how the emphasis is going to come through. The three programmes, after all, cover such very different kinds of people.'

'Tell me,' Petra said, her eyes moving back to her desk.

'Well, the first,' Jon said, 'the upper-class radicals – Burdett, Hyndman, Beatrice Webb, Cripps and so on. None of them seem to me quirky at all. Individuals, yes, but mainly with different principles, different ideas of society.'

'You should see the stuff we have on Hyndman.'

'Okay. That happens. But as I said, it's a question of emphasis. If the dissent is only a quirkiness, everything important is devalued.'

'I don't agree,' Petra said, briskly.

'I mean,' Jon said, getting off the desk, 'that it would be gutter stuff to reduce political opposition to personal eccentricities.'

'This is no gutter stuff.'

'All right. It depends how it's done. The risk is as big, if not so obvious, with the second programme, about the sexual radicals. I mean, looking at your list, they seem to range from straight libertines through various deviants to mainline sexual reformers.'

'Of course. Because we're covering the ground.'

'The Hellfire Club, Byron, Oscar Wilde, Marie Stopes?'

'And others. That's been the problem. We have far too much to get in.'

Jon smiled and turned away.

'It's not the selection or the editing I'm asking about. I know too little of all that. What I am asking about is interpretation.'

'Shouldn't that be left to the viewers?'

'No, that's what worries me. That it won't be. Because if these are only random individuals, the issues that drove them will just be pegs for their oddities.'

Petra buttoned her jacket.

'What you're forgetting, Jon, is that first and last this has to work on television.'

'No. Not necessarily.'

'This isn't a course of university lectures. It's for an audience we hope to get interested in some very remarkable people.'

'Yes, but remarkable, most of them, for what they thought and did. Not as spectacle, but as seriously alternative kinds of people and kinds of life.'

'Well, that, of course, that's been Jock's whole point.'

'Then there's a serious question about the third programme. The espionage.'

'Yes,' Petra said, and then added quickly: 'Can I get you a coffee?'

'No, thanks.'

She got up from her desk. She looked towards the door, as if Jock Allicon could be made to reappear.

'It's still the most undecided,' she said, eventually.

'Is it? But you've listed all the obvious names. Cambridge in the Thirties and so on.'

'Right. That's the core of the material.'

'As quirky individuals?'

'Well, my God, haven't you . . . ? Surely everybody has read what kind of . . .'

'There are several variations, actually, but that isn't my point. When you get to that kind of thing you've gone some way past breaking the minor conventions, or even breaking the ordinary laws.'

'Of course. But then Sir Francis Burdett was put in the Tower, as a radical. Most of the sexual reformers were prosecuted. Legality won't do as a way of distinguishing them.'

'All right. That case could be put. It's what I was saying earlier: not the quirkiness but the principles; the alternative kinds of life.'

The door opened. Allicon walked in, easily. As he passed Jon there was a sharp smell of brandy.

'Petra filled you in?' he said, settling at his desk.

'She's been very helpful, thank you.'

Petra went quickly back to her work.

'Any questions?' Allicon asked.

'We'd just got on to the espionage,' Jon said, carefully.

'Ah! *Grain Three*.'

'I was trying to say that it's a different kind of dissent, if indeed that's the word for it at all.'

'Of course it's different. It's a different programme.'

'No, but under the same title. *Against the Grain*. And that seemed to me to raise—'

'It's *Three* I want you to work on, Jon. You did say you'd work?'

'Of course.'

'Spies,' Allicon said, 'we wear with a difference. And it's for just that reason I see *Three* as the challenge. Political radicals, okay, but the streets are full of them. Sexual radicals, well they're interesting, but in a way now who isn't?'

Reaching for a photograph, Petra spilled an unsorted stack from her desk. Jon got up to help her retrieve it but she turned her back and prevented him.

'Whereas spies . . .' Allicon said, and lingered on the word.

'They've become an obsession,' Jon said.

'Right! The Sunday papers and so on. We can't help that. But it occurred to me, you know: old spies are dead. Dead and boring. Who cares who leaked the wheel?'

'Isn't it only the old spies . . . ?'

'That we know about? Ha! That's the difference, you see, about old radicals and sexuals. They're our predecessors, we're their inheritors. People queue up to remember them, even to identify with them.'

'Not seriously. How can they?'

'It happens often enough. But still the spies were pretty insoluble. Weren't they, Petra?'

Petra looked up but did not speak.

'By definition,' Allicon continued, 'the only spies we knew about were the old gang. Quirky they might be, but we all already knew.'

'So?'

'You've met Tommy Meurig?'

'No. I've heard the name.'

'He was doing your job. He knows a lot about radical politics. But they pulled him out, to help with some programme on terrorism. Still, before he went he'd come up with a lead.'

'To new espionage?'

Allicon smiled.

'We mustn't jump to conclusions. The trouble with the stuff Tommy got is that it's extremely technical. And it's still short on names.'

'We can't possibly touch that,' Jon said, coldly.

'Can't we? Why not?'

'In a television programme?'

'Ah! Television! I can hear that élitist downward inflection. Televisivisivisivi—'

'No,' Jon said, 'not television as such. But in the kind of programme you're making.'

'Jon, I don't make kinds of programmes. I make my own programmes.'

'All right, but are you saying—?'

'You'll know what I'm saying if you'll listen for a minute.'

'I'm sorry.'

Allicon pulled at his shirt again.

'It's a long shot. A very long shot. If it doesn't come off we've still got the old gang. But reading Tommy's stuff I just saw this possibility. Of some real break. Something new and extraordinary. Even if not fully established.'

'If it weren't established you couldn't dare to put it out.'

'It would get people watching. Some with more than their usual interest.'

'And you want me to work on it?'

'Jon, you said you would work. And besides, it so happens –

well, not so happens, it took me a lot of asking around – you're precisely qualified for it.'

'In what way?'

'You understand computer maths. I saw your degree in your file.'

'I know a bit of it, yes.'

Allicon laughed. He interweaved his thick fingers.

'Abandon modesty, all ye who enter here. Because in any case to know a bit is to know more than the rest of us. It's the only test, you see, to know whether it will come to anything. Tommy's dossier is here on the desk. It's a prima facie case that from wartime on there was substantial espionage, in Britain, on computer design and encoding. Espionage here, by British scientists. The file actually includes a name.'

Jon looked away. He thought for some time.

'In a television office?' he asked, eventually. 'Is that really where it should be?'

'You're thinking of what we politely call the authorities?'

'Yes. Of course.'

'What they know they're not telling. Tommy tried. But are you then saying that we should leave it? That we should do nothing about it?'

'I don't see what we can do.'

'You can read the file for a start. Tommy was honest about that; the technical stuff was beyond him. So you can read the file, assess the probabilities and if so there's a man you can see.'

Jon was silent again. As he looked around he saw that Petra had stopped work and was watching him.

'It would never fit into this kind of programme,' he said.

'I'll judge that. But if it's there and if it won't, we can still take it on its own.'

Jon got up and walked to the window. The office was below ground level. A metre from the window there was a grey brick retaining wall. He stared, half-seeing, at the dusty moss and the loosening mortar.

'I'll read the papers, of course,' he said, finally.

'Right.'

'But as for seeing this man—'

'Monk Pitter,' Allicon said. 'He's some sort of genius. A

computer genius. English originally, though he has an office in
New York now. Monk Pitter Futures Inc. He's a rich man. He
still keeps an apartment in London. He comes here quite often.'

'And this is your possible spy?'

'In the Fifties he was thrown out of his university in the States.
He was established as a communist.'

'A quirky individual,' Jon said, sharply.

He hesitated, and then walked back round the desk. He stood
undecided.

'Well?' Allicon asked impatiently. 'Because Petra and I have
work.'

Jon took a deep breath.

'As I said, I'll read the papers. I'll try to come to an opinion.
But I want to say now . . .'

'Yes?'

Allicon was stroking his grey fringe again. His plump face
was harsh.

'That I'm reserving my position. That if it gets into areas I'm
not prepared to handle, on this sort of basis . . .'

'I know, Jon. You'll cut and run.'

'Neither necessarily. But I shall have a lot of questions and
will want a lot of answers, before I do anything more.'

'Questions and answers are what we pay you for.'

'We?'

'All right. The wee buggers upstairs. But also, in this case,
from my budget, me.'

Jon pushed back his hair.

'So long as we know where we stand.'

Allicon looked across at Petra, then curiously back to Jon.

'Your father Alec wasn't afraid of asking questions.'

'Sure.'

'And Phil Whitlow, your stepfather, is never afraid of giving
answers.'

Jon smiled. He looked down at the file.

'I wasn't thinking about them. I was trying to think about the
issues.'

'No issues before facts.'

'You think so? I'm trying to understand what facts would be
an issue. Not just as exposure, I mean.'

'That's all I'm asking.'

'Is it?'

'Yes. And by the way, for the record, Phil Whitlow hasn't seen this stuff yet.'

'Though you imply he controls us. Controls us all.'

'I don't imply he controls us. I'm telling you he controls us. But the point is, these are still early days.'

'You mean you don't want him told.'

Allicon laughed, loudly. He pressed on his hands, got up and came round the desk.

'Yes, your loyalty's here, for the moment.'

'Is that how loyalty works?'

Allicon laughed again. He picked up the box file and put it into Jon's hands.

'You could be good, Jon, comrade-in-arms. Now take this pretty thread and see where it leads you.'

# ONE

1936–37

# 1

❦ ✿❀❀ ❧

## PENTWYN, AUGUST 1936

'There they are,' Georgi said, pointing.

Emma looked down at the bend in the mountain road, where the old blue bus was climbing slowly towards the farm. She and Georgi had climbed to the ridge after breakfast, while Monkey and Norman went down to Danycapel with the bus. They were lying, now, at the very edge of the scarp.

'Like a military observation post,' Georgi said.

'I suppose it is in a way.'

'This would be very good country for guerrilla fighting.'

'Yes. Though all our battles have been in cities.'

'It will spread.'

The bus slowed, at a precipitous bend. There was a puff of black exhaust smoke as the gear was changed. Emma relaxed, looking quietly down at the steep Welsh valley. The August bracken was thick and green on its slopes. The yellow gorse was still in flower, and there were scattered thorns and rowans, each isolated tree casting its shadow. Deeply cut watercourses had lichened stones and boulders at their edges. Sheep were grazing along the paths of fine grass. It was all open, bare country, but over the shoulder of the hill on the other side of the valley, along which the bus was crawling, there was a cloud of dark smoky air, from Danycapel village and the pits.

What Georgi said about fighting reminded Emma of Vienna, just thirty months ago. She had been staying with her parents in the magnificent British Embassy: living, as her brother Norman had said, like a surviving English branch of the Habsburgs. Recovering from a broken engagement, she had needed that kind of security, but it had been only a few weeks after Norman's visit, in his Christmas vacation, that Dollfuss and the Heimwehr had attacked and crushed the workers and their party.

Within the Embassy the word had been clear: avoid any entanglements; let the dust settle. But over Christmas, at parties, she had met some of Norman's Cambridge friends; Vienna, it seemed, was one of their favourite places. Through Monkey Pitter, his fellow mathematician and closest friend, Norman knew people who reached to the edges of what was already, in spirit, an underground. She had even briefly met Georgi, then a mysterious figure, half-English, half-German, who lived in the block of workers' flats that was eventually shelled. He was said to be some kind of self-defence organiser, and was treated by all the younger men with great deference.

When the fighting had started, Emma had obeyed instructions and stayed inside the Embassy, but then Georgi had got through to her on the phone and explained the need for medical supplies at the flats. Telling nobody, she had taken all she could find in the storeroom and driven down to the Stadtpark where he had told her to come. He was late and anxious. 'Is this all you could get?' he had asked, roughly. 'Yes,' she had said, abashed; she had been proud of what she had managed. He had taken the supplies and driven off. It was not until two years later, back in London, that she had met him again.

'I wonder how many they managed to get,' Georgi said, looking down at the bus.

'Fourteen put their names down.'

'It's delivery that matters.'

Emma smiled. She looked across at him: at the hard stocky body; the narrow eyes and beak of a nose; the small pointed black beard. In the light from the sun behind them she could see his hair thinned on the crown.

'Norman is very persuasive.'

Georgi looked at her, frowning.

'He is, Georgi. It's that impeccable upper-class English voice. They're all used to taking orders from it.'

Georgi frowned again.

'These are unemployed Welsh colliers.'

'Yes,' Emma said, and again smiled.

She enjoyed the irony of the contrast in class and physique. She and Norman were both tall and fair-haired. They moved and spoke as they were, daughter and son of an old diplomatic family. You could change your political allegiance but you still carried your appearance and manners. It was often entertaining, at either end of the spectrum, to watch people struggling with the contradictions. As if any of that old stuff mattered now.

'We'd better get down,' Georgi said.

'I suppose so. Are you talking?'

'Not this morning. We've got Mark Ryder; he's been in Spain. And then I thought Bert Lewis.'

'Which is he?'

'He was in the struggle against the scabs at Bedwas. You remember, I showed you the literature.'

'I know, but some of it was hard to believe.'

'It's just a factual account. To keep track of the militants a complete espionage system was started in the pit. Each conveyor, each heading, had its spy. Away from the pit, where the workmen lived, each village had its management spy.'

Emma hesitated.

'It's difficult to believe that kind of thing happens in England,' she said.

'This is Wales, actually. But it's a general tactic.'

'I liked that bit in the leaflet they put out. That we all had to choose between chaos, spying, intimidation, or normal decent relations.'

'Welsh workers, you'll find, use this moral language.'

'Good. But what's Lewis doing now?'

'He's unemployed.'

They walked fast downhill to the farm. The bus had turned in to the yard and the people were getting out. It had been Monkey's idea to buy the old bus. He had got it for thirty pounds and then worked for a week doing it up. 'My mechanical genius,' he had joked, 'has been thwarted by all this political theory.' The bus had been very useful as a baggage van for marches and demonstrations, and it had twice toured with exhibitions and speakers against unemployment and the means test.

Monkey was still fiercely possessive of it. It had once taken an official party decision to overrule his refusal to let anyone else drive. But buying it had been a great success, and so perhaps would be this other initiative of his: to rent this bankrupt farm, on the edge of the mining valleys, as a base for political work. He had been very sharp on all the details: beating down the year's rent; letting the pastures and the grazing rights to a neighbouring sheep-farmer; cleaning and whitewashing the house as a dormitory and offices; clearing the old barn for a meeting-room. What could then be offered, in the mining villages, was a good day in the country, good food, a lecture or two and some singing. 'It's always the case,' Monkey explained tirelessly, 'that any serious revolution needs a few good entrepreneurs.' Yet although his successes were solid, there were still complaints about his style.

Georgi had stopped and was counting the people in the yard.

'I make it seventeen. Do you?'

'I'm sorry,' Emma said. 'I wasn't counting.'

Georgi sighed.

'Yes, seventeen. One more than the list.'

'That's good, then.'

They went down into the yard. Monkey was stretched full-length under the back axle of the bus. Only his dirty tennis shoes and his purple socks, one with a large hole, stuck out. Norman was standing confidently at the head of the group. He was much taller than most of them, though the man beside him was bigger again, with much broader shoulders and a very thick, reddened neck: a rugby forward, Emma at once decided. He was crop-haired, square-faced, with a clipped black moustache. Smartly dressed, his gleaming white shirt buttoned at the collar, he had a striped red-and-black tie fastened at the fourth button with a thin clip-pin of twisted gold wire. Georgi made his way directly to him.

'Bert!'

'Georgi.'

They shook hands vigorously.

'All managed to come?'

'Aye, we made it.'

A girl of seventeen, tall and slender, with long black hair, was standing between Bert and Norman. Norman was smiling, happily and protectively, with his arms folded across his open-necked white cricket shirt. The smile seemed directed at the girl. Emma noticed her shyness, but there was also a self-possession about her. She was very carefully dressed, with stockings and shining black court shoes; Emma's legs were bare and sandalled. The girl's springy, almost wiry black hair was drawn back over her ears and tied at the nape with a broad yellow ribbon. The face was very strange to Emma, with finely marked, sharp features and high, prominent cheekbones. The eyes were wide and bright blue, with long black lashes. The nose was long and straight, and there was a deep groove running down to the small mouth. The skin was very white against the shining jet of the hair, except that the cheeks were a surprising bright red. On the long slender neck there was a tight string of yellow beads.

'One extra in fact,' Bert was saying, proudly. 'Jim Pritchard's sister, Nesta. Nes, this is the famous Georgi Wilkes.'

'No, come off it, Bert,' Georgi said.

'Pleased to meet you, Mr Wilkes,' Nesta said, holding out her hand.

'No. Georgi to my friends.'

'And to his enemies,' Bert said. 'And I'll tell you something, he's got plenty of both, like any good man should.'

Emma had moved away and was going round the whole group, shaking hands. She had been teased by the others for what they called her Embassy manners, and she could see the continuity. The only difference, she thought, apart from these being more real and interesting people, was that instead of moving smoothly on to the buffet she had to go, taking her turn, to the farm kitchen. While the others were having their lecture, she must cut the sandwiches for lunch.

People began drifting slowly towards the barn, although many seemed reluctant to go in from the warm, sweet air. Georgi was clapping his hands and politely encouraging the movement. As the others moved, with Bert Lewis bending his head and talking busily to Georgi, Emma saw that Norman and Nesta were still standing where they had been, though not looking at each other.

She saw them momentarily as a couple, and then dismissed the idea. Yet they were clearly conscious of each other, standing so deliberately still.

'Aren't you going to hear Mark?' Emma asked Norman.

'Yes. Fine,' Norman said.

Mark Ryder, who was to give the first talk, was a young historian. He had just won a research fellowship competition at Norman's own Cambridge college. Both Norman and Monkey Pitter had been candidates in another part of the competition, and had not been successful. Each insisted that the mathematical competition was always much stronger, especially as it was grouped with physics and there were always, Monkey said, at least four young Einsteins a year. Mark's research subject was medieval Spain, and he had been in Burgos in July, working in the cathedral library, when the Franco rising began. He had returned immediately to England and done some explanatory public writing and speaking. He was a socialist and a solid opponent of Franco, but he had declined his friends' invitations to join the Communist Party. He was always willing, however, to accept their invitations to explain the origins of the Spanish Civil War, though they had to work hard to persuade him to cut down on the more remote history, which he insisted had some relevance.

'Are *you* going in?' Emma said, looking directly and coolly at Nesta.

'I'd better not,' Nesta said. 'I only come up with my brother.'

'Which is your brother?'

'Jim. Jim Pritchard.'

'Yes, I think I've met him. But why don't you go in? It's open to anybody who's come.'

'I don't expect I'd understand it,' Nesta said.

'Of course you would. You're too modest.'

There was a slight sound from Norman. Emma glanced at him. He was watching the two young women with cool amusement.

'No, I don't know nothing about politics,' Nesta said. 'Only the bits I hear Jim and the other boys arguing.'

'What do you do, actually?' Emma asked, and then added: 'I'm sorry, I didn't quite catch your name.'

'It's Nesta,' both Norman and Nesta said, almost together. Nesta blushed and then laughed.

'I've not heard that name,' Emma said. 'Is it Welsh?'

'I expect so,' Nesta said. 'I was called it after an auntie.'

'It's very unusual.'

'Is it? I'm sorry.'

'No, I don't mean that. I suppose it's just the odd associations.' Norman laughed.

'My sister,' he said, 'is an incorrigible chauvinist.'

'Is she?' Nesta said, staring at Emma and avoiding looking at Norman.

'No,' Emma said. 'I'm just interested in you. Have you got a job?'

'Yes, I'm a clerk in the Coop. And lucky to get it.'

'Was that what you wanted?'

'Well, I wanted the money. Dad's ill and Jim's out of work.'

'But not the work itself?'

'It's all right. But Mrs Harries wanted me to go to art college.'

'Who's Mrs Harries?'

'My teacher, at the school. She said I had talent for it.'

'For drawing, you mean?'

'Well, my drawing's been the weakest, I know that, and Mrs Harries says you can't really paint until you can draw. But it's painting, really, I've been trying to do.'

'You still do it?'

'All the time. They can't stop me. It's all I bother with really.'

'That's marvellous,' Norman said. 'And never mind about art college. You just paint.'

Nesta looked shyly across at him. Emma saw her face in profile. It was like a sharp line-drawing.

'Do you really think so?' Nesta was asking Norman.

'I'm quite sure of it.'

'Only I see what Mrs Harries means, about figures and composition. And my drawing, well . . .'

There was a shout from the barn door. It was Monkey, short and awkward, with his thick glasses and tumbling dark hair.

'Come on, chaps. We're starting.'

They hesitated. Nesta looked at the ground and then up at Emma.

'Are you going to listen to it?'

'No, I can't. It's my turn to cut the sandwiches for lunch.'

'Well, I'll come and help you with that, then.'

'No, don't. I can manage. It's your day out.'

'I'd rather, really,' Nesta said, blushing.

Norman moved closer to her.

'She's only cadging your help, Nesta. Come on, I'll find you a seat. And I promise, if you're bored, just tip me the wink and I'll lead you out again. You can sit and paint the farm.'

'I've only got my sketchbook. I've got to keep trying at the drawing.'

'Well, come and draw the gang, then. It'll pass the time through the talk.'

Emma was still watching Nesta. While Norman was talking, with his easy light smile, Nesta had twice glanced at him, and then away. Emma saw that the girl's long fingers were tightly closed over the handle of her large bag, where the sketchbook was stowed. As when she had first noticed them, standing still and close to each other, Emma was surprised to see what seemed to be passing between them. One element of the surprise was that she knew Norman was still sexually unsettled. He had avoided all the more probable relationships that had come his way, in their own circle. Moreover he was still close to Monkey. On the other hand there had been a Jewish girl in Vienna: alien but clever and educated. Emma did not know how far that had gone, but it had certainly not been kept up. What then was he now doing, across another cultural distance? Though of course it was obvious what this naive Welsh girl might see in him. She waited for some moments, then:

'Yes, you go on, Nesta,' she said persuasively.

Nesta didn't answer, but as Norman moved towards the barn she walked quietly beside him, still holding tightly to her bag.

The morning passed easily. Mark's lecture was successful and there were questions and discussions after it. This overran the planned time and they went straight on to the talk from Bert Lewis. In a strong, moving, impromptu speech, he related the struggle of the Spanish people to their own experiences of struggle in the valleys. There had never in all their lifetimes been so clear a case of the realities of proletarian internationalism.

There were deep interconnections, across national boundaries, within the general class struggle. And the time was now coming close when they would have to make moves to link up these two fighting fronts. All their energies had been taken up with their own struggles, but there were moments in history when the conflict burst through into open action, with the opposing forces clearly staked out. At such times it was clear where the duties of strong men lay. The Tory government, true to its own class interests, would of course lie and manoeuvre, hide behind petty legalities, to prevent the two fronts being joined. There were some in their own movement who used the same delaying tactics to prevent any collective defence against fascism, just as all these years they had hung on to their watch-chains to soften the struggle against capitalism. But one thing they could all be sure of, friend and foe alike: when the chance of volunteering came, there would be a strong response from the best of the sons of Wales, and the most class-conscious miners would be at the head of that column. He was stating it now publicly: his own name would be the first to go down. For he was sick to death of being manoeuvred out of work in his own country, and then expected to sit on the touchline watching this first phase of the war against fascism, which was going to decide all their lives.

Nesta sat beside Norman at the back of the barn. At first she had hardly moved, and had said only 'yes' or 'no' when Norman whispered to her. But then while Bert was talking she had pulled out her sketchbook and started drawing. She had kept it turned away from Norman. She drew very fast and urgently, flipping the big soft pages. When at last he had a chance to see what she was doing, Norman held his breath. He had expected rough charcoal sketches of some of the men around them, or one of the speakers. What was there, however, was an extension of the dark vaulted shape of the barn, with its heavy stone walls and its narrow openings like arrowslits. It was now as much a castle as a barn, but seen from inside, as if by a prisoner. There was only one beam of light, from a small high window, and there were no people illuminated by it, only a strongly drawn and elongated hand, almost skeletal across the diffusing light. When she realised that he was staring at it she quickly turned the page again, and the same design began building in rapid strokes, the darkness of the walls filling in.

Emma came in and walked through the meeting to whisper to Georgi. After a few minutes he closed the discussion and said that the meal was ready. In the afternoon, he proposed, they would walk on the mountain, carrying on their discussion informally. Then they would assemble again after tea and try to move forward to some more practical decisions.

As people stood up and stretched and got ready to go out, Norman spoke quietly to Nesta.

'I had no idea,' he said. 'What you're doing is fantastic.'

She glanced up at him. Her eyes had widened, under the prominent black lashes.

'Why fantastic?'

'It's got such feeling in it.'

'No,' Nesta said. 'I can't really get it right.'

'You will. Believe me. You have. And it would be absolutely criminal for you to spend your life doing anything else.'

'I wouldn't say that,' Nesta said, smiling, and put her sketch-book away in her bag.

Most of the group carried their meals outside; they sat in the yard and on the sheep-cropped grass beyond it.

'Watch you don't eat them sheep currants,' Jim Pritchard shouted across.

There were thick sandwiches of cheese and ham, baskets of local plums, and beer from a barrel which Monkey had bought and stored in the cellar. After a full morning of talk there was not much conversation. They stretched out and enjoyed the sun.

It had been agreed that after the meal there would be a communal walk up the hill and along to the famous view by the ordnance point: looking north and east to the Black Mountains, to Eppynt and as far as Plynlimmon. They trailed out on the climb up the hill, with Georgi and three of the youngest men striding out at the front. Emma walked with Bert Lewis and Jim Pritchard. Only Monkey had not come; he had work to do on the bus.

Bert and Jim were arguing about volunteering for Spain. Bert repeated what he had said in his talk. Jim, slender and dark, very like his sister Nesta, was sympathetic but uncertain.

'It's not that I don't respect it, mun.'

'Then what?'

'It's our own fight I'm thinking about. And not just the scabs and the bloody means test. It's work I've got to get back to.'

'Slough not Spain, is it?' Bert said angrily.

'I never said nothing about Slough. We don't want their old factories. What we want is the work brought here.'

'But that's what I was saying, boy. Till we win this whole struggle, and smash capitalism, there won't be no bloody work, in South Wales or anywhere else.'

'Get war and there'll be work. Too much of the bugger.'

Emma was walking between them.

'What it is, Jim,' she said clearly, 'beyond even smashing capitalism, is stopping fascism. If we don't, we'll be back to slavery and barbarism, not just unemployment. It's coming across the whole continent. I saw it myself in Vienna. There was Italy and Germany and now there's Spain. We've got no choices left; we've got to stand against it now.'

'We got British Blackshirts recruiting even down here,' Bert said.

Jim frowned, moving his hands as if reaching for his words.

'It's what you say about fronts, mun,' he said, not responding to Emma. 'I can see that, a struggle on many fronts. Only what I don't see is sending all the best to just the one. It's like here we're stuck, just about holding on after all that's been done to us; then we get this idea there's this quick way out, going off to fight in Spain.'

'Not quick, boy, whatever it is.'

'No, not quick to win, I'm not saying that. I mean we're here on our bloody knees, and to get up and fight is a hell of a struggle. You know that better than anybody.'

Bert nodded. Emma spoke again, quickly.

'That's right, Jim, of course. But believe me, I've seen it. In every country where the workers are smashed there's that much less strength in all the others. In four or five years there could be a Fascist Europe and we'd be back to the Dark Ages. No parties, no unions, no political freedoms, and people like you and Bert in prison camps.'

'Aye,' Jim said, still avoiding looking at her.

'What Jim means,' Bert said, 'is not whether we fight it but where. Every man then must make his own decision.'

'Of course,' Emma quickly agreed.

She looked round for the rest of the party. They had taken different paths to the ridge and were widely strung out. Already, to the north and east, there was a great distance of hills, soft greens and blues in the distance. A lark was singing, close by.

Halfway up the main path, often stopping and looking at what she was carrying, Norman and Nesta were walking together. Emma stared down at them. Bert and Jim walked on, pointing out places they thought they could recognise in the distance. Emma cupped her hands.

'Come on, you two!' she shouted down.

The light wind along the ridge caught her voice and carried it away. Norman and Nesta did not look up but still walked slowly, close together.

# 2

## BLACK MOUNTAINS, SEPTEMBER 1936

'You got here, then,' Norman said, smiling.

'Did you think I wouldn't?'

He had been waiting at the bus stop outside the Brecon Museum. Nesta had been last off. She was wearing the yellow print dress she had worn for the visit to the farm, but she was carrying a brown raincoat, over her big brown bag. Norman took her arm lightly to make way through the people who were moving in different directions from the bus.

'It seemed too good to be true, that's all,' he said as they got clear.

'Why?'

'I'm notorious for bad luck,' Norman said. 'Most of the things I want somehow never happen.'

'I don't believe in luck,' Nesta said.

'Anyway I thought I'd offended you. By calling you Birdie.'

'Why should that offend me?'

'It started as Emma's silly joke, about unusual Welsh names. But then I thought it suited you, if you didn't mind.'

'Why should I mind? I'm the same whatever you call me.'

'Are you sure, Birdie?'

'Stop worrying,' Nesta said.

Norman had borrowed a car, from Monkey Pitter. They walked through to where it was parked, in the empty cattle market.

27

'Have you decided where you'd like to go?' Norman asked.

'Just anywhere. I don't mind.'

'I bought some stuff for lunch. We can have a picnic some-where.'

'I've got sandwiches,' Nesta said.

'What are they?'

'Cucumber. Is that good enough?'

'Birdie, Birdie, you're being defensive again.'

'It's what they say about our place.'

'Then forget your place for a bit. This is a day out, away from it all.'

'Yes and you've no idea,' Nesta said, then stopped and turned away.

Norman opened her door and she got in quickly. He went round and swung the starting handle. The engine coughed into noisy vibration.

'It's one of Monkey's reconstructed wrecks,' he shouted, coming round and sitting beside her. 'But it got me here.'

'Did you come straight from Cambridge?'

'Yesterday. I found a pub overnight.'

She put her bag down at her feet. Norman steered out of the market.

'How did you get your day off?' he asked, as they climbed from the town.

'I was due it because I didn't go on the outing.'

'Well then, you're having your outing now. We can still go to the sea if you like.'

'No. It's too far.'

'There's one thing I'd like to show you. It's a carved screen in a little mountain church. Even if you don't like the screen it's a lovely spot up there.'

'Where is it?'

'Oh, it's thirty miles. But we can get there for lunch. It's a wonderful screen. Mark put me on to it, Mark Ryder.'

'The historian who was talking?'

'Yes. Apparently in the sixteenth and seventeenth centuries all these rood screens were ordered to be pulled down. But this was off the beaten track; they never found it. The detail of the carving, well, you'll see that better than me.'

'I don't know nothing about carving.'

'Yes, but you've got what's much more important. You've got the eye for it.'

They were in a network of narrow lanes, with high-banked hedges. The view of the mountains above them was suddenly cut off, and they drove for some time without speaking. The car rattled but it pulled strongly on the hills.

'Actually there's more to the church than that,' Norman began again. 'It was originally a cell, where a Christian hermit was martyred. And there's a well outside it that they say is a holy well; pilgrims used to visit it.'

'Do you believe that, then?'

'About the martyr, yes. Mark is usually reliable.'

'No, I meant the holy well.'

Norman laughed.

'Probably good pure mountain water. That should be holy enough.'

Nesta smiled for the first time since she had got off the bus.

'You see,' Norman said. 'It's not so terrible after all.'

'I never said it was terrible.'

'You said in your letter you were worried.'

'Well, like you say, perhaps I ought to forget it.'

'Forget Danycapel? No, you can't, of course. But you can forget being stuck in it.'

'Can I? I don't think so.'

'You're not stuck, Birdie. Didn't I say what we could do?'

'You said, yes. Only still perhaps we're too different ever to be real friends.'

'Can't friends be different?'

'Well yes, but for you it all started with the politics. That was why you all come.'

'And found more than I expected.'

'Did you? What really did you expect us to be like?'

'Never mind the others, we're talking about you.'

'Only you ought to know, I didn't choose my politics. They was chosen for me, by the family I was born to and the place I grew up in. More like a religion, and I had that too. I don't really understand much more of one than the other.'

Norman smiled.

'But you're still yourself, Birdie. All the rest is just your place.'

'Yes and the place has made me – what you see of me, I mean.'

'Then it's a good place. Do you think I'd want to change you?'

'Well, you were saying about stuck in it.'

'Yes, because of your painting, and because these are hard times; for all of you, I've seen it, but for you especially, because you could be an artist.'

'Never that,' Nesta said, laughing.

'Of course you could. But you should realise you come from a famous people. When the Romans came up against you, you shocked them.'

'What's Romans to do with it?'

Norman lifted one hand from the wheel.

'If you knew the times we did it at school! You're the Silures, didn't you know? The Romans learned to respect your ferocity in battle, but what impressed them even more was your extraordinary independence. One of them said, I remember translating it: *Neither punishment nor kindness can turn them from their ways.*'

Nesta looked away.

'I don't know about any of that,' she said.

'They must have told you about it at school.'

'Well, I didn't take a lot of notice, but I don't think so. All I remember of history was, I had to draw an elephant. It was about Clive of India.'

Norman laughed.

'There you are, you see. Your only real life is your drawing.'

'No,' Nesta said.

'Then you're underestimating yourself. That's your only bad habit.'

'If you only knew!'

'Knew what?'

'Knew me.'

Their talk died away. Norman leaned back with his arms stretched straight to the wheel, whistling under his breath. He was wearing a crisp pale-blue shirt and matching blue trousers. His fair hair was almost yellow where it was long in the neck above the wide collar of the shirt. Whenever he had to concentrate, on some difficult part of the road, Nesta looked quickly across at him and as quickly away.

'How's your Dad?' Norman asked eventually.

'A bit better, I think. He's been sitting in the garden a lot.'

'Silicosis is a wicked disease.'

'We call it devil's dust.'

'Of course. Except it isn't the devil that sends it – any more than where we're going is a holy well.'

'I'll take him some water back. From the well.'

'Now who believes what?'

Nesta laughed and leaned back, putting her hands behind her head.

'And your brother?' Norman asked.

'Jim's fine.'

'And that friend of yours? Bert?'

She glanced across at him.

'Bert? He's all right.'

'He's an impressive man. A real fighter.'

'No, not really. It's just he's strong and people see that.'

'But he is a fighter, Birdie.'

'Oh, that? Yes, of course.'

'Have you always known him?'

'He's always been there, yes. Jim and him was always in and out of the house.'

'But not as your friend?'

Nesta hesitated.

'I've looked up to him,' she said.

'Well, you'd have to,' Norman said and laughed, easily.

They were turning now into the mountains. Norman stopped and checked his new large-scale map. Soon they were again moving along the network of steep high-banked lanes, and now the hedges and trees seemed to enclose them. Nesta leaned back and stared through the windscreen at the green canopy above. As the ascent continued, she half-closed her eyes.

They came out on the open mountain, on an earth track among bracken and whinberry, with sheep and ponies grazing across the slopes. As they got higher the track was through heather, in full flower. Nesta gazed at the heather, through the open side window.

'They say purple but it isn't,' she said, as if to herself.

'There are different kinds,' Norman said.

He was keeping his attention on the bumpy track.

'It's paler,' Nesta said.

The track dipped through the bed of a mountain stream, where a ford had been laid with wide stones. The water was shallow. Norman accelerated out of it. Two ponies, one a beautiful light fawn with a luxuriant white mane and tail, the other white with a charcoal-grey mane and tail, had been coming down to the water but now galloped away from the car.

'They're beautiful,' Nesta said.

'Yes. But you know where they end up?'

'For riding?'

'A lucky few. Most of them go to the pits.'

'Not these!' Nesta said, sitting up and looking back at them.

'Of course. It's what they're bred for.'

'But pit ponies . . .'

'They usually sell them much younger than that.'

'No, I don't mean just those two. Only I've seen the old ones, turned out, having a bit of a graze up the hill. They don't look anything like these.'

'It's the same breed.'

'Is it? Still they save the men work. All the hauling.'

'Of course.'

He was having again to concentrate on the track, where in two places there had been a landslip. Then he had to stop because an old unshorn ewe was lying in the middle of the track, with its back to them, and would not move as he jabbed at the horn. Its fleece was torn and hanging along its sides.

'She wins,' Norman said.

'I'll move her,' Nesta said, and jumped out. She ran to the ewe, shouting and jumping and waving her arms. It stirred but did not move.

'Come on, old lady, come on!' she shouted, and bent and pushed hard on its back. Very slowly, the ewe struggled to its feet and turned to stare at the car.

'Get on, then!' Nesta shouted, laughing and jumping and clapping her hands. The ewe stared at her and then scrambled up the bank, where it stopped and again turned to stare. She clapped again, sharply, and suddenly the ewe ran. She stood, laughing. She didn't want to go back to the car.

Norman had been smiling, watching her, but now his face was set. He stared down at his hands on the wheel. He had driven from Cambridge for an outing, for a date. But what desire there had been in that seemed now a generality. The perspective had altered. As he watched her jump and clap her hands he remembered his sister Emma running with a kite on the downs – a big red triangular kite with a white tail. He had been running alongside it until suddenly it had lifted and soared and he had clapped his hands. The kite had swung towards the sun and his eyes were dazzled. He felt the movements again in his body: the joy and desire he had heard others try to describe. It was a flow of reconnection, of recognition. But of this girl in front of him? It appeared so. 'If you only knew . . . knew me.'

She was walking back to the car. He stared at her, unsmiling. 'If you only knew me.' What had she meant by that? That there was some hidden self, something she wouldn't disclose to him? What he already knew of her was strange. She was so physically sure of herself, in all the ways she moved, and yet with the manner and talk of someone much younger – a very young girl or even a child. It was perhaps this that had prompted the memory of playing with Emma, that lost childhood simplicity of every physical action and feeling. For it seemed that such a flow was happening again, simply and easily, when all that he had known in this kind of relationship had been difficult, an aching physical anxiety, a pressure, and then the most obvious means of releasing it. Was this to be different, taking him back to a world alive all around him; before school, before effort; a world of soft air and quick movement and the sweet taste of release? It seemed that it might be so, yet how could he expect her to care or to respond to it? She seemed physically sure in her own world but he knew it would be very different if he touched her.

She smiled in at the window.

'Cheer up.'

'Sure.'

He leaned across to open her door. She got in, still lively and excited.

'It's not far now,' he said, forcing his voice.

'Well, as far as I'm concerned we're already there.'

In another half-hour they reached the track below the church, which was up a steep bank and largely hidden by trees.

'Shall we see it first or have lunch?' Norman asked.

He was still preoccupied and she looked at him curiously.

'I'm not hungry. Let's go to the church.'

'This is the well, by the way,' he said, pointing.

'What, that?'

He was pointing down at a small spring that flowed through the hedgebank. There was an arrangement of upright stones around it. The stones were dark with wet moss. Just below the level of the track there was a dark pool. The water was a deep peaty brown.

'That's what they came for,' he said.

'Then they must have had faith.'

'Do you want to drink from it?'

'Not from that dirty old pool.'

She bent over and reached across to the falling water of the spring. She cupped her hands and got some to her mouth.

'Go on, try it. It's lovely,' she said, stepping back.

Norman straddled the pool and twisted his head round to catch some of the falling water. Most of it went on his face but what he tasted was sweet and cool. He stepped back. Nesta was laughing at him.

'Wipe your face, then.'

He brushed his hand across his mouth.

'Birdie?'

'Yes?'

'Are you glad you came?'

'Can't you see I'm glad?'

'No, but I mean came with me.'

Nesta looked at him for a moment.

'Stop fishing,' she said, turning to walk up the path to the church. Norman made an effort and followed her.

At the church it was easier. They looked at the old preaching cross in the small abandoned graveyard. On the old headstones there were only five family names: Lewis, Parry, James, Williams, Pritchard.

'You see,' Nesta said. 'There's plenty of us.'

'Did your family come from around here?'

'How should I know? There's always Pritchards. We're all over the place.'

They examined the first names of the Pritchard headstones. Most of them were English or Biblical names, though there were also an Ifor and an Ivor on neighbouring stones.

'Where's this carving, then?' Nesta asked.

They opened the old heavy door. The church was small: smaller than the barn in which they had listened to the lectures. The Commandments were painted on the facing wall, but the plaster was flaking and the paint had faded from the original black and red. She pushed along a pew and scraped the paint with her nail. She smelled it carefully, wrinkling her nose.

Norman had walked on to the roodscreen, which crossed the whole church under a small gallery. The wood was a finely weathered oak, with a slight sheen under the light from the clear windows. It was carved in an intricate design of flowers and fruits, in long garlands which followed the spaced frameposts and in clustered panels between them. He ran his fingers over a cluster of apples. Nesta had come up quietly and was standing close behind him.

'Well?' he said, turning.

'Yes, it's lovely.'

'You don't sound too keen.'

'It's beautiful work.'

'You ought to touch it, to feel the shapes.'

'I saw you touching it.'

'And so you can't?'

'I'll touch it.'

She reached up and ran her fingers lightly along the grain.

'What do you really think?' Norman asked seriously.

'It's beautifully made. It's wonderful work.'

'But . . .?'

'No but. Only it's like a lesson.'

'You mean a Christian lesson?'

'No, it's just flowers and fruit. I meant the design.'

'Because in lessons you have to copy this kind of thing?'

'It's my fault. I'm no good at it.'

'But you are good. I keep telling you.'

'Well, not at this,' Nesta said.

They looked at the screen again, as if to remember it, and then walked together back down the aisle. There was a very old stone font beyond the door. Nesta lifted the lid and looked inside. It was dry, with cobwebs.

'What it means to me . . .' Norman said.

Nesta replaced the lid.

'. . . The screen, for example,' he went on. 'In so little a church, with only poor people living around it. Mark said there's evidence of a travelling craftsman, perhaps an Italian. But there's always that kind of story, because rich people never believe poor people can do anything. Poor people, that is, of their own country. And yet I've seen other examples of this Welsh country carving. Have you ever seen the old lovespoons?'

'Yes. At the museum.'

'Of course. That's how it's been done. The past in glass cases. So people forget what they can make for themselves. They're crammed into heavy work and told it's all they're fit for, when what they've actually made is all around them. And it's all still waiting there, the talents, the gifts.'

'You think so?'

'People think of oppression as low wages and hard work and then being put on the scrapheap. But there's another kind of oppression: killing their faith in the work of their hands and of their minds.'

'The first is enough.'

'No, it's not enough. We can fight to get that right. It will take a long time but we don't always have to wait. When I saw what you'd drawn in the barn . . .'

'No, it isn't like that, just the drawing.'

'It is, Birdie, it is. That's why I'm determined to help you.'

'You can't help me.'

'I can, Birdie. I've told you.'

'Did you come, then, to help me?'

She looked back into his face. He hesitated, biting his lip.

'You see,' she said and laughed.

'Of course I can help you,' he said, irritably.

'I'll believe you,' she said, smiling, and turned and went out of the church. She stood in the warm sunlight, so bright after the dusk of the interior. When he came out behind her she reached her hand back and took his hand. They walked slowly back down to the car.

They decided to drive higher into the mountain, for their picnic. They found a sheltered bank of heather by an old, half-ruined cottage, which had one surviving broken pine guarding it. Norman took a rug from the car and spread it where they could look down at a small stream which had cut its way into the soft red earth, in a very narrow channel. Just beyond where they were sitting the stream disappeared again under the earth, to come out twenty yards further downhill and fall over a mossy rock into a pool.

After a while they fetched the food from the car. Nesta unwrapped the thin cucumber sandwiches from the greaseproof paper. Norman spread out a loaf, a pat of butter, a Camembert cheese and a bag of apples. He had brought also a flagon of perry.

'Have you ever drunk this?'

'I've never even heard of it.'

'It's like cider, but it's made from pears. A lot of the farms still make it.'

He poured her a small amount, in a brown mug. She sipped it.

'It's nice. Very sweet.'

'But it's strong, so watch it.'

'Don't worry,' Nesta said. 'This is my day out.'

They ate the sandwiches and then some bread and cheese and an apple. Norman drained a mug of perry and Nesta helped herself to more. Norman had Turkish cigarettes, and they both smoked.

'A funny taste,' Nesta said, 'but better than Smoke Cloud.'

'What on earth is Smoke Cloud?'

'I can tell you don't live in the valleys. Threepence for ten; the cheapest going.'

'I must try some.'

'There's no reason why you should.'

She was lying on her elbow, looking amusedly across at him. He looked away.

'You can still have your politics,' she said, 'without trying to imitate everything else we have to do.'

'You don't really think that?' he said anxiously.

'It's noticeable, Norman. I mean, that that's what you think you want.'

'How do you know what I want?'

Nesta sat up, straightening her legs on the rug. He watched her for some moments and then reached out and put his hand on her shoulder. She did not move.

'You're right of course,' he said. 'I'm pretty bad at concealing what I really want.'

'Are you?'

'Birdie,' he said, and hesitated. 'You must know how I feel about you.'

'Do I?' she asked. 'All you've talked about is the drawing.'

'It was before that. From when we were standing, at the farm, when we'd got out of the bus.'

'At first sight?' she said, amused again.

'Not just sight. It was more than sight.'

She turned round on her knees and faced him.

'It wouldn't get us anywhere,' she said, earnestly.

'It could get us anywhere we wanted. I could take you anywhere, all the galleries, all the cities, all that world out there.'

'Is that what they call touring?' Nesta said, smiling.

'No, it isn't and you know it. I mean we could be together, make that kind of life together.'

'I thought you said about Europe and fascism.'

'Exactly. That makes it more urgent. It's because of the danger that loving now is so different.'

Nesta smiled.

'That's the first time you said the word. Did you notice?'

'Loving? That's right. But now it's a new kind of love, because of the danger.'

'There aren't new kinds.'

'Yes, everything feels new, in a time like this.'

'I'm not that interested in everything.'

She got up and walked down to the stream. She had to lean over to look down to the water, in its sharp narrow cut through the earth. Norman waited and then went down and put his arm round her shoulders. He turned her to him and kissed her. When they separated she was again looking intently into his face.

'It wouldn't be letting down your family,' he said, still holding her hand. 'I have enough money, since my father died, and I shall get a college job by next year at the latest. And then you could let me help them, and you could do what you should be doing.'

'It's too soon for us. Honestly.'

'No, Birdie, it can't be too soon.'

She stared at him again and then looked away, to where the stream disappeared underground. He pulled gently on her hand and she went slowly back with him. She kneeled again on the rug. Norman kneeled, facing her, and put his hands, gently pressing, on her shoulders.

'It's too soon, love,' she whispered.

# 3

## CAMBRIDGE, OCTOBER 1936

'That infernal Secretariat,' Monkey exclaimed, throwing an armful of papers into the empty easy chair by the window.

'What particular devilry now?' Norman asked, slightly turning his head.

He was lying on the soft brown hearthrug in front of the gas fire. There was a cushion under his head and his legs were drawn up to make a rest for a large sheet of drawing paper from his thighs to his knees. An unfinished equation, in large charcoal figures and symbols, was scrawled on the paper.

'Don't even look at this stuff they've loaded on to me,' Monkey said, sitting in a chair above Norman's face and looking steadily down at him.

'You brought it here.'

'It's what they're pleased to call a Party assignment. They give me these kindergarten statistics and want a professional presentation of them, by the end of the week.'

'What statistics?'

'Soviet industrial production. Need you ask?'

'And they're no good?'

'Bloody hell, they add up. All the totals in all the columns are accurate.'

'So what's the problem?'

'Georgi lectured and lectured me about a professional presentation; that it was my party duty to do it. But as I told him there's nothing to do. Believe them or not they add up. And then the only presentation would be simplification. Simplification by selection.'

'Okay. So still what's the problem?'

'They keep saying professional; and they have no idea what that means. It's a projection, really, from their image of themselves as professional revolutionaries.'

'Well, Georgi is that.'

'He is, outside the university. I told him, forget these kindergarten figures. My party duty is driving the bus to South Wales.'

'That's next week. For the hunger march.'

'Sure it's next week, but there's work to do on the bus. Not this pseudo-professionalism, seeing if Soviet statisticians can count.'

Norman yawned. His eyes were smarting from the gas fire.

'Sure. But give them something pretty. Why not a two-colour graph?'

Monkey laughed.

'I've got a cake,' he said, getting up and fetching his bag.

'Moka?'

'Moka. Do I ever neglect you?'

He unwrapped the cake and put a kettle on the gas-ring. Norman stretched out his legs and the paper slipped to the rug. Monkey stared down at it.

'No further with that equation?'

'No further.'

'It's ironic, isn't it? We already have the elegant style. Now all we need is what they can call the elegant proof.'

'Elegant is for furniture.'

'They also say beautiful, and by that time you know what they're saying. It's women.'

'Perhaps that's why we're stuck, then.'

'Why *you're* stuck.'

Norman pushed himself up.

'Don't joke about it, Monkey.'

'What else should I do?' Monkey said, and laughed.

There was a gyp-room — a small kitchen and storeroom — just outside Norman's door, at the top of the winding stone staircase.

Monkey went and fetched plates and cups. He emptied old dregs from the teapot and put in fresh tea.

'You'll be rushing down to Wales again, of course?'

Norman didn't answer. He stretched his arms and walked across to the window. An evening mist was gathering in the wide court. The lamps at the staircases had just come on. Cambridge in the autumn, with the university's year still fresh and young, had a powerful spell.

'I haven't really told you about Birdie,' he said, moving back.

Monkey laughed.

'I've seen the pretty pictures. I know what happens.'

'No, for Christ's sake!'

Norman drank his tea, avoiding looking at Monkey. As he put the cup down he turned and spoke seriously.

'You say the infernal Secretariat. I have my own reasons for agreeing.'

'What reasons?'

'Mainly that they're pushing very hard into what's really my personal life.'

'Not still our bourgeois deviations?'

'It wasn't official. It came through Emma: a sisterly word. But of course it was really Georgi.'

'What, in heaven's name?'

'To keep away from Birdie.'

Monkey spluttered into laughter through a mouthful of tea. Norman frowned and looked away.

'Even honest heterosexuals now,' Monkey hooted.

'It wasn't that. The actual words were *class and party morality*.'

Monkey laughed again.

'No, I can see they have a point,' Norman said, simply. 'As Emma explained it, Birdie's an inexperienced working-class girl. And to use a political connection for that kind of . . .'

'Seduction?'

'That word wasn't used.'

'They should try *entanglement*. Like any bourgeois family, keeping the son of the house away from the maids.'

'Do they?' Norman said, beginning to smile.

'Of course. In all the best families. Because it's Father's turn first.'

'You're a cynical bastard, Monkey.'

'Sceptical but legitimate, if you want to be precise.'

Norman went back to the window. He flopped in the big chair. After a pause, Monkey followed him and looked out into the court.

'So it's hands off Birdie?'

'In effect, yes. Not that Emma would have thought of it. She's been all the other way, almost pushing me at girls. But Georgi, I know, is very fierce about it.'

'Yes, because the core of the Party is puritan. Even their own unorthodox relationships are within the faith. Party members only. You remember how they put it to us?'

Norman looked away.

'They had to accept that,' he said, quietly. 'It had carried on for so many from school. And they couldn't just say it was illegal, since the political rhetoric was all for the illegal.'

Monkey took off his glasses and polished them with a clean handkerchief.

'You still don't understand,' he said, slowly. 'Sex of any kind is not the problem. The real and only point is that sex outside the Party would be a division of loyalties.'

'Yes, of course I see that. But with Birdie what they're saying is about class. And class, I had supposed, is what the Party is about.'

'Politically,' Monkey said.

'All right, politically. But we don't only live politically. Yet they said it was a matter of Party morality, to avoid leading on an inexperienced working-class girl.'

Monkey put his glasses on again.

'Yes,' he said. 'It's patronising. Do they think the working class are inexperienced at that?'

'Look, I'm just repeating what Emma said. In fact it's worse than patronising, because it was never like that. I didn't see her as a girl from the working class. I saw her as herself, and with this gift in her hands.'

'So you said.'

'You mean even you don't believe me?'

'I know your problems, don't I? I think the distance helped. In her case the class distance.'

Norman raised his hands to his face. Monkey looked down and then moved behind Norman's chair. There was a silence for some time, and then Norman seemed to be crying. Monkey put his hands, tightly, on the thick fair hair.

'It'll clear,' he said.

There was again a silence.

'It did clear,' Norman said, indistinctly.

Monkey moved his hands.

'You know I was glad for you.'

'Were you, Monkey?'

'Sure. I've always fostered you, haven't I?'

Norman stayed very still.

'All this crap about class and party morality,' he said, hoarsely. 'This was the flow of my own life. Can't anybody understand that?'

'Yes, I understand it.'

'All right, but now they're stopping it.'

'They can't stop it.'

'They can coarsen it, can't they? Haven't they coarsened it already?'

Monkey lifted his hands from the thick hair.

'Is that going to be your excuse?'

Norman jumped from the chair, clenching his fists.

'You bastard, Monkey! You dirty bastard!'

Monkey smiled, undisturbed.

'So I can expect you on the bus to Wales?' he said, easily. 'I might even let you share the driving.'

Norman relaxed, looking at him.

'Following the hunger march?' he asked, wiping his face.

'Picking up the weary. Carrying the baggage.'

'I don't know. I'll have to see.'

'To see about Birdie?'

Norman stepped back.

'I feel committed to her, Monkey.'

'Well, you are, of course, in a way.'

'Not in a way. In the only way.'

'With thy body I me worship?'

Norman was not really listening.

'It isn't only that. It's much more than that.'

Monkey smiled and moved across to switch on the central light.

'We're due at Paul's,' he said, looking at his watch.

'Oh Christ, I'd forgotten.'

'We have to go.'

'Of course.'

Norman fetched his big college scarf from the bedroom. He swung it round his neck. He seemed strong and active again.

They went down and through the court, out into the narrow street. They walked fast, without speaking, until they turned under the double archway to a much smaller, dark court. There was a soft light in Paul Howe's window, one floor up on the far corner staircase. As they passed under it they heard music. Norman glanced at the painted list of names and hurried up the stone stairs. He was well ahead of Monkey when he got to the big double doors.

The large room was crowded. People were sitting on all the chairs and on the floor. His sister was perched on the window-seat, looking down at the big gramophone. He knew the piece: 'Beale Street' was a general favourite. Several people greeted him casually. Behind him Monkey slid in and sat along the wall. As Norman moved away from the gramophone the hubbub of voices was much louder than the music.

Paul Howe, short and stocky with straight black hair and ruddy cheeks, was sitting by the fireplace with Georgi Wilkes and Mark Ryder. He was talking earnestly to Mark. A big fair girl touched Norman's arm as he watched. He looked more closely. He did not know her.

'You're Norman Braose, aren't you?'

'Yes.'

'Emma's brother?'

'Yes.'

'I'm Pippa Howard. I'm new.'

A man and a girl, holding hands, pushed past. Norman could have moved on, but waited.

'We nearly met in Vienna,' the girl said. 'Daddy pointed you both out but it was an even worse crush than this.'

'Was he at the Embassy?'

'At a reception. He was a Minister then.'

'Ah.'

'He probably thought you'd be friends for us.'

'Well . . .'

'Exactly. Though when I found it was Emma I had to see to join this branch . . .'

'You were in before?'

'Since last summer. I joined straight from school.'

'Good.'

'And since I found Emma I've been really wanting to meet you.'

'Fine.'

'It's so crowded here. But we must wait for Georgi's speech.'

'I didn't know there were to be speeches.'

'Just wishing Paul well in Spain.'

'Well, we do.'

'We could have a meal perhaps, later on. Unless you've got some arrangement.'

'Well, I came with someone.'

'A girl?'

'No.'

'Well, that's all right, then.'

Norman looked across at Emma. Two men were talking across her: a tall, very dark Indian and a small, plump, pale man in a black boiler suit. He was surprised how many people present he did not know. He had heard that there had been a big recent increase in membership. Emma was not listening to the talk across her. She was staring down at the record turning on the gramophone. *'If Beale Street could talk . . .'*

The record played through. Bottles of hock were circulating and the hubbub of voices was louder. A girl went to the gramophone and put on another record: 'Strange Fruit'. A few people near it stopped talking to listen. Norman closed his eyes, as the music moved from the sharp worldly bounce of exotic whoring to the slow, sad ballad of the lynch victim.

When the record ended Georgi clapped his hands and there were several calls for silence. It was very hot now in the over-crowded room. Paul Howe was sweating heavily.

'Comrades,' Georgi began, in his soft, always reasonable voice. People were shuffling round to turn towards him.

'Comrades, no speeches tonight.'

There were two or three mock groans.

'But it is a fact that Paul is the fourth member of this branch to volunteer to fight in Spain. He is also the youngest. He is still in his second year. I can perhaps tell you in confidence that he is acting against Party advice in volunteering before he has finished his degree. These are the choices now being made, comrades. We respect and honour Paul's choice.'

There was a short burst of clapping. Georgi held up his hand.

'Paul needs no words or applause from us. What he needs, with every other volunteer from the working-class and democratic movement across the world, is our solidarity. Our active solidarity, our militant support. Political, material, financial. Our pledge of effort and more effort, comrades, in the struggle which none can now escape.'

There was sustained clapping. Georgi took his glass from the mantelpiece.

'To Paul! To Spain!'

The toast was drunk and cheered. Someone called 'Speech!' but Paul waved his hand in refusal. There was a brief silence and then the many conversations began again.

'There's a good Indian restaurant we could go to,' Pippa said to Norman. 'I found it the other day.'

'Sure. I know it. Fine. I'll just have a word with Paul.'

He pushed through to the fireplace and waited his turn to talk to Paul Howe, who was still awkwardly crouched across the fender. When his turn came, Norman squatted beside him.

'This is fantastic, Paul.'

'No. I see it as very ordinary.'

'If it were ordinary we should all be going.'

'No. There are different ways of fighting.'

'Why this for you, then?'

Paul's black hair was heavy with sweat. His ruddy cheeks were bright. His large clear eyes seemed swollen.

'You're the first who's asked that, Norman.'

'Surely not?'

'Well, you heard Georgi. But that was policy. It wasn't really asking me.'

'So?'

'So I doubt if I can tell you. It certainly isn't heroism, and it isn't even solidarity, in either the romantic or the understated versions. What it actually is, I'm not sure of the word: perhaps a challenge.'

'Do you think so? Surely there are much easier responses.'

'I'm not talking about inadequacy, or any other Freudian rubbish. Intellectually and objectively, the occasion is perfectly clear. But its special claim on me, its unavoidable challenge—'

'Good luck, Paul. I'll write,' a girl leaned over to say.

Paul reached up and took her extended fingers.

'. . . I could almost say its strangeness, its alienness even. We've led sheltered lives but by any standards fascism really is alien. I mean it's not only what the Party says, that it's a barbarous outgrowth of capitalism. I think that behind the façade it's another and very powerful kind of reason, rationality – but a genuinely alien kind.'

'It's so overtly barbarous, I can't—'

'Of course. But if we defeat it in Spain it will still be active. If Hitler and Mussolini are overthrown, it will still be powerful. It has got into the human mind, even the minds of very poor and exploited people. Neither democracy nor humanism can really resist it. Its short-cuts are too attractive.'

'What can defeat it, then?'

Paul smiled. He ran his hand back over his sweating forehead and wet hair.

'My father is a parson, did you know? I can run through both litanies, his and now ours. You expect me to say *socialism*?'

'Is there any other way?'

'This isn't a debate, Norman. You try firing socialism at the Falange and the Requetés.'

'But still it's our mobilisation. Our mobilisation of the future.'

'You think that?'

'Yes, Paul. It's the only answer I can find.'

'Well, I hope you're right. But I'll tell you what I think. We have to go now as strangers to fight something alien, and the outcome, either way, will be a new strangeness. If we live to see it we shall still be strangers, to each other and to ourselves. That makes it much easier, now, for me.'

'How can it make it easier?'

'Because a line is being crossed. Because the old world is ending. Thus even survival . . .'

'It will be different among comrades. The spirit is very strong.'

'Cheering each other up,' Paul said and smiled.

'Much more than that.'

'In a strange country, wearing a strange uniform, in a strange formation. Fighting as strangers against aliens, in a bare land.'

Norman shifted his position; his knees and calves were cramped. Paul stared up at him. His unexpectedly formal words seemed to have taken a kind of possession of him.

'Did you talk to Mark about Spain?' Norman asked, relaxing.

'Yes, of course. He was very helpful.'

'Other places and new days are always blank until you arrive. Then the life makes itself.'

'Do you think I'm denying that? It's what I've been saying.'

Norman nodded. He reached out and took Paul's hand. The palm was clammy with sweat but it was also cold.

'Thanks for talking, Norman,' Paul said, now embarrassed.

'No, I'm glad. And all the best.'

'They were playing "Strange Fruit",' Paul said, getting up.

'Yes. I noticed.'

As Norman stood, Pippa was waiting for him. Several people were now leaving but the big room was still crowded. Pippa led the way to the door. Norman followed. As they got to the door Monkey heaved himself up from the place against the wall where he had been sitting since they arrived.

'Duty done?' Monkey asked. He was looking at Pippa, who ignored him.

'Hardly that,' Norman said, irritably.

Monkey smiled. He was still looking at Pippa.

'Monkey Pitter, Pippa Howard,' Norman said quickly.

'How nice,' Monkey said.

Norman hesitated.

'We're going on for a meal,' he said to Monkey.

'I won't intrude,' Monkey said, and made a quick, formal bow.

# 4

꧁ ❀ ꧂

# SPAIN, FEBRUARY 1937

'Bert!'

'Aye?'

'Did you hear that?'

Bert Lewis pushed himself closer to where Sandy Ross was lying, in the shelter of a gorse bush on the lip of the hollow they had found for a listening-post. They had been sent out after dark, a hundred yards down from the company trench. They were to try to pick up sounds of movement from the enemy infantry. During the day these had overrun and half-destroyed the three companies holding the intermediate ridge, on the long slope down to the Jarama.

Through the first hours there had been so much noise from their own lines – occasional bursts of machine-gun fire but mainly the long chipping of pick and shovel as the volunteers tried to dig deeper into the hard, dry white earth – that listening for anything else had seemed pointless. Now most of that had died down, and the night was quiet. It was very cold, with frost forming; the stars were brilliant overhead. Sitting off watch, Bert had been nodding into sleep when Sandy had roused him.

'What did it sound like?' he whispered, lying on Sandy's shoulder and pressing his mouth to his ear.

'It was voices.'

'Our lot?'

'No. It wasn't English or Spanish.'

'Moors, then?'

'Aye.'

Bert rolled away and cocked his rifle. They both listened intently. They heard voices again. Sandy whispered that they were further away. Then there was a snatch of song, in a high voice, followed by a shout and then silence again.

Bert stared across the bushy ground to the white farmhouse on the ridge where yesterday's worst fighting had been. There was a light there suddenly, standing out clearly in the dimness of starlight. He was lifting his rifle to fire at it when there was a burst of machine-gun fire from behind him. The light went out. He pulled his rifle back. It would have been wrong, he now knew, to fire himself, giving away their exposed position.

He stared again into the barely visible land. He was less than twenty-four hours into his first battle but it already felt as if there had never been any other kind of life. Since the real fighting had started, at midday yesterday, everything else had dropped away. There was only this strange dry land, among the gorse and weeds below the olive trees, and the interminable noise of the firing. He had seen more dead and wounded, in those few hours, than anyone could expect in a hundred ordinary lifetimes. The effect, after the first shocks, was to shift the mind into an unknown dimension: one in which an extreme physical alertness was strangely compounded with an overbearingly heavy fatigue and numbness. These quiet minutes of listening were like a door back into memory of a life in which people still moved and talked in what they took for normality; a life in which excitement and crisis could happen but still connected to some base from which people knew themselves and each other. That was far from this other dimension, noisy and bloody and isolated, which could only ever be known by those who, without expectation or warning, had so strangely entered it.

The door back still opened, slowly. Lying beside Sandy, staring across at the ridge where thousands of Moors must still be encamped, he was tempted to slam it shut. For it was now inconceivable that he would ever get back there, and while this was so the memories were only an encumbrance. Still they pushed through, somehow, of their own accord. Yet there was nothing beyond the top-floor office above the fruit barrows in

Covent Garden, where he had signed up, without conditions. After that the memories came quickly. The Channel ferry and the train to Paris; the free taxi ride to the big trade-union hall; then the crowds, the banners and the wine as the Red Train left for the south.

'There again, Bert.'

'Aye, but no nearer.'

He had got drinking with Sandy and a group of other Scots on the long train journey south. Many, like himself, had been on the dole, but Sandy, a communist branch secretary, had left a good job in the shipyards. They had stayed together in the buses after the border crossing, and in the kitting-out at Albacete: the thin cotton corduroy uniforms, the khaki peaked caps, the groundsheet capes, the old French tin helmets, the heavy leather belts and ammunition cases; no rifles. Trucked to Madrigueras for training, they had been put in the same company: parading and drilling and political lectures in the almost permanent drizzle; still with no rifles. The only interesting day had been when he and Sandy had tried to talk to the old men in the village, poorer than anybody they had come across on Clydeside or in the Welsh valleys. They had been shown their livelihood: the little bulbs of meadow saffron that they planted and harvested for the shreds of spice: a field of flowers for a bowl of the stamens.

There was heavy firing suddenly, away to the north, and repeated gun flashes. It was beyond the road and out of their sector. Bert settled again.

For the poor of the world – but there was poor and poor again, right down to this scratching in dry earth. These enemy Moors on the ridge above them: they had been like bundles of old brown rags through all the fighting yesterday. They wore blankets with holes for their heads to push through. They were small and swarthy. In the attack they ran weaving and ducking, like dirty paper scraps in a wind. It was not just the rich of the world and the poor lifting their rifles against them. It was now these other poor, signed up for a bit of bread in a colonial army and fighting here like devils: for their lives, for their livelihood.

There was the crump of a shell beyond, to their left. That sector had been quiet since the battle yesterday. The rifles had

been issued at last, and there were eight heavy machine-guns for
their company. They had all piled into the train of open trucks,
for the night-time journey to the south of Madrid. Then it had
been unloading and the heavy march towards the front, the
new-issue boots getting their first long go and protesting. The
assembly point, where they had tried to sleep. That boy with
the big binoculars, which he had kept hidden till they were at
the front: offering Bert a look at some bird he had spotted. Up
again, half asleep, and the climb to the plateau. Most of the men
had left their inessential stuff to collect on the way back when
the battle was over. Taking their going back for granted, as
anyone might who had not yet been in battle.

'What d'you make it, Bert?'

'Nearly two.'

'It's stand-to at three. In case the buggers come up before
dawn.'

'Give it till quarter-to, we'll get back.'

Bert crouched, thinking carefully. It can all be drawn on
paper: positions and enemy positions; lines of advance, fields of
fire. In the sun, all morning, following the paper plan, it had
been an ordinary working world, like back in the colliery,
only on strange ground. Seventy-two men in the machine-gun
company, cutting that hundred-yard trench in the hard dry soil,
behind the little stone wall. Cutting it with bayonet points and
tin helmets for shovels: someone had forgotten to bring up the
digging tools. It was work most of the men could manage: eight
out of ten of them were hard working-class lads. They had dug
machine-gun pits and then began sighting and calculating. That
boy with the binoculars again, singing out distances in his posh
English voice: a little dark, plump chap; shiny hair, very red
cheeks, you could take him for a Spaniard. It was the kind of
war you heard about: like lines and arrows on paper.

Sandy grunted and pushed himself up, stamping his feet and
beating his arms.

'I'd rather get bloody shot than freeze to death.'

'Aye.'

Bert had wrapped one blanket round his legs and another
over his shoulders and head. The cold struck only when he tried
to unbend. Everything was quiet in front of them but as they

stood they could both hear what seemed a low buzz of sound, away down to their right. They listened intently, but could not pick out any definite sounds.

'If I didn't know better,' Bert whispered, 'I'd say there was hundreds of men in that dip down there.'

'But not moving or doing anything.'

'No, I've heard it at night on the mountain back home. If there's sheep, all quiet, you pick up something that they're there.'

'Shall we try a few rounds? See what happens?'

'Better not,' Bert whispered. 'If they're there at first light they're just made for us.'

They squatted again. Now that the idea was in their minds, what they were hearing seemed clearer with every moment. Yet there was still nothing certain: only that sense of the presence of many hundreds of men in the darkness. They were probably curled and sleeping among the bushes in their bits of blankets.

Bert closed his eyes. The thought of those sleeping men, and of who they must be, had forced back the worst hours of yesterday. The company had been at ease in the long trench, looking out in the sun at the three forward companies on the intermediate ridge, and beyond them to the high cliffs of the river gorge, on which the plan of the battle had been centred. The boy with the binoculars, having finished his measurements, had been sitting near Bert. He was pointing out Madrid in the distance – a hazy frontage of high buildings that could as well have been one of the cliffs in the Jarama gorge.

'So you can see it makes sense that we're here,' the boy had said. 'Standing guard at the heart of the Republic.'

A couple of the others had smiled when he said that. In his parson's voice he sounded like the endless booming talk of the political commissar's lectures. Bert had not smiled. He could hear the same words in his own mind, as familiar inhabitants, still deeply and closely connected. The words were at a great distance from the stumpy bayonets trying to cut a trench in the white earth, and from the fatigue and muddle of all their movements so far. But that was the distance they had set out to close: from the rhetoric to the practice; from the party to the army. It was the language he had used himself, on that day at the barn, above Danycapel.

'Can I borrow your glasses and see Madrid?'

'Of course,' the boy had said. 'I'm sorry, I should have offered.'

He had then come so eagerly to sit beside Bert. The binoculars had been terrific, bringing up buildings as the sunlight caught them.

'Lovely glasses,' Bert had said, handing them carefully back.

'Yes, my mother bought them specially. They're German.'

'German? Well, they're not the only things the Germans have sent to Spain.'

'That's right. But we must use what we've got.'

He had looked so sad and embarrassed that Bert stared, trying to make him out.

'Did your Mam not want you to come, then?' he asked.

'Why do you say that?'

'I don't mean it hard, boy. I just wondered.'

He had looked then into Bert's face. His dark eyes were rounded.

'Of course she didn't want it. She thought I was rejecting her. Rejecting the kind of life she'd been making.'

'Well, that's it, isn't it?'

The boy had put the strap of the binoculars back over his head, disturbing his stained khaki cap.

'She was more right than she knew. I *was* rejecting everything. That was all it was, when I decided to come. But what I've found, since I've been here . . .'

Bert waited.

'What I've found is what *comrade* means. I would never have believed it. It's here on the ground, a real movement, not of strangers but of comrades.'

It was just as he finished speaking, and with a shattering suddenness, that the barrage had opened on the ridge and the forward companies. The artillery shells and mortars were concentrated on the ridge, and the company was safe, lying back. In the sudden weight of it they had all ducked for cover. After a minute the boy had got up to run back to his post.

'What's your name, lad?' Bert had called after him.

'Paul,' he had said quickly. 'Paul Howe.'

The barrage had intensified. The whole ridge below them, where the rifle companies were lying with hardly any cover, was already shrouded with rising dust and smoke. A great weight of explosives was continuing to pour down on it. From time to time their own men could be seen running for some cover, but under the hail of bursting shells there was none, really. Many men had run for the white farmhouse but it was easy to see, from above, that this was the ranging target for the barrage.

Bert had imagined shelling, from stories about the Great War. But this was so heavy and so prolonged that the knowledge from the stories was simply wiped out, and there was only this hellish and unbearable noise. Soon they could see wounded men being helped back from the ridge behind their line. But most of them were still there, under the endless explosions. There was a brief cheer when they saw a few planes from their own side, two bombers and three of the little Chato biplane fighters, flying beyond the ridge to the river and trying to silence the guns. They were Russian planes going in against the weight of the German Condor Legion, which they had been told had most of the Fascists' heavy weapons. The little fighters broke away and began machine-gunning the ground. The bombers swung back, in a wide arc. The heavy barrage continued, unaffected.

It had lasted for three hours. It could as easily have been for ever, imposing itself as normality. The streams of wounded coming back had got wider. There were reports of many killed. Then, in the strange silence after the artillery had stopped, there was the unforgettable sight of the infantry attack. Many hundreds, perhaps thousands, of the Moorish infantry, weaving and darting for cover up the steep slope, firing and then disappearing behind bushes and dips in the ground. They looked like bundles of rags swarming up the slope, more and more of them, getting nearer all the time. There was very little the machine-gun company could do, since their own men were between them and the enemy. There was rifle fire from the survivors on the ridge: a surprising amount of it, after the weight of the barrage. Then suddenly, over the crest of the ridge above the now ruined white farmhouse, the enemy infantry were running in great numbers, and there was a high screaming. There could now at last be machine-gun support but the battle for the ridge had been lost. There was confusion everywhere but by late afternoon the survivors had made their desperate way back. Different stories, complaints and anger were everywhere. The most common story was that a hundred and twenty-five had got back, out of the four hundred who had been there. It was on this heavy loss and confusion that darkness had closed their first day of battle.

'Bert!'

'Aye?'

'Time to get back.'

'Aye, I suppose.'

It was still dark. The stars were bright and high. They crouched and made their way up towards the edge of the plateau and the company's trench.

'Halt!' came a loud command.

'It's Bert and Sandy,' Bert shouted.

'Come on slowly, then.'

'He thinks we're Fascists,' Sandy said.

They passed the sentry: old Neil, a man of forty, an Irish republican, who had fought in the Irish rising. They found their commander and reported. They explained that they were certain there were hundreds of the enemy, in the low ground down to the right. Young Paul Howe was with the commander.

'Sir, I got that distance yesterday, there's an old dry stream-bed,' he said excitedly.

The rest of the company were stirring, along the trench. Men were sent back to bring up the machine-guns, which had been pulled back from the forward position overnight. Bert and Sandy got some bitter coffee. The guns were brought up and set into position. The stars were paler now. There was a loose grey light in the sky. They crouched and waited, looking out.

Dawn came suddenly. They could then hardly believe what they saw. In the low ground on their side of the ridge, and stretching back to the little road, there were many hundreds of enemy soldiers. As they watched more and more seemed to get up from the ground but they were not thinking of attack; they were rousing from sleep and being formed into sections. These could not be the Moors who had captured the ridge yesterday, though about half of them were Moors, in their cloak blankets; the others were Spanish Fascists of some sort. They seemed not to know that they were being looked at down gun-sights, from the edge of the plateau above them.

The whispered order passed along the trench: alignments for a box of fire, moving steadily in towards the centre. Then the machine-guns opened up. The bullets scythed into the half-awake, stumbling groups of men. There was a frantic diving for cover but hundreds were hit. Some return fire came, but for the most part the machine-guns poured bullets into an exposed and passive encampment. Bert, as a rifleman guarding the observer for one of the guns, fired until his own barrel was too hot to touch. The water for cooling the machine-guns was nearly boiling. Still the firing went on and now the survivors below were running, frantically, away towards the road, many hit and falling as they ran. As the last of them got beyond range there was a cheer along the trench. The sun was already hot above them.

Bert crawled back from his forward position. Men were standing from the trench, behind the low stone wall, stretching and pissing. Moving along, Bert met Paul. He was drenched with sweat.

'A bit of revenge for yesterday,' Paul said.

'Aye.'

Sandy came over to them, buttoning his thin corduroy trousers.

'They were there, then, Bert.'

'Aye.'

'Poor sods, waking up to that lot.'

'Aye, I suppose.'

'They were Fascists,' Paul said.

'Aye,' Sandy said. 'Little doubt about that.'

Bert was trying to wind down, after the intensity of the firing. He sat on the low wall, doing his best to clean his rifle with an old purple handkerchief. Paul and Sandy were looking down to the road, where the enemy had disappeared.

Bert heard the mortar shell as if from a distance: a low whistling and whirring sound. He flung himself behind the wall and then the explosion came almost at once. He saw the white dust rising. He waited and then slowly lifted on to his elbows. Sandy and Paul were lying sprawled, half out of the trench.

Sandy was rolling on his back and holding his hands to his stomach. Paul was lying very still.

As Bert moved towards them other mortar shells landed, along the line of the trench. He flung himself face downwards. Always, it seemed, the first move was to protect the face.

'They've got our range!' somebody shouted.

Bert lifted himself.

'Stretcher bearers!' he shouted.

He could not hear through the explosions whether anybody answered. He crawled to look at Paul, who was nearest. He had been hit on the scalp and in the throat and had died instantly. His outstretched hand still grasped the leather strap of the binoculars. Bert moved towards Sandy. Sandy seemed to feel the movement and reached out and grasped Bert's hand. The hand that he had taken from his stomach was thick with blood, and his whole body there was soaked. Bert held his hand tightly.

'Hang on, boy, I'll get help!'

He shouted again for stretcher bearers.

Sandy forced his head up a little. He looked at Bert and smiled.

'Poor sods,' he said, in a surprisingly normal voice.

'Aye.'

There was a cry along the trench: 'On guard!' On either side, along the trench and the wall, men were getting into firing positions again. One of the machine-guns started firing and the others followed it. Bert looked down where they were firing. There were, so far as he could see, no enemy at all in sight. He looked back down at Sandy. In those few seconds he had gone. His mouth had fallen open and was filled with blood. He had been wearing an upper denture and this had been pushed out, covered with blood, over his lower lip.

Bert released his hand. He wiped his palm and fingers on a weed like a dock that was growing under the wall. The firing stopped.

'On guard!' the shout came again.

Bert took the binoculars from Paul's hand and focused them along the lower ground to the road. It was still empty, as far as he could see, but then suddenly he saw a movement, no more than the edge of a blanket beside a bush, and it was gone as soon as he saw it. He focused more closely on that ground. It was as if it changed as he stared at it. What had seemed an unbroken slope had a long dip within it, running uphill, and now that he was alerted to it he could see many small signs of movement along it. Only the binoculars made this possible. He glanced back at Paul, lying dead.

He went along the trench to report what he had seen. It was evidently a stealthy advance to the edge of the plateau on their right. It seemed not to threaten them directly. But orders were given to swing the fire of the guns along that dip. It was all they could do.

Bert went back to where Sandy and Paul were lying. He touched their eyelids to close them. Then he lifted the binoculars and resumed his watch. The sun was hot now, and there was a heavy smell in the trench.

'There they are!' he shouted, pointing excitedly. A section of Moors was running from the road towards the cover of the dip. Two guns fired immediately, but most of the section had reached cover.

Now all along the line the survivors were standing to. A few of the wounded had been got back but the dead had to be left. There was a long period of quiet, as if the battle had moved away from them. There was still heavy shelling and rifle fire in the distance, and two tanks with infantry moved beyond the road and were lost to sight. It began to look as if they would hold the line without challenge.

There was then shouting behind them. Bert swung round and saw two enemy soldiers, not Moors, on his own side of the wall and the trench. At the same moment grenades were thrown into the trench, from behind but also from the slope below them. As he kneeled, lifting his rifle, Bert saw the Moors rising from the bushes within ten or fifteen yards of them. They were shouting now, and running fiercely for the trench. He fired without stopping to aim. Others were firing but there was confusion along the trench because the enemy were also behind them, shooting down from the higher ground.

It was all over very quickly. Bert had his rifle knocked from his hands with a blow on his shoulder from behind. The Moors were shouting excitedly and pushing their prisoners along the trench at rifle point. The other enemy soldiers, Spaniards, were at the machine-guns and swinging them round. In no time, as it seemed, they were firing them back towards the Republican lines.

Bert stood numb with shock and shame. It was still impossible to believe that they could have been caught like that. As he stood he was hit with a rifle butt in his back, and stumbled forward. A detachment of Moors was lining up the prisoners who could walk. They were a few over twenty, of the nearly eighty who had been in the company. They could not understand the shouted words of their captors but whenever they hesitated they were hit and pushed forward. They were being handled so fiercely that Bert thought it probable they were simply being taken to be shot.

One very small guard, with an almost square brown face, his black hair standing up from his scalp and his moustache curved from his mouth to join a narrow beard along the line of his chin, slipped quickly ahead of Bert and turned on the wall to stand level with him. He shouted and spat into Bert's face. Bert thought the shout sounded like 'Infidel'.

A Spanish officer was directing what had been the company's machine-guns. He paused and looked at the line of prisoners and shouted an order. Bert could not understand him but made out the words for 'Russians' and 'Communists'. Then he was prodded forward again, and the line of prisoners was forced to run down the slope, along the track where yesterday they had watched their comrades from the left forward company retreating. They ran a long way down, forced by their more agile guards, and were getting in among trees again before Bert realised that he was still wearing Paul's binoculars. His rifle had been taken from him but the binoculars were still around his neck. They had been bumping his chest as he was forced to run but he only now became fully aware of them. Looking for the guard, and half-turning to try to conceal his movement, he slipped the binoculars from his neck and thrust them inside his uniform tunic and vest. The casing was sharp and cold against the sweating skin.

He had not been noticed. In among the trees, the line of prisoners was halted. They were ordered to sit with their hands over their heads. The guards began talking to each other. They were not looking at the prisoners.

'Now solong,' Bert said to himself under his breath, and closed his eyes.

# 5

❦

# DANYCAPEL—WESTRIDGE,
# MAY—JULY 1937

The street of narrow grey houses ran steeply towards the open mountain. Number 27, on the western side, was already in deep shadow as Emma waited in the evening sunlight on the broken pavement opposite. Several colliers off shift from the pit in the valley bottom had already come up the street, turning in at different doors lower down, a few passing and looking at her while they tramped uphill, chatting.

'Evening,' one lad said, passing. He was no more than eighteen. He took his cap off with a flourish. There was a sharp dividing line across his forehead, between the pit dirt that ran from his throat to above his eyebrows and the pink freckled skin below his tightly curling red hair. The flirtatious greeting was easy and casual. Emma smiled but turned and looked back down the street.

Two men were walking slowly up the middle of the road. One turned off, several doors down, and the other came on towards her. Though he was in his pit clothes, Emma recognised Jim without difficulty. She had clearly remembered the lithe, dark, Italian-looking young man who had walked with her and Bert Lewis on the hill above the camp. She moved forward quickly.

'Jim?'

'Aye?'

He had stopped, surprised by her voice. He looked at her uncertainly.

'I'm Emma. You remember? The camp.'

'Emma!' Jim said quickly, and smiled.

His teeth were white against the pit dirt. He put out his hand, staring intently into her face.

'No, better not,' he said, as she reached forward to shake hands.

Emma took his hand and held it.

'Jim, I've waited to catch you. I'm going in to see your mother and sister, but I have to talk to you first.'

Jim was still staring at her. He released his hand.

'Well, come on in, Emma. You're welcome. Mam and Nesta's there.'

'I will come in, Jim. But I've got something to say to you first.'

'To me?'

'Yes. I don't know how much you know about your sister and my brother.'

'Your brother? I don't know him, do I?'

'Norman. Norman Braose.'

Jim narrowed his eyes, then looked quickly away.

'I didn't know you were brother and sister,' he said.

'Really?'

'It was all first names, see, at the camp.'

'Of course. But never mind that now. I've got to explain this whole situation.'

Jim shifted his feet in the heavy pit boots. He looked doubtfully into her face.

'You'd be better explaining it to her, I reckon.'

'I shall, Jim. I shall. That's why I've come down. But there are things it might be easier to say to you.'

Jim hesitated.

'I don't know about that,' he said at last. 'I don't see how any of it could be easy.'

'Of course not. But I know her. She's a proud girl.'

'We're a proud family. Don't mistake us on that.'

'Jim, I'm not mistaking you. But we must all face the facts. When she has this child—'

'So you know about that?'

'Only recently, Jim. Norman didn't tell me. And now he's in Marseilles, doing work for the Party, helping supplies get to Spain.'

'Is he now?'

'He wrote and asked me to deal with his letters. I found the two last letters from Birdie.'

'Birdie?'

'I'm sorry. Nesta. Birdie was his nickname for her.'

'Was it?' Jim said, and looked harder at her.

A late collier passed, an elderly man, walking slowly up the hill.

'Night, Jim,' he said as he passed.

'Emrys,' Jim answered, keeping his eyes on Emma's face.

'It's awful, I know,' Emma said. 'But whatever happens there's still all the practical arrangements. Embarrassing or not, we shall have to talk sooner or later about money.'

'Not with me you won't. You can come in and say what you've got to to the family.'

'Of course, Jim. I will. But for heaven's sake, don't take out your quarrel on me. I've come as a friend.'

'Aye,' Jim said, moving across to open the door.

Emma followed him into the narrow passage and through to the back-kitchen, where the sunlight poured through. There was a window looking out over the steeply rising garden to the fence and the mountain beyond it. Mrs Pritchard was peeling carrots in the sink.

'Jim?' she called, without turning.

'Aye, Mam. I've brought somebody to see you.'

Mrs Pritchard turned abruptly. She was confused when she saw Emma, and looked questioningly at Jim.

'This is Emma, Mam.'

Mrs Pritchard wiped her hands on her flower-patterned apron. 'Pleased to meet you, Emma.'

Emma shook hands.

'Emma's Norman's sister,' Jim said.

'Norman's sister?' Mrs Pritchard said, staring up at the much bigger younger woman.

'I had to come to discuss things,' Emma said awkwardly.

Mrs Pritchard turned away.

'I'll have to get Dad,' she said quickly. 'Jim, call your Dad. He's up in the shed, I think.'

Jim went out and up the garden. Mrs Pritchard moved quickly, not looking at Emma.

'We'll go in the front room. If you'll come this way.'

'It's all right. Anywhere,' Emma said, disturbed.

But Mrs Pritchard had gone ahead and opened the second door along the passage. The little room smelled of fabric and polish. Chairs were set around a low square table which was covered with a soft fringed red tablecloth. There were many family photographs on the walls and mantelpiece, and on white shelves opposite the net-curtained window a collection of brass jugs and harness-pieces.

'If you'd just sit you down,' Mrs Pritchard said, and went out, closing the door.

Emma waited, moving around the room. She could hear muffled voices from the back of the house. There was a long delay, and then, as she was again looking over the collection of brass, the door opened. Ken Pritchard, small, white-haired, in a waistcoat and collarless shirt, stood hesitating in the doorway.

'Mr Pritchard?' Emma said, going forward.

'Very pleased to meet you,' he said, politely.

He had a short brown pipe in his hand. His thick brown fingers were curved and slightly shaking.

'If you'd please to sit down, Miss.'

'Thank you.'

He sat opposite her. He lifted his pipe and lit it.

'You come down by train, then?'

'Yes. Through Newport.'

'Aye!'

The pipe had gone out. He looked at it and then laid it on the table.

'I shouldn't be smoking it anyway,' he said, smiling. 'The old doc warned me off it, with my lung.'

'I see.'

'It's what we call the devil's dust. Have you heard that name for it?'

'No. I'm sorry. I haven't.'

The door was still open. He looked towards it. There was a

pause and then his wife came in. She had taken off her apron and brushed her hair. She closed the door behind her, sat near her husband and waited. There was a noticeable silence.

'How is Nesta keeping?' Emma asked at last.

She had been looking at Mrs Pritchard, who did not answer.

'Pretty well, considering,' Ken said. 'The doctor said he was pleased with her.'

His wife looked angrily at him. There was another pause, while she seemed to wait for him to speak. Then she folded her arms and spoke herself.

'Jim said he was in Spain.'

'Norman? No, France. Marseilles.'

'Is he coming back, then?'

'Well, I wish I knew, Mrs Pritchard. All I got was this telegram, to see to his letters. And there were the letters from your daughter among them.'

'Nothing else?'

'Not about this, no.'

Mrs Pritchard unfolded her arms. She looked across at her husband, who picked up his pipe and got it going again.

'Then what have you come for?' Mrs Pritchard asked. Emma drew herself up.

'I felt I had to come. I didn't even know this had happened. I knew Norman had been seeing her, of course . . .'

'And that you disapproved of it,' Mrs Pritchard said sharply.

'Who told you that?'

'Nesta did. He told her you'd come from this Party of yours and that he was to stop seeing her.'

'It wasn't quite like that. I know how it must look but all we were thinking of was that she was very young and that he should not mislead her.'

'A bit late for that.'

'All right. I agree. But we knew nothing of all this.'

'When she was already pregnant by him. Didn't he tell you that?'

'No, as a matter of fact he didn't. Though perhaps at that early stage he didn't know.'

'But not later either?'

'I told you, Mrs Pritchard. He never told us at all.'

'Just run off to Spain, was it?'

'Not Spain. France. But I agree, of course. By then he must have known.'

'He knew before Christmas, when he come down here.'

'He came then?'

'Certainly. We all sat in here and we talked it over. He was to come again at Easter and they was going to get married.'

'Married? At Easter? But that may explain it. It was just before Easter he was ordered to go to Marseilles.'

'Ordered? Who ordered him?'

'Well, not quite ordered. But it was a Party instruction.'

'Them not knowing about our Nesta?'

'I don't know, Mrs Pritchard.'

'He could have told them, couldn't he?'

'Yes, of course he could have told them.'

'There you are, then. He run off.'

Emma looked down at her hands. She didn't know what to say.

'We liked him, mind,' Ken Pritchard said suddenly. 'A brainy chap and friendly with it.'

His wife looked angrily at him. He sucked on his dead pipe.

'When exactly is the baby due?' Emma asked.

'Third week in June, what the doctor said,' Mrs Pritchard replied.

'Well, I'll try, of course, to get him back in time.'

'Do you think he'd come, after that?'

'Well, he has to, Mrs Pritchard.'

'Has to is pie next week. If he was really like that he'd be here.'

'I agree. But then he didn't see these last two letters.'

'How did they alter it?'

Emma hesitated.

'I don't know. Perhaps I should speak to Nesta first.'

'I'm her mother, aren't I?'

'It's only . . . Well, all right. But they were desperate letters. That she couldn't go through all this on her own. That she couldn't stand it, being alone and ashamed among her family and friends.'

'She never said that.'

'She did, Mrs Pritchard. I can show you the letters. That was why I said I should talk to her first.'

'Except you didn't. You waited for our Jim.'

'Well, I'd met Jim. I thought it would be easier, just to start with.'

'Thought what would be easier?'

Emma put down her bag, which seemed suddenly heavy on her knees.

'I don't blame you for being angry, Mrs Pritchard.'

'I should hope not indeed.'

'No, but as I said I shall try to get him back. If he's said he'll marry her he must come back and honour it.'

'That's what I say.'

'Yes, but if he doesn't, Mrs Pritchard; or if he doesn't, or even can't, get back to England in time—'

'England?'

'You know what I mean. However it turns out it won't be easy for you. Where will she have the baby?'

'Here at her home, of course.'

'Not a nursing home?'

'Where do you think we'd get the money for a nursing home?'

'I know. But don't you see, that's where I could help?'

'No. No,' Ken said suddenly.

Both women looked at him.

'No money,' he said, and knotted his hands.

'You keep out of this, Dad,' Mrs Pritchard said, shortly.

He looked away.

'In fact I had an idea,' Emma hurried on. 'When I read her letters I knew I had to do something. If you would agree I'd be glad to arrange it.'

'Go on,' Mrs Pritchard said, watching her.

'I have an aunt who lives near Stroud. Aunt Kate. She's a widow from the Great War. I remembered her telling me she's on the committee of a nursing home. She could get Nesta in, and she'd be very well looked after.'

Mrs Pritchard said nothing. Her husband knocked his pipe out noisily in the fireplace.

'I rang her up and explained things,' Emma went on. 'It's all arranged. Provisionally of course. That is, if you and Nesta agree.'

Mrs Pritchard looked at her husband. He looked away. His thin face under the white hair was drawn with pain.

'Was that what you wanted to say to Jim?' Mrs Pritchard asked.

'Well, that and about money generally,' Emma hurried to say. 'I mean only, of course, until it can be all cleared up. But while things are as they are there will be a need for money.'

'No,' Ken Pritchard said.

He got up slowly and walked out of the room. He left the door open behind him. His wife got up quickly and closed it.

'You can't blame him for not liking it,' she said, quietly.

'No, I understand, of course.'

'I don't like it either. My own daughter. She's only a young girl still. Young for her age, I mean.'

'I know. That's what I thought.'

'She's had her disappointments, like we all have. There was her teacher, Mrs Harries, wanted her to go to art college, but no hope of that. Only now, with Jim back at work, and things beginning to get a bit easier. It's like before her life's had a chance to start.'

'I agree. That's why I thought of this arrangement. Not to put it right, but to make it that bit easier.'

'Well, it would, fair play. And then what if he came back?'

'He'd know where she was. I shall write and tell him. And whenever it is they could then get married.'

Mrs Pritchard got up. She moved closer to Emma and looked up into her face.

'I don't hold much hopes of it, I tell you straight. But you did right to come and I thank you.'

'You mean you agree about the nursing home?'

'Well, it would be better, wouldn't it?'

'Your husband doesn't like the idea.'

'Men don't have kids upstairs in these little houses.'

'And you think Nesta will agree?'

'Birdie did I hear you call her?'

'I'm sorry. It's just a nickname.'

Mrs Pritchard smiled.

'It suits her.'

'Not really.'

'She's upstairs, lying down. She spends all her time there, the little room at the back where she gets the light. She's up there painting most of the time – since she had to stop work.'

'Could I see her, do you think?'

'Yes, I'll take you up. And then you'll stay for a bit of tea. Those men of mine will be shouting for it.'

'Don't bother about me,' Emma said.

They went up the narrow dark stairs from the passage. Mrs Pritchard opened the farthest door.

'Nesta, love.' There was no reply. 'Here's a friend come to see you.'

'What?' Nesta cried, and all at once she was in the doorway. As she saw Emma her face fell.

'Hullo, Nesta,' Emma said.

Nesta stared at her. The room behind her was bright with sunlight and this was intensified by the bright yellow wash of the walls.

'She done her room up like one of her paintings,' Mrs Pritchard said.

'It's lovely. Can I come in?' Emma said.

'If you like.'

She stood from the doorway. Mrs Pritchard went back downstairs. Emma moved slowly and carefully into the tiny room, where Nesta sat on the small chair by the window; she had been working at a miniature easel. Emma perched on the edge of the narrow bed, which had a white crochet-work counterpane.

'Your mother said you still paint a lot.'

'Paint and draw. It's the drawing I've got to work at.'

'May I look?'

'If you like.'

As they squeezed past each other in the narrow space, Emma looked again at the swelling of the pregnancy. Nesta was wearing a loose blue smock, which partly disguised it. On the paper on the easel there was a nearly completed drawing of a small church with an open belfry among crowding trees.

'Is it a local church?'

'Not really.'

'It's a lovely drawing.'

'It's up in the mountains. People go there to see the carved screen.'

'Inside, you mean?'

'Yes, it's inside.'

Emma looked again at the drawing, then squeezed back to her place on the bed. Nesta turned the drawing over and sat looking out of the window. Beyond the garden there were sheep on the open mountain.

'Did he send you for something?' Nesta asked suddenly.

'Norman? No. He only sent me a telegram to look at his letters.'

'Where is he?'

'Marseilles.'

'Yes, he said he was going there. He said for a couple of weeks.'

'You saw him?'

'No, he wrote. Just a short letter.'

'When did you last see him?'

'That was before Christmas. He come to see Dad.'

As Emma hesitated, Nesta burst into tears. She let the crying come, bending her head forward into her hands. Then she began rocking on her chair. Emma waited.

'He's let you down, hasn't he?' she said at last, as the crying eased.

Nesta looked up, wiping her eyes.

'It isn't only that,' she said, looking across at Emma.

'No?'

Nesta stood and looked out through the window.

'It was when he come before Christmas. He was horrible then.'

'But I thought he agreed . . .'

'You're talking like Dad and Mam. That wasn't the worst of it. That was just my own silly fault.'

'No, Birdie.'

'It was him, it was horrible, the things he was saying.'

'What did he say?'

'It was that one bad night. He'd been out drinking with Jim. He come back and started on about Bert.'

'Bert? Bert Lewis?'

Something in Emma's voice made Nesta turn. She wiped her eyes again and stared at Emma.

'I'll tell you what it was,' she said quietly. 'Bert had volunteered to go and fight in Spain. You heard him say he was going to.'

'Yes, and now he's missing.'

'No, he isn't. We just heard from the Red Cross. I was down his Mam's. He's a prisoner in good health. The Red Cross have seen him.'

'We hadn't heard that.'

'Yes, well, his people are down here.'

'That's very good news.'

'Is it? Though I know it could have been worse. I've sent him a couple of letters and me and his Mam packed a parcel.'

'Through the Red Cross?'

'The first letter was, yes. But we've got an address now. Do you want it?'

'Yes, I'd be glad.'

'San Pedro de something. It's a prison camp. I've got it downstairs.'

'Thanks,' Emma said.

Nesta sighed. She sat wearily on her chair by the easel.

'Did Norman see Bert before he went?' Emma asked.

'No, not like that. Bert went from here in November.'

'What did he say about Bert then?'

Nesta leaned forward. Her large, light-blue eyes were wide open.

'I'd never seen him like it before. Mam says it's just he was drunk but it was worse than that. He was all dirty and hating, like a different man altogether.'

'What did he actually say?'

'He said I'd been going with Bert. He said they all knew about it, down the valley. He said I'd been only pretending with him, it was Bert I really wanted.'

Emma hesitated. She stared down at her large hand on the fine work of the counterpane.

'Did he say anything about the baby?' she heard herself asking.

'Yes he did.'

'That it wasn't his?'

'Well, he couldn't come out and say that. But it was what he meant, that was obvious.'

Emma hesitated again. The little room seemed suddenly stifling.

'And what did you say, Birdie?' she asked, carefully.

'I said of course I'd been seeing Bert. I've always known him, haven't I?'

'But surely that wasn't what Norman meant?'

'How do I know what he meant? I told you, he was just dirty and hating.'

'But he'd heard something, obviously, while he was out with Jim.'

Nesta stared at her, then jumped up suddenly.

'I'll show you something,' she said fiercely.

Emma leaned back as Nesta pushed past her. There was a picture mounted on board at the head of the narrow bed. It was turned to the wall.

'There,' Nesta said, taking down the picture and turning it. Emma stared. At first she saw only the extraordinary colours, a startling yellow and light blue.

'You're his sister, aren't you?' Nesta said. 'You can see it, I suppose?'

'I'm too close.'

Nesta propped it at the head of the bed. Emma went to the window and looked back. She seemed to feel it in her stomach before she could make it out. Then the shapes came through suddenly. It was a two-colour portrait of Norman, his head and shoulders with the face half-turned forward. The likeness was startling although the colours were so strange. The ground of face and hair was bright yellow, with small marks of light blue for features. All around the head was blue, with lines of yellow down into the shoulders, and some other yellow marks in the top left-hand corner. Emma stared at these marks and saw the shape of a tree: a broken pine.

'Well?' Nesta asked.

'It's terrific, Birdie. Absolutely marvellous.'

'But you can see it, can't you?'

'Yes, of course I can see that it's Norman. What is it, by the way? How you did it, I mean?'

'Never mind about that. It's what they call gouache. But it's what's there I want you to look at.'

'It's very like him, Birdie.'

'Is it? Do you think so? It's like what I thought he was like.'

'The features, you mean? But it is, it is.'

'No, the colours,' Nesta said.

Emma looked at her. There was now an edge of wildness in the voice.

'Did he see it?' she asked, forcing an ordinary tone.

'No, he didn't. He was going to. I was keeping it for him. But not after that night.'

'You mean what he said about Bert?'

Nesta picked up the picture and turned it again to the wall.

'You can't see it, can you?' she said, sitting on her bed.

'Yes. I told you. It's lovely.'

'It used to be lovely.'

'No, it's Norman all right. Anyone would know him.'

'Well, I didn't know him. But I knew that.'

'I don't understand you, Birdie. I'm tiring you, I'm sure. Perhaps you ought to lie down.'

Nesta laughed. There was a knock at the door and Mrs Pritchard came in, carrying a tray with two cups of tea.

'There's food downstairs when you're ready.'

'Oh thank you, Mrs Pritchard,' Emma said, politely. The woman was watching her daughter.

'Have you two had a good talk, then?'

'Yes, very good,' Emma said. 'But we still have to get to the practical side of it.'

Nesta laughed again. The other women stared at her.

'Go on, Mam, we'll come down,' Nesta said.

She seemed in high spirits. She moved quickly around the room and then followed Emma and her mother downstairs.

Nothing important was discussed during the meal. The men had already eaten and gone out. After the meal Emma wanted to talk but clearly the others didn't. She stayed awhile and then walked down to the room she had taken at the little hotel, more of a pub really, by the station. It was arranged that she would come up again the next morning.

Obviously everything had been discussed by then. Mrs Pritchard did most of the talking. The baby was expected in the third week of June. If it was still all right with Emma, and through the kindness of her aunt, Mrs Pritchard would bring Nesta the previous weekend.

'I could borrow a car,' Emma offered.

'No, the train will be all right.'

'Then you must let me meet you at Newport, when you change.'

'Yes, that would be all right. Thank you.'

Emma went through the arrangements of confirming the nursing-home booking and then writing. Mrs Pritchard would be very welcome to stay on if she could.

'No, I'll do it the one day. The men will need me back here.'

'As you wish, of course.'

Nesta sat quietly while they talked. She looked withdrawn and resigned.

'You're sure it's what you want?' Emma asked her.

'Of course,' Mrs Pritchard replied.

'Yes,' Nesta said, very quietly.

Emma wanted to talk to her again, but it was clearly no use. Soon she left to get her train. She was almost at the station before she remembered that she hadn't asked for Bert's prison address. It was too late now to go back.

As she sat in the train, going down through the many small stations and halts in the steep crowded valleys, she wished she had someone she could talk to, really talk to, about all that she had heard. Georgi would be rational, as always, but he didn't easily engage with this kind of problem. If she put it to Monkey, who would of course listen avidly, she knew what the upshot would be; she could in effect hear him saying it: 'Darling Emma, you know as well as I do our Norman couldn't manage it, whereas this miner fellow . . .' But that would be a betrayal, not least of Norman. Though none of the dates were quite certain, there was a general fit with when Norman had borrowed Monkey's car and come down to see Birdie. It was a squalid business, having to reckon like that. And the girl herself, naive, strange, in her own way very talented, was unlikely to be practising that kind of deception. If only she could have given straight answers to perfectly simple questions there would be no doubts left. Meanwhile Norman had to come back, no argument. She would get Georgi on to that.

Telegrams were sent to Marseilles, but there were no replies. Georgi himself had to go urgently to Scotland. Monkey was still in Cambridge but Emma avoided him. She had her own affairs to see to, especially an interview in Manchester for a trainee place in personnel management. She wore one of her old expensive suits. She was accepted to start in September. Her mother was still in Portugal. There was a letter urging her to come out. She wrote explaining how much she had to do.

She met Mrs Pritchard and Nesta in Newport as arranged. They travelled together to Stroud. Emma had borrowed her aunt's car and drove them to the nursing home. It was a lovely quiet place, an old manor house among trees. Mrs Pritchard settled Nesta in her room. She was still very withdrawn and quiet. She would get her medical examination the next morning. Emma drove Mrs Pritchard back to Stroud station, and saw her on to the train. Then she returned to stay with her aunt, at Westridge. She phoned the nursing home each morning and visited each afternoon. Nesta seemed glad to see her but she talked very little, except about the place and how kind everyone was. Emma, for her part, kept away from any difficult subject.

The last week of June passed. Nesta was fine but the baby was late. The daily visiting took on a strange edge through the prolonged delay. Then on the morning of the ninth of July, very early, Emma was wakened by the phone. The matron was precise. Miss Pritchard was well and had given birth to a healthy boy.

Emma ran up and dressed. Her heart was pounding with an excitement which she could not really understand. Calling briefly to her aunt she ran out to the car and drove fast, through the quiet lanes, to the nursing home. Her wheels scattered the gravel as she braked. The matron slowed her down, and she waited impatiently. Then she was at last taken up to the small bedroom at the back of the house, on the third floor: originally a servant's room but now neat and brightly furnished.

Nesta was lying with her eyes closed. She still looked withdrawn. As Emma crossed to the cradle by the bed Nesta opened
her eyes and looked up at her. Emma took her hand. It was
cold. The matron, beside them, bent over and rearranged the
shawl. Emma looked down at the tight, drawn, red face of the
baby.

'Give him to me,' Nesta said to the matron.

'Yes, dear, of course.'

She lifted the baby and put him on Nesta's shoulder. He cried
briefly and blinked.

'He took his time coming, all right,' the matron said.

Nesta smiled. Emma stared down at her: her black hair on
the pillow; the strange, still crumpled face beside it. There was
a fuzz of dark hair over the damp crown. The tiny hands were
grasping the air.

'He's lovely, Birdie,' Emma said, leaning down.

'You think so?' Nesta said, smiling.

# TWO

1944–47

# 1

❧ ❀❀ ❧

# NORMANDIE, JULY 1944

The hay meadow sloped down to the little apple orchard. At the edges of the uncut grass there were hundreds of bright buttercup flowers. In the high hedge behind which they were drawn up, wild roses had climbed in long briars, some beyond the support of the hedge and now tumbling down its sides. Their own long gun barrel was pushed in among a spray of one of the smaller white roses.

Through the long black binoculars – Paul's binoculars as he still thought of them – Bert could make out the corner of a roof beyond the apple trees. The road must run alongside the orchard and behind the high-banked hedge of the meadow. It was hot now under the midday sun. He pushed back his beret, which was rubbing along its band on his sweating forehead. He unwrapped and sucked a boiled sweet, feeling its sharp chemical taste on his palate. He looked again through the binoculars, slowly sweeping the probable line of the road and then staring into the shadows of the orchard. Everything was as still and peaceful as in any country summer. This meadow and orchard in Normandie could be anywhere between Ross and Hereford, on a scout camp.

'Cossack?'

The crackling voice was at a distance in the helmet lying on the turret by his right hand. He pulled off the beret and put on the helmet, which at once, with its radio crackle, seemed to cut him off from the world.

'Cossack,' he acknowledged.

'Confirming your lead on my arm.'

'Roger. Wilco. Out.'

He looked along the line of the hedge at the other tanks. The new young lieutenant, Angell, was fifty yards away in Condor, with Cormorant twenty yards beyond him.

Angell had arrived only yesterday, replacing Harvill who had been killed, walking to breakfast, by a sniper outside Tilly. The troop had hoped that with a new commander they would be reserve for a few days, but then there had been this flap with reports of two SS Panzer divisions – one of them the famous *Totenkopf*, the Death's Head – counter-attacking along the seam of the bridgehead, between the British and the Americans. Everything had then been pushed forward, though the centreline of the German attack was still uncertain. There was a rumour that they had broken through to the west and blown up a huge dump of diesel barrels. Somebody had said that headquarters there were already packed up and facing the sea, engines running. You could believe anything or nothing, in this mixed-up battle in which there were no real lines. Yet along this whole sector there was not even the sound of gunfire, though there was something heavy and very distant, probably bombing, away to the east.

Bert crawled down past Paddy and Sam in the crowded gun turret and crouched behind his driver.

'When we go, Tom . . .'

Tom pulled off his helmet.

'When we go, flap down, right?'

'Bugger that.'

Bert nodded. None of the drivers liked driving on periscope, with the armoured flap down, but it was much the safest way. He put his hand on Tom's shoulder.

'I'll guide you like you was a pram, boy.'

'Aye, stuck in the first bloody hedge. And you know bloody well I can't see these banks in the periscope.'

'Open your eyes a bit you will.'

'It isn't I can't see they're there, I can't judge the drop.'

'We've still got a few teeth left after your last roller-coaster.'

'Then tell me in time, for Christ's sake.'

Bert patted his shoulder. Tom was already closing his flap, adjusting his periscope, and tightening his hands on the two long steering tillers. Bert squeezed the elbow of Harry the radio operator, sitting beside Tom in the small forward compartment. Then he pushed back up past Paddy's legs.

'One up the spout, Paddy?'

'Yes, Sarge.'

Sam was already on the machine-gun, alternately whistling and chewing. Bert rose in the turret. There was no signal yet. He looked the other way to Dai in the turret of Conqueror, twenty yards along the hedge. He held his hands out parallel and then widened them. Dai nodded and put up his thumb.

There were voices again on the radio net.

'Sunray to Three. Sunray to Three.'

'Three.'

'I gather that in the next race the favourite may not even start. But the going is firm to good.'

'Wilco, Sunray. Out.'

Angell put down his microphone and lifted his arm, pointing across the meadow. Bert checked with Dai and then spoke down to Tom.

'Start engines. Then go like a bat out of hell, boy, till we're in by the cider.'

There was no acknowledgement, only the sudden shattering roar of the big diesel engine behind them and the cloud of foul smoke. They lurched forward through the hedge and into the meadow. Conqueror was even quicker away, through a hedge gap, and was widening the arc across the field. In the turret of Cossack all three were holding on as the speed increased. The long grass was hiding bumps in the meadow and they were thrown this way and that.

'There'll be eggs for sure,' Paddy shouted.

'Yeah,' Bert shouted back.

He was staring through the orchard at the building which was now coming more into view: a low farmhouse, with a stone barn beyond it.

'If the bloody chickens make off, there'll still be eggs.'

'Right, Paddy.'

There was no sign of other movements as the two tanks raced

across the meadow. The shape of the orchard now looked different, elongated towards the west, but Dai in Conqueror was already adjusting to this, going wider.

'These things were never made for fighting in fields and trees,' Sam said, as much to himself as to the others.

Bert was still staring forward.

'Tom, that bit of broken fence, you see it, this side. Get close in to that and then crawl up to the road hedge.'

They heard the engine slacken, and then there was a fast spectacular sliding turn in beside the fence.

'Bloody Brooklands,' Sam said.

Bert looked across, to see Conqueror disappearing beyond the bend of the orchard.

'Come in, Conqueror.'

'Conqueror.'

'Dai, we're out of sight but okay. Get to the road hedge if you can but do not go to the house, do not go to the house.'

'Conqueror wilco and out.'

Cossack had stopped by the broken fence. The apple trees close to them were heavy with small green unripe fruit.

'Crawl now, Tom.'

They went very slowly forward, but there was still a puff of blue smoke. There was a gate twenty yards along the hedge from the orchard. Bert stared through the tops of the high hedge and then got Tom to creep along to the gateway.

'Engine off.'

The low roar coughed and cut out. Bert took off his helmet. All the noise still trembled in his body but slowly the peace of summer came back.

'Shall I go for the eggs, Sarge?' Paddy asked.

'Not just yet, mun. I'm going to look around.'

He climbed from the turret to the engine cover and then jumped down to the long grass. He moved under the hedge to the gateway and looked cautiously out along the road. It was clear and empty in both directions and the hedge on the far side had been recently layered. He was able to look out many miles to the south, over the low wooded hills. It was deep green and peaceful as far as he could see, though as he moved to a different angle he could see smoke a mile or so west: ordinary woodsmoke, it looked. He found a position where the tank could command the road in either direction, and guided Tom into it. As Tom switched off he lifted his cover and put his head out. His face was dark red and running with sweat.

Bert put a foot on the heavy track and climbed up the front past the gun. He reached across for his radio.

'Dai?'

'Yes.'

'Anything?'

'There've been vehicles into the yard. Two or three and recent. But most of the yard's beyond the barn, I can't see it.'

'Wait.'

Bert sat in the warm sun on the turret and looked through the binoculars towards the farmhouse. He had only a very partial view through the trees, but he could see no movements of any kind. He was about to jump down again when the radio crackled.

'Sunray to Three.'

'Three.'

'Will you tell your bloody men to keep radio discipline?'

'Three wilco. Out.'

There was a short pause and then the expected call.

'Three to Cossack, Three to Cossack. Keep radio discipline.'

'Sarge!' Paddy shouted, pointing down through the orchard.

There was a puff of black smoke just beyond the farmhouse, and the sound of a powerful engine. Then almost at once there was a burst of machine-gun fire.

'Three to Cossack, I say again, Three to Cossack. Keep radio discipline.'

Bert slid down into the turret.

'Traverse right.'

Paddy swung the big gun. Sam had already realigned the machine-gun. Bert grabbed the microphone.

'Dai, was that you firing?'

'No, but there's a Tiger in that yard, probably two. And Billy's been hit.'

'Have you got him?'

'Just about. Hang on, Bert—'

There was another burst of machine-gun fire and then the unmistakable sound of tank tracks moving.

'Dai, listen. Dai. Back out now, back out. I'm putting smoke in.'

There was no reply. When the radio crackled again it was Angell.

'Cossack, report your situation, report your situation.'

'Engaging. Out. Dai. Dai.'

There was still no reply from Conqueror.

'Tom.'

'Sarge.'

'Covers down, back twenty yards, then round the back of the orchard.'

'Sarge.'

The diesel roared in acceleration. With its noise and the cover of the radio helmet Bert was now cut off from all the sounds in the orchard.

'Dai. Come in, Dai.'

Two voices cut in as he was waiting.

'Cossack, identify your situation and await orders.'

'Cossack, this is Sunray. What the bloody hell are you doing?'

The tank was lurching now from its turn, moving towards the back of the orchard. Bert held on with difficulty. He released the microphone switch and told Sam to tap Tom's shoulders and get him to slow down. Then he pressed the microphone switch and said curtly:

'Request radio silence. Emergency. Out.'

'Christ!' Paddy shouted.

He had taken off his helmet and was at the sights of the big gun. Bert had already seen what he was shouting at. There was a sudden high column of black smoke from the back of the orchard, its base just beyond their view. Bert ripped off his helmet and tried to look through the binoculars but he could not hold them steady.

'Sarge!' Paddy shouted, frantically traversing the big gun left.

Bert saw the big Tiger tank at almost the same moment. Its gun was facing at an angle from them, towards the column of smoke.

'On!' Paddy shouted.

'Fire!'

The explosion shook the turret but Bert at once reloaded.

'Fire!'

It had required the second armour-piercing shell, which struck between turret and hull. The engine of the Tiger was now on fire, and its crew were jumping out on the far side.

'Sam.'

But Sam was already spraying the area of the Tiger with machine-gun bullets. Several of the bullets, Bert saw, were hitting and ricocheting off the trees. He looked across to the meadow-hedge running back from the orchard. What he wanted to see was men running or sheltering there: the five men from Conqueror. But there was nothing of that kind, only the terrible black column of smoke, now thickening into the clear blue-and-white sky. As he watched there was a sudden explosion, followed immediately by others.

'The bloody ammo going,' Sam said, looking down at the stacks of shells that surrounded them in the crowded turret.

'Shut your gob!' Paddy shouted.

'Right,' Bert said.

He paused and consciously breathed. The Tiger was still burning but it had not brewed. He picked up the microphone.

'Tom, engine off.'

'Sarge.'

It was extraordinary how quiet it seemed, as the big tank engine cut out. The explosions from Conqueror had stopped. The meadow and the orchard were quiet again, under the spreading pall of black smoke. The silence seemed to last for several minutes.

Bert looked carefully at the column of black smoke. At near ground level it was billowing towards the orchard, as if in a north wind. But at about thirty yards up it was blowing the other way, as if from a light south-east breeze.

'We didn't lay our own smoke,' he said to Paddy.

'There wasn't time, Sarge.'

'Sure. But if we laid it now, along the line of the orchard, I could get to Conqueror and see.'

Paddy turned and looked at him. Bert saw the broad pink face smeared with grease and dirt, the staring blue eyes under the curly ginger hair.

'No,' Paddy said.

'Not the tank, Paddy. Just me slip along on foot.'

'That's what I said no to.'

'Did you, you insubordinate bugger?'

'And that's what I meant. No.'

Sam had turned and was watching them.

'Watch your front with that gun,' Bert said, sharply.

'Don't worry,' Sam said. 'I heard Dai. One Tiger, probably two.'

'Yes and that's why we can't go on in the tank.'

'We should get the bloody hell out of here,' Sam said.

'With the same objection. We'd be a sitting duck all across the field.'

'Not if we laid smoke and then drove flat out.'

'The wind's too uncertain for that far.'

'Well, we can't go into the bloody orchard and find him. And we can't stay here for ever.'

'We can stay for a bit. Remember they're probably as confused as we are.'

'Confused, that's a bloody fancy word for it,' Paddy said.

'All right. Confused and scared.'

'The bloody SS?' Sam said. 'Not those Death's Head bastards.'

'Yes,' Bert said. 'Fascists get frightened too.'

'Fascists are Italians. These are Germans.'

'And confused and scared,' Bert said. 'They probably only went into the farm for some eggs.'

He smiled at Paddy as he spoke. Paddy smiled broadly back.

'So this is what we do,' Bert said. 'In two minutes we lay smoke, lots of it, along the edge of the orchard. Then I run behind it, see if there's anybody alive there. Two minutes after I've gone you lay smoke again. For Christ's sake don't forget that. Then fast through, beyond where Conqueror is but down the line of that hedge. If I can bring anybody I will. If not, or if I'm not back, wait one minute and then through that hedge and keep its cover back to the others.'

'I still—' Paddy began.

'It's an order.'

Paddy shook his head but in the same movement began picking up the mortar smoke bombs. The radio crackled.

'Three to Cossack.'

'Cossack.'

'Cossack, disengage. Disengage.'

Bert smiled.

'Wilco. Out.'

He put aside the helmet.

'Right, Paddy, you're in command. Explain it now to Harry and Tom.'

'Sarge.'

'And Sam, no firing unless they fire. We don't want them on us too soon.'

'If they're there. I'm beginning to doubt it.'

'Good. Now the smoke.'

They fired six smoke bombs along the edge of the orchard. As the white smoke billowed out Bert climbed from the turret to the engine cover and then dropped lightly to the grass. He stopped to unhook a grenade from his belt and removed the pin, holding the lever tightly in his fist. Then he sprinted across behind the smoke, trying to hold his breath as some of it drifted towards him.

Coughing and with smarting eyes, he could momentarily not see the base of the black column, which was still thick and high in the air. Then suddenly he saw Conqueror, its near track broken, its gun lurched and pointed to the ground. It was blackened at the turret and across the engine covers; the green paint on the hull was mostly peeled but some still sizzled. One of the crew was lying directly under the barrel of the gun. One or two bullets had torn through his steel helmet and the back of his head was shattered, though there was little blood.

Bert ducked round the back of the tank. A corpse burned to an almost shapeless blackness lay under the engine cowling. Another body, still retaining some of its shape, hung halfway out of the turret, overcome there while trying to escape. He looked quickly around and even called, quietly: 'Dai.' But he was almost sure that Dai was the shapeless body under the engine, and there was no other human sound or sight. The driver and the radio operator must have been trapped inside; there could be no hope for them. He looked for identity tags on the corpse by the engine, but it was too thoroughly burned. He ran back and got the tags from the first body, turning it over. It was, as he had expected, Billy Edwards. His lips were drawn far back, showing all his teeth, but his face was otherwise unmarked.

The second smoke began landing behind him. He ran into the cover of the burned-out Conqueror. He could hear Cossack's engines now, and got ready to jump up. He was still holding the grenade, as if convulsively. He must remember to throw it before he climbed up the hull.

Suddenly there was a shell whistling above him and the crump of high explosive somewhere beyond the farmhouse. He could not understand who was firing it but there were then two more and their direction was unmistakable: from behind their squadron. Turning furiously, he supposed that the report of enemy presence at the farm had been passed to the field gunners, who would be shelling the map reference. As yet, fortunately, they were overshooting, but it was in any case time to get out. The bastards could at least have waited until Cossack was back.

Cossack was coming now through the smoke, veering wide. He ran out, waving his arms, but at just that moment there was what sounded like a heavy slap, and then a booming secondary explosion. Cossack was swung round by the impact, towards the orchard, and was then hit again. He saw the white heat as the armour-piercing shell entered its first stage. Meanwhile the field-gun shells were now coming in a barrage across the farm and orchard, the high explosive rattling among the trees.

Cursing and shouting wildly he ran towards Cossack. The turret was opening but the driver's cover was still closed. He saw Paddy's head and shouted up to him, unheard in the noise. He climbed up the hull and grabbed at Paddy's shoulder. Paddy did not turn but shouted:

'That second bugger was there!'

'Come out, Paddy! Jump!'

Paddy did not answer. He moved down into the turret again. Bert pulled himself right up and looked into the turret. Sam was sprawled on the littered metal floor. Harry and Tom were motionless in their seats. He leaned in and grabbed at Paddy.

'Leave it!' Paddy shouted. 'I think Sam's still alive.'

'She'll blow any minute,' Bert said.

Paddy was hauling at Sam's shoulders, trying to get him upright, but it was a dead weight and he could get him only half up, jammed against the gun breech. Bert reached in and pulled at Sam's shoulder but could get no real weight on it.

'Paddy, come out. Now!' Bert shouted.

'Fuck off!' Paddy shouted back, still trying to wrestle Sam's body across the breech.

There was a sudden sheet of flame, and a new explosion, as the fuel tank blew. Bert was thrown down to the grass but not before he felt across his face a flame that was more like light than touch or immediate hurt. Still shouting to Paddy, he struggled up. He was just reaching for the hold on the hull when a shell landed between Cossack and the burned-out Conqueror. He felt a sudden hammer-blow on his right knee, again without immediate pain. As he hung on to the hold a third tank shell hit Cossack. This time he saw the flash from the black shape of the Tiger in the orchard. The flame in Cossack seemed to explode, and there was a rush of choking black smoke. He saw Paddy's arm come up through the turret and then fall back. The billowing black smoke rose all around him.

Bert's face was stinging and scraped, now. His sight was blurred and he found he could see only from his right eye. His right knee was beginning to pulse, as if separate from him. Instinctively, but still shouting Paddy's name, he ran crouching for the hedge and pushed himself deep under it. The last thing he remembered was the strange dry taste of earth in his mouth.

# 2

⊰⊱❈⊰⊱

## SALISBURY, OCTOBER 1944

Nesta stood by the high, narrow, white hospital bed, looking intently down into the sleeping face. With the sheet pulled tightly to the neck, the head with its close-cropped black hair was isolated and emphatic. The sideburns, the lower cheeks, the chin and the neck had been shaved that morning: there were tiny bloodpoints among the black stubs of bristle. The nose was red and prominent above the thick black moustache. The eyes were tightly closed, but the right eyelid was delicate and blue-veined, under the bristling eyebrow. She lingered on every normal detail as a way of enclosing the abnormality of the left eye and the grafted skin down the cheek below it. There the skin colour was pale but also still faintly stained with bruising. The closed eyelid was darkly bruised and the livid skin immediately below the eye seemed to hang in an expanded socket. Nesta felt the tears in her own eyes as she gazed steadily down into Bert's face.

The heavy door swung open behind her and the young American nurse came in. She did not see at first that Bert was still asleep, as she went to the other side of the bed.

'First we couldn't get him to sleep at all, he was so excited you were coming. Then when you come, look at him!'

'It's all right. Let him sleep.'

'And have him break the place up when he finds he missed you?'

Nesta laughed. At the sound of the voices Bert opened his

eyes. He looked slowly from one to the other. The darkened left eyelid had opened to no more than a slit.

'Nes!'

He tried to push himself up on his elbows but the nurse leaned close over him, resting his shoulders back.

'Leave me be, girl. And with my wife watching us.'

'It's okay, Bertie. All your secrets are safe with me.'

She smiled across at Nesta and went out.

'Bert, love,' Nesta said, and bent over and kissed him on the lips.

He got his right arm from under the sheet and held her across the shoulders. They kissed a long time without breath.

'Come and sit on the bed this other side,' Bert said as they separated.

'What is it, your knee?'

'Aye, the bugger's so stiff. With a bit of thought they could have kept the damage down one side of me.'

'It was separate, you said. First the fire, then the shrapnel.'

'Don't talk about old rubbish like that.'

Nesta went round and sat close to him, holding his hand.

'Was the train bad?'

'Not bad. Just the two changes, Newport and Swindon. And then Emma had a car at the station.'

'She said she might wangle it.'

'It's her official car. She was taking a risk.'

'There's been one or two of them lately.'

'Risks? But you know Emma. Nothing happens by accident.'

'Aye, so she says.'

They were silent for some time, looking at each other, holding hands very tightly.

'There, I nearly forgot,' Nesta said. 'I've brought lots of things for you. All down the street they were loading me up.'

'There'll be time for that.'

'Is it all right, this Yank hospital?'

'All right? Haven't you noticed? It's food of the gods.'

'Have they said when at all?'

'Nothing definite, no. But I'll have to go back to the eye place. Perhaps by Christmas, one of them said.'

'It would be lovely to have you back home for Christmas.'

'It's kids' tales, a lot of it. The war still won't be over.'

'It will for you, love.'

'Doing what, I wonder.'

'Being looked after, boy. Like you deserve.'

Bert nodded but pulled his hand away, as if to resettle himself. Nesta watched his face intently. As he had turned the disfigurement of the damaged eye was more prominent. He lay still for some minutes and then turned suddenly to look at her.

'Did you bring him, after?'

'Dic! Aye, I said I would.'

'He must have been a handful on the train.'

'Armful more like. I thought my elbow would drop off.'

'Is he outside with Emma?'

'And the nurses. They're just stuffing him with cake.'

'You could have left him with your Mam.'

'She's got Gwyn already.'

'Aye.'

The bruised eyelid closed for a moment. Nesta stared back.

'How is he? Gwyn?'

'He's lovely.'

'Back at school, I suppose?'

'Aye, they all are.'

'In that damp old place. And the same desks as we had.'

'No, they got chairs and tables now for the infants.'

'That's progress for you.'

There was a sound at the door: a thump against it, and the noise of sliding feet.

'I'll fetch him now,' Nesta said.

As she spoke the door opened and Emma was standing there, with Dic pulling at her arm.

'Mam,' the little boy shouted and hurried towards her, trying to break from Emma's hold.

'Let him come, Emma,' Nesta said quickly, and then bent to gather him up in her arms.

'Here's your Dada you've come to see, Dic.'

The little boy took no notice, burying his face in her shoulder. She swung round and sat on the bed, close to Bert. Bert reached up and stroked Dic's back.

Emma, tall and cool in a grey linen suit, walked to the end of the bed and took off the clipboard. She looked quickly through the medical record. Then she moved to the cupboard beside the bed and picked up the various pill bottles in turn, reading their labels in the bright autumn sunlight from the window.

'Say hullo to Dada, Dic.'

Slowly and very warily the little boy turned and looked at the man in the bed.

'There, Dada's come back to us,' Nesta said, hugging him.

'Dada's in bed,' Dic said.

'For a bit, yes. Then he'll get up and come back home to us.'

'And to Nana and Gwyn.'

'Yes, to all of us, love. That'll be lovely, won't it?'

Dic continued to stare at Bert. Bert was smiling.

'Is this that map-case you told me about?' Emma asked.

She was crouching at the bottom of the cupboard. The map-case had a stained khaki waterproof cover, with a deep tear at one corner.

'That's it, Emma,' Bert said, not taking his eyes off Nesta and the little boy.

'Can I look at it?'

'Of course.'

She opened the pressed studs. There were two inner flaps with plastic on each side. There was a map inside each flap, with red and black chinagraph markings on the plastic above them. She looked at the maps carefully.

'I'm surprised they let you bring this, Bert.'

'I hid it. But none of it matters. That's Normandie, all the large-scale stuff.'

'Yes, you've got this black line on the Vire–Vassy road. It was there, wasn't it, your battle?'

'Battle! A bit of an error in an orchard.'

'What's a battle?' the little boy asked.

'Fighting,' Nesta said.

She looked directly across at Emma, who had now turned to the second flap.

'Ah, this is the one you meant,' Emma said. 'The page from your atlas.'

Dic reached out suddenly and touched Bert's mouth. Bert smiled and kissed the small fingers.

'There, he knows you,' Nesta said.

'At first sight,' Bert laughed.

'Dada hurt his eye,' Dic said loudly.

'That's right,' Bert said. 'With a bit of help, of course.'

Nesta eased away, letting Dic sit on the bed near Bert's face.

'That was it exactly in July,' Emma said, looking carefully at the large-scale map of Europe with its eastern, southern and western fronts carefully marked in red.

'I don't have a chinagraph,' Emma said, 'or I could bring it up to date. In the south we're through the Gothic Line at Pisa and Rimini. The Red Army is at Warsaw and through Transylvania into Hungary and Yugoslavia. In the west there's a long front from the Rhône valley to the Rhine.'

'Aye,' Bert said. 'Though all held up a bit for the moment.'

'It's in its last phase,' Emma said. 'The Red Army will drive through to Berlin, and in the west the Resistance will be taking over, with the Left at the head of it.'

'No front in Spain,' Bert said, looking away.

'That will come,' Emma said. 'It will have been a ten-year war, and it will have destroyed Fascism and all the systems that supported it.'

'That was the original idea of the map,' Bert said.

'Of course.'

'Except that in the end, see, it was only a sort of comforter, turning over to it. Where we actually were seemed to have nothing to do with it.'

'But it did. You know it did.'

'So we got told.'

'It was, Bert. When you were hit you were fighting the S S.'

'So they told us. What they called the Death's Head.'

Dic was suddenly restless, twisting in Nesta's arms. Bert looked back and reached out to him but he would not settle.

'I think he wants to go somewhere,' Nesta said.

'I'll take him,' Emma said. 'You have your time with Bert.'

She came round the bed and lifted the little boy to her shoulder. He cried angrily. As she carried him firmly away, he struggled and looked back, holding his arms out to Nesta. Then the door closed behind them. Nesta got up and smoothed down her dress.

'That's pretty,' Bert said.

'What?'

'Your dress.'

It was a plain orange cotton, with a wide black collar and belt.

'Your Mam made it for me. She's been good with all that.'

'Aye.'

He turned and closed the map-case, which Emma had left on the bed. He reached awkwardly down and put it away in the cupboard.

'Has she been all right otherwise?' he asked while turning back.

'Oh yes, she's marvellous. For her age, fair play.'

'I didn't mean that. I meant to you.'

'Oh that's all over and done with. Once Dic was coming.'

'She said some terrible things about you.'

Nesta looked away. She smoothed her dress again, then sat on the bed.

'Coloured up the truth a bit, admitted,' she said.

Bert laughed and reached out to touch her hair. She smiled and leaned towards him.

'Come closer, Nes.'

'I am closer.'

'No, lie on the bed. Put your head on my shoulder.'

'What would that nurse think?'

'What she usually thinks, from what I can gather. This is a warm old place.'

'Making you better I supposed it was for.'

As he pressed her hair she turned and lay along the bed, resting her head awkwardly on his arm. Bert turned her head and kissed her. She held the kiss, closing her eyes. They lay still and silent for several minutes, feeling each other's warmth.

'You're not going to sleep?' Bert said at last.

'No, though I could.'

He laughed and kissed her forehead. She moved, put her hands on his neck, and kissed him with open lips.

'It's awful having to go back,' she said. 'If you could only come back with us now.'

'As soon as I can, love.'

'I know.'

'Is Emma taking you back to the station?'

'She said she would.'

'Then she will. She's reliable, that one.'

'I know she is.'

She turned and sat up.

'It's important, isn't it, her job?'

'Aye, she's some sort of Deputy Controller, Ministry of Labour.'

'Putting women in the factories. She was talking a bit about it.'

'Aye, and she's fought for their rights, mind. She's an organiser, that one, a born organiser.'

'Is she still in your Party?'

'My Party? I'm only half in it myself, with this lot.'

'No, you know what I mean.'

'She doesn't advertise it but of course she's still with us.'

'There's been all the changes.'

'Not in the politics,' Bert said firmly. 'And especially not now.'

Nesta got off the bed and looked round for her bag. She began unpacking all the things that had been collected for Bert, and stowing them neatly in his cupboard. He watched her as she worked.

'Do you ever hear from her brother?' he asked, suddenly.

She finished arranging the upper shelf and then stood slowly. As she looked down at him he saw that the blood was bright in her face.

'No. I don't.'

'Only contact through Emma, is it?'

'No contact. Just Emma. She comes to see Gwyn.'

'And him? Norman?'

'She doesn't say. Only she told our Mam he got married.'

'She told me that.'

'Did she?'

'And that he's in some hush-hush job. Something to do with his maths.'

'Well, if she told you that's all right, then,' Nesta said, sharply.

'No need to get shirty with me, girl.'

'All the things are in the cupboard. Only use them, mind. We all want you to get better.'

He reached out and caught her hand. He smiled. Nesta was still aroused, her face bright, her eyes shining.

'I love you like that,' he said, looking up.

'Like what?'

'Like you are and always were. A beautiful girl.'

'Never mind all that. You just think about yourself and get well.'

'It's seeing you will make me.'

'No, it isn't and it won't be. You stick by the doctors.'

He turned her hand in his own, looking up at her.

'Always flat-out honest, isn't it? No sweet dreams, no illusions, even when they might help.'

'I don't know what you're talking about.'

'I know,' Bert said. 'Good people never do, about themselves.'

'That's old talk,' Nesta said.

The door opened and Emma came in. The American nurse was holding Dic in her arms. His mouth was smeared with chocolate.

'Time to go, I'm afraid,' Emma said.

Nesta leaned over and kissed Bert quickly. Then she hurried across and took Dic from the nurse. Emma looked at Bert and waved. He surprised her by lifting his arm and quickly clenching his fist. She nodded and followed Nesta and the others out.

On the way to the station Nesta had to nurse and comfort Dic. He hadn't wanted to leave the hospital, where he had been made such a fuss of and given so many nice things.

'Those American nurses are kind,' Nesta said.

'Yes, for the time being,' Emma said shortly, intent on her driving.

'Just kind,' Nesta said.

'It's like another world in there,' Emma said. 'With an American scale of supplies. Things our own working class have never seen, except on the pictures.'

'Still they let our Bert in, when he needed the bed.'

'So they damn well should,' Emma said fiercely. 'When you think what Bert's done.'

They reached the station and Emma saw them on to the platform. It was very crowded, with many soldiers and airmen travelling on leave. When the small, dirty train was shunted back in, Emma pushed through the crowd to find Nesta a place. Then the compartment filled quickly with several airmen and their kitbags. She waited and then leaned in to Nesta in her corner seat, with Dic on her knee. One of the airmen was already talking to Dic.

'Here. I nearly forgot,' Emma said.

She handed Nesta a long buff envelope.

'What is it?'

'Put it in your bag.'

'No, Emma, really. I don't want it.'

'You don't want it but you need it,' Emma said, sharply, and stood back from the door.

Dic was twisting on Nesta's knee. He was trying to get hold of a badge on the coat of the airman who had been talking to him. Nesta watched, helplessly, as Emma strode away along the crowded platform.

# 3

❧❦

# OXFORD, AUGUST 1945

Edmund Charles George Wilkes and Emmaline Matilda Braose were married in Oxford Registry Office on 9 August 1945. The marriage was witnessed by Norman Stephen Stuart Braose and Montague Kay Pitter.

Emma and Monkey strolled to the lounge of the nearest large hotel, laughing about the formalities of the ceremony and especially about the Registrar's address on the duties of marriage: what Monkey called 'the hard-Left-Protestant to anxious-secular version'. 'All the more relevant,' he added, 'since you've been living together for years.'

Norman and Georgi had gone off to look for an early evening paper. There was a rumour that the Soviet Union had declared war on Japan, two days after the Americans had dropped an atomic bomb on Hiroshima. Monkey ordered their old celebratory drink: tall frosted glasses of gin and cider.

'To you as an honest woman,' Monkey said, lifting his glass.

'Do you think it's true?' Emma asked, sipping.

'I would expect so. They are still to a large extent an Asiatic power.'

'With a socialist Europe and a socialist Asia . . .' Emma said, looking across the lounge at a large, laughing party of British and American pilots.

'Yes, with that,' Monkey said, 'there is every indication of a long and happy marriage.'

Emma laughed. Much more than the rest of them, Monkey had aged, physically, during the war years. The curly black hair was now streaked with grey. The spectacles were heavier, and the thicker lenses seemed to clench and wither the small ugly features. He now stooped more also, and this emphasised his habit of jutting his head when he spoke. Yet none of that seemed to matter: the mind and spirit were still young and bright.

'You didn't say when you'd be leaving this famous Hut.'

'I'm leaving at the end of the month,' Monkey said. 'I've got it almost fixed to get to the States.'

'What, a university?'

'I've got a friend at Cornell. So no more questions, Emma darling.'

Emma laughed.

'It's been hard enough with no questions about the Hut.'

'Oh, we can tell you all that now. We've been designing bombes.'

'Bombs! You don't mean this Hiroshima thing?'

'No, dear, not that sort. Bombes. They sort of unwind other people's mazes.'

'I don't understand.'

'Very few people could.'

'What mazes? You mean codes?'

'In that area,' Monkey said.

'Norman too?'

'Norman especially. He's been quite unexpectedly bright. So much so that they're determined to keep him.'

'Designing? You mean theoretically?'

'Of course. Algorithms. You know the poor bugger couldn't change a light bulb.'

'Has he said if he'll stay?'

'You must ask him, darling. He still has this thing about working for the state.'

'That's ridiculous, especially now with a Labour government.'

'Tell him all. He needs it. He's a political innocent. All he wants is pure maths and pure Sarah.'

'Sarah's not pure, she's just thick.'

'As you say, my love, and in all the right places. But that's it, you see. Sarah's daddy has the thread through the maze.'

'But he's some sort of naval commander.'

'Exactly. And what he commands are the threads.'

There was a loud burst of laughter from the group of pilots near the door. Looking across, Emma saw Norman and Georgi hesitating outside the glass doors. They looked an incongruous pair. Norman, tall and still very straight, with his mop of bright fair hair, looked much as he had when he was an undergraduate. Georgi looked so much older and more solid: every one of his forty years, with his balding skull and the jet-black side hair and trimmed beard. 'If you want a shorthand for popular power, say Georgi,' Monkey had joked, years before. It had been a surprise for Emma, meeting Georgi's sister by chance in a shop in London, to find that all his family called him Edmund. There was another of Monkey's jokes, that if he had been unchristened and communised, after Dimitrov, as a reborn popular fighter, he should at least have adopted the correct Bulgarian spelling. 'I didn't adopt the name, I was given it,' Georgi had replied.

Monkey was standing and beckoning to the others. Emma noticed one of the pilots, a rough fresh-faced farm boy, looking back at him with an evident but probably involuntary physical contempt. It was a drunken confidence that was shaping him: the last days, Emma thought, of that kind of fighting euphoria.

Georgi had seen them, and was leading the way across. Monkey ordered more drinks.

'We met Mark in the Broad,' Norman said. 'It appears to be true.'

'It's for China,' Georgi said. 'The two Red Armies will link up. It will turn the history of the world.'

'Except for that thing on Hiroshima,' Norman said.

'It's the land we have to hold,' Georgi said, taking a tall glass from the waiter. 'Though at least that bloody horror will have finished the Japs.'

'It will be a different world,' Norman said.

He had taken his glass but put it down without drinking.

'Of course a different world. A people's world,' Georgi said.

'That's right, Norman,' Emma added.

'I don't think so,' Norman said. 'At least not necessarily. Everyone's misunderstanding it because they call it a bomb, like the weapons they've been used to. This is not that. It is a qualitative change, in fact a qualitative regression. I am very scared of it all.'

'Do you know anything about it, then?' Georgi asked with interest.

'It's been very secret, but I've heard a few things. It is more appalling than you could begin to imagine.'

'Like these bombes you've been designing,' Emma said, smiling.

Norman started. He looked angrily at Emma, and then at Monkey. Monkey lifted his glass.

'That's entirely different,' Norman said. 'And you should, as you know, believe practically nothing Monkey ever says.'

'When I've been telling her how good you are,' Monkey laughed.

'That too,' Norman said, and lifted his glass. The others watched, amused, as he drained the long glass in a single gulping swallow.

'It'll hit you when you get up,' Monkey said.

'Trivially,' Norman said. 'In context, trivially.'

The others reached for their drinks and began discussing their arrangements. Norman was uncertain what to do. Sarah had gone down to Devon, to be near her mother when the baby was born. He was off duty at the Hut but he knew that Monkey would not want him with him. Emma and Georgi would be staying in Oxford, where Georgi had borrowed a flat. They invited him to stay with them, but he did not want this, especially after Monkey's jokes about honeymooners: 'A mature old couple like this will be even worse, you'll see, than a couple of fumbling kids.' So there seemed nothing for it but to go back to his room at the pub in the village near the Hut. Before that, however, he wanted to talk to Emma.

In the end, after more drinks, he asked Georgi if he could steal Emma for an hour or so; there was some family business to talk about. Georgi looked merely surprised. He and Monkey went off to look up friends and Norman and Emma walked through to the Parks and along the river. Norman was slow in getting to what he really wanted to talk about, but it came at last, on the little bridge over the river.

'I've been asked to stay on in this work.'

'Yes. So Monkey said.'

'He has a loose mouth, that one. But yes, it's now official. It would be a permanent appointment.'

'In the Civil Service?'

'Civil it is not. But yes, it's government work.'

'Of the same general kind.'

'I wish I could tell you about it, Em. But the end of the war won't be the end of this work. We're in the first stage of a kind of development that's going to change most things. Initially, and crucially, it will change how we think.'

'You mean beyond security and so on?'

'Security and penetrating enemy security were the wartime applications. They'll continue, of course, but the total effect will be very much wider. I said *how* we think. I meant that.'

'Then I don't understand.'

'It's not what you suppose. Just the politics and so on.'

'*Just* the politics?'

Norman looked away. A man and a small boy of six or seven were passing close to them across the bridge. He looked after them until they had gone down the steps and on to the grass.

'That's another part of the problem,' he said, looking very deliberately at Emma.

'There's no problem with the politics,' Emma said confidently. 'The Party is quite clear on what has to be done: loyal and disciplined work in support of reconstruction and the Labour government.'

'And how long will that last, do you suppose?'

'As long as it takes,' Emma said.

Norman pushed his fingers back through his loose hair. Emma smiled. He seemed still so young.

'There was hardly any vetting,' he said, 'when they shoved me into this work.'

'Well, why should there be? The Soviet Union was an ally.'

'Actually not, when they recruited me. They just wanted mathematicians, fast. But okay, that sorted out, and it lasted, didn't it, while they still needed the Red Army?'

'It must be made to last. You're not allowing for how much Europe has changed, with the Resistance.'

'Okay, it ought to last, but I just know in my bones that it won't. You can see the start of the trouble already, with the Red Army in Berlin. All right, fascism is discredited and the Left is quite strong in Europe. But nobody seems to understand how much the balance of power in the world has shifted. The atomic bomb is only part of it. The real shift is the predominant wealth of America.'

'We can deal with that.'

'How? With a reformist Labour government? Doesn't the Party think any more?'

'Not just a Labour government. But massive popular movements, all over Europe. None of us, I can tell you, is going to stand for being pushed around.'

Norman looked down. He rubbed his hand across his mouth.

'Yes? Well! But for me, you see, that's the problem.'

'Because you'll be in an official job.'

'That's the easiest way of putting it. And we can follow it up with some liberal remarks. Such as my right to hold private political views, so long as I still do my job.'

'But that's it. That's a basic civil right.'

'In what sort of world?'

'In any sort of world.'

'No, Emma. That's just a liberal illusion. Indeed I think that's the trouble. Most of us, including me, moved straight from liberalism to communism. But that was only possible, intellectually, while fascism was there as the common enemy. What will happen now is a radical sorting out. I'm just getting there early, that's all.'

'You mean shifting back into liberalism?'

Norman laughed. Emma stared at him, surprised.

'I'm just trying to tell you the sequence, Em. For ten years communist has meant mainly anti-fascist. Within the next few years it will mean anti-liberal, anti-democratic, and then in practical terms subversive, even treasonable.'

'Yes, in right-wing slander, of course.'

'No, Em, in fact! While it stays true to itself.'

Emma frowned, searching his face.

'Is that really how you see it? And then that it's going to get too difficult for you in your job?'

Norman laughed again. He turned and walked along the noisy

iron bridge. She followed, anxiously. They went down to the towpath on the other side. He picked up a willow twig that was lying on the grass. He began bending the twig between his fists. He waited for her to come up to him.

'What will you do now, Em? Having married Georgi?'

'You mean will I be leaving the Ministry?'

'Among other things.'

'Yes. Yes I shall. But not because of this nonsense of yours about communists. All that kind of thing will simply have to be fought.'

'Yet you'll leave?'

'Yes. With the Labour victory there'll be a new industrial public sector. I can get some job in that.'

'According to your convictions.'

'Of course. That's what I've been saying.'

'Good,' Norman said, and smiled.

He broke the twig and threw it down into the river. He watched it swirl, slowly, towards the overgrown bank.

'The meadowsweet is late,' he said, bending down.

'Is it?'

'Do you like the smell of it? Some people don't.'

Emma stood above him. She did not answer.

'Let me put it this way,' Norman said, still crouching at the edge of the river. 'We're moving into a world which will be much too hard-pressed, too impatient, to have time for fine distinctions. Yet it will increasingly be a world in which the fine distinctions are necessary.'

'I don't understand.'

'Well, take the Soviet Union. It's been clear since Spain and the show trials what kind of regime that is. Yet for other reasons there are millions still loyal to it. Loyal, I mean, beyond its own frontiers, and within other systems.'

'Nobody says there haven't been faults.'

'*They* say there haven't been faults.'

'Yes I know, but taking it on balance—'

'On balance will not be allowed. It will be all or nothing.'

'But that's ridiculous.'

'Yes, if you like. But it will be our real world, Emma. The one in which we shall all be making choices.'

'And so you're choosing liberalism? Just because there have been faults you'll abandon the whole thing. The working-class movement. The democratic movement.'

Norman stood up. He rubbed at his back.

'Put it that way if you like. As I said, without nuances.'

'There's no need for nuances. You've married Sarah and you're working for her father, in a secret government establishment. The rest of us, I suppose, are just the embarrassing past.'

'I told you it was a problem.'

'Oh no, brother, it's no problem for you. You just walk off, as you always have done.'

'Not just walk off.'

'Well, it amounts to that. Don't flatter yourself that you're not important. If these new developments are as big as you say, people like you will be needed, on our side.'

Norman smiled, wryly.

'Yes, that's what they said when they offered me the job.'

Emma turned, impatiently.

'You're getting frivolous, do you know that? I don't know what it is. Probably talking to people like Sarah's father. All this downbeat *bonhomie*, we grew up with it. As the servants of an old, confident state.'

'They have a certain healthy scepticism, wouldn't you say?'

'Yes, within limits, to relieve their nerves after so much subordination. But can you really choose that after the plain, straightforward, confident talk of the Party?'

'I said a problem. I didn't say a choice.'

'But Norman, you are choosing. You're telling me, in effect, that you're dropping the Party . . .'

'Distancing myself, I would rather say.'

'It comes to the same thing. You know as well as I do, once people leave the Party it's not just some shift in opinions. Their whole life style changes. And they get to sneering at the Party just to make themselves feel they're all right.'

Norman hesitated. He looked carefully at his sister. She was almost his own height. Her thick fair hair had been carefully dressed for the wedding. This softened her face, reminding him of her appearance as a girl in the Embassy at Vienna: cool, elaborate, expensively produced. The clothes, of course, were now very different: the plain light-blue linen suit; the high-necked white blouse. Their grandmother's silver bracelet was tight on her sun-browned wrist.

'No sneering,' he said, smiling at her.

She looked straight back at him, unconvinced.

'And if it's any comfort,' he added, 'I really haven't changed any of my basic opinions.'

'People often say that when they're ratting.'

'I'm trying to be very precise. And that's honestly as much as I can now say.'

She stared at him again. He turned away and walked quietly along the towpath. She fell into step beside him. After a while they talked more easily.

'Were there any very difficult questions,' Emma asked, 'when they were giving you this new appointment?'

'As you mean that, no. They seemed already to know about everything at Cambridge. In effect that's taken as the political equivalent of going wild on Boat Race Night. And after all, then it stopped. There's nothing on paper since 1940.'

'On whose paper?'

'Theirs.'

'But you've had a Party card?'

'No. Not since 1940.'

'But why?'

'It wasn't my decision.'

'Whose, then?'

'Should I really tell you that?'

'No, of course. Okay. But are you saying that it will go on like that?'

'I could please you by saying so. But no, that isn't what I'm saying. I said distancing and I mean distancing.'

'Real distance?'

'Yes, Em. Real distance.'

Emma stopped. She looked back across the river. The water was silvery, in its slow current. Willows and stands of reed jutted from the loose banks. Across the wide grass, scattered groups of people were strolling, unhurried, this way and that. She turned and Norman turned with her, to walk back towards the bridge. They went some way before she spoke.

'Can't you trust the Party,' she said, quietly, 'once they know how sensitive your position is?'

'No, I need real distance.'

'Because you want real distance.'

'You could say that.'

'But there would be nothing anyone would ask you to do which would in any way compromise you.'

Norman laughed. Emma looked at him, puzzled. He laughed again and shook his head.

'Why are you laughing?' Emma asked, seriously.

'You don't know?'

'You laughed before. As if I'd said something ridiculous.'

'It's not you, Em. Really.'

'Then what?'

They reached the iron bridge. He led the way up the rattling steps, moving lightly and quickly. He stopped in the centre of the bridge and turned to face her.

'Let's just say, shall we, that I'm drawing a line across the past?'

'How dare you?'

She was white with anger. He turned and went on down the steps. He walked away across the grass. She hesitated and then followed him. She kept a distance at first, but then hurried to catch him up.

To the west, above the city, heavy dark clouds were rising, though the sky directly above them was still a clear bright blue. The air was very warm. She saw beads of sweat on his forehead.

A dog ran up to them, a young golden Labrador. It frisked playfully, and Norman bent towards it. It bared its teeth but not in anger: it looked more like a smile.

'Pet! Pet!'

The dog answered the call reluctantly. Norman smiled, seeming relaxed.

'I had a letter from Birdie yesterday,' Emma said.

Norman continued to watch the dog.

'I wrote to tell her that I was marrying Georgi. She sent me a drawing she'd done of him, that summer at the farm.'

Norman began walking again. She stayed beside him.

'And Gwyn is well. He's doing very well at school, Birdie says. His sums and his writing.'

'That's good,' Norman said.

They walked on across the wide grass, watching the high poplars in the distance. Their leaves were beginning to stir, in a rising wind.

'She's a lovely woman,' Emma said. 'And she's painting again, did I tell you? She did a whole series of drawings of Gwyn and now she's going to classes for the painting. She said there were too many problems on her own.'

'Yes, I remember she was talented.'

'You remember more than that.'

He stopped, looking down.

'She's also very happy with Bert. He's still damaged, of course, from the war, but he's been a wonderful father to Gwyn. And now they've got this little boy of their own, Dic.'

'I see.'

'If you went down there, Norman, and saw the real working class . . .'

'I can't imagine I'd be welcome.'

'I don't mean that. I mean to see real working-class people again, to set against your kinds of doubt.'

'I was thinking of the other.'

'Well, don't.'

'Another line across the past?'

'That was drawn years ago. So leave it.'

'If you say so.'

'Did you ever tell Sarah?'

'No.'

They could now feel the rising wind, and the heavy clouds were almost over them. They walked more quickly. There was the feel of heavy rain in the air.

'You owe me some money, by the way,' Emma said.

'I'll give you a cheque.'

'It's forty-eight pounds, including this month.'

'I'll write you the cheque now.'

He stopped and felt inside his jacket.

'It'll wait till we're indoors.'

'But I'm not staying with you. I'm going back to the pub.'

'We can have a meal first, when we've collected the others.'

'Okay.'

'I send the money regularly, whether you've given it me or not.'

He again felt inside his jacket but Emma was hurrying on.

'Since Bert got out of hospital and things are a bit easier she's been putting the money in Gwyn's name, in the Post Office.'

'Is it still enough?'

'What is ever enough?'

He looked across at her. His face was twisted with pain.

'Don't worry,' she said, smiling, and touched his arm.

The wind was much stronger now in the poplars, swaying the high branches. The dark clouds had covered the sky.

'We'd better hurry, from the look of it,' Emma said. They began to run.

# 4

❧ ❀❀ ❧

# DANYCAPEL, JANUARY 1947

Nesta gazed from her front-room window across the valley. The wind had shifted overnight to north-east and a cloud of fine rain was drifting down the valley, moving within its steep slopes as if it were some separate creature: insubstantial, even ghostly; some old web of the past that revisited, down the years, this valley where almost everything else had been changed.

One thing about this house was the view – the first thing she had noticed when Bert had brought her up to see it after his uncle had died. As the top terrace, away from the others like some random idea that had accidentally materialised in light-grey brick, it had never been popular, because of the long walk up. But they had needed a place on their own, now with their three children: Bert's Mam's house could no longer fit them all in and Jim had married Pattie in the war and was living with Mam. It was a dry house, luckily, that far up, but still its main pleasure was the view.

The cloud was thickening now. Of course it wasn't the same cloud; that was raining already a mile down the valley, but it still had this shape of a creature to itself: no longer off-white and rain-grey but with more solid tones in it, at times almost silver. She couldn't think how many times she had tried to paint it, and it would never come out right. It would be either a muddling haze or then suddenly too substantial. One, she laughed, had been like a gauze at a seance; what did they call it, ectoplasm? There must be a way of handling it which would get it exactly: the drifting cloud-creature but still the valley, grey and stark, all around and through it.

She'd looked in Cardiff, at the exhibition of Welsh painters, but there was nobody had got it. Terraces, of course, and winding-gear; blackened faces under safety helmets; sweat and grime in the shoulders and biceps turning shovels and picks. The few South Wales ones, that was. For they were mostly painting the North: mountains and waterfalls; isolated boulder cottages; sheep on flatwash, green hills. This here was something else. The raincloud itself could be painted, but there must still be the sweep of the valley; the high open slope with the hundreds of scattered thorn trees and the downward lines of the water-courses; then the bed with its randomness of lines that must not be designed out; some parallel terraces but then others askew or isolated; the great black dunes of the tips, this long one running towards her with its line of slender pylons carrying the overhead wires for the tipping trucks; the engine sheds crossing that line diagonally and then the upward thrust of the smoke-stacks making a different line again; or down below these straight lines the little curves of the blackened river, with the stones and the debris on its banks. It must be through and over all these, touching, darkening, washing, that the cloud was still seen as itself.

There was an edge of sleet in it. The colour was changing again. It could have been forecast, anyway, that it would be wet for the ceremony. Bert was taking a long time, cleaning those tight demob shoes. 'No half-measures, no half-sizes' – he had shown them, laughing, but they were still taken for best. She had hung his best jacket on a chair by the stairs. When she had seen he was dressing up she had persuaded him to put on his war medals, only now they'd be under his mac. He had already decided anyway to wear his tank corps beret. Many of the soldiers did, the more insistently if it was some colliery meeting or negotiation. 'We've done things, mind. We've not come back here to rot.' It was strange, trying to follow his moods. Always this base of hard militancy, very strong and quiet: that had always been Bert. Then the frequent joking, which he often took too far, about the damage to his face. Other people said it was getting to look better but she could see it all too clearly and apart from the temporary bruising it was as she had first seen it in the hospital at Salisbury: the livid drawn skin under the expanded, staring eye socket. There was a painting upstairs that she had done as soon as she was back from that visit. It was terrible and ugly and entirely true, bitter damage to flesh that had to be recorded. She would never let him see it, or know of it. She kept it pinned over with an old watercolour of a cherry tree.

It wasn't only the joking that he used to cover the pain. It was this obedient, trusting part of his mind, in the politics especially. There had been the strange row with his Dad, when the Coal Board appointments had been announced. 'Lord Hyndley of Meads as National Chairman,' old Sam had read out from the *Herald*. 'Area Director Lieutenant-General Sir A. Goodwin Austen.'

'You're making it up, Dad,' Nesta had said, giggling.

'No, he's not,' Bert had said, 'but you'll see, it don't matter. This is the people in power.'

'Don't be ridiculous, boy,' old Sam said sharply.

'Who's being ridiculous? They put in that sort as the trimmings. Just figureheads. We've got a people's government and a people's coal industry, and it will be us, people and government, has the power.'

Bert's voice had been so intense, so forced even, that even old Sam had hesitated. Then Sam had said at last: 'They'll call themselves anything, boy, the People, the Nation, only they'll still sit on your head.'

'Never,' Bert had said, 'never no more.'

'Have you seen the new price lists, then?' old Sam had said. 'No better than they was with the old owners.'

'It's for national reconstruction, just temporary, but we shall renegotiate them.'

'They're conning you, boy,' old Sam had insisted.

'Don't you bloody say that to me,' Bert had flared. 'This has been our bloody war and now it'll be our bloody peace.'

Nesta had quietened them, but just a few days later the South Wales executive of the union had passed a vote of no confidence in the Area appointments, and Bert had agreed with this. Then the national union leadership had got them to reverse the vote, to give the new publicly owned industry a good atmosphere to start. Bert had said this made sense, when you took it all together. There had to be discipline, now the people were running things for themselves.

'Ready then, girl?' she heard his voice at the door.

'I've been ready half an hour.'

'Fetch the kids, then.'

'They've been ready too.'

She went through to the back room. Gwyn was reading in the chair by the fire. She especially wanted him to come to the ceremony. She had put him on his new brown suit from the Coop. Dic wanted to come too but he must stay with Baby Gwen at her Mam's; they would leave them on their way down. Jim and Pattie would be going, but her Mam didn't want to, and left alone in the house, widowed eight years, her main pleasure was the grandchildren coming.

'Bloody rain of course,' Bert said, pulling on his jacket.

'You've put on your medals, Dad,' Gwyn said, standing close to him.

'Aye well, your Mam wanted them.'

Gwyn nodded, holding himself straight.

They went down the steep pitch, Nesta pushing the pram with Gwen in it and Dic holding its side, Bert walking slowly, still limping, in front and with Gwyn holding his hand.

'This'll be a day to remember for you,' Bert said, turning his face from the wind.

'I know, Dada,' Gwyn said, taking the shelter of Bert's body. At nine, though his face was changing, settling into what Nesta teased him as his student's look, he was still small and light. Nesta glanced at them, smiling. It was all going well now, though it could never have been easy for either of them. Gwyn had been a toddler, slow to walk, when Bert had at last come back, released from the camp in Spain. Much later, when they started going out, Nesta had always left Gwyn with her Mam, though Bert when he called would always squat and play with him.

When Bert had got his papers for the army in July 1940 he had asked Nesta to marry him. They had very little time together before he again went away. When he came on leave Gwyn was still a little boy, who did not really know him. Bert had wanted a formal adoption, and Nesta had eventually agreed. In late 1942 Dic had been born. After the usual delays the adoption papers for Gwyn had come through in 1943, by which time Bert was in the Western Desert. He was more than two years overseas, in North Africa and then in France. He had not got out of hospital until the spring of 1945. It was only then that they were at last all together, for their real life to start. Gwen had been born next November. Gwyn, always quiet and shy, had so little time to know Bert as a father; the younger children were always more confident and demanding. Yet he had clung to Bert, whenever he had the chance, and Bert had always been kind to him.

'A funny way to make a family,' Nesta had joked with her Mam.

'You know best about that,' Mrs Pritchard had said, sourly.

'Oh, leave all that, it's done with,' Nesta had said, and settled to write her daily letter to Bert: a few words but mainly quick sketches of Dic; one of Gwyn and Dic with a big yellow ball.

They could see people making their way through all the streets below them to the loading yard where the ceremony would be held.

'What do it mean, vesting?' Gwyn had asked.

'Vesting Day is what they call it,' Bert said. 'What it means is we own our own pits.'

'*We* do?'

'It's called nationalisation. It means belonging to the people.'

'It sounds funny, vesting,' Gwyn said.

They left Dic and Gwen at Number 27, and walked on down. Now among the houses they were getting more shelter from the driving sleety rain. Nesta had got her bright blue mac turned high around her neck and a blue and yellow headscarf tight around her hair. She looked across at Bert. In the beginning of a walk he could almost disguise his limp, but as it went on it got worse; she could see the strain in his face, with the leg beginning to drag. As she slowed the pace she looked down at Gwyn, holding tight to Bert's hand.

The yard was already crowded. People had come early, moved by a sense of occasion. The band, Danycapel and District Silver, was forming up under the near posts of the rugby pitch. Jim would be among them. On the far side of the pitch was the newly painted Welfare Hall, with the library and billiards room. Between the Welfare Hall and the cinema, the Rialto, was the bowling green laid in the war: a great pride because it was fine mountain turf, dug and carted down. It was closely mowed and always a brilliant green, an oasis among the smoky and dusty grey brick. Tommy Prosser saw Bert and came across, carrying the rolled Lodge banner.

'You help me unroll her, Bert?'

'Aye, Tommy.'

Bert let go of Gwyn's hand and they unrolled the banner. The lettering of the Lodge was in white on red. Two figures of miners, in green, flanked a broad outline figure of the valley, which Nesta had sketched. At the lower edge were the mottoes: *Forward to Socialism, Ymlaen i Sosialaeth.*

'She'll flap in this wind. Can you hold her, Tommy?'

'Wrists like steel, mun,' Tommy said. Then: 'The bugger.'

As they lifted the banner the wind had turned the pole in his hands. Bert smiled, gripping his pole and taking the strain. Nesta watched him as he put out his strength, easily and powerfully. He was still big and straight in his body, the broad shoulders solid. Turned away, smiling at Tommy, his damaged face was hidden. The black army beret was speckled with light grey rain.

The band struck up and everyone turned to watch them. They marched through, in military style, with the crowd falling back. In their smart black-and-gold uniforms, with gold-braided black peaked caps, they were not all easy to recognise. Nesta knew where to look for Jim, in the middle of the column. He was holding his trumpet rigidly, his shoulders back, his face set. She smiled seeing the sharp way he thrust it forward, away from his mouth, when he was not playing: a drill so unlike all his everyday movements. The high silvery blast of the march was lifting everybody's spirits. People clapped the band in. As Jim passed close to her, looking rigidly ahead, Nesta smiled and reached down for Gwyn's hand. It was wet inside her palm. On the polished surface of the trumpet the rain was gathered in tiny globes, which then broke and ran down as the thrust of the music came through.

As the band marked time, in front of the trestled platform, the official party started to get up. Tom Parkes, in charge of proceedings as the longest-serving union official in the district – he was going from today to a post in the Area Labour Director's office – slipped on the damp wood, and others had to push and haul him up. In position on the front of the platform he held up his right arm for silence, which was already effectively there, and with his left hand struggled to pull a sheaf of papers from his inside pocket.

'By God, you see how many,' Tommy Prosser said, still struggling with the pole of the banner. 'We shall have triple pneumonia while he gets through that lot.'

Bert frowned. He was not waiting for Tom Parkes to speak. He was waiting for necessary words to be spoken: the particular voice was not important. On the platform Tom Parkes struggled with the damp sheets that the wind was blowing, and then suddenly pocketed them. He began at once to speak more clearly.

It was a day of great achievement, of the seed in bloom. The struggles of a century, in the blood of our fathers before us, were now crowned with victory. Vast rivers of coal had flowed from this valley and its neighbours to the great sea, the wide ocean, of British prosperity. And all that wealth beyond us began here, deep in the ground, where we went in the dark and ripped it with our naked strength. And we came again to the light, and looked up to the hills, and we had been left naked. The rivers of coal had flowed, but we were left stranded on their banks, old sticks and fossils, broken bits of men. Except that still, brothers and sisters, we fought. We fought through the days and the years until today, at last, we have the victory, we have the property. It is the property of ourselves, that today at last we own not only the wealth buried deep in our earth but, more important, we own ourselves.

There was loud clapping. There were other short speeches but the time for words had passed. On the flagstaff beside the platform the new blue flag was being checked and an old man and a boy were standing holding the strings. They were the oldest workman present, Billy Williams, who had been in two stay-down strikes, and the youngest boy just started, Phil Evans. Tom Parkes announced them.

'Phil Evans?' Tommy asked Bert. 'Is that Dai Evans's boy?'

'No no, mun. Roy Evans his father. A different family altogether.'

The four hands pulled on the strings, and the flag ran up and broke out. The rain stopped suddenly. Several people near Nesta laughed. The wind was still blowing, flapping the flag. Then the band struck up in the Welsh anthem: '*Mae hen wlad fy nhadau*' ('The Land of My Fathers'). The singing was slow, deep and strong. There was a loud cheer as it ended.

Then the band was moving, playing a march again, and the platform party scrambled down and formed up behind it; Bert and Tommy with their banner took the next place. As the band moved forward, to march down the long main street, people moved in to make the long procession behind it. Nesta, holding Gwyn's hand tightly, got in just behind Bert. There were her friends all around her and they were all soon laughing and talking as they walked behind the marching rhythm.

The rain started again, and everyone dispersed quickly as the march ended. As Bert and Nesta and Gwyn were making their slow way back uphill, to get Dic and Gwen, the rain was turning to sleet and even a few flakes of snow, and the wind had swung east and was now very much colder.

'For a cup of hot tea,' Nesta said, shivering.

'It's all been worth it,' Bert said.

Gwyn, pinched and cold in his face, hurried as close as he could beside him.

# 5

❧ ❀❦❀ ❧

# LONDON, FEBRUARY 1947

The snow was black in hard ridges along the gutter. On the uncleared pavement it had been trodden into patches of grey ice. Norman walked with great care until he reached the side road, where there were clear ruts in the centre. He crossed and walked in the widest rut. His shoes and socks were wet from getting out of the bus into a puddle of melted snow around a warm drain.

There was nobody about in the side street, and there were only candle lights in the houses. The power cut had still about forty minutes to go. It was the sixth week of the unprecedented cold of this winter. It was like being moved back to the darkest winters of the war, but then with very different feelings. There was no longer an outside enemy; only a beleaguered and bewildered Labour government, its confident world suddenly frozen and chaotic, falling back desperately on slogans against a natural disaster with which a still disorganised economy was unable to deal.

Norman hesitated, checking the number, at the path to Emma's door. The little wooden gate, its green paint peeling, was frozen open. The path had not been cleared and was grey with packed ice over broken ornamental yellow tiles. He pressed the bell for the middle flat. He saw her large confident writing: *Wilkes*. There was no response. Perhaps the bell was on the mains. He pressed it again and knocked. There were footsteps on the stairs. Emma opened the door. She was wearing a fur coat and a high navy-blue woollen jersey, with slacks and felt slippers. He smiled, looking at her.

'Well, come in. It's freezing.'

'I know.'

He followed her up the worn lino-covered stairs.

'God knows,' she said, over her shoulder, 'how the Russians manage, with a winter like this every time.'

'It's the abnormality defeats us,' Norman said.

'What?'

She pushed open her own door. As he followed her in she turned and looked him over.

'What are you dressed like that for?'

'I told you. A meeting.'

'It looks more like some spiv hotel.'

He took off his dark trilby hat and tight black overcoat. They already felt damp in the minimal warmth of the flat.

'It gets worse,' Emma said, looking at his dark suit.

'Bugger that. My feet are wet. Have you got a fire of any kind?'

'I've got a paraffin stove in the sitting-room. Georgi always manages to get some.'

'They're bloody frozen as well as wet. I'll go through.'

'Sure. But be careful of it. There's a saucepan of soup on the top.'

'My supper?'

'To start with. I've done better than that. I've got a swede and spam stew, more swede than spam admittedly. When the power's back on I'll reheat it.'

'Where did you get the swede?'

'Georgi. There's a comrade in Essex.'

He took off his shoes and socks, and rolled up his trouser legs. He stood near the stove, with its fierce local heat. The smell of the paraffin overrode the good smell of the soup.

'And something else,' Emma said, with a laugh in her voice.

'What?'

'Guavas. A tin of guavas. Can you believe that?'

'People probably don't know what they are.'

'That's right. I didn't myself. But if it's in a tin I buy it. And the scent, it's like another world.'

'I do know it. I forget from where.'

He took off his jacket and loosened his tie. He sat in front of the stove.

'Is Georgi away?'

'Yes. He's in Lancashire.'

'He seems to go away a lot.'

'Well of course, as a national official. And you know what he's like. He has to see to everything himself.'

'Keeping production going?'

'Are you sneering at him, Norman?'

'No. Of course not. I still follow the Party line.'

'Follow?'

'Know of, let's say.'

'It's none of it easy, for a militant working-class Party, and with the employers just taking advantage of the workers' co-operation.'

'Including the nationalised industries?'

'Sometimes, yes. Even my lot.'

Norman rubbed his feet.

'Have you got a towel?'

'For your feet?'

'All right. They're drying out.'

'Keep them away from the stove. You'll get chilblains again.'

'No, not since I was a kid.'

'Well, that's what I remember anyway. I've looked after you long enough.'

Norman smiled and looked round the sitting-room. It was a large, high room, with decorative plaster on its ceiling. There was a good mahogany table in the bay window space. The curtains were a heavy dark tweed. In the main part of the room there were two large sofas and a big black leather chair. There was a crammed white-painted bookcase along the whole of the inside wall. On the other walls there were several familiar watercolours.

'Mummy helped, I see.'

'Oh, the stuff? Yes. Though she practically had a fit when she saw this road.'

'How did she take to Georgi?'

'He was marvellous. Very correct, very European. It was like a diplomatic occasion.'

'Does she know he works for the Party?'

'Well, she's convinced he works in labour relations. She thinks labour relations are terribly important.'

They laughed, looking happily at each other. The centre light came on suddenly. Emma clapped her hands.

While she was preparing the supper, Norman laid the table. Then she came in and served the soup from the paraffin stove. For the main course she carried in the big saucepan of stew, and they served themselves from the pan on the table. Norman ate hungrily.

'What was this meeting, then?' Emma asked, wiping her mouth.

'They call it Liaison B.'

'Boring?'

'Very. But there are signs that they're all perking up.'

'Why?'

'Because a lot of them think they'll soon have another war to play at.'

'I know. They're just bastards. We should get some clapped-out troop ship and load them all on to it. Let them all steam off to their bloody America.'

He took another helping of stew.

'Only one problem with that . . .' he said, eating.

'What?'

'It'd need a lot more than one ship.'

Emma laughed. They finished the stew and she brought in the guavas. They ate them slowly, enjoying their softness. Then they carried out their plates and the pans. Norman boiled a kettle and washed up. Emma dried the plates and tidied.

'The bed's not very comfortable, but it's aired.'

'I could sleep on anything.'

They went back to the sitting-room. Each took a sofa and stretched out on it.

'This is good, Em. It's been too long since I saw you.'

'Sure. How's Sarah?'

'Very well. She loves having Alex.'

Emma smiled.

'I have my own plans of that kind.'

'What? Really?'

'Yes, it just happened. I'm due in August.'

'That's marvellous, Em. But can you afford it? I mean when you won't be earning, all you'll have is Georgi's salary.'

'Salary? In the Party? He gets the minimum industrial wage.'

'How much?'

'I'm not sure. About four pounds a week.'

'Then you obviously can't manage.'

'I've got a bit in the bank.'

'Let me know if you need any more. But at least this winter will soon be over. An end to the natural if not the political chaos.'

He leaned back, resting his head on the sofa arm. He unbuttoned his waistcoat and then after a while took it off. Emma had taken off her coat before the meal but she still had it wrapped over her legs.

'It's a game, isn't it?' he said, staring up at the plaster patterns on the ceiling.

'We'll get through it,' she said, firmly.

'Oh, I don't doubt that. But I expect it's a turning point.'

'You're always making predictions like that. You remember that day in the Parks?'

'And was I wrong?'

'Not entirely, I grant you. But the popular forces are still very strong.'

'So are their enemies. I thought that was my point.'

'They were defeated in the war. They can be defeated again.'

'It's just I have this sense people have had enough of fighting. They would be glad now of . . .'

'Yes, say. What?'

'Guavas,' Norman said, and patted his stomach.

Emma pulled her coat more tightly around her legs.

'How's your work?' she asked.

'Interesting, actually. It's beginning to move quite fast.'

'Yes, so Georgi was telling me.'

'Georgi? He wouldn't know anything about this.'

'He seemed to. He must have been talking to somebody.'

Norman raised his head. He looked sharply across at her.

'Did he mention anything specific?'

'I've probably not got it right; but that these computing machines – is that what they're called? – that were developed during the war . . .'

'Go on.'

'Well, that they were being improved, that they were finding other uses for them, that there was some breakthrough in their instructions. I didn't know what that meant.'

Norman sat up. He stared down at his bare feet.

'You don't remember who he'd been talking to?'

'I don't think he said.'

'This is dangerous, Em. I'm telling you now, it's dangerous.'

'What, these machines?'

'Not the machines. I mean this talking about them.'

'Why should that be dangerous?'

'Because unless it's just gossip this is top secret stuff. Top bloody secret, with knobs on.'

'Computing machines? How could they be?'

'I've said enough. Let's drop it.'

'All right. If you want.'

She lit a cigarette and lay back, inhaling. Norman leaned across and felt his socks, which he had left drying by the stove. They were still damp. He swore. He felt at an odd disadvantage, in bare feet.

'Can I have a fag, Em?'

'Sure.'

He lit and inhaled deeply.

'Do you see much of Aunt Kate? You're so near her,' Emma said.

'Off and on.'

'Did you know Mummy told me she's leaving us her house?'

'Us?'

'Niece and nephew. To keep the old place in the family.'

'How in hell would that work out?'

'I don't know. It'll be years. But since it's near your work you could half-rent it from me or something.'

'It's too big. I could never keep it up.'

Emma stubbed out her cigarette.

'I took Birdie there, after she had Gwyn.'

'Yes, I remember you said.'

Emma got up. She fetched a bottle of gin from a cupboard. She poured two half-tumblers. He took the drink, not looking at her.

'It appears,' Emma said, 'that there is a serious deficit.'

'What, Kate?'

'Not Kate. These new machines.'

He put the drink down.

'Look, Em, we said we'd drop that.'

'I can chat about it, can't I?'

'You're doing more than that.'

'All right, I am. Because it's time you started facing your responsibilities.'

'*My* responsibilities?'

'Yes. Because in spite of what you say there isn't any real secret about it. These things can be developed for peace or for war, and they're being developed for war.'

Norman stood quickly and went closer to the stove. He could feel the beginning of a headache, in the fumes of the paraffin. He looked back at Emma, lying full-length on the sofa.

'Have you ever heard some back-street kid talking about horses?' he asked.

'No, but what's that got to do with it?'

'It's your situation. Trying to talk about something you don't begin to understand.'

'Then explain it to me.'

'I told you, Em. I can't. Even if I were willing I probably couldn't; we'd have no common language.'

'But you agree they're being developed for war.'

He reached down and took his socks. He sat on the sofa and pulled them over his feet.

'That's twice you've agreed,' Emma said. 'Because remember I'm very used to understanding you.'

'By divination?'

'By behaviour.'

He rubbed his feet, which felt cold.

'You say *being developed*. The human brain has been developed. Would you say it has been developed for peace or for war?'

'For war,' Emma said, 'in societies like this one.'

'That's rubbish. It's general purpose.'

'And so are these machines, is that what you're saying?'

'I'm not saying anything. I'm only trying to stop you talking nonsense – and as I said, dangerous nonsense.'

Emma sat up.

'It's the danger I'm concerned with, and you should be too. While this deficit persists there is a real danger of war. All the forces that have always wanted to destroy the Soviet Union are gathering again, and now they have these two advantages: the atomic bomb and these machines of yours.'

'Christ almighty!' Norman shouted, and got up and walked away to the window.

'Well?' Emma asked, looking across at his back. He turned and came and stood over her.

'Who's been giving you this stuff, Em? It's important. I must know.'

She stared up at him, momentarily frightened by his intensity.

'Is it Georgi?' he persisted.

'Yes. I said.'

'Who did he get it from?'

'Why should he get it from anywhere? Isn't it common knowledge?'

'The general dangers, yes. This specific stuff, no. And especially – it couldn't have been your phrase – this about deficit.'

'Well, I think that's what he said.'

'But then who from, Em? English or Russian?'

'Russian? You know Georgi has nothing to do with that.'

'Hasn't he? Would you know?'

'He's my husband.'

'Yeah.'

He looked away, undecided. Then he sat on the sofa and held his head in his hands. Emma said nothing, but after a while got up and refilled his glass.

'There's so much you don't know, Em,' he said warily, as she was kneeling close to him.

'Then tell me.'

'I can't tell anyone.'

'Because it's an official secret,' she said, harshly, and moved away.

Norman laughed. She looked very hard at him.

'You laughed before. Just like that. That day in the Parks.'

'It connects,' Norman said.

'I don't see how. All you were telling me then was that you were giving up the Party.'

'Then we didn't much communicate.'

'Oh yes, I know you wrapped it up.'

He looked across at her. With the light directly above him his face looked much harder and older.

'What exactly did Georgi suggest?' he asked, neutrally.

'He didn't suggest anything. He just . . .'

'The truth, Em. I must know exactly what he said.'

'Well, he wasn't really suggesting anything. He just explained about this deficit . . .'

'The double deficit?'

'Yes. And he said what a pity it was, when we had good comrades in . . .'

'Go on.'

'Well, I don't remember exactly. He said some technical words. But I know he mentioned these machines and then, I didn't understand it, their instructions.'

'That's why it's so important to know who he's been talking to.'

'I don't see why.'

'All right, I'll tell you. The technical deficit – in electrical engineering – is well enough known, among competent people. For all kinds of reasons the Russians are years behind.'

'And that's serious?'

'Perhaps very serious.'

'Because of codes and ciphers, things like that?'

'No. Not mainly. They can cope with that. Or they think they can cope.'

'What, then?'

Norman started to speak, but then checked.

'It's no use, Em. I don't know who I'm talking to.'

'You're talking to me. I want to understand it.'

'Yes, and you'll talk to Georgi and Georgi will talk to his unknown friend.'

Emma lay back on the sofa.

'Well, and if he does?' she said, watching the smoke from her cigarette spiral towards the ceiling.

'I'm glad that's clear,' Norman said.

'Are you?'

'Of course.'

'It doesn't shock you?'

'Hardly that.'

She raised herself on her elbows. She squinted across at him, the cigarette smoke in her eyes.

'Really?'

'No. Because there's nothing I could tell you. I've never been part of this technical development. I have to know what the relays are but I could no more build or reproduce them than . . .'

'Who?'

'Does it matter?'

'No, I mean who does understand all that?'

Norman laughed.

'A pity Monkey went away,' he said wryly.

'Monkey? Really? Is that what he does?'

'It's what he did. He was brilliant at it.'

'Are you still in touch with him?'

'Not for a year or more. He's moved on somewhere. The last time he was in England he came to see us. Sarah practically threw him out.'

'Your closest friend?'

'She said he made her flesh creep.'

Emma laughed.

'Well, he does, a bit.'

'Anyway, you won't catch him. He's off on his own.'

'But he does understand these . . . relays, did you say?'

'He actually made some of the best. For the time he was doing it, I mean.'

'Is he still doing it?'

'I told you. We're not in touch.'

Emma stretched her arms above her head. She yawned.

'Okay, then.'

Norman got up.

'I'll get you a hot-water bottle. You'll need it,' she said.

'Thanks.'

When she had gone to the kitchen he switched off the light. He went to the window and put his fingers through the join of the curtains. The glare of the snow in the street under the yellow lamps was a surprise, like opening a window on to another country; a strange and bitter landscape beyond the stuffy and already familiar room. There was nobody in the street. He looked carefully both ways, and into every shadow. Then he went back and switched on the light.

Emma came in squeezing the bottle against her chest, pushing out the surplus air. Then she screwed the top back, with strong fingers.

'There!' she said, handing him the rubber bottle.

'Thanks.'

'I just wanted to get it right. The relays are what matter?'

He smiled, twisting his mouth.

'The relay systems, if you want to be precise.'

'Okay. But that's quite different from these . . . instructions, wasn't it?'

He was holding the bottle by its rubber handle. He swung it against his leg.

'Are we starting again, Em?'

'No. I just wanted to get it clear.'

He looked down at the bottle. He put it carefully on to the sofa.

'There's only one thing to get clear, so listen carefully. If, as I suspect, this is some amateur effort of Georgi's, forget it. Forget it all.'

'What do you mean, amateur effort?'

'I mean these planted questions. I mean these semi-informed references. Any serious professional—'

He stopped and looked away.

'I think you'd better go on,' Emma said.

'If it will stop this nonsense, I'll tell you just so much, and as simply as I can. Now that there are these extremely complicated relays, which can perform quite new functions, the problem is indeed what you call the instructions. What we're beginning to call a language.'

'How could it be a language?'

'It's not, in the old sense. Its base is almost entirely mathematical.'

'Which is where you come in.'

'In general terms, yes. And that's as much as I'm saying; because beyond that point this isn't stuff for amateurs.'

'Though there is a deficit there too?'

'You don't understand. The language is of no real interest without the systems.'

'Yet there could still be a deficit in both?'

'Look, Em, I'm talking professionally. In the mathematics as such, there are Soviet mathematicians who could do anything we are doing. Even if, as it seems, they're following a curious path of their own.'

'Do you know that? How?'

'There is still some international science. And in any case . . .'

'Go on.'

'No, I won't go on. What's the point? If I said we were working on a binary base and they seem, for some reason of their own, to be attempting a trinary—'

'What reason of their own?'

'I don't know. The bloody dialectic, I suppose.'

'Then shouldn't they know that?'

'They do know it. I mean the competent people. But have you ever tried telling the Russians they're on the wrong line?'

'No, I haven't. Have you?'

'Norman laughed.

'Okay. That's it, Em. Bed.'

Emma smiled, spreading her hands.

'Sure. I'm sorry if I've pestered you.'

'It's all right.'

'It isn't only this deficit, though politically that's very serious. It's also — don't you see? — that I like to know what you're doing?'

'Is it?'

'And I wouldn't dream of asking you to do anything — what

did you say? – dangerous. It would never be any more than just coming to talk to me.'

'You're not serious, Em?'

There was a husky catch in his voice. She watched him, calmly.

'Yes, my dear. I'm serious.'

'Then you must be mad. You and Georgi both.'

'Just leave us to decide that.'

He picked up the hot-water bottle.

'Which is my room?'

'The door on the right.'

'Goodnight, then.'

'Goodnight, dear. Sleep well.'

He walked quickly to the bedroom and closed the door firmly behind him. The bed was one he recognised from childhood, with a carved oak head. It was heavy with good old blankets. On the mantelpiece there was a framed photograph of his mother and father, in the garden of the Vienna Embassy. Beside it there was another photograph that he did not immediately recognise. Then he saw Emma's writing in the bottom margin: *Birdie and Gwyn at Danycapel, 1946*. He stared at the smiling woman and the solemn, half-turned-away child. He picked it up and then quickly put it back. He undressed rapidly and slid into bed. Then he realised that he had left the hot-water bottle where he had put it down to look at the photograph. He cursed and put out the light.

# THREE

—◦⟶❧❀⬭❀☙◦—

## 1955–56

# 1

❧✿❧

## DANYCAPEL, MARCH 1955

Nesta was alone on the long board platform, sitting on the edge
of a luggage trolley. After the train had stopped a porter came
through and shouted 'Danycapel, Danycapel!' in a long tenor
cry. She got up and spoke to him, and then saw Emma getting
down from her carriage. She ran along the platform and threw
her arms around her. Emma, flustered, had to let her suitcase
drop to the boards.

'Emma, love, I'm so sorry.'

Emma looked down at her.

'Thank you, Birdie.'

Nesta moved and picked up the suitcase. Emma tried to get
it back. They walked down the platform. Emma gave her ticket
to the porter.

'And Bert, well, he was more upset than . . .'

'Yes, Bert and Georgi did a lot together.'

'And those awful bikes. I told Bert it wasn't right of the Party.
They should have let him have a car.'

'No, Georgi loved his motorbike.'

'That's true. But they're not safe. I wouldn't let Bert on
one.'

'Let me have my suitcase, Birdie.'

'No, really, it's nothing.'

'I'm still perfectly strong, you know.'

'Well, of course you are. I can see you are.'

Emma reached across and took the suitcase. They walked uphill from the station, past the cinema.

'Only I hope you don't mind,' Nesta said, 'I got to pick up Gwen from school. It was just an awkward time for the train.'

'There was no need for you to meet me, Birdie.'

'As if I wouldn't. After what you've been through.'

It was just two weeks since Georgi had been killed; outside Walsall, late at night, in heavy rain, in a collision with a lorry. He had been brought back to London to be cremated. There would be a memorial meeting in another four weeks; the Party was organising it.

'How's Bert?' Emma said.

She was striding along the narrow pavement, her head pushed forward into the wind. She was wearing a heavy white raincoat.

'He's not too good just lately,' Nesta said. 'He gets a lot of pain from his leg and he's had flu twice this winter. And his nerves, I don't know, it's all been a strain on him.'

'I'm sorry. But you're well anyway.'

'Me? Yes, of course. Nothing ever happens to me.'

She was hurrying to keep up with Emma. She was very much thinner than when Emma had last seen her, two years before. Her face seemed altered, with the shining black hair cut close to the head. The big eyes were more prominent and the small bright mouth more emphatic. Her sky-blue raincoat was tightly belted at her waist. There seemed hardly room for a body inside it.

'And the children?'

'Well, there! You'll be pleased with Gwyn.'

'Yes, you said in your letter: how well he was doing at school. I want to talk to you both about that.'

'Then Dic, well Dic, he's thirteen, you know what that is. Either sulking or shouting; well, they have to don't they? He even shouts at Bert and he'd fight me if I let him.'

'Not like Gwyn?'

'No, Gwyn's the quiet one. Like he's got to work to prove who he is.'

Emma looked sharply across, but Nesta's expression had not changed. When she saw Emma's glance she smiled.

'Not far now,' she said, and turned a corner towards the school. As they turned they were exposed to the wind, a cold east wind blowing down from the mountain. The narrow streets were still wet with rain, and there were drifts of low cloud along the dark ridge beyond the tip. But there was also a fitful sunshine, gleaming now along the grey street and the narrow pavements.

'Little Gwen,' Nesta said, 'she's lovely. Her Nan's girl.'

'I thought when I saw her she looked very like you.'

'Her and Gwyn, yes. Only Gwen, see, has got her Nan's character. Well, she spends so much time there, she's bound to.'

'Why does she spend time there?'

'She has to, between school and me finishing work, and then more than that the Saturdays and all the school holidays. These teachers have it cushy.'

'You're still working at the Coop?'

'Yes. Today's half-day.'

'Do you like it there still?'

'Well, not so much with this new manager. He's one of the loud ones, but it's all right.'

'You still go to your art classes?'

'No, not now.'

'Why not, Birdie?'

'They shifted the time. But I'm not worried. I still paint a bit on my own.'

'You need a full-time course, at an art college.'

Nesta laughed.

'Aye, and I might too, when the kids are grown up.'

'You couldn't manage it before?'

'Well, it's obvious, isn't it?'

The school was in sight now, and they were meeting other mothers on their way there. Nesta called across to several of them. Then she stopped, suddenly.

'What is it, Birdie?'

'I'm a fool, that's all. I never asked you about your Bill.'

'That's all right,' Emma said, smiling.

'Did it hit him very hard, about his Dad?'

'I don't know, Birdie, I really don't know. I told him, of course, and I heard him telling it to one of his friends. But at eight, I don't know, they keep it in to themselves.'

'You didn't think to bring him down? We'd have loved having him.'

'Oh no, he mustn't miss school.'

'That's right.'

'Mrs Mansell is very good with him. Better than I am really.'

'I don't believe that.'

'She is, Birdie. I've got no false pride about it. She knows how to run the house and get proper meals and look after clothes. She did almost everything for Georgi.'

Nesta nodded. They had reached the school yard, behind its high pointed iron railings. There was a bell sounding.

'Now the charge of the Light Brigade,' Nesta said, pushing her face close to the railings.

There was a silence and then a sudden shouting run of boys, a few pushing and throwing missed punches as they ran. A group of girls came after them, more quietly, and some went over to a corner of the yard to skip. They were nearly all out before Nesta at last saw Gwen, walking head down, carrying a cotton bag, deep in talk with another small girl.

'That's her friend Phyllis,' Nesta said. 'You'd have laughed, Phyllis was the black cat in *Dick Whittington*. Well, she looks it really. So do our Gwen, come to that.'

'Oh, she's very pretty,' Emma said.

'Phyllis?'

'No, Gwen. Your Gwen. She's as pretty as you, Birdie.'

'Me!'

The two little girls had stopped, their heads still close together. The two women watching them through the railings waited, smiling, but as the close talk continued, and the other mothers and children were going off, Nesta moved.

'Gwen, come on,' she called, going in at the gate.

The little girl looked up, said a few words to her friend, and then walked sedately to her mother.

'Hello, love,' Nesta said, bending and kissing her hair.

Gwen walked along beside her.

'You remember Auntie Emma.'

'Hello, Auntie Emma.'

Emma smiled and reached down to shake hands. Gwen adroitly moved her bag from her right hand to her left. As the women turned, she walked quietly between them.

In the long pull up to the house they met Dic with a group of boys.

'Don't be late for your tea, mind!' Nesta called, from the other side of the street.

'No, Mam!' Dic called back, but he scarcely looked at her.

'Let me take a turn with your case,' Nesta said. 'This old pitch, it jellies your legs.'

'It's perfectly all right,' Emma said.

There was nobody at the house when they arrived. Bert was off shift but had gone to see someone. Gwyn's school bus, from down the valley, didn't arrive till nearly five. Nesta took Emma upstairs to the back bedroom.

'I hope you don't mind this, it's small but you get a good view of the mountain.'

'It's fine, Birdie, thank you.'

'And I'm sorry but it would be easier if Gwen slept in here with you. We've got a little bed Bert can put in the corner.'

'No, that's fine.'

'Only she said she'd go down to her Nan's but I thought better not, she's not too well.'

'That's your mother, is it, or Bert's?'

'Oh, my Mam, yes. Bert's Mam, well, she still tries, but she never has thought much of me.'

'Really?'

'Since before we was married – but no need to go into all that.'

Emma hesitated.

'Do you mean because of Gwyn?'

Nesta went over and pulled back the counterpane.

'The whole thing,' she said quickly.

She smiled and went out, but then stopped on the stairs.

'Come down for a cup of tea,' she called, 'before all our noisy men get here.'

Bert was the first to arrive, while the women were just finishing their cups of tea. When Nesta called he came into the front room, stopped as he saw Emma, and then walked stiffly across, holding out his hand. Emma got up.

'Emma, I'm more grieved than I can say.'

'I know, Bert. Thank you.'

'He wasn't only a good comrade. He had the kind of knowledge the movement never has enough of.'

'That's right. He did.'

'I always said, even when we'd been arguing, Georgi's one of the very few you could call a strategist.'

'That's right. He was.'

'And to lose him like that, well . . .'

Emma released her hand and sat down. She had been shocked by Bert's appearance. It had overborne his words. There had always been some shock, seeing his disfigured face after an interval in which it had blurred. But with some thickening of the features it now looked very much worse. There was an area of dark puffy skin around the hanging left eye, and that whole side of his face seemed more twisted. The skin on the rest of his face had blotched and reddened, and the face and stomach were now badly overweight. As he had walked towards her she had seen his effort to overcome the limp, which seemed to drain him of strength, though he was still big and solid, with the firm heavy shoulders. His black hair was cropped close and some of the scalp showed through.

'In one war or another,' she found herself saying, and then regretted her words.

'How do you mean, Emma?'

'All I mean, Bert, is this unending struggle. We've all taken our losses.'

'Exactly, Emma. Exactly.'

Nesta got up.

'There's still some tea in the pot. Would you like some?'

'No, no, I'll wait for the meal.'

'It's in the oven. We'll just wait for the boys.'

'Aye, that's it.'

Bert turned to Emma and laughed.

'The reinforcements, I call them.'

'Well, they are,' Emma said, 'growing up in this house.'

Nesta got up and went out. She found Gwen already laying the table in the kitchen.

'That's a good girl.'

'Nan showed me.'

There was a bang of the front door and Dic rushed through

and up the stairs to the lavatory. A few minutes later Gwyn walked in quietly. Emma had seen him in the street and hurried out to meet him in the passage.

'Auntie Em.'

She kissed his cheek. His skin was cold. She held his wrists and looked him over. His thick curling black hair was still cut quite short, though not as closely as when she had last seen him and protested that he must let it grow. His narrow bony face had crease lines above the nose and beside the mouth that were surprising on so smooth and fresh a skin. His body was filling out, and he looked sturdy in his closely buttoned dark-grey blazer. When he saw her he had put down the black leather briefcase she had given him for his fourteenth birthday. His voice was now fully broken and deep.

'There you are,' Nesta called, from the door of the kitchen.

'Mam.'

Bert was still standing in the front room, looking out at the street. As Emma stood aside to let Gwyn past, the boy stopped at the open door.

'Hi, Dad.'

'Gwyn boy.'

'I got travelling reserve to West Mon.'

'Never! That's bloody marvellous. Except you ought to have been in.'

'Not really. John and Gareth are up to two stone heavier.'

'Where do you play?' Emma asked.

'Lock.'

Bert was watching Emma. She went back in to join him. Gwyn went on upstairs, and passed Dic hurrying down. They pushed at each other, Dic laughing.

'Don't be long, Gwyn, I'm putting the tea out!' Nesta called.

'Right. I'll just change.'

Bert was still watching Emma, with an open curiosity. She became embarrassed, and flopped into a chair.

'You reckon he's coming along?' Bert said.

'Yes, of course, he's fine.'

'You ought to get Nest to show you his exam marks. Those mocks he done. He got straight A's.'

'She wrote and sent them, Bert, yes. That's one of the things we must talk about.'

'How d'you mean, Emma?'

'What I mean, Bert, is I want him to put in for Cambridge.'

'Cambridge. You mean for university?'

'Yes. Why not?'

'Well, his school's advised him for Cardiff. He's got an interview I think Nest said.'

'I want him to go to Cambridge, Bert. I want him really to fly.'

Bert again stared curiously at her. She turned away from the look on the damaged face.

'Right, are you coming or not?' Nesta called.

They got up. Bert stood back for Emma at the door. The kitchen table was crowded, the chairs jamming against each other. Gwen was sitting near the stove on a low stool. The boys sat together between Bert and Emma. Nesta served from the stove.

'It's just sausage and mash and broccoli, Emma. I hope that's all right.'

'Oh, that's lovely, Birdie.'

Nesta put down Emma's plate.

'The plate's hot, mind.'

'Why do you call Mam Birdie?' Gwen asked, from her stool.

'Hush now,' Bert said.

'Because we're very old friends, Gwen,' Emma said, smiling. 'It's what I've always called her.'

Nesta served the other plates: first Bert, then Gwen, Dic and Gwyn. She brought her own warm plate, in a hold of teacloth, and sat down.

'You haven't got much, Mam,' Gwen said.

'You get on with your own, never mind other people's.'

Bert and the children began eating.

'How is it at work, Bert, these days?' Emma asked.

Bert had his mouth full. He had to swallow to reply.

'Oh, much as usual, Emma. A bit quiet, to tell you the truth.'

'You on the same job?'

'Aye, more or less. Only I'm charge lampman now. That brings it up one grade.'

'All the surface rates are lower?'

'No, no, it depends on the job. Only but for this bloody leg I could be cutting coal.'

'Is the union pretty good?'

'Union!' Bert said, putting down his fork. 'Well, that's a long tale for now. But I'm still, you see, a marked man. One of the boys from the Shakespeare.'

'The what?'

'It's a pub,' Gwyn said, 'where the unofficials used to meet.'

'The unofficials?'

'What it is, Emma,' Bert said, 'is the Saturday overtime. We been working three years now to ban it, and we was winning actually. Only national union policy, you know how it is.'

'They're against you.'

'Oh aye. Only not so much the policy, at least I don't think so. It's being an unofficial group, almost a shadow leadership. That's what they won't have.'

Nesta leaned forward.

'Finish your food, Bert. You can talk after.'

'Yes, I'm sorry,' Emma said. 'I'm interrupting your eating.'

'Don't worry about that, girl. There's a lot of things wants interrupting.'

The boys had already cleared their plates. Gwyn got up.

'Sorry, Mam. Homework.'

'You'll stay and have some icecream?'

'No. No, thanks. I got some wicked stuff tonight.'

'Bags yours,' Dic said.

'Aye, all right, kid.'

He went quickly upstairs. The others finished their meal.

'Bert, you and Emma go in and be comfortable. Gwen and me can wash up.'

'No, I must help, of course,' Emma said.

'Not a bit of it. You're our guest, aren't you?'

As Emma hesitated, Dic pushed back his chair.

'I got table tennis down the Welfare, Mam.'

'All right.'

'Don't you have homework, Dic?' Emma asked.

'Aye but I done it. We had a free period. Old Roberts had a fainting fit.'

'Mr Roberts? Never,' Nesta said.

'Well, they give out it's flu but he's the sort has fainting fits. They sent that new one, Lewis, but he took one look at us and thought better of it. He just said get on with your homework.'

Nesta laughed. She reached across and ruffled Dic's hair.

'Dic Lewis, you're a liar,' she said, still laughing.

'I'm not, Mam. Honest.'

'You think I don't know my own son?'

'Well,' Dic said, 'there wasn't really any homework. Because Roberts is off and he's the only keen one.'

'What about the other subjects?'

'They say they're letting us find our own pace.'

Nesta pulled his head to her shoulder and put her hand on his cheek.

'Lovely. Go on, then.'

Dic smiled and hurried out.

'Right then, Emma,' Bert said, and led the way to the front room. They sat opposite each other. He reached down and switched on two low shaded lights.

'What do you think of my fireplace?' he asked, getting out his pipe.

'Sorry?'

'The fireplace. I put it in over the summer.'

Emma looked at the fireplace. It had a wide stone façade, with lined pointing, and a dark slate mantelpiece.

'You did that yourself?'

'Aye. In the end. There was them porridge tiles before.'

'Porridge tiles?'

'You know. Only Nest wanted the stone.'

'It's lovely,' Emma said.

She lit a cigarette as Bert drew on his pipe. There was a long silence.

'The Party'll miss Georgi,' Bert said at last.

'Yes, I'm afraid so.'

'Is it still all right up there, you reckon?'

'It's very good. The campaigns have been good.'

'I've heard a few arguments.'

'Well, of course there've been arguments. But the majorities are still solid. There's only one worrying thing, but it's still very small. Among a few there's a definite anti-Soviet tendency. At a time like this, of all times.'

'You mean with the German re-armament?'

'Of course. That's what makes it so unforgivable. Not that there haven't been mistakes . . .'

'Aye.'

'But the thing is, the thing they won't see, the Party is still of and for the international working class. What these others represent is something different: a sort of liberalism really, like some of it was in the Thirties.'

'Anti-fascism, that was.'

'Of course, and so we got in these liberals, who had nothing else in common with the international working class. So now, with the Cold War, they go back to their own colours; saying that the Soviet Union itself is a tyranny . . .'

'Not Party members saying that?'

'Oh yes. Though only a few. They have no understanding of the disciplines of building socialism, because for them, of course, daily life was never a struggle.'

'That's right.'

A lorry went by in the street. The window frame rattled. The noise broke the exchange. They sat silent for some time.

'Is your brother still in the Party?' Bert asked, suddenly.

Emma sat up.

'Norman? Oh no. He left at the start of the war.'

'He's all right, is he?'

'Yes, he's very well.'

There was a sound at the door. Nesta was standing there, holding Gwen's hand.

'She's being silly,' Nesta said. 'She won't come in, because we've got visitors.'

'Only one visitor, Gwen,' Emma said, holding out her arms.

Gwen moved closer to her mother.

'You go and sit on the stool by your Dad,' Nesta said.

'That's right, lovely,' Bert said and shifted his leg.

Nesta followed the little girl in and sat between Bert and Emma. There was a long silence. It was Bert who broke it, clearing his throat.

'Emma says you showed her our Gwyn's results.'

'Yes, I told you I was writing to her.'

'She thinks he'll do well for university.'

'Well, he will. The school's always said.'

There was another silence. Gwen, on the stool by Bert's legs, was looking up into his face. In the shaded light he looked very dark and heavy. His face was in shadow.

'I want him to go to Cambridge, Birdie,' Emma said.

The child moved quickly and looked hard across at her.

'Emma's been explaining about it,' Bert said.

'Well, not really, Bert. But I do want to make the case for it. There's no difference really, when it comes to the grant, between Cambridge and anywhere else. So that side of it isn't a problem.'

'It's a more expensive sort of life there,' Nesta said.

'Not these days, Birdie. And that needn't be a problem. What is a problem, and you'd have to put this to Gwyn, is that it means another year at school. Another term, anyway, for him to take their entrance exam.'

'You mean instead of his A-levels?'

'No, after his A-levels. In December I think it is.'

'Would it be the same subjects?' Nesta asked. 'No Latin and that?'

'Well no, he's got a Latin O-level.'

'Just about,' Nesta laughed.

'So that it would be his same science subjects. He could do it, Birdie, I know he could do it.'

'That's more than I could,' Nesta said, and again laughed.

There was another silence, before Bert spoke again.

'What do you really reckon, Emma, is the advantage of him going to Cambridge?'

'It's the best, Bert. That's all. Why shouldn't he have the best?'

'Best at these sciences he's doing?'

'Yes, best at them especially.'

A shoot of pain crossed Bert's face. Nesta watched him, anxiously.

'And the thing is,' Emma went on, 'I know Mark Ryder, you remember Mark . . .'

'You all right, love?' Nesta asked Bert.

'Aye, sure.'

'It's your leg, isn't it?' Nesta said.

'Aye, a bit.'

'You must get it up on the stool again. Gwenny, love, come over by me.'

'No, I want to stay by Dada.'

Nesta got up quickly and went and picked up Gwen, putting her back in her own chair. Then she lifted Bert's damaged leg to the stool. She pushed up the leg of his trouser and laid her hands on his knee, rubbing gently.

'Don't fuss me, girl!'

She stayed kneeling by him, gently rubbing the damaged knee. Emma, looking round, saw Gwyn at the open door, looking across at Bert and Nesta.

'There,' Nesta said, and pulled the trouser down again, settling the leg on the stool. She went back, picked up Gwen and swung her round to sit on her knee.

'As I was saying,' Emma went on, 'Mark Ryder, you remember him, he talked about Spain that summer at the farm, he's an admissions tutor now and—'

'Mam,' Gwyn interrupted.

'Come in, son,' Bert said.

'No, I can't stop. I only come to ask Mam if she'd seen my ink rubber.'

'That green one,' Nesta said. 'Damn, I'm sorry, love, I pinched it for that pony I'm doing.'

'Can I go in and get it?'

'Course you can, love. I'm sorry.'

Gwyn went back upstairs.

'Only it's this one old pony,' Nesta said, excitedly, 'she's just these grey and black lines, the mane and tail specially, only I messed her up, more fool me.'

'Just drawing?' Emma asked.

'Well, pen drawing and a wash. She's just along, you can see her, I give her grass over the wire.'

'I give her grass,' Gwen said. 'Mam showed me to hold my hand flat.'

'Or she'll bite off your fingers, won't she?' Nesta said, cuddling her.

Gwen smiled and pushed in closer. Nesta rested her cheek on the soft hair.

'We interrupted you, Emma,' Bert said.

'No, Bert, that's quite all right.'

'I'd have been glad, really, if Gwyn could have stayed. It's for him to say in the end.'

'Well, of course it is, Bert. But he's very quiet and modest, you don't need me to tell you. I simply think it could make a world of difference to him. To be there with the very best of his generation, it could pull out all he's got.'

'But staying on school next year?' Bert said.

'Well yes, he'd need to work for the entrance. I'm sure the school would do it, and if they wouldn't there's other places. Then after December he could get a job till the October, see a bit of the world.'

There was a silence. Nesta held Gwen very close, waiting for Bert to speak.

'It's for you to say, girl,' Bert said, shifting his leg.

'Whatever's best for him,' Nesta said quickly.

'I remember him,' Bert said. 'Mark Ryder you mentioned.'

'Yes of course, he spoke the same morning as you.'

'He seemed a tidy chap.'

'He is. Very good. Of course the university as it is now, the best they get to is what they call independent Left.'

'A bit detached, you'd say?'

'But very honest. Mark's very honest, and if I asked him he'd see that Gwyn was all right.'

Bert laughed. Both women looked at him, surprised.

'We had a discussion at District about Welsh nationalism,' he said, still smiling.

'Really?'

'There's more of it now, in the Party even, than there was before the war.'

'But they were almost fascists, weren't they?'

'Well no, I wouldn't say that. And we've got our own national-ism, mind. If we wasn't Welsh, we'd be a different Party down here.'

'I understand that.'

'One young chap, Owen Harries Maesteg, he said this, I remember it. Coal, slate, water, brains: that's Welsh industry for you, and all for export.'

He laughed again, shifting his leg.

'Well, the brains can come back,' Emma said.

'Aye,' Bert said, smiling. 'Maybe.'

Nesta got up, lifting Gwen. She was very slender and wiry against the light. The black hair was like a cap.

'Bed for this young lady,' she said.

'Damn, I got that bed to bring up,' Bert said, rising.

'I can do it,' Emma said quickly. 'You stay where you are.'

He stretched his arms and slowly swung his bad leg.

'Nothing to it,' he said.

Emma stood and faced him.

'We can talk again about Gwyn,' she said, confidently.

'No, Emma, no need. We've took it as far as we can.'

'I'd go with Birdie to the school, to see his headmaster.'

'Aye, that's kind.'

He went out and down the passage to get the wire bed from the shed.

'You got the mattress?' he called up to Nesta.

'Aye, it's in our room. I been airing it.'

'Righto then, we'll soon have it fixed.'

Emma waited at the bottom of the stairs as he carried the bed back. She put out a hand to it as he turned round the end of the banister but he lifted it easily, away from her, and carried it up, whistling.

# 2

❧ ✿ ❧

# CAMBRIDGE, JANUARY 1956

Emma knocked again on the high inner door. The white-painted oak stood invitingly open but she could see no light at the edges of the second door, though it was already quite dark in the late winter afternoon. She looked again at the name painted above the door: *Dr Ryder*. She heard some sound from inside but could not make it out. She pushed the door half-open and called.

'Mark?'

'Yes, who is it?'

She looked across the almost dark college room. She could see no one.

'Emma!' Mark said, from somewhere beside the fireplace. She could now see him getting up from a deep chair.

'Can you see in the dark?' she asked, laughing.

'Oh, is it? Sorry.'

He switched on a table-lamp. It had a thick gold shade and its light was dim and diffused.

'I'm disturbing you, obviously.'

'No.'

'Do you sit in the dark thinking, or what?'

He got up. He was taller than she remembered, but also much heavier. He was wearing a dark red high-neck jersey and grey trousers. He had a pipe in his teeth.

'It's good to see you again, Emma.'

'See is putting it a bit strong.'

'Oh! Do you want more light? Of course.'

He went past her to the door and switched on the centre light. They stood looking at each other in the suddenly bright room.

'That's better,' Emma said.

'Good. Now come and sit down. Have a glass of Madeira.'

'Is that a change of fashion – Madeira?'

'I don't know. Is it?'

'It was always said that if you see a face in Cambridge you push a glass of sherry at it.'

'I prefer Madeira. But if you want sherry—'

'Mark, it's me! Don't fuss.'

He glanced sharply across at her. He indicated a chair. When he had got the drinks they sat facing the empty fireplace. The room was very warm, from some noisy central heating.

'It's been a long time,' Mark said.

He gave his glass a token lift. Emma waited. He looked away.

'I want to know, Mark,' she said.

'Know?'

'Gwyn Lewis?'

'Yes, of course. Lewis. Oh, he'll be all right.'

'You've given him a place?'

'It wasn't a problem. His marks were just about good enough and the science people liked him.'

'Did you like him?'

'From an interview? I don't know. I have serious reservations about interviews.'

'But you must have got some impression.'

He put down his glass. He had not touched the wine.

'Impression? Well, yes. I got a fairly clear impression of a resentful, uncertain, even rather sullen boy.'

'Perhaps you read that in. From what I'd told you.'

'On the contrary. What you said, on the phone and in your letter, was that he was very lively, talkative, interested in everything.'

'So he is. In Danycapel.'

'Well, I said I have reservations about interviews.'

Emma drank her wine. He noticed and picked up his own glass, but then put it down again without drinking.

'Anyway,' Emma said, 'if he's got his place . . .'

'Sure, fine!'

'Did he mention his family?'

'No. Why should he?'

'Well, I explained the situation.'

'Yes. I tried to forget that.'

'Forget it? Why?'

'In fairness to him.'

'That's one way of putting it. Are you sure it isn't a wider problem? That all those memories embarrass you?'

'They don't embarrass me. Why should they?'

'You haven't joined the great stampede to do dirt on the Thirties?'

'No. Why should I? What we did in the Thirties was right.'

'We? But then, you were never so close.'

'That must be it, then.'

'You must have some feelings about it. You were there at the farm, with Bert Lewis and Norman. It must touch you still, surely?'

'You mean there with his two fathers,' Mark said, getting up.

'That's very sharp, suddenly.'

'I expect it is.'

'Do you disapprove of us all so much?'

'I don't disapprove. I merely disagree.'

'On what, Mark? That's never really been clear.'

'On the identification of socialism with the development of the Soviet Union.'

'Not that Trotsky line, surely?'

'No, not Trotsky. Wasn't he part of the same thing?'

'Then what? The Labour Party?'

'Yes, from 'forty-five to 'forty-seven.'

'And then?'

'There isn't a name for it. That's what these false links did to us.'

'No, you can't say that, Mark. Mistakes perhaps, but the links happened, as history. You can't just pretend they didn't.'

'I don't pretend they didn't. I just said we should drop them.'

'Thus becoming anti-Soviet. Very conveniently for the time.'

'Not anti-Soviet. Simply choosing our own socialism.'

'Morris and Methodism?'

'And the British working class.'

Emma got up. She looked around the comfortable room.

'Well, at least I'm glad you put it like that.'

'Did you doubt it?'

'Not really. Not at an ideal level. In the way you would see it from Cambridge, I mean.'

'Yes, I know you mean that. I'm prepared to face you down on it.'

'Very sharp again?'

'Yes; and I'd remind you, Emma, it was you brought young Lewis to Cambridge. You picked him up, from that Welsh valley, and decided he should come here.'

Emma's voice rose.

'And why not? I wanted the best for him. I've always done what I could for him, since Norman—'

'You didn't have to tell me about Norman and his mother. I wouldn't have known.'

'But then—'

'Yes, Emma. But then.'

She moved away from him and sat on the edge of a chair.

'You're saying I was after some privilege, some favour?'

'Well, weren't you? We both knew.'

'You mean if he'd just applied in the ordinary way . . .'

'It would have come out the same. But of course he would never have applied.'

Emma picked up her handbag. She looked quickly around the room.

'Mark,' she said in a rush, 'I don't know why we're quarrelling. We've got nothing to quarrel about.'

'I agree.'

'I know it could be said that I've done too much for him. I met him in London last night, I put him up at the flat, I drove him down here this morning. And I was at the porter's lodge, waiting, when he came out after his interviews. I got him a taxi to the station.'

'Well?'

'His mother was very glad that I was seeing to it all.'

'And he?'

'He was a bit impatient, when he came back out to the lodge.'

'I can't really remember his mother. Bert Lewis, yes, very well. I remember him speaking in that barn.'

'Was it Bert Lewis's son, then, you thought you were admitting?'

'No, because you'd told me about Norman.'

'I know. But essentially, I mean.'

'On what I had to do with it, which was not the main decision, I was admitting the boy.'

Emma prepared to leave. She was moving towards the door when she turned and looked back.

'You remember Monkey Pitter, of course?'

Mark smiled.

'Would one be likely to forget him?'

'Would you like to see him again?'

'Monkey? Well, why not?'

She came back towards him.

'It's ridiculous, really. This crossroads of Cambridge, where we were all young. I was hanging about, just filling in time till Gwyn was finished, and a man bumped into me in the doorway of a bookshop. A very small, ugly man, talking back over his shoulder to some assistant who'd annoyed him.'

'Monkey?'

'Instantly Monkey. And yet I hadn't seen him for years, he's been in the States – officially, still is.'

'Officially?'

'I only got a few bits of it, you know what he is. He works in New York. On the Stock Exchange, he said, but that was probably only a joke.'

'He was at a university. I know someone who met him.'

'Yes, well, he said that too. He said they'd found him out.'

'Nothing more specific?'

'No. But I'm having a meal with him, this evening. Why don't you come along?'

'No, I wouldn't push in.'

'It's not a tryst, for God's sake.'

'Where's he staying?'

'I've got a number. I'll ring him if you like.'

Mark hesitated.

'Yes, Emma. I'd be glad to see him again.'

'I'll fix it,' Emma said.

They met at seven, in the bar of Monkey's hotel.

'Do you know those buzz machines?' Monkey said, shaking hands. 'Your little ball bumps into a coil, and your life lights up. Then it cannons away and bumps into another. Another equally spectacular light.'

'Social mechanics,' Mark said.

'Don't spoil it, Mark dear.'

Monkey went to the bar. He did not ask what they wanted. He brought back three frosted glasses of gin and cider.

'The only progressive drink,' he said, lifting his glass.

'It's lethal,' Mark said.

'The story of our times.'

Menus were brought to them in the bar. As they were looking through, Monkey said:

'To your heart's desire, my children, and simply ignore those sterling scribbles. You have a friend who is affluent.'

Mark frowned.

'What is it you're doing, Monkey? Emma was saying—'

'No more,' Monkey said, lifting his hand. 'Not a whisper of backstairs gossip.'

'But we're interested,' Emma said.

'So you should be. It's particularly instructive. When that foul little academy sold me out—'

'Wait,' Mark said, 'we haven't got that far.'

'And may you never!' Monkey said. 'A foreign red corrupting the youth of America!'

'The university said that?'

'Only when it was their turn. It began in the State Senate and continued in the newspapers. Names were named.'

'Were you involved at all in their politics?'

'Politics, I can fairly say, I have never been involved in.'

'Oh, come on, Monkey. We've been politicking together.'

Monkey smiled, looking deep into his glass.

'You may think so, Mark, but what have I ever been but a useful mechanic and quartermaster? I would have done as much, if asked, for the Church Army.'

'That simply isn't true,' Emma said.

'All right, and why should I lie to you? But it comes to the same thing. From the time I arrived there I had no political connections. I spent my blameless days with my head in my marvellous machine.'

'Is that one of these computing machines?' Emma asked.

Monkey glanced at her, curiously.

'Then what could they have against you?' Mark asked.

Monkey did not answer. He was still looking at Emma.

'Was it just some general smear?' Emma asked.

Monkey finished his drink.

'They keep files,' he said, shortly. 'And it seems they've put paddles on them.'

'You mean from here?' Mark asked.

'Where else?'

A waiter came and took their orders. Monkey leaned back in his chair. Mark and Emma were silent for some time.

'What do you do now?' Mark eventually asked.

'By way of gainful employment? That's simple. I take the gainful seriously.'

'In what?'

'There is an innocence in historians,' Monkey said, smiling at Mark. 'Kings before Fuggers. That's your motto, wouldn't you say?'

'What are Fuggers?' Emma asked. 'Or did I hear it wrong?'

'Fuggers were once bankers but now, Emma dear, they are large financial corporations. So large, the sweet things, that even their fat fingers can't count high enough. But then here is this wandering scholar with his philosophical machine. He can not only do their counting, he can out-analyse and out-predict their little hunches.'

'You work for one of these corporations?' Mark asked.

'Nothing so subordinate. I'm a new breed, a mutation. I'm, roll it, an independent financial consultant.'

'And successful?'

Monkey laughed.

'Let's just say your units are my factors.'

'I don't understand,' Emma said.

'He means,' Mark said, 'that he's rich.'

The waiter came back to call them for dinner. They went into the half-empty dining-room.

'And no more business,' Monkey said, 'until after the coffee. You must learn the rules of commercial palaver.'

They talked through the meal, about other things. Emma spoke a little about Norman. Monkey seemed not interested. He responded more to Mark's answers about his current work. He had done all he meant to on Spain, and was now working more generally on the Mediterranean.

'Not even one last little book on the Civil War?' Monkey asked, after some eager questioning on the Mediterranean work.

'It could hardly be little.'

'Then big. Think big.'

'It's too soon,' Mark said.

Monkey leaned back in his chair.

'Do you remember that nice boy Paul Howe?'

'Paul, yes,' Emma said. 'He was killed on the Jarama.'

'He talked to Norman about being a stranger, in a world of strangers.'

'He was very young,' Mark said.

'Do you think so? I'd say he was old. He was twenty years ahead of us, and old before his time.'

'Dead before his time,' Emma said. 'Like the millions of victims of fascism.'

'That too,' Monkey said. 'But we've come out the other side, into a quite staggering revival of capitalism, which will go on for at least twenty years. And then those of us who lived, as Paul didn't, will be the real strangers. We shall go on saying the things we learned to say and it will be just strange talk, in a strange land.'

He took off his glasses and rubbed his eyes. The eyelids were reddened. The skin under the eyes was livid.

A waitress came and cleared their plates. As they were eating their fruit Emma said:

'Bert Lewis was with Paul when he died.'

'Bert Lewis?' Monkey asked, as if from a great distance. He seemed suddenly very tired.

'He was at the meeting in Wales. He was taken prisoner in Spain and then wounded very badly in Normandie.'

Monkey nodded. He took another apple and began peeling it.

'I remember now. A big miner, very devoted. He married Norman's friend.'

'Birdie, that's right.'

'Was she called Birdie?'

Emma was about to answer when the waitress came for orders for coffee. The conversation died away. After coffee Monkey insisted on brandy. Emma eventually accepted but Mark continued to refuse. Monkey was quiet, drinking his brandy, but then his mood suddenly changed again.

'You'll say I've sold out, Emma dear.'

'No, Monkey.'

'Yes, Monkey. Can you doubt what Georgi would have said?'

'You know that Georgi . . .' Mark said to him, anxiously.

'Yes. I was shattered. That's my point, Emma. Can you be faithful to Georgi and not say I've sold out?'

'You were victimised,' Emma said.

'And survived it, wouldn't you say, rather well?'

'You had to make your living.'

Monkey laughed.

'It's the innocence that's so touching. Not just kings before Fuggers: revolutions before Fuggers.'

'What else,' Mark asked, 'ever breaks them?'

'Ah, but you see I'm a Marxist,' Monkey said. 'A Marxist and not a liberal historian. What breaks capitalism, all that will ever break capitalism, is capitalists. The faster they run the more strain on their heart. Moreover it helps that they've forgotten they have a heart. Perhaps even never knew.'

'This is persiflage, Monkey,' Mark said, irritably.

'Of course, but very serious persiflage. I told you I could out-analyse and out-predict.'

'What, in stocks and currencies?'

'As immediate dealing, yes. And especially futures. The only futures they think are left. But they make what Emma so politely calls my living. Still the real analysis is way below that.'

'What, then?'

'It would take hours. I will if you like. But briefly, they profit more by making more, and that more is always more than the poor, even the improved poor, can buy. So depression? Not this time. They're beginning a credit bonanza that would have made their fathers jump out of windows. They'll do new record times, run faster than anyone thought possible. And then the heart will give out.'

'What heart?'

'What heart would you expect? It will look like money, though it won't actually be money. But you can be sure of one thing: it will be quite fatal.'

'When?' Mark asked.

'Oh, a long time. Long enough for us to grow old and miserable.'

'Then what kind of hope is that?' Emma said. 'As against the real struggle now.'

'All the hope we've got, Emma dear. But enough.'

Emma looked at Mark. She had drunk more than she was used to, and was feeling the effects. She was also impatient with Monkey. Mark, who had drunk less, was withdrawn and tired.

'Time to go, my children,' Monkey said, getting up.

They pushed back their chairs. He walked over to the desk to sign the bill. Mark fetched Emma's coat and his own.

'How's the boy, Emma?' Monkey asked, coming up to them.

'The boy?'

'Your boy.'

'Oh, did Norman tell you? Yes, he's fine.'

'Eight now?'

'Rising nine.'

'You have someone to look after him?'

'I've a housekeeper, yes. Today was rather special. Gwyn came to see Mark for his interview.'

'Gwyn?'

'Gwyn Lewis,' Mark said. 'From Danycapel. Norman and Birdie's.'

'Of course,' Monkey said.

He walked with them through the lobby to the edge of the street. The air was wet and cold. He looked around quickly.

'Those political files I was mentioning . . .'

Only Mark heard. Emma was looking along the street. Mark waited.

'What ought to be known and perhaps isn't . . .' Monkey continued.

Emma had half-turned and was now listening to him.

'Some of our dear Russian friends,' Monkey said, and saw Emma wince. 'Some, only a few but some, have done the great good thing. They have chosen freedom. And the price of freedom turns out to be not eternal vigilance . . .'

'What are you talking about, Monkey?' Emma said, anxious to go.

'. . . not eternal vigilance, but names. Little lists of names.'

'Not in your case, surely?' Mark said, seriously.

Monkey smiled and looked out at the street. A crowd was coming out of the cinema and filling the opposite pavement.

'They don't print the lists in the papers,' Monkey said, 'if at all. That comes later.'

Emma had again stopped listening.

'Well, yes, it is late,' she said decidedly. 'I have to drive back to town. Good night, Monkey. Thank you for dinner.'

'Thank you for everything,' Monkey said, and bowed.

# 3

❧❧❀❧❧

# WESTRIDGE, JUNE 1956

The house was hidden from the narrow country road. Through closely planted lilac and laurustinus the sharp gradient of the curving drive took them to high ground, from which they could look out over cypress and sycamore to the meadowed hillside above the river. Emma made for the house but Norman stood, holding the keys, looking across to the wood and to a Friesian herd in one of the high fields. The young bullocks there were running, for no obvious reason. He watched them run and veer at the hedge, wait, and then run fiercely again.

'Are you coming?' Emma called.

'Sure. But you really ought to stand and let this have its effect on you.'

'What effect?'

'You don't see it?'

'Well, it's always been pleasant but apart from that . . .'

'I'd call it civilisation.'

'That's ridiculous. It's a nice country view but surely civilisation . . .'

Norman walked to the old stone porch, selecting keys from the bunch. He stopped to run his fingers over the weathered surface of the stone. There were two keys to the old oak front door: the big key of the nineteenth-century lock, which had been a replacement, and the thin shiny key of the recent lock, put in after the burglary.

'Kate was so scared after the break-in,' he said, opening the door.

'She was scared before it, poor Auntie,' Emma said. 'Every time I came to see her it was how all decent society had collapsed since the war, with all these terrible—'

'Which war?'

'Right. She meant this last one, when she was finally down to the Hodgsons, and then when they started living out.'

'Poor Kate!' Norman said.

They stood in the hall. The air was stale; it was a hot late June. Emma looked up the old oak staircase.

'Those treads are bad,' Norman said. 'Though it would be a shame to carpet it.'

'That will be for Sarah to say.'

'You think?'

'Of course. Wives make those decisions.'

He opened the door to the drawing-room. A vase of lilac near the window had gone over. There was an edge of green on the little remaining water. Emma had crossed to the dining-room.

'That little Cotman's very nice,' she called. 'You'll want it, I suppose?'

He came across to her. Their voices sounded loud in the unoccupied house.

'I thought we'd agreed, Em. You and Sarah will divide all the movables.'

'Well, you'd better keep the Cotman. I associate it with the house, from as far back as I remember.'

'Yes, we had good times here as kids, didn't we? Having been thrown to grandparents while the old man served the King.'

'We weren't thrown. They loved having us. Kate too, we saw more of her than of Mummy all those early years.'

'*My sister's children,*' Norman mimicked, lifting his chin.

Emma laughed.

'Still,' she said, 'what else do you expect? Those Great War widows had a hell of a time. *When my Malcolm was killed:* you remember how often she said that? And then as the elder sister it was particularly hard for her. She just stayed on here; keeping it going, she used to say.'

'She'd been late marrying?'

'Yes. There'd been some other affair. Definitely not to be spoken of – though Mummy told me a bit of it, those last days in hospital.'

'Poor Kate!'

They walked through to the kitchen.

'This at least will have to be ripped out,' Emma said.

'A pity in a way.'

'Not a bit of it. This is not a kitchen for a lady to work in. It's the sort they set up on the assumption of servants.'

'Sarah has some plan.'

'So she should. As a priority.'

They went up the back stairs, as so often as children. They walked along the narrow corridor, opening the bedroom doors. The air in the bedrooms was especially stale.

'This was mine. Still called mine,' Emma said, opening the last door. There was a high, narrow, brass single bed with a white counterpane. A mahogany washstand with a green jug and basin stood under the small diamond-paned window.

'Not a thing changed.'

'We can still call it yours, Em. If you'll ever deign to come and see us.'

Emma sat on the edge of the bed.

'I slept here that week when I'd brought Birdie to the nursing home.'

'Did you?'

'I remember running like mad to answer the phone and then rushing over to see Gwyn.'

'Yes.'

'I remember thinking, when I got back: I'm going to be like Kate, a fussy and perpetual aunt.'

'It didn't happen.'

'What didn't happen? Oh, I see what you mean. It's true, I had Georgi, and then Bill came along; but at that time I felt it. With you in Marseilles, quite as inaccessible as Daddy had ever been . . .'

'And also on foreign service,' Norman said, smiling.

'Don't make a joke of it, Norman. Don't ever make a joke of it.'

He went out of the room. She followed him. He stopped to look in the central front bedroom. Through the broad window he could see, at an even better elevation, the view he had been admiring from outside. She came and stood beside him.

'To get up and see that every morning,' he said. 'I still can't believe my luck.'

'Not luck, dear, just inheritance.'

'Well, inheritance is luck.'

'In fact, Norman, you've always been lucky. Much more than you deserve, if you really want to know.'

'Luck isn't deserving. That's the distinction.'

'Is it? I really don't know. What I was saying about feeling like Kate it's come true in a way. She lost her Malcolm and I've lost Georgi – if in a different kind of war.'

'I know, Em. It was terrible.'

'It was that I foresaw it, really. He was always pushing himself, on that bloody motorbike. Always another meeting, another contact, another crisis. Yet at a different level I thought he was indestructible. From that night in Vienna he was like the Party itself, rock hard.'

Norman put his arm over her shoulders. She moved and released herself.

'Don't fuss,' she said. 'And don't worry. It's passed to me.'

'What? The hardness?'

'The firmness. The Party's firmness.'

'That at least is not like Kate.'

She looked round at him.

'You think not? I keep getting this misplaced idea of class, from these younger ones since the war. They make it subjective, though they're supposed to be Marxists. But class is objective: objective membership and objective affiliation.'

'I know. At least I know the argument.'

'What they especially don't realise is the kind of clarity, the kind of hardness if you like, that we learned in what was our own class. To grow up in what was very consciously a ruling class . . .'

'We've been over this.'

'Yes, but now so often you forget it. You think your professional *couche* is a viable political alternative. But it isn't and can't be. Once you've seen the world from a ruling-class point of view, you always know the real score, you see through all the little evasions and compromises, and you know in your own life that you just have to be on one side or the other. There aren't any other real places.'

Norman moved to the door.

'This sounds more like Georgi than you, Em.'

'Well yes, of course, he helped me to see it.'

'When you started having doubts?'

'Not doubts. Not political doubts. The politics were obvious. But yes I suppose I did agonise . . .'

'About all this?'

'This is just a house. All right, it's a privileged house, and there are working-class families without the chance of anything. But we all work from where we are, and if there's one thing Georgi taught me . . .'

'Yes?'

'It's what we can give to the Party, wherever we come from: what can be given, especially, by those of us who know how the ruling class thinks.'

Norman walked on.

'Well, they don't think like Kate any more,' he said, over his shoulder.

'Not directly, of course. She was a survivor, an inheritor, but she had that same iron will.'

'To preserve her portion.'

'To preserve it for us. That was her loyalty.'

'She certainly managed that.'

'It's a spirit I can feel. In a quite different cause.'

'Well, I hope so, Em.'

'You ought to feel it too, now you'll have the comfort of living here. Given what you can still contribute, if you'll only get back to seeing the world straight.'

Norman paused at the head of the stairs, then walked on down, running his fingers along the old dark oak of the banister. He stopped at the foot of the stairs and looked back at his sister. She waited, halfway down.

'It's a different war, Em. If war is even still the right

word. It's longer range, it's different weapons, it's different tactics.'

'Not so different as all that. As long as you're still really fighting it.'

'Well, as to that . . .' Norman said, then changed his mind and walked on.

They went out to the porch. He relocked the heavy door. They got into the car.

'Lots of money details when we get back,' he said.

'It's all settled, isn't it?'

'You'll have to look through the papers.'

'We're keeping Sarah for lunch,' Emma said.

They did not talk while Norman drove back. He had bought a suburban house, jointly with Sarah, in 1946. As he parked the car in the narrow entrance, in front of the concrete garage, he closed his eyes momentarily, thinking back to the stone porch and the view of the meadows over the trees.

Sarah had come out when she heard the car. She spread her arms and kissed Emma warmly. As he moved across to them he realised that he had not consciously seen them together before. They were the same height, and there was some similarity of features: the high forehead, the long straight nose, the firm chin. Sarah was nearly ten years younger, and her eyes and mouth were both prettier and more lively. The hair too was very different: Sarah's heavy dark-brown curls contrasted with Emma's severely cut straight fair hair, though that too, he now noticed, had darkened.

'Darling,' Sarah said, as he came up to them, but her attention was still on Emma.

'We feel awful,' Sarah continued, 'at least I feel awful, that Norman and I are getting that beautiful house.'

'We're sorting out the money, for Christ's sake,' Norman said, impatiently.

'I know you are, darling, but it isn't the same. It's the house itself, the old family house. I'm sure Emma feels it.'

'I do a bit,' Emma said, 'but this is the only way to manage it. I have to live in town anyway.'

'But you must still think of it as a home from home, Emma, and come down whenever you'd like to.'

'Well, thank you, Sarah.'

'He won't ask you, I know, but I'm asking you: you promise?'

'I promise.'

They had lunch in the small front room that was kept as a dining-room, though normally they ate in the dining area next to the kitchen. Sarah had prepared chicken, a potato salad, tomatoes and strawberries. She had chilled and opened a bottle of Moselle.

'In fact, with that big house . . .' she said, as she was serving.

'It's not all that big,' Norman said.

'It's big by comparison with this one. And having to run it on my own . . .'

'You'll get a cleaning woman.'

'I've told him,' Emma said, 'you must have an entirely new kitchen. That museum piece—'

'I know. And it's fixed. I've had a builder over there.'

'Oh, good,' Emma said, and gave her a hard look.

When lunch was finished she got up to help Sarah with the plates and dishes, but Sarah waved her away.

'You and Norman have all this paperwork.'

'It's not much. I'll give you a hand.'

'No, really. I'd prefer it.'

Emma looked at Norman.

'You ought to sit in on the paperwork, darling,' he said to Sarah.

'There's no need, but I'll come in a minute. Until I have to fetch Alex from school.'

Norman lit a cigarette and took a file from his desk. He sorted the papers on the table. Emma put on her reading glasses.

'Right,' Norman said, 'the valuer's report. You've had your copy of that.'

'Yes. He sent me the top copy.'

'Thirty-four thousand. That's excluding all furniture and pictures and so on. You and Sarah will agree how all that's to be divided.'

'We've got the probate list for all the items.'

'Yes. Okay, but remember the house value has come up from probate.'

'They always do that. Low for probate, I mean. The house valuation was specifically in terms of our dividing. And for the furniture and so on the relative values will be the same.'

'Sure, okay.'

He set one sheaf of papers aside.

'Ah yes,' he said, staring at the next sheet. 'Monkey insisted that I tell you—'

'I know. He rang me: that regardless of the valuation I'm being thoroughly cheated.'

'Then I'm glad I remembered to mention it.'

'Don't worry. I would have. But as I told him, what he's saying is just guesswork.'

'If you think so. Though he's got rather rich by something more than guesswork.'

Emma lit a cigarette.

'I understand it, you know, perfectly well. He says the house will appreciate in value much faster than anything I'm likely to do with my money – the money I get from half its present valuation.'

'It's a professional opinion.'

'It's also an interested opinion. What he's really saying is that I should give him my money to speculate.'

'To invest. I mean, he's doing it for me.'

'Invest or speculate, Norman, it's the same kind of thing. I can't imagine how a socialist, which he undoubtedly once was—'

'Still is.'

'If you say so. What he's actually doing is playing in this filthy market: stocks, currencies, commodities, God knows what. Do you think I'd let my money be used for that?'

'Well, what will you do with it? In a capitalist economy?'

'I thought the bank—'

'Which is not a capitalist institution?'

'If you'd let me finish. I shall get the bank to advise me. And I shall go for something like National Savings or government funds.'

'The state also not being capitalist?'

'There is some distinction in the public sector.'

'A very fine one, in fact. Still, it's your money and your decision. All that matters is that he's warned you; and that I've passed it on.'

'I don't need warnings. Certainly not from Monkey.'

'As you wish. Though he's the only person we know who has any idea what's really happening.'

'I don't accept that. He's simply justifying himself.'

Sarah came back in, and sat at the table. She crossed her arms over her full breasts.

'I haven't another copy of the papers, darling,' Norman said. 'Would you like to share mine?'

'It's all right. I'll just listen.'

'We're well on. I have just to explain to Emma where her seventeen thousand is coming from.'

'You don't have to,' Emma said.

'I think you should know. We should all know where our money comes from.'

'It's a mortgage, isn't it?' Sarah said.

'Yes, but that's the point. There was no hope of my getting an ordinary mortgage for that amount. They determine it not only by the value of the house but by the applicant's salary in relation to the scale of repayment. I doubt if I could have got more than five or six thousand at the outside. That was where Monkey came in.'

Emma happened to be looking at Sarah as Monkey's name was mentioned. She was surprised by Sarah's immediate physical reaction. The lips compressed and blood seemed to drain from the skin on either side of the nose. The forehead was creased and the eyes seemed to pull back from the world, to go into neutral. Emma nearly spoke, about her own attitude to Monkey, but the reaction was so strong and so deep that she thought she would do better to say nothing. Norman, it appeared, had not noticed.

'What Monkey could arrange,' he continued, handling the papers confidently, 'was a mortgage still below the valuation of the house but more than enough to pay off Emma. In fact it's for twenty-five thousand.'

Emma was startled.

'But then he could get the whole house. Get it cheap, in fact, if you couldn't repay. You've said yourself you can't repay that amount from your salary.'

'Do you think we didn't work that out?'

'I bet he worked it out. Suppose you died? Where would Sarah be, with the house going to him?'

'No, that's taken care of. The seventeen, as half-share, is linked with an insurance on my life, and the other half she'd get anyway, by my will.'

'You've made a will?'

'Yes, Em. That had to be part of it. I'll explain the rest of it, if you'll give me a chance. Only your seventeen is covered by the insurance, representing the mortgaged half of the house.'

'I thought you said twenty-five.'

'Exactly. The other eight is invested, and it earns the repayments on the seventeen.'

'Is meant to earn: you mean invested by him?'

'Of course invested by him.'

Emma was indignant.

'Then why should he give you eight thousand, over and above the seventeen of the mortgage?'

'He's not giving me eight thousand. The mortgage—'

'Do you understand this, Sarah?' Emma asked.

Sarah shook her head slightly, as if to regain attention. She looked at Emma and gave a mechanical smile.

'Not really,' she said, 'but I'm sure Norman does.'

'It's incredibly simple,' Norman protested. 'The true mortgage is for twenty-five, while the nominal, tied to the insurance, is for seventeen. The balance of eight earns repayments on the seventeen.'

'Suppose he loses it all?'

'What, the eight? He won't lose it.'

'No, but suppose he does. Then you won't have the money to repay on the seventeen.'

'It's very improbable, but even if it happened, in some temporary fall in the market, I'd have enough to keep it going for a year or two until the market turned up again.'

'And suppose it didn't turn up?'

Norman sighed. He pushed the papers away.

'Well, then I'd have to shoot myself, wouldn't I? To get Sarah her half of the house.'

'Don't say things like that,' Sarah protested.

'Well, Sarah, you ought to ask him these questions,' Emma warned.

'I said, Emma, I don't understand it. But I'm not alone in the world, you know. Our family's very close. I should never be left in real trouble.'

Norman lit a cigarette and got up. He went across and stared through the window. A big laundry van was stopping at one of the houses opposite. There was a black car parked on the same side, a few doors down. He shifted to see past a branch of rowan. A man was sitting in the driving seat, his head bowed.

'Finish it now you've started,' Emma said.

He looked round.

'Finish what?'

'Explaining this business.'

'I've already explained it. And you began by saying you didn't have to know. You can just take your seventeen thousand and run.'

'That's not fair,' Sarah protested. 'It was as much Emma's house as ours. Her aunt left her the same half-share.'

'That isn't the point,' he said angrily, looking again at the parked car.

'Maybe not,' Emma said. 'Perhaps the real point is why Monkey is giving you eight thousand.'

'He's not giving it to me. The whole twenty-five that he's raising is covered by the mortgage.'

'But what isn't covered,' Emma said, pausing to scribble figures on her papers, 'is the interest he's forgoing on the eight that will be, you say, earning for you.'

'Technically, yes,' Norman said.

The black car started up. He watched it signal and pull out.

'Not technically. Actually.'

'In his kind of world . . .' Norman began, but then it was as if he had lost the thread of his argument. He looked out again at the street.

'Exactly,' Emma pounced. 'In his kind of world: manoeuvring, calculating, speculating, cheating . . .'

Norman was staring past her. Sarah got up. She looked intently at him; looked over him, in effect, as a mother might look anxiously at a child. He stubbed out his cigarette and came back to the table.

'I must go and pick up Alex,' Sarah said.

'Is it that time? Shall I go?'

'No, you stay with Emma.'

She smiled and went out.

'When you even think,' Emma said, 'about these sums we're discussing. It's more than a working miner would get in a lifetime.'

'The point bears both ways,' Norman said, abstractedly. 'It bears on us both.'

Emma looked away.

'All I was trying to explain,' he resumed, with an effort, 'is that there isn't just crude interest. There's handling fees, there are commissions for introduction, there's the over-the-top if you can move money to and fro very quickly.'

'He still has to raise the twenty-five.'

'Look, Em, if you despise that world – and I'm not saying you're wrong; even Monkey didn't choose it, he was pushed into it – at least don't double the contempt by pretending you understand it better than they do. It's a skilled professional world, and becoming more so every year, every day. So concede at least that he knows what he's doing.'

'I've never doubted that,' she said, getting up. 'It's what you're doing that worries me.'

He looked down at his papers.

'The risk, you mean? Well, as to that there have been worse.'

'With this sort of money?'

'I wasn't thinking about money.'

Sarah had started the car and backed out, but Emma still went across and closed the door. Norman took no notice. He was still staring down.

'I want to help, you know,' Emma said.

He didn't answer.

'Has Monkey got some hold over you?'

He looked up and smiled: a small bitter smile, with no opening of the lips.

'Or have you got some hold over him?'

He got up from the table. He stretched his arms above his head. He did not speak.

'Tell me,' she insisted.

'There's nothing to tell.'

'I don't believe you.'

'Well, that's your problem.'

He walked to the window again. He could still see the laundry van, further down the street. Emma came up quietly behind him, and touched his arm.

'Look, I know there's something,' she said.

'Do you?'

'A few minutes ago, when you came back from the window, you looked frightened to death.'

He turned and looked at her.

'No,' he said.

He walked quickly back to the table and picked up the papers. He put his own file back in his desk.

'Do you want a drink?'

'No. We'll have tea when Sarah gets back.'

He poured himself a small whisky. He sipped it and watched her, looking over his glass.

'You think I'm not political,' he said, quietly. 'You think that's so because I'm not out at Party meetings and so on. But if you really want to know, it all still rages inside.'

'Inside isn't politics.'

'You think so? I'll give you an example. These Khrushchev disclosures about Stalin . . .'

'Of course that shocked everybody.'

'It shocked the Party, obviously, at being caught out in a lie.'

'Not a lie,' Emma protested. 'How could we have known?'

'How could you not have known – anyone in or near the leadership? Even I knew it. I've known it since the aftermath of Spain.'

'*God that Failed* stuff, I suppose?'

'No. But while it shocked me then, it doesn't shock me now. What does shock me, even frighten me didn't you say . . .'

'The full details are awful, of course, but it's all being put right, it's all being corrected.'

'How do you correct the dead? But I mean beyond that. To the already disillusioned, the already sceptical, comes a new fear.'

'What fear?'

He emptied his glass.

'I doubt if I can explain it. There's a whole long sequence of misconceptions and errors, some of them crimes. Unless you're armoured by blind faith you watch it as it goes, you try to unravel it. But still as you unravel it you are knitting something else. Knitting up some new position, some new personality. And all that is your actual growth.'

'Are you talking about yourself?'

'Yes. Among others. I mean that this process happens, the new condition is really reached. Yet still in memories inside and in records outside . . .'

'What records?'

'Still in both, I'm saying, there's a continual threat. And when any of it comes close it's a tearing, a tearing from that past, from that otherwise composed and lived-through past . . . Can you understand me at all?'

'You mean guilt,' Emma said. 'But that gets us nowhere. We have to put things right and go on.'

'By being reborn or something?'

'Of course not being reborn. That's mysticism.'

'Exactly. So the past is still there, inside and outside, and it tears.'

The car was coming through the gate. They heard the doors slam and then the front door opening. Alex ran ahead of her mother and went straight to Norman.

'I got two house points for my tables.'

'I told you,' Norman said.

He bent and kissed the top of her head. She stayed close to him. She was tall for her age, and had Sarah's features and hair.

'Say hello to Aunt Emma, Alex,' Sarah said from the door.

Alex went across and shook hands. Emma crouched to be near her.

'You're going to go and live in a marvellous house, Alex.'

'I know.'

'You'll be very happy there. I was a girl growing up there myself. It was marvellous.'

'Why were you there?'

'Because my mummy and daddy were abroad. So every school holiday I went there.'

Alex looked closely into her face.

'Why is it called Nayles?'

'They're not sure. They think it's an old family name.'

'It's a funny spelling. When Daddy came and told me—'

'Alex, go up and wash,' Sarah said. 'There'll be tea in a few minutes.'

Alex turned obediently. Emma smiled across at Norman, still pleased by the child.

'And you've cleared up all your business?' Sarah asked Norman.

He was still holding his whisky glass. He put it down.

'Yes, darling. We've got as far as we're going to.'

# 4

❧✦❀✦❧

# LONDON, NOVEMBER 1956

'Gwyn! Gwyn!'

Emma's voice was lost at once, in the noise of the crowd across Trafalgar Square. From the distant platform, on the far side of the column, a loudspeaker voice echoed wordlessly against the surrounding high buildings. Emma pushed across, through people who were lifting their heads to try to see and hear. There was a burst of clapping, from people nearer the platform, as the echoing voice ended. Emma reached out and just managed to touch Gwyn's shoulder.

'Aunty Em,' Gwyn said, surprised as he looked round.

There was a push of people trying to move sideways to get a better view. All that was really in sight, above the placards and banners in the crowd, was the wide banner on the opposite side of the plinth from the speakers: *No War Over Suez. End the Tory Intervention Now.*

Emma was pushed back but Gwyn squared his shoulders and pushed through to her. Across the other bodies she saw Mark standing and watching them. She waved. Mark took his pipe from his mouth and eased his way through.

'How marvellous!' Emma said, holding Gwyn's arm with both hands.

'Aye, it is pretty good.'

'The demo? Yes, marvellous. But I meant finding you. You didn't say you were coming down.'

'A whole gang of us come. Came. It was all a bit last-minute.'
Mark was standing smiling at them.

'And Mark,' Emma said.

'Emma.'

'This takes you back a bit, I expect.'

'No.'

'I mean the size of it.'

'Sure.'

There was now another, more penetrating voice from the loudspeaker, but most of the words were still indistinct. There was a loud burst of laughter from many of the hundreds nearer the platform.

'Though it is a sacred place,' Mark said.

'Trafalgar Square?'

'Yes. Even against the column and the lions. Since Bloody Sunday it has been a sacred place.'

'That's a historian's point of view.'

'Or in fiction. Four years ago, wasn't it, 1952, Morris had the English Revolution start here.'

'Morris,' Emma said, 'was a Utopian.'

Gwyn stood, half looking at them, half turned towards the distant speaker. He was wearing a blue raincoat over his grey suit. On his fine white shirt was a silk college tie. His thick, curling black hair was cut close to the skin on his nape.

'I should be with my branch,' Emma said. 'But I was late. I'm getting old.'

'Nonsense, Aunt Em,' Gwyn said politely.

Mark was looking over the crowd. In a change of wind they could hear some of the words of the speaker: '. . . the unanswerable and unstoppable demand of the entire British people to end this criminal intervention now'. Emma and Gwyn clapped. Mark hesitated and then also clapped.

'If not all, then maybe enough,' he said, smiling.

The others did not respond. There was another change of speaker: a harsh and indecipherable but evidently angry boom.

'It's being here that matters,' Emma said.

'Sure.'

'I reckon,' Gwyn said eagerly, 'it must be like what Dad used to talk about, with Spain and the hunger marches and the Popular Front.'

Mark smiled sceptically, and briefly closed his eyes.

'Yes,' Emma said, 'I'd say so; with some differences, of course. But after all they've tried, we're still here. You just wait, this stupid war will be the end of them.'

Mark shrugged doubtfully, but was interested in watching Gwyn.

'Let's hope so anyhow,' Gwyn said.

There was some disturbance on the far edge of the crowd, in front of St Martin's. People were pushing away; a policeman and an ambulance man were trying to get through. The loudspeaker voice stopped and there was clapping from near the platform.

'Can you see what it is?' Emma asked.

'Someone ill, I think.'

'Well, with a crowd this size . . .'

A young man came pushing through, selling a socialist paper. Its banner headline was *Law Not War*. A fine drizzle was starting. Gwyn turned up the collar of his raincoat; the first rain gleamed on his shining black hair. Emma, in her heavy white raincoat, took a plastic headscarf from her pocket and pulled it over her thick brown hair. Mark, glancing at her, saw through the plastic how much her hair had darkened in middle age. One of the things that had stuck in his mind, about both her and Norman, was that exceptionally bright golden hair of their youth: an image of something, he had often supposed; an image he had always partly suspected – at once an heroic and a gilded age.

'Mark, you'll get wet,' Emma said.

'No more than damp.'

He wore a jacket and high-necked jersey, with old baggy corduroy trousers. The fine rain was settling in drops on the tweed shoulders and sleeves.

Another speech ended. Another began. In the area of the disturbance an ambulance had drawn up in the street. They could see a stretcher being carried. With the rain and the new speaker many in the crowd were now beginning to drift away.

'You mustn't stay, Mark. You'll catch your death.'

'Within days of the Third World War?'

'Sir, you don't really think that?' Gwyn interjected.

Mark smiled. He was keeping his head down now against the rain.

'Well, with this *and* Hungary . . . No, I don't really think so. Because with *both* Suez and Hungary, there's a stand-off.'

'You can't compare this kind of war with what's happening in Budapest,' Emma said, sharply.

'Compare, Emma? Yes: and contrast; yet still with the solid similarity that each is an aggression.'

'To control a counter-revolution!' she said angrily. 'Can't you see it's all part of the same thing? Each the same kind of imperialist manoeuvre?'

'Which way?' Mark asked, moving his long index finger like a pendulum.

'This attempted coup in Hungary, this faked intervention in Suez.'

The rain was getting heavier. Many more people were leaving. Mark shook his head.

'It makes one wonder,' he said quietly, 'why we're on the same demonstration.'

'You've not fallen for these stories about Hungarian freedom fighters?'

Mark looked at Gwyn, who was hanging his head.

'I always fall for freedom stories,' Mark said, smiling. 'And when I've checked them out they usually begin by being true.'

'Begin, yes . . .' Emma said, but the rain was now sweeping the square. 'We'll have to get some shelter,' she shifted to saying. 'Mark, come and have some food with us. And Gwyn, you too, it would be lovely.'

Gwyn shifted his feet. He looked exposed and miserable.

'I really can't, Aunt Em. See, I got to meet up with the others. That's my transport back.'

'You can go by train.'

'No, really, Aunt Em. I promised.'

She looked hard at him. She did not conceal her irritation.

'Well, you come Mark, anyway. I've got the car.'

'To be put right on freedom?' Mark asked, easily.

'Oh rubbish! We're old friends. We've been through worse than this.'

Many people were now pushing past them. There was already a big queue at the entrance to the Tube.

'Okay,' Mark said.

They said goodbye to Gwyn and walked, with difficulty, through the crowd, making their way to the back street where Emma had parked her car. She got a towel from the back seat and insisted on Mark drying his hair. Then she set off, driving fast.

'Anyway, Norman will be glad to see you,' she said as she waited at a pedestrian crossing. Many people from the meeting, some still carrying placards, were hurrying across through the rain.

'Norman?'

'Yes. He's been looking after Bill.'

Mark was silent for some time. He watched the swing of the windscreen wiper closely, as if counting its strokes.

'You mean,' he said at last, 'you asked that boy back, knowing Norman was there?'

'Yes. Why not?'

'You mean they know each other? They meet?'

'No, they've never actually met.'

'But then how could you, Emma? It would be appalling for the boy.'

She glanced across at him. He wished that she would look at the road.

'It has to happen some time,' she said, reasonably. 'And perhaps better just casually than in some great arranged confrontation.'

'However it is, it will never be casual.'

'That's Freudian stuff,' Emma said. 'Between grown-up people . . .'

'Which he as yet is not.'

'You don't think so? You find him immature?'

'Christ, of course he's immature.'

'No, you mean socially. The class thing. A working-class boy in upper-class Cambridge.'

'He can deal with that – given friendship and time. But this other—'

'You see,' Emma said, changing up and accelerating on a

length of clear road, 'it is this Freudian stuff. Subjectivity before class, it's the whole post-war rot.'

Mark went silent. He sat uncomfortably, feeling his trousers drying against his legs. At last she pulled in and parked.

'We have the whole house now,' she said, cheerfully. 'Or didn't you come here while Georgi was alive?'

'No, I've not been before.'

'It was worth buying it. There was a rather nasty little land-lord. I let the top floor and there's a room we use for meetings.'

She pushed the street door open. It was unlocked. Mark followed her up the stairs, which were close carpeted in crimson. The paint of the banisters and of the walls was a gleaming white.

'Good,' she said, opening a door on the middle floor.

'Norman!' she called.

'Here,' came a familiar voice.

Norman was sitting with Emma's son Bill at a mahogany table in the bay window. They were both staring down at the chessboard that lay between them. The large red and white pieces were carved ivory.

'I've brought Mark,' Emma said.

Norman got up quickly. He came across to Mark, and they shook hands.

'And this is Bill,' Emma said, proudly.

The boy looked casually across at Mark. His face seemed old for nine. He had very thick, curly black hair. His skin was sallow. He wore large, black-rimmed spectacles.

'How was it?' Norman asked, as Mark was greeting the boy. 'But first let me get you a sherry.'

'Mark's wet,' Emma said.

'No,' Mark said, 'it's all right.'

'Take your jacket off at least.'

'Sure.'

Emma was hanging up her raincoat. She called from the landing.

'Don't ask Mark about the demo, Norman. He thinks we should have been outside the Soviet Embassy.'

'I have been,' Mark said.

'Ah, you see it that way?' Norman said, handing him a glass. 'I expect you're right.'

'Don't indulge him,' Emma called. 'This stampede back to liberalism is more than I can take.'

'Ah, but we're all finding that's where we now are,' Norman said, lightly. 'Back to 1935. The League of Nations and the sanctity of frontiers. It will have to be pacifism next.'

Mark looked at Norman, and spoke very deliberately.

'I went to the Soviet Embassy as a socialist. To oppose the military suppression of a popular revolution.'

'Oh God!' Emma said, coming back.

She took a sherry from Norman and walked across to Bill.

'Who's winning?' she asked cheerfully.

'Can't you see?' Bill said, looking up.

'You mean Norman's winning?'

'Yes and he gave me a knight and a pawn.'

'You're still learning, darling. It'll come.'

Bill got up, irritably. He pushed over his king and hurried from the room.

'Is he all right?' Mark asked.

'Oh, fine,' Emma said. 'Now do sit down.'

Mark sat on one of the big sofas, Norman on the other. They exchanged news and mentioned friends: the easy general talk of this kind of meeting. Yet Mark seemed withdrawn and absent. After so many years, he found it hard to focus Norman, though it was not a problem of unfamiliarity. On the contrary, in dress and manner Norman was like so many of his Cambridge colleagues; it was only the memory, the probably false fixed image, that was incongruous.

Seeing Norman was reminding him of what one of his more awkward and sceptical graduate students had said: that these are men who weather beautifully. The face was still fine-drawn and handsome, still relatively unlined. There was a patina of some sort on hair and skin, harmonising exactly with the well-cut and uncreased clothes.

Lacquered people, Mitchell had gone on to say, but that was clearly wrong. There was nothing artificial in the appearance. It was wholly straightforward and natural; genuinely all of a piece. Presumably the politics now were cut from the same cloth. Emma, by contrast, seemed stuck where she had been as a girl: the Party line as unquestioned as the original beliefs of her class.

But not this man: he had become used to living in a consensual professional world. He wore his minor qualifications easily, and would be supremely confident in his immediate skills. A half-inch of the brain would have been left quite open and tolerant.

Mark pulled himself up. This was becoming complacent, as he sat observing the same easy rituals, making the same reassuring conversational moves. He saw Gwyn's face suddenly: tense, narrow, high-cheekboned and Welsh. He saw it with rain running down it. He thought momentarily of tears; but whenever it might be, in Emma's evident intention to bring them together, there would be no physical recognition between father and son: no recognition of any kind, if it came to that. They were of different classes, of different societies, of different peoples whatever that meant. Had there even, perhaps, been some error? Some false story, some misunderstanding? It was almost easier to believe that than to think of Gwyn as this man's son.

'You look thoughtful, Mark.'

'It's a professional habit. Don't let it deceive you.'

'I still sometimes envy you Cambridge. Whenever I'm there—'

'Yes, Norman, it shows best on visits.'

'Not only on visits. There is still a certain cool purity.'

'Which we renounced, right? Which we chose to move beyond.'

'Some of us,' Norman said. 'Some of us. For a time.'

'Well,' Emma said, returning from the kitchen, 'there's sausages and some lettuce, and some nice oranges to follow. Will that suit you, Mark?'

'Fine.'

'And Norman brought some overpriced plonk. I've opened it, by the way.'

'In fact a decent burgundy,' Norman protested.

'So not exactly High Table . . .' Emma said.

'But Broad Line,' Mark said, laughing. 'Anyway that image has to go. The two fixed images of Cambridge are High Table and what you said, you remember: seeing a face and pushing sherry at it. In practice, even leaving the work aside, we spend ten times longer in meetings than doing either.'

'You too?' Norman said. 'I've got the next three solid days of meetings. That's why I came up.'

'I'll burn the sausages, then,' Emma said. 'And I'll take Bill's up to his room. He prefers it when there are people in.'

'Which happens often, I suppose?' Mark said, trying to relate to her.

She laughed. 'There are more meetings in this house than in your two places put together. How else do you suppose any serious politics survives?'

When she had gone, Norman sat quietly for a time and then, without explanation, got up and left the room. Mark found a book and settled to reading. He was becoming involved in the contested origins of the Korean war when Norman came back, carrying the wine and a bag of oranges. Emma followed with a dish of sausages and a colander of lettuce.

'Okay, we'll get some bits,' she said, collecting plates and glasses and knives and forks. Mark helped by lifting away the chessboard and pieces.

'Shove it anywhere, Mark,' Emma said.

'They're beautiful pieces.'

'Yes. They were Daddy's. One of his Eastern postings.'

Mark could find no clear surface. He eventually settled for an unused corner of the floor. Norman was already at the table, distributing the food. The sausages were indeed burned.

They ate in silence for some time. On a second round they finished the sausages and Norman refilled the wine glasses.

'You saw Monkey in Cambridge, I gather,' he said, leaning back.

'Yes. With Emma.'

'How did you find him?'

'Amusing. And clever of course.'

'Yes, he has spirit, that one. After what he was put through.'

'He told us something of that.'

Norman sipped his wine.

'The persiflage,' he said. 'Isn't that what you called it?'

'Did he pass that on?'

'Did he? I'm not sure. Perhaps Emma mentioned it; but you see, after trial by newspaper, after expulsion from the university, and then after solid and prolonged official interrogation, you either collapse or you play Monkey's trick, that the whole thing is ludicrous, parodic even.'

'Sure,' Mark said. 'Though he always talked rather that way.'

'It depends when you date the beginning of the ludicrous. All I mean is, what happened to him was serious.'

Emma took oranges from the bag and passed them round.

'I've met a few others involved in that witch-hunt,' Mark said.

'No, I doubt if you have,' Norman said, quickly. 'The general red-baiting, sure. That hit all sorts of people. But this was more specific.'

'Shall I put some more light on?' Emma said, getting up.

'No, leave it, Em. This is cosy.'

'All right. Anyway Mark likes dim rooms. Don't you, Mark?'

'Sitting in near darkness,' Norman said, taking over. 'It's a marvellous restorative. You sink back into your body. Into yourself.'

Mark smiled at brother and sister in turn. Behind the smile he considered and rejected the impression that their talk was arranged, even rehearsed. He could have taken it that way, but for a clear sense now that Emma wanted it to stop.

'What happened, you see,' Norman said, turning his glass in his fingers, 'is that a Russian defector informed American intelligence there'd been a steady leak of material from that place Monkey and I worked in during the war.'

'When the British and the Russians were allies, for God's sake,' Emma said, excitedly.

'That wasn't quite the point,' Norman said. 'It was all, of course, very secret. And with that sort of thing it's difficult to determine, from that kind of hint or allegation. The deciphering, for example . . .'

'Should we be talking about this?' Mark said quickly.

Norman smiled.

'Yes, in general terms there's no reason why not. I mean, take the deciphering. We had to unwind a very complicated German apparatus, and were eventually able to do it because the Poles had captured one for us. But then it always seemed likely, with the Russians in Poland, that they also had an example and could, like us, unwind it. So some technical indication, which you could say had been leaked, might in fact have been what they were getting themselves.'

'Except that the defector said otherwise?'

'The defector said otherwise, but that will be a job for some especially good historian. Here and in the States there are now a whole lot of defectors, announced and unannounced. There are so many that in places you almost trip over them.'

'They're scum,' Emma said.

'They include scum. But there is also a dialectic. An arbitrary and unpredictable regime throws off arbitrary and unpredictable defectors. For example, Mark, have you ever looked at what happened to some of the senior Russians who served in Spain?'

'Not properly. I heard one or two things.'

'It was bad. Very bad. But then that's my point. Some of these people really know things; others make plausible guesses that may or may not be reliable; others again will say anything for asylum. You can then see the problem with checking.'

'And the problem with allegations – if the general atmosphere is bad.'

'Exactly, Mark. I knew you would understand this.'

Mark opened his hands.

'Not understand. Just see the problems of understanding.'

'Quite. To which you would have to add the problem of assessing a kind of technical information which only a very few people in fact understand, and those, for the most part, themselves involved in it.'

'Of course.'

'So that it was difficult either way: either to prove or disprove. That's where Monkey was caught.'

'Caught?'

'In the difficulty of either proving or disproving. There was indeed a coincidence of certain technical developments, though the British development was very much more advanced – although on lines on which others could and would have advanced. You see the kind of nightmare it is.'

'Sure.'

'The leak, if there was one, was in the engineering. That is, if the defector could be believed. And Monkey, you see, was one of the few at the heart of that.'

'So they threw the book at him?'

'More than the book. They flew over two British interrogators. He was grilled for several weeks.'

'But survived it?'

'Oh yes, he survived it.'

Norman picked up the wine bottle. There was only a little left. Mark and Emma declined. He poured the last half-glass for himself.

'The problem was, in the end,' he said, lifting his glass, 'one of the few possible leaks they could really pin down – I mean from a development which they knew hadn't otherwise been duplicated – happened nearly two years after Monkey had left the project.'

'He wasn't still working on any similar line?'

'At the university? Yes. That's what they kept pushing at him. But it was in a rather different direction. Where he ended up, in fact, when they'd done their worst. In the commercial development – the line that led to business computers.'

'Which the leak wasn't on?'

Norman laughed.

'You'd do well at this, Mark. You ask the right bloody questions.'

'I'm not trying to quiz you.'

'No, I know, but you're right. From inside the field there aren't really separate lines. I mean at the most fundamental levels, at the leading edge where Monkey certainly was.'

'So?'

'So that's from inside the field. A classics graduate or an ex-Indian policeman might well see it differently.'

'Might be brought to see it differently?'

'It's what I said before, about proving or disproving. The only relatively hard evidence was from a date when Monkey had no direct knowledge of what was being done, secretly, in the official establishments.'

'No direct knowledge?'

'Right. And the people at our place . . .'

He hesitated. Mark, watching him, realised how badly he had misjudged him, from the composed appearance. This was a man in high tension, which the manner only temporarily covered.

'You weren't questioned yourself?' he asked.

'During Monkey's interrogation? No. Because they knew that my own work is miles away from all that.'

'I thought perhaps simply as his friend. I mean they do track guilt by association.'

Norman drained his glass, leaning his head back.

'Yes,' he said. 'Yes, they do.'

'But not you,' Emma said, pulling the orange peels together. 'Only Monkey. So thank God for that.'

'Except—' Mark began.

'Yes, Mark,' Norman interrupted quickly. 'I thought you would get there.'

'What are you talking about?' Emma asked, impatiently.

'Mark has realised,' Norman said, 'that a classics graduate and an ex-Indian policeman may retire, baffled, from a shower of technical bullshit, but sooner or later . . . Why don't you tell her, Mark?'

'If I knew what to tell.'

'Come on. Give intelligence its due. It doesn't often get it.'

Mark lifted his empty glass to his mouth. When he realised that it was empty he kept it pressing against his lower lip. Norman spoke more loudly, with an edge of the wine.

'Do you know, Mark, that biological hypothesis? It's probably rubbish but I sometimes take it seriously. That at a certain stage in hominid evolution a serious virus disease attacked a still primarily animal brain. In one line it produced a mutation, which we now call human intelligence.'

Mark smiled, behind his glass.

'The point is,' Norman laughed, 'a small human minority was especially badly affected. Indeed they continue to suffer from its undoubted ravages. Fortunately, however, the great majority of people got over it very quickly. In many cases they made a complete recovery: the happy and healthy most of us.'

'I don't know what you mean,' Emma said.

'You would have to take the slightly afflicted as inoculated,' Mark said, smiling.

'Yes,' Norman said, with a loud laugh. 'Capital!' He got up from the table, stumbling slightly. 'I've got some cognac in my bag. I'll fetch it and we'll drink to the virus.'

'We've drunk enough,' Emma said, anxiously.

Norman did not answer but went to his bedroom. Emma gathered the plates and dishes together. Mark got up to help but she told him not to bother.

'Perhaps I should go, Emma. I've got to drive back.'

She hesitated. He looked round for his jacket. Then Norman came back, with the cognac.

'I should be going back,' Mark said.

'Of course. But have a drop before you go.'

'I don't know that I should.'

'Yes, have just a drop and tell Emma what you were going to.'

'I had nothing to tell Emma.'

'You had to tell her, surely, that any link from a place where the information was available—'

'Shut up, Norman!' Emma said angrily.

'. . . would mean, not guilt by association but guilt by transmission.'

Mark looked away.

'To a sufficiently amateur mind,' Norman added. 'And we have to deal with amateur minds.'

He took the wine glasses and poured cognac into them.

'I don't want any,' Emma said quickly.

'Well, it's all poured out now.'

He handed a glass to Mark, took his own and lay back on the sofa.

'What you were mentioning about meetings,' he said, looking up at Mark.

'Yes?'

'I now have two or three days of it.'

'So you said.'

'Out there in the streets it's Suez and Hungary, seven days that once again are changing the world. While in some boring room, with the most profoundly boring people, we'll have the classic delayed response. Where was this one, where was that one, in 1944, in 1947? With all that spurious precision.'

Mark put his glass on the mantelpiece. He pulled on his jacket.

'Officially and formally?' he asked, looking down.

Norman nodded.

'Officially and formally what?' Emma asked.

'Ask Mark,' Norman said.

'How would Mark know what you're talking about?'

'By listening,' Norman said.

Mark hesitated. He buttoned his jacket.

'It being different, obviously,' he said, gently, to Norman, 'since you are still officially employed?'

'Yes. I should have followed Monkey to the financial markets.'

'I hope you don't do that. Oddly he spoke about mutation too, but his is one we can do without, given the state of the world.'

'The other difference being, quite clearly,' Norman said, pulling himself up, 'that the criteria of proof and disproof can be different. Very different.'

'I had supposed that,' Mark said, holding his look.

Norman turned to Emma and smiled. 'I'll see Mark down.'

'Oh, good.'

Mark and Emma said good night. She waited to be kissed on the cheek.

'You've restored my faith,' Norman said, putting his hand on Mark's shoulder. 'My faith in intelligence. You really have.'

# 5

❧ ❀ ❦

# WESTRIDGE, DECEMBER 1956

As Norman switched off the ignition the engine continued to run. It ran for several seconds, then coughed and died.

He sat with the keys in his right hand, and with his left hand rubbed his eyes. There was a strange car, a big red estate model, drawn up close to the porch. He got out, slowly. His legs ached with cramp.

In the light from the porch lanterns the weathered honey-coloured stone was especially mellow. He looked along the façade. The maturity of the house had its familiar reassuring effect: surprising even when anticipated; a secure coda to the jagged restlessness of the day.

He went in, carrying his locked briefcase. He was putting it away, in the safe behind the Cotman in the dining-room, when Sarah called from the hall.

'Norman?'

'Here, darling.'

'Come through. We're in the drawing-room.'

He walked across, tossing the keys in his hand. Sarah was standing, smiling, in the centre of the room.

'Lady Fferris ran me back,' Sarah said.

'Yes, they gave me your message. A bit garbled but that's what we're there for.'

He could see a woman's head above the back of the nearest chair. The white-blonde hair was long and straight.

'Apparently you knew each other in Cambridge,' Sarah said, still smiling.

He moved forward. The woman in the chair turned.

'Hullo, Norman.'

'Pippa!'

There was a short silence.

'I'll get your sherry,' Sarah said.

'Thanks,' Norman said. Then, to Pippa: 'Long time.'

Pippa smiled. His first impression was that she had not changed at all. Perhaps it was her hair, which was still in a girl's style.

'Too long,' Pippa said.

He went on looking at her. What he now noticed was the high bulging of her cheeks. It was as if curved slices of apple had been applied over them, and this had compressed the eyes which, brown, small and hard, seemed far back. The lips also had thickened; a rosepink lipstick accentuated them. There were a few small brown hairs on the edges of the upper lip.

Sarah handed him a sherry.

'But then,' Pippa said, 'we only came to these parts last summer. When Jack inherited.'

Norman appeared to consider this.

'From his uncle,' Pippa said.

'I'm sorry. I should know them.'

'No earthly reason why you should.'

Sarah perched on the edge of the long sofa. Norman went deliberately across and sat very close to her.

'We all lose touch,' Pippa said. 'But when I saw Sarah's name on this new committee . . .'

'Is that the handicapped children?'

'Mentally handicapped.'

'And money's being raised for them?'

'What else?'

There was another silence. Pippa was looking very closely at Norman.

'We've only been here a few months ourselves,' Sarah said. 'Though we didn't have far to come.'

'It's a lovely house,' Pippa said. 'Does it have much land?'

'Only this cross between a wood and a garden,' Norman said.

'My grandfather sold off all the farming land. After the First War.'

'Yes,' Pippa said, 'a lot of our substance went then.'

Norman smiled. She looked away from him.

'Jack's family was lucky, they always are. But it's all changed now anyway. We had to take in the home farm and really run it. For the money, I mean, not just for the cream and the eggs.'

The telephone rang in the hall. Norman got up to answer it but Sarah was before him.

'It's almost certainly for me. There was a message from Judith.'

'She's all right?'

'Later,' Sarah said, and hurried to the phone.

They heard her answer but then she was quiet, listening. Pippa waited for some moments and then put down her glass. She looked across at Norman, smiling.

'Well, you bugger, how are you?'

Norman smiled.

'As you see.'

'You look bloody awful, actually. You look worried to death.'

'Overwork I suppose.'

'I can't think what else. You've got a lucky marriage.'

'Yes. Sure.'

'You don't deserve her but that happens to all the nice women.'

Sarah hurried back into the room. She was upset and flustered, pulling anxiously at her necklace.

'It was Judith,' she said to Norman, and then: 'I'm sorry, Lady Fferris . . .'

'Pippa.'

'Pippa. Yes. It's my sister Judith. She's expecting her second and it seems to be coming early. Her husband's abroad. He's a Marine in Aden. Now it seems she has to go in tonight, so I must go over and hold the fort.'

'Is it far?'

'No, just outside Gloucester.'

'I'll run you over,' Pippa said, getting up.

'Oh, no need for that, thanks. I can take the Morris. But I do really have to dash. I'm so sorry.'

Norman got up slowly.

'Sarah, why don't I drive you over?'

'Darling, you know you can't. You have to pick up Alex at half-seven. You can get the old Ford out.'

'Sure. At the Jarretts, is she?'

'Yes. Half-seven.'

Sarah moved restlessly. She obviously wanted to hurry off but didn't know how to get away.

'Anyway I'll be running along,' Pippa said.

'There's no need. Really! You stay and talk to Norman.'

'Another time,' Pippa said.

Sarah dashed upstairs and came down buttoning her coat. Norman gave her the car keys. She hurried out to the car and drove off. It was now quite dark but she was twenty yards down the drive before she switched on the headlights.

Norman and Pippa stood in the porch, watching the car out of sight.

'Lucky indeed,' Pippa said.

'Stop patronising her, Pippa.'

'Christ, can you think that? About someone that delightful?'

'You see. Delightful!'

'Well, all right. Any of the good words there are.'

'Okay. But you don't have to tell me.'

'I think I do. You probably still think loving kindness is a bourgeois illusion.'

'Why should I think anything so stupid?'

'It was common form. I remember Emma saying it.'

'Emma and you and Magda and Dot and Ingrid and . . .'

Pippa laughed.

'Is Emma still in the Party?'

'Of course.'

'I don't know, of course. But then didn't she marry Georgi Wilkes?'

'Yes. Did you know he was killed, on a motorbike? Nearly two years ago.'

'Oh, God, I'm sorry. I didn't like him but I'm sorry.'

'Why didn't you like him?'

'He was like your friend Pitter. A creepy sort of manipulator. A wanting-to-be-boss man.'

'That's not remotely like Monkey.'

'Perhaps. I just thought they were both revolting.'

Norman smiled.

'Not our sort, Pippa?'

'Yes, Norman. Not our sort. But I'm sorry for Emma. And now the Party will have her for life, serving the sacred memory.'

'You can't be serious, saying that about Emma. She thinks for herself.'

'So we all thought, all thinking for ourselves. And we were just kids being taken for a ride.'

'No, that's ridiculous. We were more nearly right than anyone else at that time.'

'Oh, sure. All those ghastly old people. But still we were wrong.'

'If you say so.'

'Surely you don't still believe in the Party? With your sort of job?'

'I'm not still a member, if that's what you're asking.'

'I'm not asking. But if I were forced to guess, I'd say some sort of social democrat, liberal even.'

'I see. And yourself?'

'I'm a Tory, isn't it obvious? I know who I am and where I belong.'

'Which you didn't then?'

'Which I didn't then. Though I still respect the Party. I'm the kind of hard Tory who's learned to respect it. Because they and we are the only people who've faced it: that there are sides and that we must choose.'

Norman shifted his feet and rubbed his eyes. Pippa stared across at him.

'Go back in. I'll make you some coffee.'

'No, Pippa. No, really.'

'You needn't look so frightened.'

'I'm not frightened.'

'I'd say you are. It was the first thing I noticed. But whatever it is, for Christ's sake there's no need to be frightened of me.'

He smiled.

'I mean,' Pippa said, 'remember Aldeburgh.'

'Remember what?'

'Yes, I thought you'd forgotten. A functional forgetting.'

'Aldeburgh! Of course. I didn't catch the name.'

She smiled and put her hand on his arm.

'I'm going to make you that coffee. You look like death.'

'It's a headache, that's all.'

She went back into the house.

'Don't worry, I'll find the kitchen.'

'No, I'll get it.'

He followed her through. She took off the bulky sheepskin jacket which she had pulled on for the car. She began opening cupboards.

'It's here,' Norman said, finding the beans and grinder.

'No, damn all that stuff. Have you got this new powder?'

'Yes, I think I brought some back from the States.'

She filled a kettle and switched it on. He found coffee powder and milk and sugar. She sat on the edge of a stool by the kettle. She looked across at him.

'How old is your daughter?'

'Alex? She's eleven.'

'So it did come all right? In the end?'

'What?'

'Or perhaps it was just Sarah. Some more or less immaculate conception. I could believe that.'

'What in hell are you talking about, Pippa?'

'Crude stuff, darling. Crude stuff.'

He looked away.

'I see, yes. Aldeburgh.'

She pushed herself down from the stool.

'Indeed Aldeburgh! It took me two bloody years to get over that. Because I thought, you see, that it was *my* fault. It made me more damn wretched than you could believe possible.'

Norman did not look at her. He went across to the dresser and picked up two large black mugs. The kettle came to the boil and Pippa made the coffee quickly and impatiently, rattling the spoons around the mugs.

'Shall we go back to the drawing-room?' she asked, not looking at him.

'Of course. As you like.'

'It will seem less intrusive there.'

'Intrusive?'

'Well, a woman's kitchen is quite as private as her bedroom.'

She walked quickly back to the drawing-room. He followed her. She went back to where she had been sitting. He sat opposite her. He sipped his coffee. The mug was very hot to hold.

'I've been badgering you, Norman.'

'No, I'm sorry. It's just that I'm tired.'

'Weighed down by all these secrets?'

'No, I doubt that.'

'What about this garden of yours? How are you going to manage it?'

'Oh, that's not a problem. I'm really looking forward to it. There are already some very good trees and there's a collection of lilacs that my aunt started. I'm going to really work on them, do a book on them if I can.'

'Making even the gardening intellectual?'

'Oh no, I shall be doing all the work myself.'

'You look as if you need to. After Cambridge and all that it took me years to learn, but it's only physical work that can keep people sane.'

'You do a lot yourself?'

'Yes. Since we came down here. But we had years in London and I watched it through. That sort of indoor-to-indoor life and just artificial exercise. If you look it's obvious. Those people are sick to the soul.'

'I've heard the theory. Intelligence as a viral disease.'

'It isn't intelligence at all. It's just an unhealthy combination of physical stagnation and mental abstraction. A world made out of paper and money. Nobody ever out of breath.'

'All right. If you're doing it. But I remember that kind of talk from the Party. An intellectual idealisation of physical labour.'

'Exactly. One bloody intellectual nagging another about what neither would ever by any chance do.'

'Perhaps. But what it really left out was the history of actual labour. What it really comes down to, in working-class lives.'

'Sure, but when did the Party ever understand that? They made their pitch for the workers, but only as intellectuals. It's only the Right, anywhere, who know what labour and the physical are.'

'Yes. That's exactly what the fascists used to say.'

'And then ballsed it up with their own sick ideas. You need a traditional Right to keep it straight.'

'I see what you mean about hard Tory.'

'Well, don't think up arguments about it. Just notice that we're winning.'

He finished his coffee and put his mug in the hearth. He let his eyes follow the lines of the high carved stone fireplace. Pippa was watching each of his movements and he felt very self-conscious.

'Right then, I'll be off,' she said, getting up.

He rose at once. She collected the mugs and walked through with them to the kitchen. She pulled on her heavy jacket as she went to the front door.

'I'll be seeing Sarah again,' she said, turning. 'I don't know about seeing you.'

'These things work out.'

'You think so? I don't think so. I've been lucky myself but I can see that most of it is still bloody ridiculous, just as I saw it at school.'

'Getting older makes that worse. Seeing the same follies the third or fourth time round.'

'I don't see it like that. I expect there to be follies. I'm past those perfectionist fantasies of the Left. But it's just all this business of relationships.'

'Business?'

Pippa paused, looking down.

'Well, Norman, most of it is. We follow our own tracks, make our own lives, but then we have these odd contacts with people who are bits of our past. We bump into them, unexpectedly, and then we move on. So that . . .'

'Unexpectedly?'

'Well, whether or not. You don't want to be with these people. You don't wish you'd stayed with them. But you say nice to see you, mustn't leave it so long till next time, and . . .'

'Look . . .'

'And in fact it churns you up because you can see that there's no connection, no real continuity anywhere. These odd people pass out of sight but they go on solidly eating and sleeping and then you look round in the street and there they are again, much the same. A few minutes and then off, a few years and then on. It's all bloody meaningless.'

Norman hesitated, watching her. The thick cheeks had reddened.

'It just means that you want something different, Pippa. Some different order of life.'

'I doubt that too. The Party was the fantasy that there could be something different. We've all seen through that. But it was how they picked us up, you remember?'

'No, it was always more than that.'

'For you and me it was no more than that. And in our case, for sure, there never was going to be anything more.'

Norman smiled and lifted his hands. Pippa pulled on her large hide gloves. He followed her out.

'Don't forget to pick up your daughter.'

'I shan't.'

'And give my love to Sarah. I hope her sister and the baby are all right.'

'Fine.'

She got into her car. She started the engine and then suddenly switched it off. She wound down the window.

'Actually there is one question.'

'What's that?'

Pippa looked away. Her gloved hands were tight on the steering wheel.

'The one and only question. Where actually did you go when you came back from Spain?'

He stared down at her. He took his time to answer.

'From Spain? I was never in Spain.'

She turned and looked up at him. By some trick of the light her eyes seemed to have receded, above her bulging cheeks. Her voice now was hoarse.

'You went to Marseilles for the Party, right?'

'Sure.'

'You went just before Easter. You were supposed to get back in June. We were going to Scotland.'

'I remember.'

'You didn't come.'

'No, I couldn't. I was ordered to stay on in Marseilles.'

'You bloody well were not.'

He looked closely at her. Her mouth was still moving, wordlessly. Her face was twisted with some pain.

'Well, who do you think's best likely to know?' he said, steadily.

She put a gloved hand up to her face. The big glove was shapeless as she rubbed at her eyes.

'I'm sorry, Pippa,' he said.

'Yes, I expect you are. And I don't really want to go through all that again. But still there are things I must know.'

'Well?'

She looked up at him. She had recovered control of her face and her voice.

'I've been trying to tell you. After that fiasco in Aldeburgh I was pretty hysterical. When you hadn't come back, by July, I got in touch with Emma. She said you were still there, though she'd been sending you telegrams and you hadn't replied. She said you were probably too busy.'

'I was very busy. Getting clandestine stuff through that chaos at the port.'

'I got on a train, Norman. I went to the address. Yes, you had been there, until the middle of May. Then you had left, they told me, for Spain.'

'Then they were wrong,' Norman said, shaking his head and smiling.

'I don't think so. I went back to Paris. They were very sticky. They would give me nothing more than your Marseilles address.'

'So?'

'So I went back to Marseilles. I asked around. But apart from that simple Mme Bourget at your lodging nobody would tell me anything. So in the end I had to come home.'

She looked up at him again. There was some pleading in her face.

'Pippa, there had to be security. It was getting trickier and more dangerous all the time.'

'I know that. I cried myself to sleep on it, night after night. So that by the end of the year, when somebody told me that you were back in Cambridge, I was ready to understand everything.

I was even, against advice, going to come down from Scotland to see you.'

'But you didn't,' he said, sharply.

She looked angrily up at him now. He had a fixed, soothing smile.

'Norman, you really are a bastard. You know why I didn't. First you were only in Cambridge for two or three days. Then you went off somewhere else, you and Pitter. And second . . .'

He moved impatiently.

'Second, you bugger, I heard about that Welsh girl and her baby. And that you weren't there either.'

Norman said nothing. She shifted her right hand and reached for the ignition.

'I won't give you the satisfaction,' she said, fiercely. 'I'm past caring where you were. But I do take notice that now, when none of it matters, you're still lying to me.'

'Lying? I'm not lying. Lying about what?'

'About Spain.'

'I told you. I wasn't in Spain.'

'Yes and that's the lie. Ross Morrison saw you there.'

'Ross Morrison? Do I know him?'

'He knew you. From Cambridge. And he was back in the base camp at Albacete, wounded, when they started re-examining all the volunteers' papers and histories. A sort of purge, he called it.'

She waited. He said nothing. There was still a faint smile.

'He saw you very clearly. He was in some difficulty and he wanted to appeal to you because you seemed to have some authority. But when he asked for Norman Braose he was told there was no one of that name in the camp. When he pointed you out he was told that your name was Edward Davies.'

Norman shrugged.

'There's always that kind of mistake. In that kind of chaos.'

'It wasn't a mistake. You were there, on a false name, and you were working with the Russians checking the Englishmen's histories and papers.'

Norman shook his head.

'This is absolute fantasy, Pippa.'

She gazed into his face. Her lips were compressed and pushed forward. She switched on the car engine. He waited and then leaned towards her.

'Where is this Ross Morrison now?' he asked, casually.

Pippa pushed the lever into gear.

'Oh no you don't, you bugger. The lying is enough.'

'I keep telling you it isn't a lie.'

'You're worried now that I might tell someone. That I might embarrass your gentle middle age and your sneaky job.'

'What sneaky job?'

'Well, don't worry, I shan't. Any more than I'll have a girlish chat with Sarah about Aldeburgh. Not out of any regard for you, but simply from contempt.'

He leaned closer, trying to answer, but she let out the clutch and skidded sharply forward. The engine roared as she raced down the drive.

# FOUR

—⟡—❧—❀◯❀—☙—⟡—

## 1968

# 1

⊰❁⊱

## LONDON, FEBRUARY 1968

The young man was stretching his legs across the damp pavement, his canvas shoes partly blocking the entrance to the gallery.
He was sitting on a pile of newspapers. His hair was long
and blond, falling around his narrow and bristled face. Nesta,
looking down at him, saw that the colour of his hair, in its long
waves, varied between a bleached whiteness and a warm brown.
She crouched and spoke quietly to him.

'You'll get bad sitting there in the damp.'

He looked up at her, puzzled.

'No, Ma'am,' he said, in a surprisingly deep voice.

'You American?'

'So they say.'

'Are you waiting for somebody? For a friend?'

'Ma'am, we're all waiting for friends.'

Nesta looked back up at Gwyn. He had turned away. She
hesitated and then stood.

'Are you sure you don't need help?' she asked, leaning over
again. The young man did not answer.

'Leave him, Mam,' Gwyn said impatiently.

'No, he worries me, Gwyn.'

'If you were more often in London you'd know you can't
worry. There's thousands like that.'

'Well, there shouldn't be. This is a civilised country.'

'It's the civilisation he doesn't like.'

The young man moved and smiled. Gwyn nodded and looked away. On the glass doors of the gallery there was a line of identical posters: *Four Working-Class Painters*, in large red type under Nesta's sketch of the Danycapel valley, with the two heads of miners in green.

'Including this,' Gwyn said, nodding towards the posters.

'Well, he's here,' Nesta said, 'he must have come for something.'

'And stayed outside. Like you yesterday at the opening.'

'Well, I didn't want the speeches.'

'Or the drinks?'

'Nor the drinks.'

She tightened the belt of her shiny, plum-coloured raincoat. The February afternoon was damp and mild, under a low hazy sky. There were drops of rain on her hair, which was swept up off the face and into a pleat at the back. A prominent streak of grey marked the crown.

'As it was . . .' she said, and then stopped.

'Yes?' Gwyn encouraged.

'Up here I suppose it means something, saying working-class painters . . .'

'You had that argument with Emma.'

'Yes and I know very well, if it wasn't for calling it that, nobody would be bothered to show off my pictures. It's the politics, I know that, but none of them was painted for politics.'

'Go on, Mam, you're still flattered.'

Nesta laughed, but then checked as she looked again at the young man on the pavement. He had belched and was now gulping with what seemed a full mouth.

'Don't you think we should get an ambulance?' she asked Gwyn, quietly.

'And get him busted?'

'What d'you mean?'

Gwyn reached across and put his arm under her elbow.

'Mrs Lewis,' he said, 'you're late for your work.'

She resisted his move forward.

'And then going round listening to what people are saying about them,' she protested.

'Then don't go near your own. Just look at the others.'

'Yes, it's only fair play to do that.'

Gwyn pushed open the heavy glass door. A neon sign, *Partisan Gallery*, hung in the foyer. He went across and bought tickets at a counter heavily loaded with pamphlets and news-sheets. He took a copy of the catalogue, which was being sold for Medical Aid to Vietnam. He waited for his change.

There was no one else in the foyer. He made for the short flight of steps to the gallery. He offered Nesta the catalogue.

'No, you just tell me what's in it.'

'About you?'

'I know that. About the others.'

At the top of the steps was a low rectangular room, brightly lighted from above. The grey walls were crowded with the many exhibits. An elderly woman was walking slowly around the otherwise empty room, stopping and staring, shifting her distance.

'This one,' Nesta said, beginning at the beginning. It was a very large black-and-white drawing of a shipbuilding dock, the human figures tiny on the lifts and scaffolding of a hull in construction.

'John Sowerbutt,' Gwyn read. 'Forty-seven. Born in South Shields. Began work in . . .'

Nesta wasn't listening. She had gone eagerly forward along the whole line of very similar drawings. Now she was walking slowly back.

'What do you think?' Gwyn asked.

She looked across at him, surprised.

'Very good,' she said, brightly.

'Are they?'

'Well, you can see as well as I can.'

Gwyn looked again.

'It's very striking, all that scaffolding. Only the people seem a bit lost. Insignificant.'

'Well, that's what it is,' Nesta said.

'How d'you mean?'

But she had again gone forward. When she came to her own exhibits she glanced rapidly over them. They had hung them more or less as she had asked. The sketch for the banner, which had been reproduced on the poster, had been made too prominent, but beyond it there were the two series she really cared about: of the raincloud that was moving like a creature through the valley – none was quite right but they made a comparison with each other – and of the best ones, the ponies behind the wire fence of the mountain: the strange heads and the lines of light and shade in the manes and tails.

'They say pit ponies in the catalogue,' Gwyn said, coming behind her.

'Well, they're not. I told Emma and that Carl.'

There were voices behind them on the steps. Nesta looked quickly at the two pictures that turned the corner of the gallery: the ink sketch, with some wash, of a small church with an open belfry among crowding trees, and the much larger oil which had been developed from it; the church almost disappearing among the heavy dark green of the trees and a much larger sky above it, an intense blue with yellow-edged clouds.

'Carl said he preferred the sketch,' she said over her shoulder.

'Do you?'

'How should I know?'

Two young men and a young woman had come in behind them, talking loudly. Nesta crossed, nervously, to the opposite corner.

'These are nice,' she said hurriedly.

She was looking at a collection of small, bright watercolours of a girl's head with flowers: the same features, even the same happy tilt of the head, were in several, though the flowers varied. Some she did not know; they looked tropical.

'Maggie Krwycziak, twenty-seven, born Chicago,' Gwyn read. Nesta was still looking closely.

'Now settled in North London and . . .'

There was a loud laugh from the group behind them. Gwyn looked round. They were laughing to each other, one of the young men holding the young woman's extended fingers. Nesta had moved on, to a very large painting of a huge and distorted bird flying above and overshadowing a tangle of leaves and flowers: a few at the edges still bright but most grey and dying under the shadow.

'Vietnam,' Gwyn read from the catalogue.

'It says,' Nesta answered, pointing.

Looking closer Gwyn could see that distorted letters had been formed in the tangle of branches. He could make out two words, *Nam* and *Cong*, but there was another too misshapen to make out.

'The same artist, Maggie Krwycziak.'

'Well, I can see that.'

'Do you like it?'

'No, I don't.'

'Why?'

'I think it's a shame.'

'What, the war or the painting?'

There was a loud burst of talk from behind them. The young woman was looking closely at Nesta's series of ponies, but the men seemed not to be talking about them. Nesta had turned, following Gwyn's look, and as he glanced back at her he saw her face go white.

He looked back where she had been looking. A middle-aged man and a young woman had come up the steps and were looking easily around. They were both tall, and conspicuously well dressed: the man in a dark blue overcoat with a thin velvet collar; the young woman in a tailored tapestry cloak.

Nesta had moved on. She was walking quickly down the long wall, staying close to it and hardly looking at the pictures. He hurried to catch her up. She stopped suddenly.

'What do you think of this?' she asked, beckoning him closer and leaning forward to a wide poster drawing. Gwyn focused it better from a distance: the curve of a march, with banners, and high warehouse shapes in the background.

'Paul Connolly, thirty-four, born in Liverpool,' he read from the catalogue.

'Never mind that, look at it. It's lovely.'

'Do you think so? I'd been getting the impression this wasn't your kind of art.'

'There's no kinds like you mean. Look at that strong drawing.'

'If you say so, Mam, but it's a stereotype, isn't it?'

'I don't know what that means,' Nesta said.

As she spoke she glanced quickly past him, at the people on the other side of the room. She took his arm. He could feel the hard pressure of her fingers. The Connolly drawings had a common style and theme, of marches and demonstrations, one of a platform of speakers with a single dark figure pointing to the sky. Then at the end and turn of the wall there were four pencil portraits: beautifully drawn, he could now see; the faces old, hard and lined.

'We've seen enough,' Nesta said.

He looked at her, surprised.

'I was hoping we could walk round again,' he said.

'No.'

'Why not? We're not all as quick taking it in as you are.'

'I'm not quick.'

She was now talking without thinking, her mind elsewhere. The colour had come back into her face but she seemed to have pulled into herself even more closely. She even now, as he watched, pulled the belt of her raincoat tighter, around her thin waist.

'Is it something else upset you?' he asked.

'I don't want to talk about it.'

'Is it these other people?'

She looked up at him.

'Why do you say that?'

'I just wondered. You said it might upset you.'

She passed her hand quickly across her face.

'I want to go,' she said.

But she still did not move. Impatiently, she looked away from his face and back at one of the portrait heads: an extraordinary drawing, he could now see, in which the head, seen from the side, was like a rock slab, almost without features, though in a lighter pencilwork there was a bristle of close-cropped hair and what seemed almost incidental features, occupying so little and so subordinate a space on one side of the dominant shape of the skull.

She clutched at his arm again. As he turned he looked across the room, where more people were entering. He saw among them a man of about his own age whose face he instantly recognised. It was only at a second stage that he realised the recognition was from television.

It was the young Labour politician Alec Merritt, who had

become prominent last year in a public demonstration. He had burned a Whip's notice and flung the ashes in the face of the Labour Foreign Secretary who had been defending the American war in Vietnam. There had been controversy about whether the paper was still burning when he had thrown it at the eminent head and he had said, on television: 'It wasn't, but I wouldn't have minded if it was. It might have given him some idea of napalm.'

This had been widely denounced as a shameful violence, but in the strange cross-currents of these years it had made him, simultaneously, a television celebrity: a man to be brought forward into the statutory circle of uncomfortable armchairs to be stared at and interrogated and display radical dissent. Merritt had gone along with this process, boldly and cheerfully. He had even revelled in the internal mechanics of the process. Gwyn remembered an occasion when he was being solemnly attacked by the interviewer for what was called his endorsement of violence, and he had replied, smiling – he was a handsome young Saxon, broad-shouldered and dressed as if for golf: 'It's curious you should say that, for your producer Philip Whitlow was telling me, just before we came on, that flinging that paper was the best bit of political television there'd been in years, and you were standing between us, smiling accordingly and sagely nodding your head.'

Gwyn stared across at him. The screen image riveted the attention. He was walking quickly forward from the group with which he had entered towards the well-dressed middle-aged man and young woman, who were standing looking at Nesta's pictures. The young woman turned as he came up to them and lifted her face. He smiled and kissed her close to the mouth, then shook hands with the older man.

'What's so interesting?' Nesta asked, looking up at Gwyn and increasing the pressure on his arm.

'It's just I know that man.'

Nesta moved forward.

'That man with those two over there,' Gwyn said. 'He's Alec Merritt, the Labour M P.'

'Is he?' Nesta said.

She did not follow his look.

'You must have heard of him,' Gwyn said.

'Yes, Emma told me.'

'Emma?'

'Yes, when they got married.'

Gwyn waited, feeling entirely baffled. His mother turned away. He looked back across the room. The three people were still by her pictures. The older man was looking closely at the oil of the church among trees. The other two were strolling, back and forward and further out and in. Gwyn thought, watching them, that they had a distinctly proprietorial, inspecting air, but he did not want to think badly of Merritt.

'If you won't come I'm going without you,' Nesta said. As she spoke she risked a glance down the length of the gallery. When she saw the three with their backs to her she had a much longer look. Then as the older man straightened from his close look at the oil she took her hand from Gwyn's arm and made for the steps out. Embarrassed, he followed her. He caught her up on the steps. They did not speak until they were through the foyer and out of the glass door to the street.

The young American was still on the pavement, but he had slipped sideways and was now lying on his elbow, staring up at the passers-by. The low cloud was thickening towards a misty drizzle. Nesta pushed her hand over her hair and let out her breath.

'What is it, Mam? Tell me,' Gwyn said anxiously.

'Well, he can't be left there whatever you say.'

'Him,' Gwyn said, looking down at the long sprawl. 'Can't you see that he's happy?'

Nesta shook her head.

'It's not him,' Gwyn said. 'It's those people in there.'

'Is it?'

'Those two people Alec Merritt went up to. You know them, don't you?'

'Never mind that now,' Nesta said, and walked off along the pavement.

He hurried and caught her up. He took her arm. She seemed glad but did not look up at him.

'You know them,' he repeated.

She quickened her pace.

'Yes, and you don't,' she said quickly. 'That's what's so bad about it.'

He walked in silence for some time.

'They didn't look at you,' he said. 'They didn't seem to know you.'

'No, only the pictures,' Nesta said and suddenly laughed.

'I can find out, Mam, you know. I can find out who Alec Merritt married.'

She looked up at him, searching his face.

'Alec and Alex they're called. That sounds nice, don't you think?'

'Alex who, then?'

'Well, Alex Merritt.'

'No, stop fooling. You know what I mean.'

'You think I'm fooling? I'm not fooling.'

'Well, tell me, then.'

'Alex Braose.'

She had spoken so quietly that he had to replay the words in his mind. They had reached the subway to the Underground. People were hurrying and pushing past them. A newspaper seller was shouting some strange cry: words he could not make out.

'Braose? You mean the man . . .?'

She looked anxiously up at him.

'Yes.'

He stood quite still, then turned as if to go back. But it had been an instinctive movement. Once he thought about it he checked. He looked across at her again. There was colour back in her face, and her thick black hair was shining in the light rain. She held his look, with an expression he could only record; he could find no immediate word to describe it. If it had not been for the situation, and his own sense of it, he would have said a kind of exultation: a hard, self-centred, extraordinarily physical pride.

'I'm sorry, Mam. I was stupid.'

'No need for you to be sorry.'

'No, I'm sorry for you. It must have been awful.'

'Awful for him, perhaps,' she said, smiling.

'You said that as if you enjoyed thinking so.'

She smiled. There was no mistaking now the extraordinary, delighted self-possession.

'Jill and Lyn will be waiting for us,' she said, busily.

'No, they won't. We were in and out in five minutes.'

'Well, they'll still be waiting. That's what family is.'

She hurried, skipping, down the steps. Several people turned and looked at her, interrupted in their preoccupied oblique hurrying. He followed and pushed close to her. He looked at his watch. Jill would have collected Lyn from playschool and be back at the house. Lyn would look up and laugh when her Nana from Wales rushed in and immediately sat on the floor with her, drawing. Yet all around him and behind him there was this largely indifferent rush and crossing of people, and within it, suddenly, his own complex history.

'Come on, boy,' Nesta called.

# 2

❧❀❀❀❧

## LONDON, MARCH 1968

Dic leaned over to cut up Lyn's bacon and fried bread, on the plate which had pink roses around its border. She was tracing the garland of roses with her little finger, appearing more interested in them than in the food. Jill, carrying Dic a large mug of strong tea, intervened.

'Get on and eat it, love, now your uncle's cut it up for you.'

'The bread's hot.'

'Then eat the bacon. And let Uncle Dic eat his.'

Lyn picked up her fork.

'If he can manage it after last night,' Jill added, laughing.

'On that drop of London beer!' Dic protested.

'More than a drop,' Jill said. 'Look at your brother.'

Gwyn was standing by the stove, holding a fork, mechanically turning bacon in the frying pan. In his grey dressing gown, with his thick black hair tousled, he looked still half asleep. His face was very pale.

'Rugby and beer, it'll be the end of the Welsh,' Jill laughed.

'Aye, and he wasn't even playing,' Dic said. 'Christ, I'd like to see him in one of them mauls. Though, fair play, it's softer up here than when we play each other back home.'

'What's a maul, Mam?' Lyn asked.

'When these men all shove each other. And punch each other if nobody's looking.'

'Don't tell such things to this innocent child,' Dic protested.

'Innocent!' Jill exclaimed.

Gwyn had walked solemnly to the table, holding the pan of bacon stiffly at his waist.

'Take the plates to it, why don't you?' Jill said.

He didn't answer. He forked the bacon on to Jill's plate and his own, then sat heavily. Jill fetched two mugs of tea.

'You'd better forget that demo,' Jill said.

Gwyn didn't answer.

'Aye, well I don't mind,' Dic said. 'It's only these students.'

'Not altogether,' Gwyn said.

His voice was hoarse.

'Playboys from what I've seen of them,' Dic persisted.

'Yes, but you haven't seen them. All you've seen is the telly.'

'That's right, Dic,' Jill said, supporting her husband.

'Aye well, I said I'd go, on the way to the train,' Dic said, agreeably.

'Vietnam is our Spain,' Gwyn said, heavily.

The others hesitated, pulling back from banter.

'Only it was both for our Dad's generation,' Gwyn went on. 'The struggle in the pits and the struggle for Spain.'

'We know, love,' Jill said quickly.

'They're not going to fight in Vietnam, though, are they?' Dic argued.

'No, but if we can just stop it from this end.'

'Eat your bacon,' Jill said.

Gwyn's eyes were almost closed. It was not only the physical tiredness, after the drinking with Dic and the rest of the team last night. For Jill it was also the sign of one of the moods he had fallen into, in these last weeks: since he had taken his mother to the exhibition.

It was not like him to be withdrawn and brooding like this. But he wouldn't talk about it. All he ever came out with was some heavy, general political statement. This had never been necessary between them. From when they first met, in his first job, they had seen the world the same way. Her family experience of politics, in Swindon where her father was in the railway works and a union branch secretary, had been close enough to his own to make basic discussion and argument unnecessary. Since they'd married he had taken much more interest in the new kinds of intellectual socialism. But it had been taken for granted that this was an extension of the old union and labour politics, even when it was much more concentrated on international events: Cuba and China and now Vietnam.

None of this had been a difficulty. It was only this very recent phase that had cut some part of him off from her. She had tried several times to discuss it directly, to lead on from what he was apparently saying. But past a certain point he went stubbornly silent, most of his energy turned inward to something else that was preoccupying him.

Lyn finished her breakfast and left the table. Gwyn reached out, quickly, as she passed him, and stroked her hair.

'And I expect Emma's given her marching orders,' Dic said.

'What?'

'Emma. Giving out her orders for the demo.'

'No. It's not the Party,' Gwyn said quickly.

'Well, we had it at the branch, we had a speaker about Vietnam.'

'Yes, but this is different, Dic. Well, in London it's different.'

'How could it be different? It's the same bloody war.'

Gwyn looked down, trying to overcome his tiredness.

'Yes well, it's how to stop it. There's big differences on that. Whether to negotiate or go for victory.'

'Isn't that for them there to decide? They're doing the bloody fighting.'

'Right,' Gwyn said, 'that's what I've been arguing. But I think mainly the Party's worried because so much of the campaigning is being done by what they call Maoists and Trots.'

'Splitters,' Dic said, nodding.

'No, not splitters. It isn't like that any more. There's no one big thing to split.'

'There's Wilson's government,' Jill said, 'supporting the war.'

'No, I meant on the Left,' Gwyn said, frowning.

'Well, it needn't worry you, mun,' Dic said. 'Unless you've joined the Party again.'

Gwyn put his hands on the table.

'No. No. And I won't.'

'All right, I'm not trying to recruit you.'

'It might be different at home,' Gwyn said. 'And of course with Dad.'

'He don't mind. He says you've got your own work.'

'But I still am political. And I'm trying to explain how it is in London and in the universities.'

'Like I said. Students.'

'And like I said, not only students. And I'll tell you this, kid, they're impressive. They're really standing up to fight.'

Dic drained his large mug of tea. Jill got up to refill it.

'Aye well, Dad says that,' Dic said, easily. 'How it was in the Thirties. How good these students was then.'

'Yes,' Gwyn said, and then went silent.

'That's how Emma come, wasn't it?' Dic persisted.

'Yes.'

'And fair play, she's stuck with it.'

'Yes. Yes she has.'

'Even if she does think this lot . . .'

'It's just that the Party isn't leading them,' Gwyn said, sharply.

'Well, what do that matter if we're all on the same side?'

'It's that, Dic, which is the question. Are we?'

Dic stared at him, baffled. Jill came back with the tea. She had heard what Gwyn said and had seen that the question wasn't directed outward but back in on himself. His mind was tying up again, on whatever it was that preoccupied him.

'Well of course we bloody are,' Dic said, putting his mug down noisily.

'Aye, I suppose,' Gwyn said quickly.

'All right, then,' Dic said and got up.

Gwyn stayed at the table, warming his hands around the hot tea. Jill got busy with clearing the table. She worked around him, from time to time glancing anxiously at his face. As the light fell from the window she could see the dark hard bristles on his neck. The corners of his mouth were pulled down. His eyes were half closed again.

'Have a bath, love,' she said, 'it'll ease you.'

'What?'

'A bath.'

'Aye.'

He didn't move but as she again reached across him he looked and said suddenly:

'Perhaps after all there are two quite different traditions.'

'Which, love?' she asked, stopping.

'And not only different traditions, but quite different people carrying them.'

'Which traditions do you mean?'

'They find common cause, at certain times, and objectively, always, they have need to. But still through people who are basically different from each other.'

'We're all different from each other.'

'Like if Vietnam is our Spain, objectively that is quite clear. And even the sectarianism can then be incidental. But still the different people . . .'

He stopped and looked up at her.

'In effect, different classes,' he said, his eyes searching her face.

'Who? Us?'

'No, not us. It's what follows those moments of temporary fusion . . .'

A pain crossed his face and he got up abruptly, pushing his chair back.

'Love,' she said, reaching out to him.

He smiled, touching her.

'Is it a headache? I'll get you some aspirin.'

'Thanks.'

Dic was watching them from the door.

'I'm sorry, kid,' Gwyn said, quickly.

'It's the morning after,' Dic said.

'Aye, the morning after, the year after, the generation after. It's all bloody after.'

'Forget it, mun.'

'You think so?'

He took the aspirin from Jill. He washed it down with the last of his tea. He went and dressed.

'You sure you don't mind going?' he said to Dic.

'If you are, I will.'

'All right, then. Sure. Because I really feel that I must.'

They found Lyn's coat and walked out with her across the park at the end of the street. The metal track of the slide which was her favourite was too damp to slip on. Gwyn pushed her on the low box swing and when she was tired of that Dic went with her on the roundabout, holding her tight and whirling the old machine with kicks from the asphalt. Jill walked across the park and joined them. Dic got Lyn on one end of the seesaw and persuaded Gwyn on to the other, but it wouldn't balance and they had to change ends, with Gwyn holding Lyn to make up Dic's weight. Jill was cold watching them, in the damp March morning.

They walked back with Lyn on Dic's shoulders. Jill had put a roast in the oven. Gwyn and Dic shared the Sunday paper. There was a short front-page paragraph about police arrangements for the demonstration. There was a report of the busmen's strike in Liverpool, where a wage agreement had been frozen by the Prices and Incomes Board. A road haulage strike was about to begin. There were letters protesting about the cutting of supplies of milk to secondary-school children and about the new Immigration Bill. In Vietnam there was regrouping after the Tet offensive. More reforms of socialism were being discussed in Czechoslovakia. Production was getting back to normal in the Shotton steelworks, after the lay-off of seven thousand production workers. It was reported and denied that by the autumn the Coal Board would be announcing another twenty-five thousand redundancies in the pits.

Jill had insisted on a full Sunday dinner, centred on roast lamb with honey and cider. The house was warm with the smell of cooking.

'We don't get you here that often,' she said to Dic.

'Don't worry. At this rate I'll be up again.'

They sat to table talking and laughing. Even Gwyn, for a time, seemed relaxed.

Gwyn and Dic were late setting out for the demonstration. They went by Underground to Marble Arch and then through the streets towards Grosvenor Square. By the announced timing the march would be there, but already three streets away there were groups of people moving that way, with placards and rolled banners. A young man with an armband came back on a motor scooter.

'How big is it?' somebody shouted.

'Ten thousand at least but keep going.'

Dic laughed.

'Not bad,' he said to Gwyn.

'Sure.'

'Only what strikes me . . .'

'Yeah?'

'It's like a picnic, mun. Daps and sandals and miniskirts.'

They were walking behind a group of students, who were unfolding a red banner in the wind along the canyon of a street. Most of them were wearing the soft shoes that Gwyn and Dic called daps. Big white letters spelled *Revolutionary* in the folds.

'It's the mood,' Gwyn said. 'Informal.'

Dic laughed.

'The revolution in daps!'

'They're all right.'

'Of course they're all right.'

As they turned a corner they could hear the chanting ahead: the lively rhythm of 'Ho, Ho, Ho Chi Minh!' and the deeper, less carrying 'Victory to . . . NLF!' Two girls passed them, running, in black pyjama suits. And now they could see the crowd ahead, at the entrance to the square. Dic quickened their pace.

'I don't want to miss this.'

'It'll last.'

They pushed into a march coming in from the right. The banners and placards were all up now, and the whole column was chanting. There were police lined along the pavements, three deep, watching. The column slowed on the edge of the square.

'Keep moving,' came a shout from behind.

They shuffled slowly forward, trying to press into the already crowded square. Then there was shouting from behind them and the police were moving in from the pavements, narrowing the line of march.

'Horses!' somebody shouted, and Gwyn and Dic, looking

back, could see mounted police coming in from a side street.

They pressed forward, but the column was breaking up in the general crowd of the square. The Embassy steps were black with lines of foot police, with more mounted police in front of them. The chanting was now much louder and angrier. There were scuffles near the steps.

Still pushed from behind, but linking arms with four others, Gwyn and Dic moved to try to get round the most crowded press near the steps. It was slow going, but they went some distance. Then there was a swirl in the press and just ahead of them they could see a double line of police, close with linked arms, blocking their way. They tried to stop, but the pressure from behind them was too strong. There were pushes and sideways movements but still they were pressed inexorably forwards towards the line of police.

'They'll have to make way. Get in and push the buggers,' Dic shouted.

'No, boy, watch it.'

A girl had fallen behind them, and was shouting that she was hurt. A very tall young man was calling over the heads of the police, in an authoritative upper-class accent:

'Who's in charge of your detachment? I want to know who's in charge. There are injured people here and I want to know who's in charge.'

His words were almost lost in renewed angry shouting from near the steps. The mounted police behind them had come closer and there was a further irresistible heave from the packed crowd. Gwyn found himself pushed close up against the line of police. He was less than a foot from the face of the young constable opposing him.

'I don't want to push into you,' he said breathlessly.

There was no change of expression or reply. Dic, behind him, held on firmly to his shoulders.

A tall, fair young woman, a couple of places along, was trying to argue with the police.

'Why don't you let us through? We can't go back and we're being pushed.'

'Yes, let the women through,' Dic shouted.

The young woman turned and looked angrily at him.

'I'm talking about all of us,' she cried.

Dic pushed forward close to her.

'You hear, copper,' he shouted. 'Let the women through.'

'Stop that,' the young woman shouted.

Dic looked at Gwyn, puzzled. Gwyn was now exerting all his strength, trying to hold back from being pushed into the police who were so close to him.

'I'm asking you reasonably,' the young woman said to the line of police. 'People are being crushed. You must let us through.'

She was directly facing a dark young constable, who like most of the others was saying nothing but simply standing close with linked arms.

'Please,' she said, and then shouted with pain.

She turned, white-faced.

'You stamped on my foot,' she said in amazement to the constable.

There was no expression on his face.

'You deliberately stamped on my foot.'

'Get out of it, girl, let me tell the bugger,' Dic shouted.

Faces along the police line hardened as Dic pushed forward.

'No, boy,' Gwyn called.

Dic had pushed himself in front of the young woman. In the press of bodies she was trying to look down at her sandalled foot. Dic was half a head taller than the dark young constable he now faced. He glared at him. Nothing was said.

Then there was high angry shouting behind them, and the sound of horses' hooves on the roadway. From another part of the crowd there was a loudly defiant chant. Voices took it up from all over the square, but there was again a sudden break as the crowd heaved. Those close against the police line were pushed relentlessly forward. Dic put his arm out to steady himself against the constable's shoulder. He pulled his arm back quickly.

'Once more,' the constable said quietly.

'Once more?' Dic repeated. 'Look, copper, if you want it you can have it, only don't stamp your bloody great feet on young women.'

'Leave it, it's all right,' the young woman said.

There was a sudden momentary silence, in their immediate area. Beyond the police lines there were vans drawing up, and somebody shouted that there were dogs. Gwyn eased himself sideways, and put his hand on Dic's arm. Dic swung round, aggressively, but then saw who it was.

'You see this bugger,' he said to Gwyn. 'He deliberately stamped on her foot.'

'We're all pushing and shoving,' Gwyn said.

'Deliberately,' Dic repeated. 'Look at him.'

There was again a pause, and then things happened so quickly that Gwyn was bewildered. On some signal that neither of them had noticed, the linking arms of the police immediately in front of them were dropped and three other policemen, in crash helmets, rushed through and grabbed Dic. Gwyn got his arm up to try to hold him but Dic, struggling, was quickly pulled through the line, which then, with linked arms, immediately reformed. Jumping to see over the heads of the line, Gwyn saw Dic being frogmarched to one of the waiting vans. He was thrown roughly inside.

'That's my brother you've got,' he shouted. 'Let me through.'

But the stolid line had reformed, as if nothing had happened. Gwyn felt sweat start all over him. He looked hopelessly around. Then he tried to make his way back through the crowd, to get out and find Dic.

People cursed as he tried to push through them. In the centre and near the steps the crowd had stabilised, and were shouting and chanting together. Gwyn pushed slowly on past them but then came to another ruck, where a very young crowd were pushed as he had been against a single line of police, with mounted police beyond them.

He jumped to look all around. It seemed that the whole demonstration was surrounded. Then there was a shout and people were running through a gap in the line where two constables had fallen. Gwyn ran with them. An arm reached for him, as he ran through, but he evaded it and was away.

He turned down a side street, away from the horses. When he had made his distance he stood getting his breath back. He tidied his hair and clothes, to be as respectable as possible when tracing Dic through what might be several police stations. Behind him, from the thousands in the square, the shouts of 'Victory!' still resounded.

# 3

### ❧❀❦

## LONDON, MARCH 1968

'It was no good,' Gwyn shouted angrily, while he was still pushing open the front door. 'I waited two hours and then . . .'

'It's all right,' Jill called, coming through from the kitchen. 'He's released.'

'What?'

'Yes, Emma rang up. Somebody paid his fine so they let him go.'

'Who paid it? I would have paid it but he told me not to. Did they ask him if they could pay it?'

Jill came close and put her hands on his shoulders.

'I don't know, love. Only what Emma said.'

'But she didn't say who?'

Jill laughed. She turned her face away, shyly.

'I think she did but you know how I am when she talks to me. I'm just back in school and like jelly.'

He put his arm across her back and held her close.

'Actually,' she said, 'it sounded like it was paid by a monkey.'

'Ah!'

'Does that make sense?'

'Probably. She has a friend called Pitter. The older ones call him Monkey though everyone else calls him Monk.'

'Well, just so long as I'm not going daft.'

'You going daft!'

'Oh and she said he's at her place. We can collect him whenever it's convenient.'

He caught her eye and she laughed again, helplessly. She said something that he could not make out through the laughing. Then she took a deep breath and said it again.

'Like a parcel!'

Gwyn smiled.

'Well, it is,' Jill said.

She turned. Lyn was coming downstairs, slowly, taking a step at a time.

'Careful, love,' Gwyn said.

'She's all right,' Jill said. 'In fact this morning she was showing me she could jump.'

'On the stairs? No, young lady, three is much too young to go jumping on stairs.'

'*You* run up them,' Lyn said. 'And down.'

'Aye but I'm old,' Gwyn said and went and stood below her.

She jumped into his arms and he swung her round.

'Are we going, then?' Lyn asked.

'What, for Dic?'

'Well, you know how it is with collecting parcels.'

'I haven't eaten.'

'Okay, but then we ought to go over.'

'We? Are you coming?'

'Of course we're coming. Aren't we, Lyn? We've been stuck waiting here all day.'

They ate bacon sandwiches in the kitchen and then set out. The traffic was thinning and the rain had stopped. Gwyn couldn't park anywhere near Emma's door and he had to carry Lyn as they walked back. The front of the house was newly painted, in grey, with a glossy light-blue front door. Jill pressed the bell.

Bill Wilkes, Emma's son, came to the door. Jill, standing a step below him, looked up and up.

'We're the Lewises,' Jill said. 'For Dic.'

Bill gazed down at her. He was so very tall that she could not help staring back. Lyn had turned her head into her father's shoulder. Bill looked at Gwyn and nodded.

'That's okay, come in.'

Jill turned to take Lyn, but she began struggling in Gwyn's arms before reaching out for her mother. She was looking apprehensively up at Bill and now began to cry.

'It's just with strangers,' Jill said.

'No,' Bill said. 'It's because I'm too tall. I often have that effect.'

'Not too tall,' Jill said, stroking Lyn's hair.

'Six six and a half,' Bill said. 'And yes it does cause problems.'

He stood aside. Jill went in, talking soothingly to Lyn, who was growing calmer. Gwyn followed and closed the door.

'They're all in the music room,' Bill said.

'All?'

'It's a general celebration, for all our hero-victims. Heroine-victims too, come to that.'

There was the sound of piano music from beyond the tall ground-floor door. Gwyn hesitated.

'We only came to fetch my brother.'

'Yes, Dic. You said. He's in there. In fact well away.'

Gwyn turned and moved away from him. Jill had taken Lyn to the stairs and was sitting on the lower step, talking quietly to her and wiping her face.

Gwyn had seen Bill only once, briefly, several years back, before he had gone up to Oxford. What had then been an adolescent face, curiously ugly and unformed, with heavy brows, a broad nose and a very large loose mouth, had now settled into hard crude features: primitive, Gwyn found himself thinking, though what that really meant he did not know. He had black, close-cropped hair and heavy black spectacles. In this as in most other ways he seemed very unlike Emma. His father, Georgi, Gwyn had heard a lot about but never seen even photographed.

'Right, then,' Bill said, seeing that Jill and Lyn were ready. He opened the door and bowed them in.

The buzz of conversation came first, with the piano music beyond it. The room was long, made by knocking down the wall between the old front and back rooms. At the far end, double glass doors opened on to a yard bright with daffodils. The walls were hung with a crimson flock paper. The fitted carpet was white. At three points along the ceiling hung small, glittering glass chandeliers.

There were some fifteen people in the room. Gwyn could not at first see Dic. His attention was caught by the man at the piano: a small, grey-haired, wrinkled-faced man, smiling up at a young woman as he played. Gwyn knew the piece as Debussy, one of the Preludes. Its freshness came curiously from the hunched player.

'Gwyn, my dear,' Emma said, coming forward and kissing him lightly on the cheek.

'Jill,' Gwyn said, half-turning.

'And Jill, how lovely.'

She bent to kiss Jill's cheek. Jill was still holding Lyn in her arms. Emma put out a finger towards the child's face. Lyn turned away, into her mother's neck.

'Now, who do you know?' Emma said. 'We're such a mixed lot, since events have brought us together.'

Gwyn was staring at a man he recognised: Alec Merritt. He was standing with a glass talking to a young woman with long black hair which almost covered her face. He was poised as he listened. His fawn denim suit was pulled in sharply at his waist.

'Well, Alec and Alex of course,' Emma said, and directed Gwyn and Jill forward.

As Bill crossed between them, carrying a bottle of red wine, Gwyn stared at the black-haired girl. That could not be her. Then as Alec Merritt moved he saw another woman who had been standing behind him. It was the young woman he had seen in the gallery. He felt a sudden breathlessness. She was draining her glass and then, though it was obviously empty, still trying to pour it into her mouth. As the black-haired girl laughed, Gwyn saw a bitter, contemptuous expression cross Alex's face. She was staring at her husband's long back.

'Alex dear,' Emma called, moving forward. 'And Alec. Look who's come. Gwyn Lewis and Jill.'

'Mr Lewis,' Alec said, turning and extending his hand.

'Dr Lewis, if you please,' Emma said.

'Sorry, Dr Lewis. My wife.'

He turned as if presenting Alex. She looked quickly at Gwyn

and held out her hand. It was hot and damp as he touched it.

'And Jill, did I hear?' Alec said easily. 'No more doctors?'

'No,' Jill said, still carrying Lyn. 'Just the nurse.'

Alec laughed happily. Alex looked again at her glass but then stepped forward to greet Jill. She looked affectionately at Lyn and spoke to her quietly.

'But will all ninety stick to it? Stick to forcing the leadership to change on Vietnam? Have they really got the guts?' the black-haired girl asked insistently.

'Ah yes, Marie, Gwyn,' Alec said quickly.

Marie nodded.

'I know *you* will,' she said, warmly, to Alec, throwing back her long hair. 'And perhaps a dozen others. But, on previous form, the rest . . .'

'Oh, come on,' Alec said, 'they're all pretty reliable. It's just this constant problem of loyalty to a Labour government.'

'To a government that's an accomplice in genocide?'

'Of course. But also to a government that still offers to embody the labour movement, the trade-union and working-class movements.'

'This is crap,' Marie said.

'Sure it's crap. They no longer embody even that. But it takes time for people to unhook themselves. Unhook themselves from old habits. Don't you think so, Gwyn?'

'If it was a matter of loyalty we'd be sticking to quite different people,' Gwyn said. 'Not to that gang in power.'

'Exactly,' Marie said. 'And Alec, really, only you . . .'

Gwyn let the words fade out. He was looking past Alec to Jill and Lyn. They had gone to sit on a deep sofa, and Alex had joined them and was leaning over, talking quietly to Jill. Gwyn breathed deeply. She looked older than when he had seen her in the gallery. Her face was more lined and strained. Beside Jill, with her plump red cheeks and springing dark hair, she looked tired and faded, though the face was still handsome and the clothes – a dark red suit – were elegant. Elegant and confident, he found himself shaping to say. But it was other words that pressed closer. My sister. Half-sister. Sister. It seemed, as always, impossible to believe. To know, to be convinced, to have no room for doubt, but not, as between brother and sister, to believe. Half-brother and half-sister. She seemed not even to know.

'Excuse me,' he said briefly to Alec, and walked away down the room.

He then saw Dic on another sofa: legs stretched out, head back, with a small, very pretty girl sitting by his head.

'There you are then, kid,' he said, crossing and standing above them.

'Big brother,' Dic laughed.

'You all right, then?'

'Aye, now.'

'Did they treat you all right?'

'In the gaol, aye. Though before, at the station, I had two buggers at me in the cell.'

'What sort of buggers?'

Dic laughed and then grinned at the girl.

'Not those buggers. Uniformed buggers.'

'Why didn't you say in court?'

'Because it was after the court. They're not daft, you know.'

'They're not all like that.'

Dic shook his head.

'If you say so. Only listen now, our Gwyn, you see Mitzi. This is Mitzi.'

'Hullo.'

'You just ask her, go on, what she was charged with.'

Gwyn hesitated. Dic and Mitzi smiled, looking up at him.

'Obstruction?'

'This little?' Mitzi said, pointing at herself.

'Breach of the peace?'

'No.'

'Give up?' Dic said.

'Yeah, give up.'

'Assaulting a police dog,' Dic said, and as he spoke, Mitzi joined in with the last words.

'I don't believe you.'

'Honest,' Mitzi said.

Gwyn shook his head.

'So what happened?'

'Well, they read it out in court,' Mitzi said, 'and then somebody in the gallery laughed. There was this old woman magis-
trate and she had a long look at me and said case dismissed.'

'I should think so. Was there really a dog?'

'Yes, an Alsatian. He came at me and I hit him with my
handbag.'

'You should have had me to look after you, girl,' Dic said.

'No thanks.'

Gwyn waited. He heard the piano. It was still Debussy.

'You okay, then? About coming back?' he asked Dic.

'Yes, I'm very comfortable.'

'Only Jill and Lyn come with me, I don't want to keep them
too long.'

'I can get back on my own.'

'Aye. Well I'll ask again before we go.'

He walked on down the room. He had seen Mark Ryder by
the piano. He now recognised the piece: 'Sounds and Scents of
Evening'. The grey, hunched man was playing it very softly. His
long fingers were delicate. Mark nodded to Gwyn, and they
stood together watching the playing.

'So!' Monkey said, turning from the keyboard as he ended
the piece, and smiling up at Mark.

'That was delightful, Monkey,' Mark said.

'Yes. Of course. It comes from my innate gentleness.'

He was looking interestedly up at Gwyn.

'You've not met?' Mark said.

'No,' Gwyn said quickly.

'This is Gwyn, Monkey. Gwyn Lewis,' Mark said, carefully.

'Whom I have known all his life,' Monkey said, and smiled.

'You know nobody, Monkey,' Mark said. 'You only know of
them.'

'Such a tired little distinction,' Monkey said, stretching his
fingers. 'And from a historian so pathetically self-cancelling.'

Gwyn moved across.

'I may be wrong, Mr Pitter,' he said, 'but I believe I have to
thank you for paying my brother's fine.'

'Your brother? Who is that?'

'Dic. Dic Lewis. He's over there on the sofa.'

Monkey turned and looked.

'Ah yes, with the little girl who assaulted the dog.'

'I offered to pay it myself but he made it very clear that he didn't want it paid.'

'There were several who said that. But with the young there must always be someone to ease them off the hook of their conscience. So reckless they can be, at that age.'

'Well anyway, I'm sure you intended to act generously.'

Monkey nodded to Mark, as if in approval of some performance.

'It's very good of you to say so,' he beamed up at Gwyn. 'But for the health of the social order somebody has got to finance heresy. And in the matter of generosity, and things of that kind, it is often easier to take from a stranger than from a brother, or even a half-brother.'

'Play something, Monkey,' Mark said heavily.

Monkey's eyes were shining.

'Well, perhaps. But all this simple beauty has been, as you see, disregarded. Perhaps I should have struck up one of those rousing songs.'

'Yes, Monk, please,' came another voice.

A tall, fair girl had come up behind them. She was holding hands with a young man.

'Yes indeed, sir,' the young man said.

Gwyn glanced at him. He looked remarkably like the young American who had been lying on the pavement outside the gallery.

'Do you know "The Family of Man"?' the girl asked.

'Intimately,' Monkey said.

Suddenly Emma was there, and he turned to her.

'These young people are asking me for political songs, Emma. But I wouldn't abuse your hospitality.'

'There's always been politics in this house, Monkey.'

'But that's my point, dear. Politics of a certain colour, which unless I'm mistaken isn't being worn this season.'

'If you mean the Party, you're being ridiculous.'

'Am I? But I have the strong impression that a gravely weakened Party is now tagging along behind any column it sees moving: Trotskyites, Anarchists, Flower Children, New Left.'

Emma glared at him.

'You've been out of the country, Monkey. You don't understand. Nobody is tagging along behind anybody else. This is a broad, spontaneous, voluntary movement.'

'Oh dear,' Monkey said.

'There are differences,' Emma said, 'but in many ways it's just like the late Thirties and the Popular Front.'

'Not in any way,' Mark said.

'And if it were,' Monkey said, 'we'd all have to pray that it wouldn't end so badly.'

'What do you mean, ended badly?' Emma said, indignantly.

'Mark's the historian. Ask him.'

'It would take too long,' Mark said.

'When he writes his history of Spain, for example.'

'I'm not writing one.'

'You will, Mark, you will. When all the truth comes out. When we have all the facts about our Russian friends there.'

'This is just Cold War rubbish,' Emma said, angrily. 'Stuff you've picked up in New York.'

'No,' Monkey said. 'I picked it up from the Russians who survived it. Some of them indeed in New York. And telling tales, Emma, about what they did and who they worked with.'

'That's all very old stuff,' Gwyn said sharply.

Monkey looked up at him, curiously. Then he nodded, as if in approval.

'In any case, Emma,' he said, brightly, 'the main difference should be obvious, to anyone who really knows the Party. In the Thirties a Trotskyite was a skunk or worse. But now, even tonight in this room, I'll bet you at any level there are more of them than of us. And you're even pretending to like it.'

'You're impossible, Monkey. You're just living in the past.'

'It's a result of watching the young. Watching their bright faces in the same confident errors.'

Mark intervened, impatiently.

'This is just depressing. Both of you. This is a celebration, isn't it? So more music, Monkey.'

Monkey turned back on the stool.

'There is one song.'

'Great!' said the young American.

'Completed by myself, more in anger than in sorrow. But

political, and singable. I stole the tune, as seemed only appropri-
ate, from "The Lincolnshire Poacher".'

'Not that,' Emma said.

'Yes, please,' said the girl.

Monkey struck a chord. He looked round as if at a public
performance.

'*When* . . .' he sang, in a deep, clear voice.

Several people stopped talking to listen.

> '*When Trotsky trotted his droshky down the Kingsky Prospekt
> wide*
> *The Party had a "crise de coeur" and withdrew to the Whim to
> hide* . . .'

Emma had walked away, angrily, but other people had come
closer.

> '*They called the Secretariat, to consider what to do,*
> *But first they ordered some Moka and a chocolate sponge or
> two.*'

Mark laughed. Gwyn looked at him, puzzled, as if by some
private joke.

> '*Some said: "We'll just ignore him, the fellow must just be cut;*
> *He's down in the dustbin of history, the lid must be quietly shut."*
> *But others were all for action, their faces were raw and red.*
> *They said: "We must not only cut him, we must cut the bastard
> dead."*

> '*One very vulgar fraction proposed to throw a bomb.*
> *But the Party was out of dynamite, and the shock troops lacked
> aplomb.*
> *Then up stood Comrade Chamberlayne* . . .'

As he sang the name, Monkey turned from the piano, beaming.

'Chamberlain?' Mark protested.

'No relation,' Monkey said, smiling.

> '*Then up stood Comrade Chamberlayne and showed them the
> way to go,*
> *They must all go out in the streets and cheer and pretend it was
> Uncle Joe.*'

For the first time there was a general laugh. Hearing it, other people converged on the piano, among them the tall figure of Bill Wilkes. Monkey savoured his audience, timing his pause.

'So . . . *that is just what happened, as Trotsky trotted by.*
*They made quite a demonstration, though nobody else knew*
*why.*'

There was again a loud laugh, and Monkey waited before moving to a much more rapid pace.

'*But it's nothing to the hullabaloo and the awful bloody row*
*When Trotsky trots his droshky down the Kingsky Prospekt*
*now.*'

Other voices took up the last rising '*now*', and then there was loud clapping. Monkey stood from the piano and bowed.

'Monk, sir, you missed your profession,' said the young American.

'My two professions,' Monkey said, smiling. 'I was also the best computer designer in the free world.'

'But then renounced it all,' came Bill Wilkes's deep voice, 'just for the love of money.'

'As you say,' Monkey replied. 'For that precise passion.'

People were moving around uncertainly. The party seemed likely to break up. Emma clapped her hands.

'People! People! There'll be food very shortly. I'll just go up and see Mrs Mansell.'

New groups formed. Bill came over and talked earnestly to Mark. Gwyn, finding himself alone, looked along the room. Dic was still with Mitzi. They were close on the sofa. They had not got up for the singing. Two men moved and Gwyn saw at the far end of the room Jill and Alex still sitting together, with Lyn between them. They were talking quietly. Alec Merritt and the girl he had been talking to seemed to have gone.

There was a gentle touch at his elbow. He turned to see Monkey Pitter. He looked different, suddenly, standing with his left hand holding his right wrist, his body small and vulnerable, his face deeply lined.

'A word, Gwyn, if I might.'

'Of course.'

'You must forgive my public performance.'

'There's nothing to forgive.'

'If that were only true.'

He held tightly to Gwyn's arm and guided him towards chairs by the glass doors to the yard. They sat facing away from the room. In the centre of the courtyard there was a big tub of daffodils. There were still drops of rain on the yellow trumpets and the leaves.

'You know Norman has retired,' Monkey said, quietly.

'Norman Braose?'

'Don't spell it all out, Gwyn. And don't think I'm fishing. I know the whole story. I have often felt for you.'

'Yes. Thank you. But given the way it went, it concerns me very little.'

'I hoped you might think that. If you mean it,' Monkey said.

Gwyn found himself being examined by very deep brown eyes, enlarged behind the thick lenses of the heavy spectacles.

'I mean it.'

'Good. Then consider this. He has now retired. Full of years and dishonour.'

Gwyn looked at him, startled. The lined face was very serious.

'You say that about your friend!'

'Yes. Who but a friend is in a position to say it?'

'But still what you're saying is ridiculous. I was told he'd retired, but in that kind of work they often retire early. He had his knighthood five years ago. He has his comfortable pension. So neither years nor dishonour.'

Monkey took off his glasses and polished them on his cuff. Gwyn noticed for the first time the fine silk shirt.

'You're very trusting,' Monkey said.

Gwyn looked more closely at him. With the glasses off the eyes looked weak and raw.

'No. Not really.'

'But you are, Gwyn. You accept these public accounts.'

'Should I not accept them?'

'It depends. You said it was not your concern.'

'Not my personal concern. I have had a quite different father.'

'Of course. And your mother. Whom in fact he loved.'

'Then why did he desert her?'

Monkey replaced his glasses. He inspected Gwyn again.

'I joke with these people back there,' he said. 'But under the jokes I am saying something about the politics. Something they still don't want to hear.'

Gwyn hesitated.

'Is that your answer to my question?' he asked, facing him.

'It is the basis of my answer. He was a most dedicated communist.'

'Braose!'

'Certainly.'

'Well, in some adolescent phase, maybe. The usual public schoolboy revolutionary.'

'Yes, that too. To begin with.'

'But in fact he didn't go on with it. Not as my father did. Not as Emma did.'

'I accept Bert Lewis.'

'But not Emma?'

'Emma is sincere. But for her it is social work. She has never left her own class.'

'And Braose has, I suppose!'

Monkey sighed. He turned and looked back along the crowded room. His eyes rested on several men. Gwyn waited.

'Do you know that young American?' Monkey asked.

'No, though I might have seen him once before. At the gallery where my mother's pictures were exhibited.'

'Yes, I'm sorry I missed that.'

He continued to stare at the young American. Gwyn became embarrassed. It was some time before Monkey withdrew his close attention.

'I have a reputation for rudeness, among so many other vices,' Monkey said, with a trace of his ordinary speaking for effect.

'Yes, I got a few vague hints.'

'That's indeed what you got. But this now is the rudeness, since I have no possible right to say it. When I said that I have known you all your life I was not joking. Your life, I mean, has been there all the time as a central, an essential fact. But what I have further to say is what you do not yet know: that you have been deprived of your history.'

'I don't agree. My mother was very honest about it.'

'About herself, of course, and as far as she knew. But let me put it in this way. You have been deprived not only of your natural father but of what he was doing and has done.'

'I don't understand.'

'That's just what I'm saying. But I would like you to believe that it has been heroic in its way.'

Gwyn stared, open-mouthed. He barely heard Emma clapping her hands again and directing her guests upstairs for food. Monkey sat quite still, watching him, but then Emma noticed them.

'What are you two talking about, then?' she asked briskly.

Gwyn was disturbed by her voice.

'Come on, you two,' she called, impatiently.

Monkey touched Gwyn's arm and they got up.

# 4

❧❀❧

## DANYCAPEL, OCTOBER 1968

'Here's Gwyn come,' Pattie shouted.

Nesta, wiping her hands on a teacloth, hurried along the
passage and reached up to kiss Gwyn on the cheek.

'How is he?' Gwyn asked.

Nesta put her finger on her lips.

'Oh he's a lot better,' she said, lifting her voice. 'The trouble
now is just keeping him in bed.'

Pattie smiled and pointed upstairs. Gwyn nodded. It seemed
always to be like this when Pattie was around. The plump girl
who had married Nesta's brother Jim was now, in her late
forties, fat and lively: always, it seemed, up to one of what she
called her games: often in the form of 'not letting on' about
something which she had decided might upset someone.

'Have you seen his lovely car?' she said to Nesta.

'No.'

Gwyn could see how worried his mother actually was. He
watched her hesitate and then make up her mind.

'Can you stay a bit longer, Pattie?'

'As long as you like, Nes.'

'Only Gwen will be home in an hour. If Gwyn, now, could
run me down to the shops, it'd be a real help.'

Pattie laughed.

'See what it is, Gwyn? Once she hears about this lovely car
of yours she wants a ride in it.'

'It's just an ordinary car, Auntie. And if Mam's got shopping . . .'

'Get away with you, boy. She's still like these bits of girls. If they saw King Kong on one of those big motorbikes they'd flip up their skirts and hop on.'

'Catch me,' Nesta said, 'I'm respectable.'

She fetched her coat and came back quickly. She took Gwyn's hand.

'Back soon, love. Pattie's here,' she called up the stairs.

There was a distant gruff 'Aye' from the front bedroom, where the door stood wide open.

They went out to the car. There was a late, golden light along the whole eastern side of the valley. The steeper western side was black, with a sharp hard line at the ridge. Down the crowded bed of the valley there was drifting black smoke, from a fire on waste ground behind a garage, and along the line of the river thin swathes of early autumn mist.

Nesta did not speak until they were in the car, and even then she glanced nervously back at the house.

'Best drive on round the corner.'

'Which shops do you want?'

'Never mind the shops. Gwen's bringing all that.'

'Then why are we here?'

'Round the corner,' she repeated.

Gwyn drove on and pulled in to a bus-stop.

'What's all this mystery?' he asked, pulling the handbrake even tighter.

Nesta patted his arm.

'Don't get ratty, now. Only you can't say nothing, in the house, without him hearing it.'

'What wouldn't you want him to hear?'

'How ill he is, Gwyn.'

Her voice changed as she spoke. Tears had started into the corners of her eyes.

'Well, I knew that. From what Gwen said on the phone.'

'Aye, the chest infection, that's all they thought it was. But they're giving him drugs for that.'

'What, then?'

Nesta hesitated. Tears were now rolling down her cheeks.

'It's his heart, Gwyn. When the doctor was examining him, it showed up. There's still got to be tests, mind. They'll have him in hospital once the chest is cleared up. But the doctor come to me in the kitchen and asked whether he had any history of it.'

'Heart trouble?'

'I told him no, not that I ever knew of. But he said there must be and then he started asking about his face.'

'It couldn't be that. It's much too long ago.'

Nesta waited, looking hopefully at him.

'Do you really think so, Gwyn?'

'Well, I don't *know*. But it's twenty-four years. And it was never mentioned, was it?'

'No, though they push all these names at you; you know how it is.'

'But still he's never complained of it?'

'Him! Complain!'

The low October sun, now just touching the dark western ridge, was blurred and refracted on the rain-stained windscreen, above the arcs which the wipers had cleared. Street lights were coming on, in the valley below.

'I know nothing, that's my trouble,' Nesta said, suddenly.

Gwyn waited.

'There must be words,' she said, brokenly. 'Words somebody knows. To say what I feel.'

'About him?'

'Well, that's obvious. I don't mean that. I mean to say what I feel of him. What I know has happened to him.'

'You mean the damage from the war?'

'Well, we can all see that, on his face and then his limping. But it isn't only that sort of damage.'

'Disappointment, do you mean? A sadness that it happened to him?'

'Of course it is, but he don't listen to that. He's a man that's always carried things, his own share and some of the rest. And he'll go on carrying, and not notice any of it till after he's dropped.'

Gwyn was silent for some time.

'Yes, but what can we take off him? What load, Mam? What share of the load?'

'Oh you can't, Gwyn, no.'

'If it's money . . .'

'It isn't money. He never asked for much.'

Gwyn smiled, sadly.

'What is it?' Nesta asked.

He rested his hands on the wheel.

'I live in the wrong place, Mam. I was smiling to think of him as they would think of him in London: as one of these aggressive militants, these subversive and greedy communist workers.'

'They don't know Bert up there. I don't know what you mean.'

'That's because you live in the right place.'

'Here?' Nesta said, pushing her hand towards the valley, which was now rapidly darkening, with lights springing along it.

'Among people,' Gwyn said, 'who don't need it explained.'

'Well, that's where you're wrong, Gwyn. You give us too much credit. We don't understand hardly one thing that's happening to us, and them that make out they do are just in it for themselves.'

'Politicians and parsons?'

'More than them.'

'Who, then?'

'Well, like you saying we understand. I don't understand. Bert don't understand. All you can say is we stick by each other.'

Gwyn put his hand on her arm.

'But that's saying everything, Mam.'

'No, it isn't. You're just talking like Emma. That's all we get, whenever she comes here. How we're the real life. How we really understand things. How much stronger she feels when she's been here.'

'It's her politics, that's all. There's only a few places she can still hang on to her simple beliefs.'

'Well, I don't mind that. Good for her. Only saying we understand things, she says it but that's all. Whenever she comes, it's just to tell us we do.'

Gwyn sighed but did not answer. Nesta pulled her arms tightly folded in her lap. A bus passed, up the hill. The engine was burning oil and the smell hung in the air, penetrating the car.

'You'll see it when you talk to him,' Nesta said. 'Something's broken. Something's old and broken. If it was a machine you could put your hand on it.'

'Perhaps these tests in the hospital . . .'

'Well, of course. Only don't say nothing about that. All he knows is the chest trouble.'

'Right.'

She unfolded her arms. She looked across at him uncertainly. She took out a handkerchief and carefully wiped her face.

'Just one more thing.'

'Yes?'

'Try not to talk about . . . well, you know. Emma.'

'He usually asks about her.'

'Yes he does but I don't just mean Emma. I mean all that side of it.'

'The politics?'

'No, not the politics. He takes that like syrup.'

'What, then?'

'All that other side of it, Gwyn. Your side of it.'

'My side?'

She moved impatiently.

'Don't drag it out of me, Gwyn. Those people we saw in the gallery.'

'Braose and his daughter? Alex Merritt?'

'I know who they were.'

'Well, of course you do.'

'I don't want your Dad having to carry any more of that.'

'Of course not.'

'It was my fault with the pictures. Only Medical Aid to Vietnam, that's good. It was Medical Aid to Spain, when we was at that farm. And then it's all back into it again.'

Gwyn waited. A burst of heavier rain was now blurring the windscreen.

'It upset you, of course, Mam, seeing Braose.'

'I don't know about that. All I know is it upset your Dad.'

'You mean Bert?'

'Well of course I mean Bert.'

'But, Mam, you've always told me . . .'

She looked angrily across at him. Her eyes were very large.

'Don't be daft, now, Gwyn. Of course Bert is just your

adopting father. But I'll tell you something else. He's been the only real father you've had.'

'I don't need telling that, Mam.'

'All right. So don't upset him.'

'I'll try not to. But did you tell him you'd seen Braose?'

'No, I didn't. Of course I didn't.'

'Then how could it have upset him?'

Nesta stared at Gwyn. She was still angry but there was now also a hopelessness. How could she ever make him understand things? Couldn't he see that when people were really living together what passed between them was much more than the words? She opened the door, as if to get out of the car. Then she changed her mind and slammed it shut.

'Drive back now.'

'Yes, of course.'

He turned the car on the hill. There was more traffic now, and he had to wait for some time. But he did not speak again. He had reached some point, with his mother, where he could go no further, where he dared go no further.

There were lights in the front bedroom when he pulled in again. Bert had made a white plank fence at the edge of the pavement and planted a bed of different-coloured heathers above it.

'You can go straight up,' Nesta said.

'Right.'

He hung up his coat and walked quickly upstairs. The door to the front bedroom was ajar. He knocked quietly.

'Who's that? Dic?'

'No, Dad, it's Gwyn.'

Bert was lying propped on pillows on the single bed furthest from the window. He had bright red pyjamas buttoned to his neck and a yellow plaid shawl around his shoulders. He was wearing reading glasses but watching the television set in the corner by the window. There was a cartoon, with the sound off.

Bert held out his hand.

'Glad to see you, boy.'

'And you, Dad.'

'Only I thought just now I heard Dic. I heard the car come.'

'That was me.'

'No, you just come. There was another car, drove up and then off.'

'That was me too. I took Mam down the hill.'

'Aye.'

Bert's eyes moved back to the cartoon. Gwyn sat on the edge of the other bed and turned to watch it. Bert laughed.

'Only you know what he's been up to?'

Gwyn thought for a moment that Bert meant the bear in the cartoon. He turned and smiled, sharing the enjoyment of the chase.

'They bust in on the Labour conference,' Bert said, smiling.

'Well, I heard that. And that it was miners.'

'It was our boys in the front of them. Dic rang up and told our Gwen.'

'Demonstrating against the closures?'

'Aye, that and all the rest of it. They didn't mean to, mind, they just went there to picket, and they'd got some bit of a leaflet. But then they thought bugger it, that lot in there, and in they went and stopped the session.'

'Well, I know how they feel.'

'No, you don't, boy. You got to be here to feel it. Look at this valley now: two pits left from seven. And if we don't fight the buggers there'll soon be none.'

'I thought Three Cocks was all right for ever. Well, I know that, I saw the geological report.'

'Down to the one, you mean? Rationalisation.'

'No, Dad, I didn't mean that.'

'You talk to Dic when he's back. He'll tell you. He'll be back tonight, certain.'

His last words were hoarse and brought on a fit of coughing. His eyes flooded with tears. He pulled off his glasses. The damaged flesh of the hanging eye was an ugly dark red.

Gwyn waited until the coughing eased. The little table between the beds was covered with jars and bottles and packets of medicine.

'Can I get you anything, Dad?'

'What's that?'

'Any medicine?'

Bert wiped his eyes and looked hard at Gwyn. It was as if, still, he was surprised to be seeing him.

'Well aye, a spoon of that linctus.'

Gwyn sorted among the bottles.

'This one?'

Bert moved impatiently. Gwyn found a spoon and poured the dark sticky liquid.

'Come on, then.'

Bert waited. Gwyn leaned forward and put his left hand on Bert's shoulder, among the folds of the yellow shawl.

'Open wide.'

Bert smiled. He had his teeth out. The inside of the mouth was a soft pink, against the dark stubble above the lip and on the chin. Gwyn carefully inserted the spoon. Bert lapped it clean.

'Thanks, boy.'

'No bother.'

The television screen had changed to a nature film. Three fox cubs were playing at hunting: running and twisting, mouths snapping at head and neck.

'While you're here,' Bert said.

'I'm sorry?'

'While you're here, I said, there's something I want you to have.'

'Never mind that now, Dad.'

'But I do mind it. There's a grey cardboard box, can you see it, on top of the wardrobe?'

Gwyn looked up. He could just see its edge.

'Give it down to me here.'

Gwyn went and reached down the box. It was thick with dust. He went to the open door and brushed it off with his fingers, then blew at it.

'Aye, it's been a long time,' Bert said.

'What is it?'

'Give it me here.'

He took the box between his large hands. His knuckles were white and swollen, standing out on the discoloured rough skin.

'There. See?'

A large pair of binoculars lay on cotton wool in the box. Bert began fingering the strap.

'Are they yours?' Gwyn asked. 'I've never seen them.'

'No. I put all that kind of thing away.'

'From the war, are they?'

'No, not the war. They're much too good for them to give us in the war.'

'What, then?'

Bert pulled at the strap and held the binoculars flat in his palms.

'They're German glasses. The best.'

'Did you take them from the Germans?'

'No. They belonged to a boy from Cambridge. Paul he was called. Paul Howe.'

'How did they come to you, then?'

Bert turned the binoculars and gripped the long black barrels. He looked up at Gwyn. His damaged eye was almost closed.

'I want you, Gwyn, to hold on to these glasses. They come to me the year you was born. He was a boy of eighteen, nineteen. Straight from Cambridge. He'd never done anything hard in his life.'

'It was in Spain, was it?'

'In Spain. His mother had given him the glasses. He was killed there in front of me. I've had them ever since.'

'Paul Howe, you say?'

'Aye, that was his name. There's now two of us remembering him.'

'Perhaps there are others.'

'Aye I expect his family. His Mam didn't want him to go. It was all very hard.'

Bert moved in the bed. He winced as pain shot through his knee.

'Can I get you comfortable?' Gwyn asked, anxiously.

Bert leaned back on his pillows.

'I want you to keep these glasses,' he said. 'I want you to remember what a communist was like.'

'Remember? I don't need reminding.'

'Perhaps you do, perhaps you don't. But I read, you know, and I listen. I know what they think of us.'

'That's always so in politics.'

'Aye, politics! That's all they make of it. But this was a boy getting killed. If that mortar hadn't got him he'd be a man coming fifty. He'd be walking around to take part in their discussions.'

There was a long silence.

'The year you was born,' Bert repeated.

'Yes.'

'I took them with me, over to Normandie. I looked through them from old Cossack trying to see that bloody Death's Head.'

'Death's Head?'

'*SS Totenkopf*. They told me that's what it means.'

'When you were wounded?'

'Aye. More bloody fool me.'

He turned his head on the pillows. The damaged eye was now in shadow. He was breathing hard. Gwyn stayed silent, hoping he would rest or even sleep.

'Only when I was in that fight with the scabs down Bettws,' the hoarse voice came again.

'Rest now a bit, Dad.'

'Old Vanny Prosser it was, an old chap of sixty. And he give me this pick handle, a dirty old thing, and he said he'd had it against the horses, 1910, 1911.'

'Horses?'

'Police horses.'

'So why did he give it to you?'

'He didn't say. He just give it me.'

'So you could use it?'

'No, no, we had plenty of picks.'

'What did you think, then?'

'I didn't. At that age you don't.'

He rolled again on the pillows. He felt for the binoculars and grasped them.

'You'll know better than me,' he said, with his eyes closed, 'but I don't reckon much to this memory they call history.'

'Why's that?'

'History, I don't know. Your aunt Emma's always saying it. Only what I've noticed is you get this story, this record, this account they call it. And of course you can soon take it in. Aye that was Tonypandy. That was Bettws. That was Spain. That was Normandie. You know it all, you know what I mean?'

'Aye.'

'And you know nothing. Like a birth certificate, or a diary. Accurate, granted . . .'

'Not always even that.'

'Aye but still when it is you know what it means you to know. And it still isn't none of it what it was. That was why old Vanny give me the pick handle.'

'To feel it? Through the actual thing?'

Bert sighed.

'Aye. I suppose that's what he meant.'

'And did you?'

Bert opened his eyes.

'No. Not then.'

'And the glasses?'

'I expect so. I mean I can feel it, but it isn't in them.'

'It is now you've told me.'

Bert smiled.

'I'm glad to hear you say that.'

'Well, I mean it.'

'That's all right, then. Only when your Mam come back, from showing her paintings in London . . .'

Gwyn sat up stiffly. Bert noticed the movement and stopped. Gwyn felt the pressure in the room. He did not trust himself to speak.

'We told you, fair and square,' Bert said, deliberately, 'once you was old enough to know.'

'It's all right, Dad. It isn't a problem.'

'She was crying about you, that time she come back. I don't know what you'd said to her.'

'There was nothing. We'd had a good time.'

'You may think so but I know better. She was crying about you like she was when I first come back.'

'Come back from where, Dad?'

'From Spain.'

The nature film had ended. It was the beginning of the News.

'You know what I wanted?' Bert said, suddenly.

'No?'

'I wanted you never to know.'

He turned with an effort, and stared at Gwyn. His damaged eye was a dark hollow.

'But, Dad, I would have been bound to. Later.'

'Because you was born before we was married? That happens all over. Nobody would ever have thought twice of it.'

'But still you didn't arrange it like that.'

'Your Mam wouldn't have it.'

'Did she give any reason?'

'Yes, she did. She said she'd stick by the truth.'

'It would have come out anyway. With the adoption. And it's on the birth certificate.'

'There's lots of things on paper. It's what we believe matters.'

Gwyn moved his hands and linked his fingers. Bert spoke again, harshly.

'And it could have been that. When he come down here he tried to make out you was mine.'

Gwyn looked up, holding his breath.

'Even Emma tried that,' Bert went on, angrily.

Gwyn forced himself to speak.

'So Mam had to stick to the truth, Dad. To protect you.'

'Protect! No, boy. She *wanted* you to know.'

'Why, then?'

Bert hesitated. When he spoke his voice was again hoarse and tired.

'It would take us too far.'

'How take us too far?'

'Into what we was, with people like that.'

Gwyn looked down. He thought for some time.

'But is it really that?' he asked, quietly. 'I respect her, you know I do. Love and respect her. But she was still so very young. That sort of thing happens. It's hard to say but almost anybody would say it. Just an adolescent affair.'

'No. Don't you ever talk like that.'

'I'm trying not to talk like that. Do you think I don't feel it? But I'm trying to be objective about it. Just to understand how it happened.'

'How it happened was not what you call an affair. I knew her, didn't I? She was not like that.'

'I don't mean it as wrong.'

Bert knotted his hands on the sheet.

'It was real, believe me. And it was to be kept going.'

'I don't understand.'

'Kept going in you. By you knowing who you was.'

Gwyn held his look for a moment, and then had to turn away.

'And by letting Emma come and watch over you,' Bert went on, harshly. 'To turn up when you was ready and get you back to Cambridge where you belonged.'

Gwyn leaned forward, angrily.

'No, Dad, I've never seen it like that.'

Bert pulled at the sheet. He was coughing again.

'Take these back with you,' he said quickly, and thrust out the binoculars.

'Of course, Dad, if you want.'

He reached out and took the binoculars.

'It was how it was all done, Gwyn. You can't deny that.'

'Yes, perhaps, but it wasn't what *I* did.'

'So you say.'

'As for Emma, she came just as much to see you.'

'Did she?'

'Well, of course. For the Party.'

'You think that?'

'You always said so, didn't you? And that the Party was your life.'

Bert leaned forward, clearing his throat. When he sat up again, there was loose spittle on his lips.

'That's what I meant, boy,' he said with an effort. 'That it would take us too far.'

'I don't understand.'

'Well, we used to think we needed them. The runaways.'

'Runaways?'

'Runaways from their class. Isn't that what they were doing?'

'And you didn't want them?'

'Yes, we did but still they used us.'

'Not all of them, surely?'

'I only know where we fetched up.'

'It's been difficult all through.'

'Difficult, aye.'

He pushed himself up on the pillows. He closed his fist on the yellow shawl.

'You talk to Dic,' he said harshly. 'He'll tell you. Like we know now we got to do it by ourselves.'

'Yes. But because it's very difficult we all still need help.'

Bert struck his fist on the bed.

'Aye, from that Pitter on the Stock Exchange! From that Braose in the government spy place!'

He stopped suddenly. Gwyn stared and then looked round. Nesta was standing very still in the open doorway. Neither man had heard her coming. She looked across at them for some moments, without speaking.

'You all right, girl?' Bert asked, in a softer voice.

'Me?' Nesta said. 'There's nothing the matter with me. Only we cooked the supper. Gwen's bringing it up. And Gwyn must come down and have his.'

'We've had a good talk, Gwyn and me,' Bert said, and smiled.

'Aye, I heard a bit of it.'

She was very pale. She had tied her long hair back at the neck, in a thin yellow scarf. Her eyes were unusually large.

'Come on, Gwyn, then.'

'Yes, Mam.'

'And Dic will be in about eleven,' she said quickly to Bert, going over and rearranging his bed. 'He rung up Gwen at the school. They're back in Ponty only they've stopped to report.'

Bert smiled at her.

'Aye and a drink, I expect. They deserve it.'

'That's right,' Nesta said.

She came back towards the door and stood waiting for Gwyn to go out.

# 5

❧ ❦❧ ❧

# LONDON, DECEMBER 1968

'Ah Gwyn, you've come to see Norman.'

'That's right.'

Bill stood filling the doorway of Emma's London house. Gwyn stared up at the large cropped head and the heavy black spectacles. The big mouth had moved into what was perhaps a welcoming smile but which from its cast, and the big teeth, suggested also a grimace. The wait on the doorstep lasted some seconds beyond the conventional delay.

'Come in, then, why don't you? He's up in Emma's sitting-room.'

'Is your mother here?'

'No, she's working. I thought she would have told you.'

'Yes she did, actually, when she rang.'

'So no problem?'

It was perhaps only Bill's great height, and the ambiguity of the smile, which suggested an edge of contempt. It was a manner Gwyn had noticed whenever Bill was speaking to others. But then it had seemed habitual: a rougher version of Emma's unforced assumption that she was right. Ten years older than Bill, Gwyn felt himself placed in a position of being observed and corrected. He thought, by some connection, of Mark, with whom he had been in that formal relationship; yet from that abstracted, self-hiding, self-determined man there had never at any time been any edge of rebuke.

'Can I find my own way up?'

'Can you? The first door on the right from the landing.'

'I have been up before.'

'Then I'll leave you to it.'

He walked slowly up the crimson-and-white staircase. It was odd and wrong to be preoccupied by Bill when he was moving inevitably towards this strange encounter with Braose. Yet his mind could not pull away from it.

There was great force in Bill Wilkes, over and above his manner. It had been no surprise that he had done brilliantly in his Finals and that there was already talk of a research fellowship. His was the justified assurance, at least in his case justified, of a settled, achieving intellectual caste.

He stopped and breathed out heavily. He must bring his mind back to what really concerned him. The sitting-room door ahead of him was closed. On the landing, he now noticed, was a framed poster of the Partisan exhibition, with Nesta's green, inward-facing heads of miners. His eyes moved back to it as he knocked quietly at the door.

There was no reply. He half-opened the door and looked in. A man was sitting in the pool of light from a reading lamp, a heavy volume propped on his knees. Relaxed in a pale fawn cardigan and open-necked light-blue shirt he seemed more slight, more frail than the confident figure Gwyn had seen strolling, ten months ago, in the gallery. The lean handsome face, under the loose fair hair, was immediately recognisable from the resemblance to Emma. There was a frown of concentration in the attention to the book.

Gwyn hesitated and then pushed the door wider. He stepped into the room and waited. The man suddenly looked up. There was now a different kind of attention in the face: not the outward-moving scrutiny of print but a sharp, inward-directed concentration of faculties.

'Dr Lewis?'

'Yes.'

'Gwyn?'

'Yes.'

There was a silence, while they looked at each other. Then Norman looked away as he carefully turned his book over and laid it face down on the carpet beside his chair.

'I have some back trouble. Forgive me for not getting up.'

'That's perfectly all right.'

'Do sit down yourself.'

'Thank you.'

There was another wait. Norman smiled and looked across.

'You've been here before, I suppose?'

'A few times.'

'Yes, of course, you've seen Emma so often.'

'Yes.'

'I've always heard about you from her.'

'Yes.'

Norman lit a cigarette, from a black packet. Gwyn watched the short, red-tipped match spurt and flare.

'Do you?' Norman asked, holding out the packet.

'No. Thanks.'

Norman inhaled deeply and seemed to gather strength.

'Where are you now?' he asked, confidently.

'At work, you mean?'

'Yes.'

'I'm at Stockwell.'

'Ah yes. That's good. I've always heard it spoken well of.'

Gwyn stayed still and spoke formally.

'I was with the Coal Board but with this closure programme I found too many contradictions.'

'Of what kind?'

'Well, centred on just one. On what I could report, scientifically, as a geologist, and what I knew, more generally, as the issues.'

'Of course. And how did you resolve that?'

'By leaving, I suppose.'

Norman smiled.

'It's a familiar kind of problem. For the few of real conscience.'

'Well, at least I didn't go to the oil industry. Which is where the real money is.'

'Of course. And in the circumstances I'd say Stockwell is the entirely correct decision.'

'Thank you.'

The atmosphere was now easier. It was like the more informal kind of work interview. Gwyn held himself carefully to that.

'Of course, stupid of me,' Norman said suddenly.

'I'm sorry?'

'I was so sad to hear that Bert Lewis had died.'

'Yes.'

Norman looked at him sharply. Gwyn waited.

'I believe, you know, that we are still getting casualties, from those terrible years.'

'From the war?' Gwyn prompted.

'Yes, the war, but also all that went before it. For men like Bert Lewis the war began in Spain.'

'He always said so, yes. Though it was the wounding in Normandie that really damaged him.'

'Yes,' Norman said. 'That was very bad. But also, I'm sure, the long strain before that. The long strain of struggle.'

Gwyn looked away. He had wanted something like that to be said at Bert's funeral, but there had been only the short, standard religious service before cremation. The whole family had thought this was right and by local custom it undoubtedly was. But how strange that the necessary words had come from this man in front of him, so distant in every way from what the words really meant!

'Will your mother be able to manage?'

Gwyn heard the words as if in an echo chamber.

'Manage? You mean financially or what?'

'In every way. Including, of course, financially.'

'She'll be all right. We've made some arrangements. And besides she's very resilient and independent.'

'Yes.'

Norman stubbed out the cigarette. He looked past Gwyn at the door, which was still standing half-open. Gwyn again waited.

'I remember her also as gifted,' Norman said.

'Yes. She is.'

'My impression was confirmed when I saw her work in that exhibition at the Partisan. You went, of course?'

'I went with her. She was shy about it.'

'Was she? She had no need to be. That pony series was very beautiful.'

'I thought so.'

There was another pause. The older man seemed abstracted, and it was Gwyn who broke the silence.

'Actually we were there at the gallery the same day as you.'

Norman sat up, convulsively.

'You mean you and your mother?'

'Yes. Of course I didn't know you. But she saw you come in with your daughter.'

Norman clenched his fist on the matchbox he was holding.

'But there was hardly anyone there. A rather noisy young group and then Alex's husband came in.'

'We were on the other side. We left quite soon.'

'While I was actually looking at her pictures! For I hardly looked at the others.'

'Yes. That's where you were.'

Norman lit another cigarette.

'I'm sorry about that,' he said and inhaled. 'I simply didn't see her.'

Gwyn didn't reply. Norman was looking across at him, as if waiting for something. Gwyn averted his eyes.

'Would you have wanted to see her?' he asked.

Norman got up. He seemed to move without strain or stiffness. He went over to the window and looked down at the street. Finally he turned and came back to stand in the centre of the room, behind a long brocaded sofa.

'It has been a very long time,' Norman said.

'I know.'

'Of course you know.'

He moved away again, restlessly. He circled and came back to his chair.

'I hear you've been talking to Monkey Pitter,' he said, sharply.

'Yes. At a party downstairs. And then a few days later he rang me up. He said you'd be glad if I came to see you.'

'I know. We discussed it. And with Emma, of course.'

'Well yes, and I knew Emma better.'

'It was still some time before you came.'

'Yes. Because of the death of my father.'

Norman looked at him, frowning. Then his face cleared.

'Of course. With Bert dying.'

Gwyn again averted his eyes before speaking.

'I would not have come before that,' he said, firmly.

'I see. Why?'

'I'm not sure, really. I suppose I thought that it would have seemed disloyal.'

Norman stubbed out his cigarette. Energy seemed to be flowing back to him.

'But not now?' he asked eagerly, as if in an intellectual argument.

'I said, I'm not sure.'

'Not disloyal, for example, to your mother?'

'Perhaps. But I told her.'

'And what did she say?'

'She said nothing at all.'

'You mean she was indifferent.'

'No, I don't mean that.'

Norman nodded and threw down the matchbox. He brought his hands together and interweaved his fingers. He rested his chin on them, lightly.

'There are so many things which you and I would be expected to say . . .'

'I have no expectations,' Gwyn interrupted, harshly.

'Exactly. The main difficulty is mine.'

'Yet eroded, surely? Over thirty-one years.'

Norman smiled. He unclasped his fingers.

'How long would that be in geological time?'

Gwyn found himself returning the smile.

'Faults can widen and deepen,' Norman added, enfolding Gwyn's response.

'The analogy doesn't help,' Gwyn said, stubbornly.

'Of course not. Though I was trying to move on from it.'

Gwyn looked away. As he spoke he found that he was listening to his voice.

'There is probably nothing at all to be said. I mean by this date and to me.'

Norman jerked back his head. There was a very sharp look, now, in his narrowed eyes.

'I expect you're right. Though Monkey seemed certain . . .'

'Of what?'

'Of the need for some acknowledgment. That at least, if nothing more.'

'What he said to me was that you had genuinely loved my mother.'

Norman hesitated.

'Yes.'

'Did you?'

'I said, yes.'

'A yes to be followed no doubt by a but.'

'Are they not all?' Norman said, and smiled ruefully.

'Not all.'

Norman nodded. A car was hooting in the street. He looked round, as if searching for something.

'You said, just now, that your father had died.'

'Yes.'

'You meant Bert, of course?'

'Yes. He was both actually and legally my father.'

'When you say actually, you mean that he brought you up.'

'Yes. Isn't that what a child knows?'

'Of course. And is loyal to.'

'Exactly.'

'The biological paternity then being . . .?'

He paused, staring at Gwyn.

'Insoluble,' Gwyn said, sharply.

'You can't really mean that.'

'I mean that any problem it creates is insoluble.'

'Because it's over and done with? Surely not?'

'Because it's over, anyway.'

'Exactly. It's over, but it isn't done with.'

'It could be.'

'How?'

'By leaving it alone.'

'But then you haven't left it alone.'

Gwyn flushed and got up. He stood looking down at Norman. His heavy shoulders were tensed.

'I should go.'

'No, please.'

Gwyn stood very solid and tense.

'I'll get you a drink,' Norman said. 'Would you take a dry sherry?'

'Thank you.'

Norman went to a sideboard. There were bottles and glasses on the top but he opened a cupboard and took out another bottle and two finer glasses. As he was pouring he spoke easily, back over his shoulder.

'It's unknown country, isn't it, interrogating the past?'

'Even when enough of it is known?'

'I wasn't meaning the past itself. I was meaning what happens when it begins to be interrogated. That is always genuinely unknown.'

He turned as he spoke the last words. His eyes were shining. He held out the glass and Gwyn took it.

'The traditional analogy is with harrowing,' he went on, pleasantly. 'I mean as the tines cut deeper and begin to drag through.'

'I've no real experience of it,' Gwyn said, embarrassed.

The contrast between the words and the light tone disconcerted him.

'No,' Norman said. 'Well, I may at least have spared you that.'

'I don't understand.'

'And will never do so, I hope.'

Gwyn moved, uneasily.

'Look, sit down again,' Norman said. 'Enjoy your drink. Tell me what you're doing at Stockwell.'

'Not much yet, actually. It's a new set of problems.'

Norman had his arm stretched out towards the chair. Gwyn hesitated and then sat.

'You'd come within Official Secrets anyway?'

'Yes, formally.'

'But not in practice?'

'There's one section does some very secret work. But most of mine, as yet, is for construction.'

'No links with the oceanographic people?'

Gwyn looked at him, sharply.

'Yes. So I've heard. In some of the secret work.'

'Only part of it's secret,' Norman said, confidently. 'There's the work on fishing grounds, and now of course they're looking for oil.'

'Most of that has been published.'

'Exactly. But there's also a link there with underwater communications, and then from that, curiously, to submarines.'

Gwyn put down his glass.

'You're very well informed. Do you know some of the people?'

'I know Masson.'

'Ah! From the top.'

'You could say so. I've known him since school. He was always my junior. He has always also been good.'

'Well, as I say, I only know my own small area.'

'The comfort and the excuse of the subordinate!'

Norman was smiling as he spoke. Gwyn was again disconcerted by the contrast between the words and the manner.

'Not an excuse,' he said, tightly. 'I've nothing to justify or apologise for.'

'But suppose you had?' Norman said, eagerly.

'It would depend on what it was.'

'Exactly. But say, for example, you were in a situation where your loyalties were divided. Where you could feel the pull of both but had still to choose one or the other.'

'I told you. I had that problem at the Coal Board.'

'Yes, and left. But suppose you couldn't simply leave? Suppose you had to go on with it and simply live with the difficulties?'

'Doing something wrong, you mean? Something wrong either way?'

'It can easily happen. And what does it mean, then, to choose between loyalty and conscience?'

'I would hope to be strong enough to act by conscience. I would have to live with myself.'

'You would also have to live with what the choice implied. What it implied and what it led to.'

'Yes.'

'Where it leads is often surprising.'

'Well, most things are.'

Norman leaned back. Gwyn, glancing at him, was surprised to see how confident and relaxed he had now become. This was a man fully attuned to his class and position, accustomed to an unstressed authority and respect.

'Let me get you another sherry.'

As Gwyn hesitated, Norman took the glass and refilled it.

'What I most notice,' he said, handing Gwyn the glass, 'is that hardly anyone quite does what they profess to believe in.'

'Well, it isn't a free-floating world. We have to accept some restraints.'

'From employers? From the state?'

'From other people. Of various kinds.'

'Yes, but you see that ought to modify the beliefs. If it doesn't there's something wrong.'

'No. We can still try.'

Norman smiled.

'Gwyn, let me give you an example. Your brother was arrested on the Vietnam demonstration. Your half-brother I should say.'

'Dic.'

'Yes, Dic. Now ask yourself, when a crowd can be assembled to confront something evil . . .'

Gwyn prepared to intervene but then hesitated.

'. . . when such a crowd is assembled,' Norman continued, strongly, 'in a clear demonstration of physical force by mass presence . . .'

'Presence, not force. A demonstration by presence.'

'Which however the police will not tolerate. They surround you, they press you back, they try to disperse you. And your brother resists.'

'Well . . .'

'He resisted.'

'Only under provocation.'

Norman snapped his fingers.

'This is childish,' he said, smiling. 'What do you think the police will do? What do you think the police are for?'

'It was a shock to a lot of us, seeing them behaving like that.'

'Then you do have something to excuse. Ignorance! Simple historical ignorance!'

'Times change.'

'You thought! But all right, what follows? You find they are like that, but you still believe in your right to assemble, against an evil war.'

'Of course.'

'So then why do you not act as you believe? You are asserting a right against them. Why not be prepared to act against them? To act, I mean, effectively.'

'It was quite effective.'

'It was also absurd. There were more of you than of them. Why didn't you press *them* back, disperse *them*?'

'Because we were neither prepared nor equipped.'

'Exactly. Because you were not really acting as you believed. I tell you, Gwyn, I have seen this all my life. It is the line each generation arrives at. They must make their own decisions but they are required to be consistent. If they come to believe that they must fight, then they must learn how to fight.'

'I know what you're saying. But there must still be some hope for legitimacy.'

Norman smiled.

'There must still,' Gwyn continued, 'be the right to peaceful protest: peaceful marches, peaceful assemblies.'

'And when they resist this? When they actually prevent it?'

Gwyn jumped up and faced the older man. He was still trying to control himself but he knew that his temper had at last broken.

'Men like my father fight,' he said angrily.

'Yes. Bert did. He fought all his life.'

'And was damaged and made ugly by it. You should have seen him there, dying. What right have you got to talk?'

Norman's lips moved but there was no sound.

'Did you fight in Spain?' Gwyn asked, fiercely.

There was no answer.

'Did you fight in Normandie? Did you fight the fascists anywhere?'

Norman turned away. He walked across to the window and looked down into the street. He was silent for some time. Gwyn watched his slim, now slightly bowed shoulders. He saw him turning back to the room. The face was pale now, and deeply lined.

'What you've just said is understandable, Gwyn.'

'I think so.'

'Though you still haven't answered my general question. All you've done is displace it to Bert.'

'Because he did what you're only talking about.'

'There's still yourself to consider. You can't go on living on your father's reputation.'

'Are you entitled to say that to me?'

'I don't know. It's quite a question. But my general argument is perfectly clear. That we must all try to do what we really believe.'

'It's just the talk makes me angry. The talk about fighting when it's nothing of the kind.'

Norman hesitated, watching Gwyn carefully.

'There are other ways,' he said slowly, 'beyond what you call legitimacy.'

'What would you call it?'

'Well, give it its names. The established laws. Even the established loyalties.'

Gwyn stared at him. The manner was now wholly changed: sad and quiet.

'Yet I'm glad,' Norman said, 'that you still have some hope for legitimacy. I have reason to believe it is much the better way.'

'Except, as you said, when we are forced to fight.'

'Yes. Surely?'

His voice was now barely audible. He was clearly extremely tired. He stood looking at Gwyn and then suddenly held out his hand. Gwyn took it and felt the surprisingly firm grasp.

'I have many good wishes for you and for your mother,' the quiet voice said. 'I cannot send such wishes. I no longer have the right. But I have them.'

Gwyn nodded, and then released his hand.

'I should be going.'

'Of course. Let me see you down.'

He led the way out of the room and down the stairs. As he was near the bottom of the flight he said over his shoulder:

'You know Alec Merritt, then?'

'No, not really. I just met him briefly.'

Norman stopped in the hallway, and glanced back.

'My daughter Alex told me she had a long and interesting talk
with your wife.'

'Yes. Jill.'

'And your little girl. Lyn?'

'Yes.'

Norman walked on towards the door and then stopped again.

'Alex and Alec have a son. My grandson. He's just six.'

'Good.'

'He and Alex are with my wife. At our home in the country.'

'What's his name?'

'Oh, didn't I say? Jon. Well, Jonathan really.'

'I see.'

Norman turned and looked into Gwyn's face.

'They're there because Alex and Alec are breaking up. Divorc-
ing.'

'I'm very sorry to hear that.'

'No, don't bother. He's a worthless man.'

'He's been very successful.'

Norman smiled.

'He's been quite intolerably promiscuous. As perhaps also
even in his politics.'

'I don't know about that.'

'It has become much more than Alex can stand. She's insisting
on the divorce.'

'Yes.'

Gwyn was now deeply embarrassed. He stared past Norman
at the door. Norman noticed his attitude and nodded, briskly.
He moved and opened the door. Gwyn pushed past him and
then turned to say goodbye.

'I think of Jon, you know,' Norman said evenly. 'One more
son without a father.'

# FIVE

—❧❧✿◯✿❧❧—

## 1984

# 1

❧ ❦ ❧ ❦

## LONDON, 7 JUNE 1984

'Dr Lewis, I understand that you are the natural son of Sir Norman Braose.'

Gwyn stared at the square glass ashtray on the corner of the shining teak desk. A shaft of sunlight had struck through the broad metal window to illuminate a moulded corner of the glass. It was possible that there would be some prismatic effect, on the bare white wall behind him and to his left.

'Though it is not actually down in your file.'

Gwyn shifted on his hard chair.

'Should it be?'

He glanced at Meele as he spoke. He knew that he was being closely observed, in the bright light from the window. But after the one quick glance he looked beyond him, to the trees in the public garden. In this exceptionally hot dry summer the branch of a big lime tree was already, in early June, hanging with light brown, shrivelled leaves. A tobacco colour. He brought his look back to the ashtray.

'Well, there's nothing secret about it,' Meele said. 'It's on your birth certificate.'

'Which you have examined?'

'Dr Lewis, that's my job.'

Gwyn shifted again on the chair. The lightweight dark suit which he had put on for what was politely described as the interview was no protection against the hardness of these official chairs, with their curious conventional version of the human seat. The rise in the centre, between the legs, was normal enough. It was the insistent hard smoothness behind it, where the weight was really taken, that was arbitrary.

'Then as a fact it's no problem,' he said, glancing again.

'Indeed. As a fact.'

'But whether relevant to what we are supposed to be discussing . . . ?'

'Exactly, Dr Lewis. That is for you to say.'

Gwyn looked down at his hands. Meele might suppose that he had schooled himself, had perhaps even been trained, to concentrate on this or that contingent object while being questioned about himself. Yet to begin with it had not been conscious. It was a habit he had developed that Jill had first noticed and talked about. Surprised, he had put it down to his scientific training and practice, but she would not accept this: 'It's only when you're under some pressure, some personal pressure.' He would not want to admit this to Meele.

He had not been seriously worried about what was called the interview; concerned and concentrated, but not worried. He had been vetted, as they called it, twice before: on his original appointment, when it had been little more than an extended version of small talk, and then again when he had been transferred to the new division, to work with the oceanographers.

This third vetting, he could see, would be considered more important. Certainly Rivers had seemed to think so, in his unduly repeated insistence that it was no more than routine. Promotion to head of division would be more than scientific, since one element of his responsibility would be the bearing on public policy. Neither part of the work, he had accepted, could be had without the other. Theoretically the science could be done without the bearing on policy, but that was not how, in practice, the machine worked.

He remembered the standard internal joke: your youth for science, your middle age for public policy. Yet also, in fairness, the science in this case was a matter of policy from the beginning. After extensive and controversial mainland testing of possible sites for the deep deposit of the more dangerous nuclear wastes, there was now an urgent and technically very difficult exploration of the possibility of drilled ocean-bed deposits: now the main work of his division. The questions of public policy did not have to be invented; they were already being openly argued. The division's own work had been described, in the press and in pamphlets, as preparation for gross dumping in the ocean: poisoning the seas which are the common inheritance of mankind.

The work they were actually doing was not that; was indeed a way of trying to avoid just that recklessness. Yet in both policy and technology the connections with major issues were complex and unavoidable. Gwyn's early fascination with the technical problems of reading the deepest cores had temporarily excluded the wider issues, at least while the work was being done: always uncomfortably, in those rough western seas. But being the head of division meant that the big issues would inevitably come back. There would at the very least be complex problems of interpretation. For none of the evidence was likely to come out in the form of the 'yes/no', 'safe/unsafe' answers on which people outside the investigation insisted. But then, since he wanted the promotion, since it was in strict terms overdue, he must accept the shape in which it came, and as part of that shape what Rivers primly called the interview: the positive vetting, perhaps now intensively done.

He had not expected a man like Meele. There was the standard joke about Security: the classics graduates and ex-colonial policemen. Actually his earlier questioners had looked like, and probably were, very ordinary, mild, constrained civil servants: probably shunted sideways from some more testing constructive work. Meele, at first glance, was very different. To begin with he was, in dress and manner, part of the upper layer of that generation which, with some astonishment, Gwyn had seen growing up behind him. The very expensive City suit, the healthy confidence of skin and voice, the profound self-assurance of manner and gesture, seemed to belong in a different, moneyed or orthodox-political, world.

Gwyn recalled the earlier transitions: the trivia that were still in some sense a real history. At Cambridge, in his first three undergraduate weeks, he had worn a suit: a Coop suit, admittedly, but dark blue and conventionally cut. There had then been the transition, which had seemed universal, to jerseys and jeans, longer hair, anoraks, and this had been, until well into the Seventies, the normal dress at work except for a few special occasions: a retirement party, a meeting with government and especially local-government officials, a working-day funeral. Then, gradually, and at first seeming merely a few local eccentricities, the suits had come back, even at work: in the office, anyway, though of course not on sites. Now, in these last years, with a younger generation coming through, the whole armour of civil righteousness had again been put on. What in the Sixties to mid-Seventies had looked, if seen at all, like tailor's dummies, were now walking and talking with an evident conviction that they had inherited and come to possess the earth. Most of this, at first, had been in the worlds of money and of straight career politics. But it had extended until the middle-aged who had persisted in the manners of their youth not only looked out of place but often plainly inadequate. It was the position of any informality against any insistent convention, of any kind of loosening against any strict uniform.

So that he should not really have been surprised to see Meele as he was. It was only that he had supposed, as at the edge of his mind always, that the Security people would be, like so many orthodox police, reserved, cautious, undemonstrative men; even, in bad cases, hardbitten, cynical, embittered. This outgoing, assured, essentially smooth man did not appear to match the job; yet that also had been the surprise, for from the beginning of the interview, establishing the details of the work of the division, the broker's manner had not concealed, had even as it continued supported, a better than adequate level of scientific knowledge, including a lot of recent and reasonably well-understood information. And then, with that flow established, and Gwyn happily shifting to reassurance, Meele had paused and looked down at his papers and made that still astonishing and freezing remark: 'Dr Lewis, I understand that you are the natural son of Sir Norman Braose.'

The shaft of sunlight had moved from the corner of the glass ashtray. It was now making a barred, wedge-shaped quadrilateral across the desk and Meele's spread of papers. Gwyn looked up.

'I don't see how it could possibly be relevant.'

Meele smiled.

'Very well. Then we'll leave it, shall we? I've just one or two other general points.'

'Please.'

'Well, there's the obvious question about your general attitude to the policy of developing nuclear energy. Many well-informed and entirely loyal people are, we all know, opposed to it.'

Gwyn relaxed.

'It's difficult,' he said. 'I suppose really I'm agnostic on it. Or you could say agnostic to sceptical. But I don't see that as affecting the work I shall be doing. If no more nuclear stations were built, we should still have large quantities of existing waste to dispose of. And on the choice between mainland deposit and ocean bed I have a very clear preference, if our work on the shelf comes out as I expect.'

'You mean you would be against mainland depositing?'

'In those circumstances. If ocean bedrock drilling proves practical. Or rather not so much the drilling, which can be done, but the subsequent monitoring, which is our main current problem.'

Meele smiled and nodded.

'Of course. I only asked, in passing, because I see that you attended a protest meeting, in mid-Wales, against one of the test deposit sites in the area.'

Gwyn sat up straight.

'How on earth did you know that?'

Meele smiled.

'Is that really what you should be asking me?'

'I suppose not. But it was entirely by chance that I went to that meeting. We'd been on holiday near Aberaeron and we were driving home. The car broke down, just outside Caersws. We got it towed in and we found a hotel. My wife and daughter and one of my daughter's friends.'

'Yes?'

'We had an unexpected evening on our hands. I saw a poster for this meeting and my wife and I went to it.'

'You didn't otherwise take part?'

'Not at all. Though I admit I was tempted. Aside from the general rhetoric they had one real point, about earthquake probabilities in the area. But through no fault of their own they hadn't enough really hard information.'

'And you had?'

'As it happened, yes.'

'But you didn't, for example, feel it was your public duty to disclose it.'

'It wasn't so much that. But I hadn't expected to be there. People who had were very anxious to speak. And what they were saying wasn't actually wrong.'

'So you left it?'

'I left it.'

'Though in the hotel bar afterwards you talked to a Mr Evan Davies and some of his friends, about just these points.'

'I don't know the name. A lot of people went to the bar, and my wife and I went too and got into the obvious conversations.'

'I see. But do you remember, for example, Mr Davies saying that he had heard a rumour that on one of the test drill sites they had not just taken samples of rock but had actually deposited, secretly, a sample of low-risk nuclear waste, to observe the effects over time?'

'I remember somebody saying that. I said at once that it was nonsense.'

Meele looked up and smiled.

'Yes, Dr Lewis, that agrees with my information. But I understand that you then added – what were the exact words? – that you *wouldn't put it past some of them.*'

Gwyn stared at the elongating wedge of light.

'Did I say that?'

'Well, that's my information.'

'But this is absurd. Do you really employ people to hang around bars listening to casual conversations? Especially on matter of no conceivable security interest.'

'Are you sure of that, Dr Lewis?'

'Yes. The civil energy programme, at this level, is a matter of open public policy.'

'For those of goodwill, of course. But you must know that there is concern about terrorist access to these sites.'

'You mean . . . ? But you can't be serious. Not in the case of sealed deep deposits.'

'It's an uncertain area. We would be foolish to overlook any possible risk.'

'But the risks are not in that. The real risks are to the people living around these sites.'

'Real risks?'

'Measurable risks.'

'And your sympathies are with these locals?'

'With them as people, yes. That is the point of all our work.'

'Exactly. So that of course you didn't imply that some of your colleagues would behave as recklessly as was alleged?'

'I know that they wouldn't.'

'Then why did you say it?'

'I don't agree that I said it. If I said anything of the kind it would have been as a joke.'

'A joke.'

'If it was said at all, yes.'

'I see.'

Meele paused and looked over his papers. When he looked up again he smiled.

'There's really very little else, you'll be glad to hear.'

'Good.'

'You went on CND marches in the Sixties. You were on an anti-American Vietnam demonstration in 1968. Your brother, half-brother, was arrested. But—'

'Might I say something?'

'Of course, Dr Lewis.'

Gwyn pulled back from the smile. He shifted on the chair, clenching his fists to control himself.

'You say this is only your job. Very well. But may I observe, and please record this if you wish, that this kind of pettifogging eavesdropping and recording is not only irrelevant to real national security, it is actually an insult to it, and potentially even a threat.'

Meele smiled.

'Of course, Dr Lewis, I will note what you say.'

'Thank you.'

'And may I add, personally, that I entirely take your point? What is it, after all, this fairly normal record of a young man's political protests? I often think, in fact, that we should be more suspicious when there's nothing at all of that kind.'

'I don't know about that. But the real security of our people has to include their civil liberties.'

'Precisely. And my point relates to that. Would some really dangerous group or individual go along to marches and demonstrations of that kind, at which they know even from the newspapers they are liable to be photographed and put on file?'

'I have no idea. I don't know any such people.'

Meele smiled.

'And you can add to your list if you like,' Gwyn continued vigorously. 'I attended two support meetings for the 1974 miners' strike. I also attended a fund-raising meeting for the NUPE strikers – the dustmen and sewermen – in the autumn of 1978. Moreover, in the current miners' strike, I have been helping in the collection of money for the families.'

Meele smiled again.

'I'm sure I have no need, Dr Lewis, to take note of things of that kind.'

'No, I want them taken note of. I want them on the record. Because they are perfectly normal, legitimate activities. If anyone says that they are not, the sooner it's in the open the better.'

'Quite so.'

Meele paused. He pulled together his papers. He looked at his watch.

'And that, thankfully,' he said, smiling, 'seems really to be that.'

'Good.'

Gwyn made to get up.

'I've asked them to bring us some coffee. It's due. Would you stay and share a pot?'

Gwyn hesitated.

'Even with your inquisitor?' Meele added, lightly.

Gwyn smiled.

'Yes, of course. Thanks.'

Meele pressed the bell on his desk. Almost at once a tall young woman carried in a tray of coffee. Meele got up, poured and served. As Gwyn held the cup in his hands, waiting for it to cool, Meele who had gone to the window and was looking out at the trees turned and said easily:

'I'm sorry about the Braose business.'

Gwyn leaned forward and put the cup on the table.

'You realise I had to ask.'

Gwyn looked away.

'No,' he said.

'Oh, but I did. It's the kind of thing that can upset people. Make them behave unwisely.'

Gwyn got up and faced him.

'Is this still part of our official interview?'

Meele smiled, but thinly. His eyes dulled.

'How would you wish to regard it?' he asked, with a new edge.

'I had understood we were finished.'

'Well, as you say. But I wanted you to know why I had brought the matter up.'

'Which you have not told me.'

'Exactly. But I was coming to it. Look, do drink your coffee.'

'It'll wait.'

Meele went back to his desk and sat down. Gwyn remained standing.

'I'll be frank with you, Dr Lewis. I was interested to see just how you would react.'

Gwyn ignored this.

'That is my only excuse, really, for raising it quite so brusquely.'

Gwyn squared his shoulders.

'You mean how I would react to an act of personal rudeness.'

'Oh come on, it was hardly that.'

'You could have made it even brusquer and just called me a bastard.'

Meele smiled.

'All right. It may have seemed like that. But you'll be interested to know that I found your reaction quite admirable. As again indeed now.'

'I don't care what you bloody found. And it still has nothing whatever to do with my work.'

'Ah well, as to that . . .' Meele said and looked up.

Gwyn waited, meeting his look.

'I took all your earlier points,' Meele said. 'And of course I found them convincing.'

'There were no points. I just said that it wasn't relevant. That it had no connections whatever.'

'Ah well,' Meele said, and paused to sip his coffee. 'But unfortunately on that there isn't only my opinion to consider.'

'Whose, then?'

'You would not expect me to tell you that. But I can assure you, as man to man, it would really be very helpful, and especially as it happens to you, if I were in a position to understand it.'

'Understand what? He is my natural father. There has never been any secret about it.'

'At what age were you told he was your father?'

'When I was fourteen.'

'By your mother, presumably?'

'By my mother and my father. For by then, of course, I had been legally adopted.'

'Of course. Herbert Lewis, who had married your mother.'

'Yes. And then later by Mrs Wilkes, who had always been kind to me.'

'Emma Wilkes? Braose's sister?'

'Yes.'

'Who had taken what might be called a family interest in you?'

'Yes.'

'But you didn't meet Braose himself?'

'Not then. Not when I was young. But many years later, after my father had died, I did go to see him. It was disastrous.'

'You mean after Herbert Lewis had died. What year would that be?'

'Nineteen sixty-eight.'

'And you say you found it disastrous?'

'Well, not overtly. But he talked and talked at me, and about nothing I really wanted to know.'

'What would you have wanted to know?'

Gwyn stopped. He looked round the bare office.

'I'm sorry,' Meele said. 'I can see that this is painful.'

'Yes and moreover it's none of your business,' Gwyn said, turning away.

'I know,' Meele said.

'What I wanted, if you must know, wasn't general remarks about this and that. What I wanted, and it was fair, was just some honest explanation. Had he really loved my mother, and if so why had he deserted her?'

Meele looked away.

'Yes, of course,' he said, sympathetically. 'After all, I suppose this isn't something you can discuss with many people.'

'You mean that's why I'm talking to you?'

'Not at all. But I can see just how much it means to you.'

'Not in the way you think. And I can talk about it. I talk about it to my wife. I used to talk for hours with Emma Wilkes.'

'But not with your mother?'

'No.'

Meele smiled.

'I understand,' he said, quietly.

Gwyn looked down at his coffee. He didn't want it. He wanted to turn and go. Yet he was still in some way held.

'I'm sorry,' Meele said. 'It would not, I assure you, have come up at all if some of my superiors had seen it as I do.'

Gwyn sat down, nervously, on the edge of the hard chair.

'Some of my older colleagues,' Meele continued, 'were formed, you see, in a quite different world.'

'We have all seen change,' Gwyn said, and at once regretted the banality.

'Not only their minds but their lives,' Meele continued, 'were formed, fixed, by the Cold War. I mean the real Cold War, not this re-run. And then it's easy for people like that to get stuck in the past.'

'It's more than a re-run, this Cold War. With some it's a deliberate and very dangerous continuation.'

'Of course. They would be the first to agree with you.'

'But still of no possible relevance to me.'

'You mean it's just sins of the fathers and that kind of thing?'

Gwyn stared at him.

'No,' he said. 'I mean that it has no possible connection with my work. As you must see yourself, having gone so carefully through it.'

'Of course,' Meele said.

He lit a small cigar, then offered the packet to Gwyn. Gwyn refused.

'No possible connection,' Meele continued, 'as we both see it.'

'Exactly.'

'Except that in their perspective . . .'

He paused.

'In their perspective,' he went on, leaning forward and tapping his cigar on the square glass ashtray, 'there is without question a long-term secret operation to penetrate every department of state and official institution. Including scientific institutions.'

On the last words he smiled, deprecatingly.

'It's a fantasy,' Gwyn said. 'And then a fanaticism.'

'It is indeed often that. But the problem is that from the past, when their minds were formed, they have really, when you look at it, very solid evidence indeed.'

'As you say, from the past.'

'One has to see their point of view,' Meele said, tolerantly. 'For you and me these old scandals are history. We read about them at school. But for them, and for these others they suspect, it's bound to be different. And it's difficult simply to refute them. Many of the people concerned are, after all, still alive.'

'So they pursue these old hostilities to the edge of the grave?'

'And beyond it,' Meele said, smiling.

He drew deeply on his cigar.

'But still,' Gwyn said stubbornly, 'with no possible relevance to me.'

Meele looked down at his papers. He smiled.

'Did you know,' he asked lightly, 'that Norman Braose recommended you for your job at the Institute?'

'What job? When? That's impossible.'

'Your first job at the Institute. After you had left the Coal Board.'

'In sixty-six? But I'd never even met him.'

'So you said.'

'Because it was so.'

'I don't doubt you, Dr Lewis. But the fact remains, it is in the files, that while Masson was Director, Braose wrote to him recommending you.'

'Well, I knew nothing of that.'

'Though it's a fact that you didn't apply for the job. You were approached.'

'Yes. By Masson. And he said I'd been recommended by my old Cambridge supervisor, Tomkins.'

'Of course. I know how these things are done.'

Meele looked down again at his papers. Gwyn felt his heart thumping. He made an effort to sit still.

'Yes,' Meele continued. 'Jacob Tomkins. Who is the brother-in-law of your tutor at Cambridge, Mark Ryder.'

'Was. Tomkins died last year.'

'I see. And Mark Ryder, do I have it right, is the Marxist historian?'

'He says just historian.'

'Of course.'

Meele smiled. He continued to read interestedly from his papers. Gwyn intervened impatiently.

'Whether Braose recommended me I have no way of knowing. It would in any case count less than what Tomkins said. He knew my work.'

'Of course.'

'If he did it was probably . . .'

He hesitated. Meele looked up.

'Well, we've been through all that,' Gwyn said, hurriedly. 'It may just have been, what, guilt. Going back to the beginning. That he had done nothing for me.'

'Of course,' Meele said. 'Though it's obvious from the letter that he knew you needed a job.'

'Not from me.'

'We've agreed to that. But then from whom?'

Gwyn hesitated.

'Perhaps,' Meele said, 'from his sister? From Mrs Wilkes?'

'That's possible. I really don't see how else.'

'Mrs Wilkes, with whom you were in regular touch?'

'Yes, as I said, we had been from the beginning.'

'Mrs Wilkes, who is still a senior member of the Communist Party?'

'Yes. There's no secret whatever about that.'

'Mrs Wilkes, who was Emma Braose and who married George Wilkes, an official of the Party in its International Department?'

'Yes. He died in an accident in 1955.'

'In a period,' Meele said, 'of great interest to my colleagues.'

Gwyn stared at him.

'Perhaps it is. It still has nothing to do with me. This is all prehistory. It has nothing to do with my work.'

'Yes, I take your point,' Meele said, and stubbed out his cigar.

'What you're trying to imply,' Gwyn said bitterly, 'is some whole network of guilt by association, though my only guilt in the matter is that I was born.'

Meele smiled and nodded.

'I'm glad you said that, Dr Lewis. It is, I am convinced, the essential point.'

'Then why bring all this other material up?'

Meele closed his file.

'We're not our own masters, Dr Lewis. Like everyone else we have to follow certain routines.'

'And disciplines, I hope. Disciplines of relevance, for example.'

'Of course, though in our case . . .'

He broke off and smiled.

'. . . though I shouldn't bore you with this,' he said, disarmingly.

'I've had the effect,' Gwyn said stubbornly. 'I might as well know the reason.'

'Well, you mention relevance. But by definition, you see, we have to try to connect things which have been quite deliberately kept secret. It is only because of this that we have to probe, suggest, even speculate.'

'All right. I see that. But then introducing Braose was an extreme speculation. Because the only possible connection was personal, and when you had got that, what else?'

Meele stood up. He smoothed down the tails of his jacket, which were creased where he had been sitting.

'You mean, of course,' he said, 'that there's nothing else

against him. Nothing other than that he abandoned your mother and yourself?'

Gwyn got to his feet. He nodded, preparing to turn away.

'But then that, you see,' Meele said, coming round the desk, 'is the most difficult assumption of them all.'

Gwyn stiffened as Meele came close to him.

'Because from the period we were discussing,' Meele continued, evenly, 'there are very substantial questions about what Braose was doing.'

Gwyn risked a glance at him. The face and manner were still open and pleasant.

'For a fact,' Meele continued, 'we know that very important material was passed to the Russians, from the government establishment in which he and his friend Pitter were working.'

Gwyn looked into his face.

'What kind of material?'

'It isn't my field. But as I understand it, some decisive material on early computer theory and design.'

'Most of that was fairly open. From the bits I've read of it.'

'Yes,' Meele said. 'You know Pitter, of course?'

'Pitter?' Gwyn repeated, his mind elsewhere.

'Monk Pitter. He's now a financial consultant.'

'I know. I met him. Twice, I believe.'

'Yes. Twice.'

'He approached me. To talk about Braose.'

'I know.'

'It was the personal problem. He was a kind of intermediary when I first made contact with . . .'

'Your father,' Meele said.

'Yes. In that sense.'

Meele smiled and turned to fasten his briefcase. He glanced at the garden.

'Still no relief from this hot dry summer,' he said, casually.

Gwyn waited, awkwardly. He could feel the sweat in his hair.

'All right?' Meele said. 'Fine. We'll leave it at that.'

Gwyn turned and faced him.

'But we can't leave it at that.'

'You mean about your clearance? Well, that takes a few weeks to work through.'

'No. I don't mean the clearance. I mean what you're alleging about Braose and Pitter.'

'Which, as you've correctly insisted, has no connection at all with yourself.'

'If it has no connection, then why—'

'Yes,' Meele said, quickly, and picked up his briefcase.

Gwyn looked at him, perplexed.

'I said more than I should have, no doubt,' Meele said.

'But having said it . . .' Gwyn insisted.

Meele moved towards the door.

'It having been said, you're curious,' he remarked, lightly.

'Much more than that. If it's true.'

'Oh, it's true all right. But tracking back, in a complicated field, these things are always difficult to establish beyond all doubt. I mean whether it was these two men working together, or one through the other, or perhaps only one of them. But that the material was passed there can be no doubt at all.'

'And nothing has been done about it?'

'Some things have been done.'

Gwyn was looking again at the square glass ashtray, now in heavy shadow.

'The only misfortune might be . . .' Meele was saying.

Gwyn turned towards him.

'. . . If ever, for example,' Meele continued, smiling, 'some question came up about your own work.'

'We have been through that.'

'Exactly. Though I didn't raise the question that when you are head of division . . .'

He paused. Gwyn stared at him.

'I should have, I suppose,' Meele said. 'But it's a relative formality. That as head of division you will have some overlap of material with others interested in those depths.'

'No. We keep quite separate.'

'Very wisely. But I've heard there's a good deal of interest in the kind of ocean-bed communication you particularly have been working on.'

'Interest from whom?'

'It will come through channels.'

'If you mean submarines and submarine detection systems . . .'

'Something like that,' Meele said, and moved further towards the door.

'We keep quite separate,' Gwyn said, firmly.

'Of course. And all I meant was that if some question came up – I don't only mean security, it could even be just dissent . . .'

'Policy dissent, do you mean?'

'Policy dissent, interavailability of material. It might be anything.'

Gwyn stepped back.

'Why are you raising this now? At the very end of the interview? Actually on your way out?'

'Because that's my judgment of it. It's a fairly remote possibility.'

'You said misfortune.'

'Ah, that,' Meele said, and again smiled. 'I meant only that it would be a misfortune, if some difficulty of this kind, affecting you, ever by chance came up . . .'

'Go on.'

'. . . if intruding into that, infecting it one might even say, were this quite unconnected material about Braose and Pitter.'

Gwyn clenched his fists and looked away. The sun was now high on the trees in the garden. The lower branches were in shadow.

'That sounds to me very like blackmail,' he said, sharply.

'No,' Meele said, and touched his arm. 'No.'

'That it would then be used against me,' Gwyn insisted. 'Even dribble its way into print, as so many of these things do.'

'That would indeed be very distressing. For you, obviously, but perhaps even more for your mother.'

Gwyn stepped towards him. Meele smiled and moved away. There was some difference now in his manner. His confidence and assurance, which had been smooth and even conventional, seemed to have hardened into some more absolute conviction: not the manner of superiority but its cold fact.

'I'm not leaving it like this,' Gwyn said, roughly. 'I shall take it to—'

'Good day to you, Dr Lewis,' Meele said, and opened the door and walked out.

# 2

❧❀❧

# LONDON, 18 JUNE 1984

'Gwyn? Bill. Bill Wilkes.'

'Oh, hullo.'

'Do you think you can come over. We're at Emma's.'

'Come over? When?'

'Now.'

Gwyn pushed the phone away. He waited, collecting his thoughts.

'Gwyn, are you there?'

'Yes. When you say we . . . ?'

'Mark's here. With Emma and me.'

'Mark? But—'

'I know. He still thought he should come and see us.'

'He had no right. I was—'

'Come and tell him. Will you?'

Gwyn looked along the familiar hallway. The mirror reflected him standing holding the phone. Jill was out at a meeting. He looked away from the mirror to one of his mother's pony drawings, well lighted beside the hallstand.

'You mean come over now?'

'Yes, Gwyn. It's important.'

'It's difficult just now. I'm expecting Jill back.'

'But you can't start something like this and just leave it.'

'I start it?'

'But you did, for all practical purposes. And it can't be left as it is.'

Gwyn looked again at the drawing of the pony. There was a brilliantly caught tiredness in all its lines. Or perhaps more than tiredness: the fatigued bewilderment of the ageing animal behind the wire.

'I'll come,' he said and put down the phone.

He wrote a quick note to Jill and went out for the car. As he drove he could still hear that peremptory voice on the phone, its hard ruling-class accent exaggerated by the machine. Yet that was the least of his problems. The only important question was why Mark Ryder had gone to them.

After the shattering encounter with Meele he had spent hours talking with Jill, taking it through from the beginning, admitting to emotions which for years he had only intermittently recognised and which he had always appeared to control. What had never been allowed to come through as itself was a straight anger, an aggressive anger, against what he found himself calling, to Jill, the Braoses: including Emma, as Jill was quick to point out. Over and above the personal resentments it was a straight, bitter, unreconstructed class anger. But as this came through he found himself still making moves to control or soften it: moves he had learned, over the years, in his own transition. He had only ever fully noticed them when he was back in Danycapel, and especially with Dic.

For this basic anger had seemed to be left behind when he had left home. It was not beliefs or positions he had then left behind; these could be packed and taken. It was the thing itself; the active alignment. Without that, in the world in which he had come to move, the beliefs and positions were matters for explanation, argument, even qualification, and he had always defended this, even against Dic, as being necessary for entry into a wider, more diverse, differently committed world: the fight for the high ground, as he had once incautiously said, and been jeered at by Dic: 'while we're still bloody underground'.

It was not that he was now renouncing his new ways of seeing and arguing. It was that bursting out under them was this long repressed class anger, of a kind which he knew would seem absurd anywhere beyond its own sites and communities. At one level this could rejoin the open beliefs and positions: the settled critique of a hard and now destructive capitalist state. But also, in more complicated ways, it was coming through, as he had put it, against the Braoses: that is, even against people in that other and hated class who in terms of beliefs and positions were already on his side: 'our side', as he had without thinking put it to Jill.

Yet the Braoses were often quicker than his own people to talk the hard general language of class. Where Bert or Dic would say 'our people' or 'our community', the Braoses would say, with a broader lucidity, 'the organised working class', even still 'the proletariat' and 'the masses'. Trying to discuss this with Mark, for it had been no use with Emma, he had been told, kindly enough, that the shift to generality was necessary. What could otherwise happen was an arrest or a relapse to merely tribal feeling. And he had wanted even then to object: 'But I am of my tribe'; except that he had seen, with examples, and from the lessons of repeated political failures (the betrayed trust of a tribe in leaders and parties who had offered to speak in its name), the general solidity of the argument.

None of that seemed to matter now. He had expected Jill to say that his anger against the Braoses, his suddenly released anger, was personal: that it expressed his long resentments against the man who had deserted him and his mother, and against what Jill called Emma's matronage. So that the wider class feeling would be only a vehicle, through which these personal feelings could flow, could be displaced and even handled. Yet this was not what Jill had said. It was personal and social, she had assured him, in one seamless cloth. 'For they have always been our enemies, whatever they professed. If not our open enemies, then our actual or prospective controllers. And always they've lived on our blood.'

It was a sign of the long shift, and of his present confusion, that he had been both glad to hear her say this, feeling confirmed at some deep, indeed inaccessible level, and at the same time wary, qualifying, sceptical: wanting to except them, or some of them, or to acknowledge their disinterest and goodwill. Jill would have nothing of that. They were all enemies and damaging, whatever shapes they assumed.

'Him I can see,' he had agreed. 'But Emma? She's tried very hard to be kind.'

'She's actually been kind. But for her reasons, not yours.'

'Does that matter, if the kindness is given?'

'It's mattering now. When you see what you've really inherited.'

And that indeed had been the spur: Meele's allegations. He had come to think that he should not really have been surprised. Looking back he could see that this was what Monkey Pitter had been trying to tell him, way back in '68; not just trying, actually telling him, if he had had ears to hear.

But then came the doubts. Had it only really registered, only come to be taken seriously, when it was directly connected with his own security and success? Was not his anger now tinged with fear, his angry talk with panic, because his own interests were threatened?

'Of course it's that, love, but why be ashamed of it? It was always your life they were disposing.'

So their long talk had continued, until one morning, waking early, he had said:

'Mind you, we're simply assuming that what Meele says is true.'

'Of course it's true. Can you doubt it?'

'I feel I ought at least to test it. But then how? Who can I really talk to?'

It was then that he had thought of taking the story to Mark Ryder, who had known Braose and Pitter since before the war. If anyone could estimate the likely truth of the story, without prejudice but also without betraying a confidence, it would surely be Mark. And indeed he had listened, when Gwyn had sought him out in Cambridge, with exemplary sympathy and care. He had made hardly any comments, merely asking some factual questions. He would think it over, he had said, and would then get in touch. Gwyn had returned, feeling some of the weight lifted from him.

Then the phone call just now: Mark here in London with Emma and Bill; the whole story presumably passed on. As he drove he felt bitter about Mark: bitter and quite extraordinarily surprised. It was at the very least a breach of confidence, even a crude betrayal. What he had said to Mark had been private, as so often in the old days, when Mark was his tutor. Yet where, when it came down to it, would Mark's loyalties really lie? He was at some political distance from Emma but they were still very old friends. The concerns of a younger generation were probably subordinate to that.

Still, for whatever reason Mark had done it, what Gwyn had now to face was what he had manoeuvred to avoid: a direct confrontation with the Braoses. Yet of course, he pulled himself up, it was not yet that. Though difficult, this would be peripheral. The only real confrontation would be with Pitter and . . . In the hesitation the names flicked, as so often, through his mind – Braose. Sir Norman Braose. Norman. My . . . My natural father.

The gate was off its hinges. As Emma had got older the front was less well tended. He walked up and pushed the bell.

A young man in his early twenties opened the door. He was tow-haired, fresh-faced, with big gold-rimmed glasses.

'I'm Gwyn Lewis. Bill rang. Bill Wilkes.'

'They're upstairs. You'd better come in.'

As he was stepping inside, the tall figure of Bill appeared at the head of the stairs.

'Jon! Is that Gwyn? Send him up.'

Gwyn hesitated.

'I'm Jon Merritt,' the young man said, putting out his hand.

'Pleased to meet you.'

'I'm a sort of second cousin. I keep some of my stuff here.'

'Merritt?'

'Yes, my mother was Alex Merritt. But look, I'm sorry, I must rush. This week is Finals.'

'I see. What are you reading?'

'Maths. My last fling. Then out into the world.'

'To do what?'

'I've got a sort of job. As a television researcher.'

'That sounds interesting.'

'I doubt it. But it's a crust.'

Bill came down a couple of steps.

'Look, Jon, don't keep him. We need him up here.'

'It's my fault,' Gwyn said. 'Chatting.'

'Okay. But come on up.'

'It's an old Danycapel habit,' Gwyn said, between them. 'We talk to people when we meet them.'

Jon grinned. He lifted a heavy case and went out. Gwyn walked up the stairs, and followed Bill as he turned.

They went together into the familiar sitting-room. In the late evening there was only a dim light. Emma was sitting with her back to him. She didn't look round. Mark was on the far side of the room, lying back in a wide chair. He had looked drawn and frail when Gwyn had seen him in Cambridge. He seemed now almost tired to sleep, though he lifted his hand to greet Gwyn.

'Will you sit here?' Bill said.

He indicated a space on the big sofa beside Emma. Gwyn went across to it. Emma did not turn her head.

'Drink,' Bill said.

'If you are.'

'We are. Whisky?'

'Thank you.'

'Straight?'

'Please.'

Bill poured the drink and carried it across. Then he sat in the big armchair by the fireplace. Gwyn remembered sitting in it, many years ago, when he had come to see . . . The names flickered again. Norman . . . Sir Norman . . . Norman Braose.

'Mark wants to say something first,' Bill announced.

'Yes,' Mark said, shifting. 'I'm sorry, Gwyn, but the more I thought about it the more I was certain we couldn't keep this to ourselves. I tried to ring you but . . .'

'It's all right, Mark. I understand.'

Mark smiled, sadly.

'And with that over,' Bill said, 'we can get down to cases. This was Meele you saw? Robin Meele?'

'I didn't get his first name.'

'I know him. He's a particularly unpleasant example of this new Far Right in Security. He was already so at Oxford.'

'I didn't get that impression.'

'Because you're so naive,' Emma said suddenly.

Gwyn shifted and looked at her. She looked away.

'In any case,' Bill said, 'he seems to have taken you for the proverbial ride.'

'In what way?'

'Can't you see it? The whole point of him doing this routine vetting, which he wouldn't normally be on, was to plant this story and frighten you with it.'

'For what purpose?'

'Oh God! To draw a line. To clench their own. To make sure that you know they can control you.'

'But how could they control me? By simply planting a story?'

'Do you think he was telling you the truth, then?'

Gwyn hesitated. He looked across at Mark.

'Well, as I tried to explain to Mark . . .'

'Yes,' Bill said. 'That you didn't know. That you were worried and upset—'

'Well—' Gwyn protested.

'Well nothing. This is how they operate. And like a fool you fell for it.'

Gwyn clasped his hands and put them between his knees, leaning forward.

'I didn't fall for it,' he said slowly. 'But there was just enough in what he said for me to want to know more. And especially since I realised, as I heard it, that I had heard something very like it before. In fact here, in this house. Downstairs, back in 'sixty-eight.'

He paused. The others were watching him.

'It was Pitter,' he said, in a rush. 'He sought me out and just said it.'

'Said what?' Bill asked.

'Well, I remember how he started. He said that Norman had retired, full of years and dishonour.'

Emma grunted contemptuously.

'He's just filth, that man,' Bill said.

'Well perhaps, but he went on to say that Norman had been a very dedicated communist and that it was a pity I'd been deprived of knowing what he had really done.'

Bill laughed.

'Which you at once took as a confession of espionage?'

'No, not at all. In fact at the time it didn't really register. But then later, when I came here and met . . . Norman, there were things he said that I suppose must have lain in my mind.'

'What things?'

'It's a long time ago. But he talked a lot about the law and legitimacy, and about the failure of most people to act right through as they believed. And then he talked about sparing me what he called the harrowing.'

Gwyn hesitated again. Mark, he noticed, had covered his eyes with his hand.

'What he said he meant by harrowing was interrogating the past.'

Emma turned and looked at Gwyn's face.

'Go on,' Bill said.

'Well, that's it, essentially. As I said, at the time not much of it registered. But then when I heard what Meele said, and began thinking it back . . .'

'Exactly,' Bill said. 'He played you like some dumb fish. He knew all about these personal difficulties and resentments and—'

'Wait, Bill,' Mark said.

The strength and depth of the intervening voice was surprising. They all turned to him.

'Before we limit this,' Mark said, 'to what Gwyn can report . . .'

He was pushing himself straighter in the chair as he talked. His eyes moved between Bill and Gwyn.

'I should explain,' he continued, 'that I came not only because I thought Gwyn had a problem, but because when he told me Meele's story I also had reasons to remember.'

'This wasn't where you started,' Bill said, coldly.

'No. And I still don't know where it ends. But I'd better make clear that this isn't only a problem about Gwyn. I mean about whether he should or shouldn't have believed Meele.'

'Isn't that what we're discussing?' Emma said, confidently.

'Only partly, Emma. Because as you, in fact, have good reason to know, we have heard some of this quite directly from Norman himself.'

'What was that? When?'

'It was here in this room, as a matter of fact. In 'fifty-six, after the Suez demonstration.'

'That's a long time ago.'

'Yes, but I remember it very clearly. He told us that he was facing several days of what he first called meetings and then in effect interrogations. And what he told us was at stake was quite remarkably similar to what Gwyn has now got from Meele.'

'I don't remember anything like that,' Emma said.

Mark hesitated. He looked hard at Emma, who returned his look openly.

'You must remember some of it, Emma.'

'No, Mark. I don't. I remember nothing of the kind.'

Mark spread his hands.

'And even before that,' he went on, quietly, 'when you and I met Monkey in Cambridge. We had a meal together. Monkey then in effect told us the same story.'

'I remember him fooling about. Talking as usual for effect.'

'He had his effect on me. That was why, later, I listened so carefully to Norman.'

'And made up your own version of it,' Emma said, raising her voice.

'Why also now,' Mark said, 'I listen very carefully to what Meele told Gwyn.'

Emma stood up.

'I didn't think you'd desert us,' she said, looking down at Mark.

'I came to help,' Mark said.

Gwyn thought how close he now looked to exhaustion. The voice was still strong, but as if going on outside his body: a still practised voice, in a being becoming detached from it.

'How exactly?' Bill asked, trying to resume control.

'Well, what has been done is done,' Mark said, with an effort. 'But if what you say about Meele is true there must be some motive, some plan, behind reviving what by now is an old story.'

'I've explained that,' Bill said. 'There *is* a motive. It's a controlling operation on Gwyn.'

'So you said. But how can you know that? Or rather how can you know that is all it is?'

'Because I know the whole story,' Bill announced, calmly.

Mark and Gwyn stared at him.

'Yes,' Bill went on. 'From the beginning. That's why I can construe all these carefully leaked versions, and know what each is being used for.'

'What story do you know?' Mark was the first to ask.

As he spoke, Emma smiled and looked contentedly across at Bill.

'The key to it all is Monkey Pitter,' Bill said. 'For the fact is that from 1943 at latest Pitter was indeed passing material to the Russians.'

'Who were our allies,' Emma interjected.

'Of course. But then Pitter was more than an ally. He had the mentality – it's part of his extraordinary intelligence – to detach himself from conventional considerations, from what he always genuinely saw as the peripheral, and to concentrate only on the moves in the game.'

'It was more than a game,' Emma said.

'For him it was not. Yes, he had what others call beliefs, but which were for him primarily intellectual positions. He played with great skill and subtlety on that basis, and he played alone.'

Mark began but then restrained a question.

'It was then part of the logic,' Bill continued, 'that at the end of the war he should move to the States. That was where the real action was going to be, and he got cover to take part in it.'

Mark could no longer restrain his question.

'But did Norman know about this?'

'At that time, no.'

'Then when?'

'In 'fifty-three to 'fifty-four, when American security had at last got on to Pitter. Through a defector.'

'And he was then interrogated himself?'

'Inevitably. They had been close colleagues and close friends. And Norman, by this time, was in very secret and sensitive work.'

'The interrogation cleared him?'

'Yes. Eventually. That was the stage he was in, Mark, in 'fifty-six, when he was talking to you.'

'He was frightened then. Genuinely frightened.'

'Of course. Because quite apart from Pitter there were these other things they could use against him. The politics before the war and still, of course, Emma.'

'They'll use anything,' Emma said. 'They're entirely unscrupulous.'

'But still he was cleared?' Mark asked.

Even his voice was now tiring.

'Yes,' Bill continued. 'The more readily because, when it came to it, they couldn't even make it stick against Pitter. They got close enough to force him out of his cover, and to dry up most of his contacts, but they got nothing against him that would ever stand up as a case. Partly because the field was so difficult, and Monkey, evidently, played the science like a master. He had to get out, of course, but he got out and by applying the same mentality he then made himself rich.'

'End of story,' Mark said.

'No,' Bill replied. 'I only wish that it were. Because in the mid-Sixties they got on to Pitter again. There were other defectors, bringing unchallengeable material, and there were now much better qualified people to do the interrogation.'

'British or American?'

'Both.'

'Yet it never became a case.'

'There were reasons for that. It was by then nearly twenty years back. It was very complicated between Britain and America. And in any event what they had in mind was something much better than a case, which by this time, remember, was a kind of scandal, reflecting as much on governments and on the intelligence services themselves as on the ageing individuals concerned.'

'So what was better?' Mark asked.

Bill paused. He looked slowly around the room, holding the attention of each of them in turn.

'They knew their man very well,' he said slowly. 'All they had really to offer was that Monkey should change places on the board. Take the black pieces instead of the white.'

Mark pulled himself back in his chair. There was open pain in his face.

'Yes, Mark,' Bill said relentlessly. 'From 'sixty-five at latest he was working for them. For the Americans.'

'Directly, are you saying?'

'Directly. And consider the advantages. He had a good Left pedigree, he had old Left friends. And that he was something of a buffoon was a bonus: nobody took him quite seriously.'

Gwyn leaned forward. His hands were again tightly knotted between his knees.

'So that when he came to this house? In 'sixty-eight, for example . . . ?'

'Yes, then particularly,' Bill said, and took a paper from his pocket. 'Because in just those years there were not only anti-war Americans but others, refugees, from Germany especially – I've got several names here – that he could help to put away.'

There was a long silence. Emma went across and drew the curtains and switched on another sidelamp. It was Mark who eventually spoke. His voice had recovered some of its strength.

'There were several bad cases at that time,' he said.

'Certainly. And from inside information.'

'Yes, it had to be someone, or more than one. But will you tell me, Bill, precisely, why you believe you know it was Monkey?'

Bill folded the paper in his lap.

'It took some years,' he said. 'But there were two routes. First, that in 'sixty-seven, quite suddenly, Norman was interrogated again.'

'And . . .?'

'He was confronted with material that could only have come from Pitter. It was a very skilful blend of the true and the false.'

'The true being . . . ?'

'Well, when he had stopped being a communist, for a start. That had never been said, in terms, but it was generally understood that it was in 1939, at the beginning of the war.'

'And it wasn't?'

'It's complex,' Bill said. 'In a way he was never a communist. He was just an anti-fascist. But for many reasons, including in fact Emma, and perhaps, Gwyn, even you, though you couldn't possibly have known about it, he hung on as . . . what? I suppose fellow-traveller still gets it exactly.'

'Until?' Mark asked.

'It was a drift,' Bill said. 'You'd have to ask him. But I'd say till 'fifty-six or so, and then it slowly melted away.'

'That's right,' Emma said. 'But he never became anti. He just went back to being a liberal.'

Mark had got out his pipe. He tried to light it, repeatedly, but his lighter would not spark. Gwyn leaned forward and offered him matches. He took the box, hardly noticing. His hands were moving restlessly on the lighter and the pipe.

'Norman retired early,' he said, still preoccupied. 'In fact at just that time.'

'Yes.'

'Was it forced?'

'Effectively yes.'

'Because he had kept in touch with his sister, and held broadly Left views until the Fifties?'

'I said a blend of the true and the false,' Bill continued. 'And that is the heart of the matter.'

'What was false?'

As Mark spoke he darted a match at his pipe.

'The extraordinary concoction,' Bill said, 'that Gwyn got from Meele.'

'That they were both in it, Norman and Monkey, but that they couldn't be sure of who played which part? Yet you have just told us that they had nailed Monkey.'

Bill looked at him coolly. The pipe had gone out, and Mark stuffed it into his pocket.

'They knew that,' Bill said. 'Monkey knew that. But they could put it as they wanted to bring pressure on Norman.'

'Successful pressure.'

'Well . . .'

'They forced him to resign.'

'In a way, yes. But then you see he wasn't reluctant. From back in the Fifties, when he got that lovely house, and the wood and the garden that actually meant much more to him, he wasn't interested any more, he even preferred going.'

'With pension?'

'Yes, with pension.'

'Because they couldn't prove anything? Or what?'

'Because the ruling tactic was pressure. As I said, by the Sixties they didn't want more scandals. They simply wanted to ease out all the doubtful people, the liberals, the old reds.'

Mark leaned forward so abruptly that Bill stopped for a moment.

'The ruling tactic was pressure and the ruling means was slur,' he then hurried to say. 'In effect they were clearing out what they saw as a bad old gang. And that extended, believe me, to the softest kind of liberals.'

'No more than that?'

'No more than that. He kept his knighthood, he kept his pension, he retired to write his book on *Syringae*.'

Mark pulled out his pipe again. He lifted his lighter, which flamed at first strike. The smoke rose around his head.

'You said two routes,' he remarked quietly.

'To Monkey Pitter, yes. Though, by the way, Norman was always reluctant to blame him. He has never accepted what Pitter became.'

'You have, however,' Mark said.

'I knew little of that part at the time. But from 'seventy-four, as you know, I started working on the penetration, indeed the actual espionage, that doesn't so often get mentioned. I mean not from the Great Bear but from the old Bald Eagle.'

Emma smiled.

'Most of my stuff, as you've seen, was right back to the Cold War. The agencies and individuals whom the Americans bought and financed, and beyond that the penetration . . .'

'Of the Left.'

'Of course. But then there was also some luck on our side. After the endless Russian defectors, telling their tales, there were now a growing number of American defectors, coming out of their agencies, and they also had tales to tell.'

'I know,' Mark said. 'I've read them.'

'You've read what's been published. There's a lot of other stuff, some of it legally very difficult. And our own authorities were quick to turn some of these inconvenient Americans out.'

'Yes.'

'From two separate sources, Mark, separate and unconnected, we got the truth about Pitter. Monk Pitter, as of course the Americans all called him.'

'That he had been an American secret agent?'

'That he was still an agent. Behind the excellent cover of a rich, elderly, Lefty buffoon.'

Gwyn interrupted. The anger he had set out with was again coming through.

'You keep saying buffoon. I've only met Pitter twice but I never thought that of him.'

'Yes,' Bill said, confidently. 'And of course he paid your half-brother's fine.'

'He did, and I thanked him.'

'Of course. It was cheap at the price.'

Gwyn raised his voice.

'So that the only guilty man, in this entire business, is Pitter? That's very convenient.'

'Not convenient, Gwyn. Just true.'

'So you say. But it's only what you say. These things get so twisted you can explain them any way you like.'

'I can?' Bill said, smiling.

'One can. One. You see I've learned your bloody lingo.'

Bill got up. He went across to the sideboard and came back carrying the whisky bottle. It was an old malt. He filled Mark's glass first. Emma refused. He moved to stand over Gwyn, holding the bottle in front of him. Gwyn reluctantly picked up his glass.

'Of course we all understand,' Bill said, as he was pouring, 'that you have other reasons for thinking badly of your father.'

Mark moved to protest but already Gwyn had pulled his glass away. Some of the whisky spilled at his feet.

'*Braose bradwr,*' Gwyn said angrily.

'What does that mean?' Bill asked coolly, moving away.

'He doesn't mean it,' Mark said.

'Mean what?' Emma asked.

Mark looked questioningly at Gwyn. His face was hard-set now, and brick-red under the thick grey hair.

'*Bradwr* is Welsh for traitor,' Gwyn said and got up.

Emma stared at him, shocked.

'I'm going,' Gwyn said.

'You just don't want to hear the facts,' Bill said, from the fireplace.

'I'll find my own facts,' Gwyn said, and moved towards the door.

Emma stood indecisively and then hurried after him, catching at his arm. He turned and looked into her face. She waited.

'I'm sorry, Emma,' he said. 'It's never been your fault.'

'It's all right, Gwyn. I understand.'

'But do you also understand that these are things I must know?'

'But Gwyn, you've heard Bill explaining it. It really couldn't have been clearer.'

'Except,' Bill intervened, 'to an already prejudiced mind.'

'No, Bill,' Emma said, turning. 'You should know how Gwyn feels. But just to prove it, Gwyn, I'm going to tell you something even Bill doesn't know. I wasn't going to, but you have a right to know what your father actually did and didn't do.'

'My father,' Gwyn said, 'was Bert Lewis.'

'Of course, dear. I know what you mean. But I've always been close to Norman. That's why I'm so convinced that none of these stories are true.'

Gwyn waited.

'Is that all?'

'No, it isn't all. But what I'm telling you now is quite difficult. Nobody else at all knows it. It was in 1947. That terrible winter. And Georgi and I, by chance really, had got talking with . . . well, never mind the name but we were given a very clear picture of what was called the deficit. I remember that word particularly, in this very new technical field. I don't know all the names but what they now call computers, data processing, information and guidance systems.'

'A deficit where?'

'Why, in the Soviet Union, of course. It was—'

Bill stepped forward decisively.

'Emma! Mother! Leave it at that.'

Gwyn glanced up at him. Beyond him he could see that Mark was on the edge of his chair, his hands covering his face.

'Gwyn has a right to know, Bill,' Emma said firmly. 'And it's the end of the story that matters. Because you see, Gwyn, though Georgi was very cautious about it I'm afraid I wasn't. I suppose I didn't realise quite what was involved. I mean it sounded like just general scientific and technical business.'

'Which in effect it was,' Bill said, supporting her but still standing close.

'Of course. And it seemed to me obvious that I could ask

Norman. He would understand it, anyway, and he would know who else we could talk to.'

Gwyn looked into her face. The hard lines of rest were now softened with reminiscence. She was almost smiling. In some trick of the light he saw how much her now white hair had thinned. The kindly, trusting expression was one he had seemed always to know.

'So I put it to him. I explained about the deficit.'

She paused. Mark was pushing himself from his chair.

'And he just hit the roof. He was as angry as I've ever seen him. He told me, at once, to keep out of anything of that kind. He explained how secret and how dangerous it was. He would have nothing to do with it. In fact he dismissed the whole business as just the meddling of amateurs.'

Gwyn noticed Mark look sharply across at her. She was touching his arm again. She was smiling.

'So you see, Gwyn, I know for a fact that he would never, never, do anything of that kind. I mean even for his sister, who was out of her depth. Which of course I now see that I was.'

'Thank you, Emma,' Gwyn said, 'for telling me that.'

'Yes,' Bill said, 'it's very useful confirmation.'

'So don't misunderstand us, Gwyn,' Emma said, kindly, 'don't think the worst of us. It has really, honestly, never been like these devils are saying.'

She leaned forward and kissed his cheek. He turned, embarrassed. He looked through to Mark and raised his arm for goodbye.

As he moved to the door Bill followed him closely. On the landing Gwyn noticed that Nesta's green heads of miners had disappeared. Where it had been hanging there was an embroidered African landscape. He pushed on down the stairs.

'We'll talk again,' Bill said, at the door.

'Sure.'

'I've got a few things to check and I'll be in touch again.'

'Fine.'

'But above all, Gwyn, don't worry. It's just a stupid try-on. They can't touch you with any of it.'

# 3

❧❀❀❦

## LONDON, 8 JULY 1984

Gwyn carried up the Sunday paper with the breakfast. He put
the tray on the duvet and opened the window. The morning air
was already hot. The grass and the street were dry and dusty.

'Did you get back to sleep in the end?' Jill asked.

'No. I was awake straight through. That's why for a change
I fetched breakfast.'

'The same worries?'

'The same worries.'

He got back into bed. They divided the paper. Gwyn took the
sport and business pages.

'One for pleasure, one for politics,' he said, wryly.

'Politics? All that money stuff?'

'You see how much there is of it. And that's right. That's now
where all the real politics happens.'

'I can't look at it. It sickens me.'

'Yes.'

They ate and read for some time in silence. Then Jill moved
suddenly, almost tipping the tray.

'What is it?' Gwyn asked, irritably.

'Look,' Jill said.

He pushed his own crumpled pages away. He felt sweat start
on his forehead and neck. This was a moment he had never really
acknowledged but now knew he had expected and dreaded.

He looked across to where Jill had turned a page towards

him. He saw the big headline: *Revolution Again in the East?* He stared as if identifying a wrong page. Then he saw the large name, Alec Merritt, and recognised the photograph.

'Is that it?' he asked, recovering.

'Yes. I've often wondered what had happened to him.'

'He lost his seat last year. Don't worry, they'll find him another.'

Jill turned and looked at him.

'What is it?'

'Nothing.'

'Oh, I see,' she said. 'The connection with Alex and then with—'

'No,' Gwyn said quickly. 'They've been divorced for years.'

'It could still remind you, love.'

'I don't need reminding.'

'Then why look at this as if . . . ?'

'Because it's rubbish.'

'You haven't even read it.'

'I've read the bit in idiot type. For our slower readers. For our readers.'

'And you're sure it's rubbish?'

'That while workers' revolutions in Western Europe are a lost cause, a new phase of socialist revolution may be already under way in Eastern Europe, behind the old bureaucratic façades?'

'He's been there,' Jill said. 'For three months.'

'And it's still rubbish. Why do you think this lot print it? To help the workers' cause along? He's just easing his way in. An acceptable Leftish entry into the new Cold War.'

'That's just prejudiced, Gwyn.'

'Yes. Prejudiced. Prejudged. Because I now know that whole gang.'

'What whole gang?'

'That successful metropolitan and university Left. Past and present. The whole family of them.'

He pushed out of bed. He went to the chair by the window and started dressing. Jill watched him, anxiously. When he had finished dressing he went to the door.

'Are you going somewhere?' she asked, controlling her voice.

'Somewhere's about it.'

He stopped and looked back at her. She smiled. He hesitated and then sat on the side of the bed.

'I'm sorry, love.'

'It's all right. I know what it is.'

He got up, restlessly. He walked to the window. When he spoke his voice was almost too quiet to hear.

'I decided in the night that I must go and see Pitter.'

'Pitter? Why Pitter?'

'Because I've run it all through and it doesn't add up. I've been told these different stories but there's no way, no way at all, I can choose which one of them to believe. So something, some key fact, must be missing. I have to try to get hold of it.'

'Why should you expect Pitter to give it you? Either way, in either of the stories, he was mixed up in it. Do you think he'll just tell you if you ask him nicely?'

'I shan't ask him nicely. And I shan't necessarily believe what he says. But in anything like this the only way is to hear all the versions. The truth can come out when you compare them.'

Jill waited. Then she moved the tray and slipped out of bed. She walked over and stood behind him, joining her hands around him. He stood very still.

'Do you think I shouldn't see him?' he asked, quietly.

'You already know what I think.'

'That I should leave the whole thing? Just let go of it?'

'Of course.'

'But you know why I can't.'

'No, I don't know. All I notice . . .'

He turned, still inside her arms. He put his hands on her soft bare shoulders.

'That it's about him?' he said, quietly.

'Well, it seems to be.'

'And that I could go and ask him but it's the one thing I won't do?'

'Something like that.'

'And you think that's wrong?'

'I think you've got your own life, your own family. You should let go of all these others.'

'When it affects who I am? Who I really am? Not just these old acts and deceptions. Not that general politics at all. But here, now, me.'

Jill tightened her hands on his waist.

'It isn't, love, it isn't,' she said, whispering. 'You are Gwyn and we love you. All the rest is just them.'

He was silent for some time. She kept holding him close.

'It's no use,' he said suddenly. 'I just have to know.'

'Then go to see *him*, Gwyn. Go to see Braose.'

She felt his body stiffen against her.

'I'll come with you, love,' she said. 'We can go and do it together.'

He waited, thinking. Then he gently eased himself away.

'I'll get the directory.'

He went downstairs. It took her some moments to realise the implication. He came back with the book open and sat and dialled at the extension. She sat on the edge of the bed, near him.

'Dr Pitter? This is Gwyn Lewis. You may remember we—'

There was a long pause. Jill watched him listening.

'Yes, well I would be glad of a talk. Whenever it's—'

There was again a long pause. He held the receiver very tightly to his ear. She noticed how much his forehead had been caught by the sun. Even with the grey hair he looked younger, suddenly.

'All right, then,' he said and put down the phone.

His eyes and mouth were wide open as he looked across at Jill.

'He'll see me this afternoon.'

'Really?'

'He said he'd been waiting for me to call.'

They stared at each other.

'What does that mean?' Gwyn asked at last.

'It's beyond me, love. You'll have to just go and see.'

She dressed and they went out for a walk in the park at the end of the street. Gwyn didn't want to talk, and she just stayed close to him. After a salad lunch he drove off. Although the day was so hot he had put on a business suit.

Pitter's flat was in a close near Park Lane; on a Sunday it was easy to park. Gwyn rang and spoke into the security phone. The

heavy door was opened and he walked through to the elevator.
It was padded with green velvet, virtually noiseless.

At the fifth floor he stepped out to a high mahogany door,
with a grille shielding it. As he watched the grille slid back. He
knocked on the door. The big brass knocker was shaped to an
ape's face.

The door opened and there again was the small, grey, hunched
man: looking hardly at all older than when Gwyn had last seen
him. Pitter smiled warmly but did not offer to shake hands.
Gwyn followed him through to a room where the slatted blinds
were almost closed and a fan was working. There was some
scent in the air of the room: a sharp tang. The furniture was
elegant; light woods and a great deal of glass. The walls were
hung close with paintings in light frames. There was a computer
and a television set but no books in the room.

'Spritzer,' Monkey offered.

'Thank you.'

'Have you noticed it yet?'

'Noticed what?'

Monkey smiled and walked across to the end wall. He turned
on a spotlight. There was a large oil of a church among trees
and an intensely blue sky with yellow-edged clouds. Gwyn got
up and looked closer at it.

'But I thought . . .'

'A Canadian gallery?'

'It was what they wrote and told her.'

'A harmless deception. I did so very much want it. How is
she, by the way?'

'She's well. She's working very hard in the village.'

'The emergency feeding? Of course. After four months of the
strike!'

'They're very close in Danycapel. They look after each
other.'

'Yes,' Monkey said, switching off the light. 'And the Canadian
gallery paid a good price, once they knew it was for the miners'
strike fund.'

He led the way back to their chairs.

'I should not have disconcerted you,' he said, settling comfort-
ably, 'by admitting that I had anticipated your call.'

'That's all right,' Gwyn said hoarsely, and coughed to clear his throat.

'There is no mystery about it,' Monkey continued imperturbably. 'Mark came to see me. He was extremely agitated. He became even more agitated when having retailed these stories he realised that there was nothing I would say to him.'

'Nothing?'

'Nothing. To him. And I am not sure that he took my point, though he is a subtle man, when I said that an explanation was due to only one person: yourself.'

'That isn't right. If any of it is true a lot of people are owed an explanation.'

'In some itchy way, perhaps. But of those that are available only one man positively needs an explanation: yourself. One woman perhaps also: your mother. But I've assumed, I think correctly, that she would not really be interested.'

'You've assumed a lot. About everything.'

Monkey smiled.

'Yes, I knew you would feel that. But tell me, am I right? Mark didn't get in touch with you?'

'Not since I saw him with Emma and Bill.'

'Exactly. Because as a scrupulous man he doesn't know what to advise. Without reliable facts he risks making things worse, whatever he does. And that, my dear Gwyn, is the point we have all arrived at. For it is the end of the story that makes its telling impossible.'

The rotating fan seemed to stir the light scent in the room.

'Except, you said, to me?'

'There are no exceptions. But in your case, probably wrongly, I think the risk may be justified. Or even if it is not, we must accept the consequences. You have an unanswerable need to know, and since you have come and asked you shall know.'

'I can be trusted, I hope,' Gwyn said, doggedly.

Monkey smiled and shook his head. He settled again in his chair.

'Please listen closely,' he said. 'I shall not repeat it. And to begin with, anyway, do not interrupt.'

'Of course,' Gwyn said.

He stared at the bars of the blinds. Signal lights switched on the computer behind Pitter's head but the display screen was blank.

'It began in Spain,' Monkey said. 'Norman was initially sent to France, by the Party, to help organise the passage of men and materials. With his acquired advantages – I mean as the son of an ambassador and with good German and French – he became more and more useful. You must remember that his attitudes were simple: he was helping to defend a legal government against a fascist rebellion. Nothing that he could do was too much. And that of course was where it all started.'

He lit a cigarette. The smell of Turkish tobacco drifted across.

'He was working in Marseilles. It was at just the time when you were due to be born. Emma was sending him frantic telegrams. He wanted to come back. If I say that he was ashamed, deeply ashamed, I am not trying to make a case for him. He was disturbed and immature, but briefly, and genuinely, he had loved your mother. Not with a mature love, he wasn't capable of that. But through all those years he had been in effect impotent, and was to become so again. In that one brief relationship he knew some difference in himself: a difference that he experienced as love. But he was then immediately subject to pressures from others. He was told by the Party – it was Emma who brought it to him – that he should stop exploiting the inexperience of a young working-class girl. Since he already half-believed this of himself – as I said, it wasn't a mature love and he was more conscious of his own release than of her except in relation to that – he complied; indeed, did worse. He went to Danycapel, he got drunk, he insulted her. The order to go to France was the one simple thing in his confusion. He was ashamed but he was also frantically busy; the one often helps the other.'

There was a click from the computer. Monkey leaned back and touched a switch, watching a run of digits go through and stop.

'It was at this point that there was a shift of dimension. It was a critical period in Spain. For some bad and some good reasons – bad that the Party was increasingly monopolistic, indeed in some ways paranoiac; good that there was indeed some reason to reassess and determine people's loyalties – there was a hard investigation beginning, among the foreign volunteers. People now say that the Russians began it, but there were also Spanish party people and, crucially, some of the French. Indeed it was the French who first approached Norman. With his English and other languages he was an obvious choice. He was asked to go to Spain, under an assumed name, and help conduct the investigation.'

Monkey paused. He looked across at Gwyn, as if inviting him to say something, in spite of his earlier instruction. But Gwyn was sitting dazed, unable to speak.

'It sounds much worse now,' Monkey went on, 'than it did to him at the time. The Civil War was going badly. There were some real traitors, as well as ordinary political opponents. He was certain, in himself, that he would know the difference.'

Gwyn lifted his hand. Monkey paused, but Gwyn did not speak.

'It's the history of our times,' Monkey said and waited.

Gwyn could look only at the carpet between his feet: an intricate, indented pattern of ferns.

'He did what he could,' the steady voice continued. 'But the political complications were beyond him. Not beyond him intellectually, but socially without any doubt. And morally also, I think. Certainly he now thinks so. But the fact is that from that work in Spain – work is the easy word, it was political counter-espionage, under a false identity – he moved into a world that was to determine the rest of his life. When he eventually came back to England – he came at once to see me in Cambridge – he was committed to what he still thought of as political counter-espionage. I can take credit for telling him, immediately, that back in his own country, outside that special situation, it would inevitably, and very soon, be much more than that. For he was now to work, you see, under direct instruction and control from the Russians. As indeed he went on to do.'

Gwyn shifted in his chair.

'Was it a sort of blackmail?' he asked, carefully. 'Because they knew what he'd been doing in Spain?'

'No,' Monkey said. 'You mustn't try to excuse him. He didn't want it excused. There was still a war against fascism, an extending and terrible war. He had chosen his side and he would stick by it. He discounted all the difficulties, including I may say his political doubts, which he expressed very readily to me. And of course he admitted what he called the moral problem: to be doing secret work, to be acting deceptively, when there were, after all, other ways of fighting fascism. He spoke often, in those days, of Bert Lewis. And of course of him and your mother. That memory was there all the time.'

'Just as memory,' Gwyn said bitterly.

'Yes, Gwyn. You if no one else, except of course your mother, are entitled to say that. And in fact it was there that Emma could help him. In a way he was used to, from when they were younger, he let her substitute for him, where he knew he was inadequate.'

'She didn't know about his commitment to spying?'

Monkey smiled.

'You use the hard word. Very well. But no, she knew nothing. He told no one but myself. He didn't even know that there were others sharing his position.'

'Why, then, did he tell you?' Gwyn asked, quietly.

Monkey sat very still.

'He had always told me everything. We had always shared, he once said, both our lusts and our equations.'

Gwyn turned away.

'But you are right,' Monkey continued, steadily, 'it was more than that. He could tell me because he knew that whenever it became necessary I would help him, indeed join him.'

He looked across, candidly. Gwyn held his look.

'Moreover, Gwyn, there was this. There was no general solution to what he had called the moral problem. But there was, we soon agreed, an intellectual solution. What he and I might be able to do, in the opportunities likely to open to us, was indeed a special case: one in which others, however brave, could not volunteer. As indeed it turned out.'

Gwyn felt in his pocket for his handkerchief. Monkey watched the movement intently.

'You've been told,' he went on, 'what we were able to do. It was much more than we had foreseen, because of the speed at which the technology developed, but still it was of a kind we had expected. And I want you to understand that, as it went on,

I was much more active than he was, since it happened that what I was doing was more useful to our side.'

'*Our* side?'

'Indeed. The Russians were our allies. Our only enemies were the fascists.'

'In the war.'

'Yes. In the war. A war in which, when you look at the whole record, good men did virtually everything, including many things they would never otherwise have done, to survive and to gain a victory.'

'Yet it didn't end with the war?'

'You are quite right. I want no easy ways out. But we re-assessed our position, with a good deal of care. We thought it was only a matter of time before the alliances shifted again and the Russians would be either the actual or the nominated enemy. We decided that we at least would not be part of that shift. And I want you to understand that we were not afraid of what others would then say of us. We brought the word out quite openly. We looked at each other and we spoke it, in the cant of the time. We said *treason*. We said *traitors*.'

'In bravado?'

Monkey smiled, but bitterly.

'You could say so, no doubt. But the political equations were exceptionally complex. Traitor, without doubt, is a definable quantity. There are genuine acts of betrayal of groups to which one belongs. But you have only to look at the shifts of alliance and hostility, both the international shifts and within them the complex alliances and hostilities of classes, to know how dynamic this definable quantity becomes. There are traitors within a class to a nation, and within a nation to a class. People who live in times when these loyalties are stable are more fortunate than we were.'

'Not only in times. In places,' Gwyn said.

'That too,' Monkey acknowledged. 'But be clear about it, Gwyn. This is a narrative, not a confession. So I had better make it clear what we actually did. I went to the States, to continue my line of work, but I was still used as a consultant and between us a great deal of information was passed.'

'Through him, you mean, or what?'

Monkey's face hardened.

'That affects others. I cannot tell you. But if you happen to be thinking about Emma . . .'

He paused.

'All that Emma did was give us a very bad scare. She and Georgi had concocted a naive operation and she actually asked Norman . . .'

'I know that,' Gwyn said. 'She told me. And I still don't believe it was an operation. Naive if you like, though why more naive than—?'

'She didn't intend espionage,' Monkey broke in. 'Her mind had got no further than some vague idea that all science should be shared. Georgi too, I suppose, though he wasn't a fool.'

'But why was it so different from what you were doing?'

'Because they had chosen a different activity. They were known and active communists. Thus they had a different loyalty: to be a party in and of the British working class. They had also a different danger: that they would compromise with that loyalty, compromise and disperse it, and also, of course, that if they did they would be more readily and more damagingly detected.'

'Because they were open and you were not?'

Monkey paused and adjusted his rimless spectacles.

'Gwyn, how can I explain this? It was never what you are thinking. Georgi and Emma had chosen a different road, a political road, just as Bert Lewis had chosen to fight fascism in battles and struggles. Ours was a different choice, neither political nor military. What we were doing, indispensably, was operational. It was in a quite different field and equation.'

'I can't accept that.'

'I'm not asking you to accept it. I am asking you to look at a fact. What we were doing was not as communists. We did not see ourselves as communists. It had begun there, of course, but it was now in a wholly different dimension.'

'A Russian dimension. A kind of treason. That's what you're really saying.'

'Not even that. This was a dynamic conflict within a highly specialised field. It was vital to prevent it, through imbalance, reaching that exceptionally dangerous stage in which, by its own logic, it passed beyond nations and classes and beyond all the loyalties that any of us had known. Except, perhaps, in the end, a simple loyalty to the human species.'

'Which nevertheless it now has.'

'Which in weaponry it has. That was implicit, from the beginning, in our development of guidance systems. Each was a stage towards what we now have: a state of computerised war. And in that situation every imbalance, every deficit, is dangerous. But then not through our dereliction. At least, not from anything that we then did.'

'I distrust that kind of argument,' Gwyn said stubbornly.

'Then distrust it. I am not trying to persuade you to anything. I promised only to explain. But in fact what I have been telling you is far from the worst. Indeed in a way it is an old story, with new names. Others did more than we were able to, and some of them were exposed and are notorious. Yet none of it, I assure you, stops there. For we now come to the defectors, and to the way they changed us. Defectors: that other quantity as traitors, in yet another equation.'

He waited. Gwyn was frowning with concentration.

'Where I was, in the States, there was already a high-rank Soviet defector, who had been in Spain. He passed various names, among them an Englishman from Cambridge called Edward Davies. In England they started tracking back. They could find nobody relevant of that name. But of course they came across two names that interested them: my own and Norman's. It was Norman they questioned first, and then me because of our work in the war. But they had very little to go on: enough, in that climate, to get me out of my university but in Norman's case, at first, nothing. Indeed they seem to have ended by thinking him useful, as a reformed spirit. They even sought his help, genuinely, in trying to trace Edward Davies.'

Monkey smiled and shook his head, as if resigned to folly.

'Edward Davies was the name Norman had used in Spain. We laughed. But then two other things happened. Another defector brought information indicating that our kind of work had been passed. A much harder interrogation resumed. And right in the middle of it a woman turned up who had known Norman in Cambridge, a woman in fact with a grudge against him, and she knew the whole thing, through another volunteer who had seen him in Spain and using his false name. If she had passed that on, then, we would probably have been finished. But she didn't, though he fully expected her to. He was very near breaking all that year. It was 1956. We were all being changed.'

Monkey got up and refilled their glasses. As he went back to his chair he was shuffling his feet.

'Yes,' he went on, 'and Norman especially. We survived the interrogation but this woman, now, was a friend of his wife's and they saw each other quite often. Moreover the marriage he had made, to a very different kind of woman, a woman without and not wanting politics, was developing in new ways. They had just moved into a very beautiful house. The crisis of 'fifty-six, from the Stalin revelations to Hungary, had finished what was left of his earlier politics. Will you believe me if I tell you that what came out of that period, in the official mind, was that there had been this dangerous and probably treacherous Pitter but that Norman Braose was a good liberal, who had been over-influenced by friendship and nearly misled?'

'He had given up working with the Russians?'

'No. He had not given it up, though he now did as little as possible.'

'Because he wanted to be comfortable? Not pay his accounts?'

Monkey frowned.

'Gwyn, you are describing a whole epoch. The misled and aggrieved liberal was loud in the land.'

'Admitting what they thought were their errors.'

'Yes, when they had to. It depended on the errors. Norman's, don't you think, would have been a little more than that?'

'So he went on playing his double game?'

'Yes, but as a wraith. The disturbance, the passion, the beliefs of any kind, shrivelled inside him. To an occasional knot in the gut.'

Gwyn leaned forward, his hands clasped tight between his knees.

'Yet when I saw him,' he said, 'though of course it was much later, what came through was a self-possession, an assurance, a manner of total confidence.'

Monkey threw up his hands.

'It's the style of the country,' he said, laughing. 'The English gentleman, the English scholar. It isn't for nothing that they have superb tailors. That style can cover anything.'

'He was still your friend?'

'Yes, he needed me. Among other things I kept his investments afloat.'

'But this isn't what you told me, when we met at Emma's. You said that he had been a most dedicated communist. You said that what he had done had been heroic in its way. You said it was an inheritance I had been deprived of.'

'Up to 'fifty-six, did I mean?'

'How do I know what you meant? What you have told me today deserves none of those terms.'

Monkey looked away, distressed. He got up, slowly, and walked along the room to the wall with the painting. He switched on the light and looked carefully over it. Then he put off the light and walked back.

'It was the rhetoric of 'sixty-eight,' he said, sitting again.

'I don't accept that.'

'What do I care what you accept?' Monkey said angrily. 'What I am telling you now is the truth.'

'Evidently a variable quantity. In different equations.'

'Indeed,' Monkey said, harshly. 'But now one last thing and I have done. On that wraith, as I have called him, there descended in the Sixties a new pressure. First another defector, with more traceable information. It needed all of what you doubtless think of as my guile to protect him, to protect both of us, from that. But the record of suspicion was lengthening, and then in 'sixty-seven there was yet more information. Moreover it was of a kind which now excluded me but pointed quite directly at him. He now had no chance. They pressured him until he broke. He confessed everything he had done: in fact more than he was obliged to. He also, for good measure, confessed what I and others had done. All of it, of course, in return for a guarantee of immunity from prosecution.'

'For you too?'

'That didn't arise. And I then knew nothing about it.'

'You mean they didn't come after you?'

Monkey spread his hands.

'Only one thing Bill Wilkes said was right. That by then, for internal reasons, they didn't want prosecutions and publicity. And I was no danger to them. I was impeccably employed in making money.'

Gwyn smiled.

'Unfortunately that wasn't the case,' Monkey added, sharply, 'for at least two others. They were pushed out of their jobs, on much worse terms than he'd got.'

Gwyn hesitated.

'Then when did you get to know this?'

'Of course, the precise question: because you haven't forgotten Bill Wilkes's version: that I had been turned, that I was an American agent.'

Gwyn waited, watching him. He now suddenly had the confidence to examine him directly.

'Were you?'

'No.'

'Do I have any reason to believe that?'

Monkey extended his hands.

'Well, I don't know how I could prove or disprove it. The fact is, on your question, an American agent did come to see me, in the early Seventies. He had seen all this material. It was from him I first learned all that Norman had done. But his motive was not to pursue me. He was about to resign. He even wanted, against my advice, to go public. And he had come to warn me not to think it was finished. There were still internal disputes, among both British and Americans, about the decision to give Norman immunity. There were groups who believed this kind of immunity was itself a betrayal, to cover up people who were still inside but involved. He wasn't sure if these groups could win. He was in any case heavily opposed to them, politically. They were trying to drag everything back to the old Cold War.'

'They failed, presumably?'

'Did they fail? In fact they lost that particular internal battle. But they then had another resource. Other people were beginning to inquire into this whole period. In fact Bill Wilkes among them, wholly innocently but naively. And what then developed was a technique which you can check for yourself: the feeding of some of this concealed internal material to selected scholars, authors, journalists, who would then, as they could, make it public.'

'Perhaps that's so. But in your case it hasn't gone public.'

'Yet,' Monkey said, and stared at Gwyn with suddenly shining eyes.

Gwyn waited.

'Bill Wilkes,' Monkey said, 'got it muddled. He was never, of course, one of their chosen channels. He was reading the same facts, but from left to right. But have you reflected that what Meele so incidentally disclosed to you—?'

'No,' Gwyn said sharply. 'You can't persuade me of that. Because if it was as you say he would have had all the facts. The full facts from the confession.'

'Of course he has them. You don't understand the technique. Yes, the earlier operators tried feeding whole stories. But many of the people involved were still alive. Publication was very dangerous. So the later operators became more subtle. They would pass on hints and suggestions, one end of a thread. They would let the researchers flatter themselves that they were tracking down the unknown, discovering it for themselves.'

'But in my case? With Meele?'

'Well, they guessed quite correctly. That you would be disturbed by it. That you would start stirring things up.'

'Not for that sort of reason,' Gwyn said, indignantly.

'Are you sure, Gwyn? I mean, you hate him, don't you?'

'Braose?'

'Your father. Your deserting and treacherous father.'

Gwyn got up. He looked around, impatiently, at the elegant room.

'In fact,' he heard Monkey saying, 'the whole operation seems to be already under way. They don't positively need you, though of course they might still try to use you. But the day before you saw Meele – I checked the dates with Mark – I had a visit from a pleasant, ruffled, informal young man: a television researcher, called Meurig. He was working, he explained, on a documentary about the Left in the Thirties. He had been given my name.'

'They do that sort of thing all the time.'

'Coming to me, for God's sake? And with an oh-so-casual interest in Sir Norman Braose?'

'You think he wasn't genuine?'

'Well, he works in television. I checked. And there is some sort of programme, though not quite the one he described. The programme is in fact on espionage.'

'Would he make that sort of mistake?'

'Meurig? Perhaps. Or perhaps deliberately. What you must understand is that the security service puts its own people in to every important organisation. That would of course include television, which is a very good cover for planting some story and for getting others to follow it up. Or else, using that cover, to approach people, in some beguiling way, and try to flush something out.'

As he spoke he stood up. He came close to Gwyn. The almost grotesque lines of the face had hardened. The look was implacable. As Gwyn froze, disturbed by his closeness, the sharp tang of the scent in the air of the room came through more strongly.

'You've taken a risk in telling me all this,' Gwyn managed to say.

'Not from recording. That has been checked. But in any case I am very used to risks.'

'Then what do you now expect me to do?'

Monkey smiled, and extended his hands.

'If I were you, Gwyn, I would do nothing. I would try to forget all about it.'

'Because that's how you have lived.'

'Forgetting, no. But moving when I had to, and for my own reasons, yes.'

'Including today?'

'If you want to think so. My tolerable reason was that I thought you should know the truth.'

'And your intolerable reason?'

Monkey smiled.

'It isn't that bad. It's just a hope really, though it is also my most urgent advice. That you should not go to him.'

'To Braose?'

'To your father. Where you would, in your disturbance,

undoubtedly have gone. Perhaps sooner, perhaps later, but you would have gone.'

'And why should I not go?'

'Because it would be a move in their game. One more move to drag it all out.'

'I don't see that. I would go for personal reasons.'

'Don't, Gwyn. Do not. In the sense you mean there is no person there for you to see.'

'I don't understand you.'

'He is nothing. He is a name. The man and the father are entirely burned out.'

'You're asking me to pity him.'

Monkey closed his eyes and then rubbed them vigorously.

'No,' he said, turning away and still rubbing his eyes, 'don't pity him. Leave that to those who love him.'

# 4

# DANYCAPEL, OCTOBER 1984

Gwyn signalled and swung the car into a layby, on the Heads of the Valleys road. The big lorry which had been pressing close behind them for several miles hooted repeatedly as it sped past.

'On its way for another scab load!'

Gwyn switched off the engine. He didn't answer.

'It's a cash bonanza, carrying imported coal,' Jill insisted.

'Aye, I suppose.'

He reached to the shelf for the binoculars which he now always kept by him. He had been driving slowly because he had been watching, ahead, a high column of smoke. The light was poor, in the late October afternoon. The dense smoke was rising and spreading into a loose grey cloud.

'What are you looking at?' Jill asked.

She was lively and expectant, wanting to see Gwyn's family in Danycapel and to hear all their news.

'That smoke,' Gwyn said shortly.

'Oh, I expect they're just burning the hill.'

Gwyn got out. He was moving as if his whole body was tired. He lifted and focused the long black binoculars, but could see little more, against the light. Yet he could at least judge the distance better. The fire was near the edge of the big forestry plantation at the top of the valley. He moved back to the car. A bedraggled ewe, which had been nuzzling at the overflowing

326

litter bin, crossed in front of him and pushed its head into the
open door of the car.

'Come to see what we've got?' Jill called, brightly.

Gwyn scuffed the gravel to try to make the sheep move.

'People feed them from cars in the summer,' he said. 'It makes
them daft and dependent.'

'It's only a poor old ewe,' Jill said, forcing a laugh.

She had picked up what seemed an unreasonable anger in his
voice. Gwyn pushed forward.

'Get out of it,' he shouted.

The ewe moved reluctantly. It had missed the summer shear-
ing, and patches of its wool, streaked with grease and dirt, were
hanging loose. Two heavy lorries passed, at high speed, their
metal bodies empty and rattling.

Gwyn got in, holding the binoculars carefully in front of him.
He went on staring down at them.

'What was it?' Jill asked, watching him.

'The smoke? It was by the forestry.'

'What did you think it was?'

'I don't know. I suppose I come here expecting it to look like
a battlefield.'

'Not like that it isn't.'

He turned the binoculars in his hands.

'Bert had these. In Spain and then in Normandie.'

'Yes, you told me.'

'They originally belonged to a boy from Cambridge, who got
killed in Spain.'

'Yes, you said. A boy called Paul Howe.'

'Bert gave them to me because he wanted me to know the
connections. To feel the connections.'

She didn't answer. Through most of the summer it had been
like this, often in much the same words. He was not so much
trying to remember the past. Most of the memories were very
clear. It seemed more that he was trying, endlessly, to arrange
and rearrange them. Those words about the connections had
been spoken again and again, yet each time as if he had only
just thought of them. As the silence continued she forced herself
to speak.

'You remember watching the dolphins with them?'

He turned and stared across at her. She smiled. In August, near Aberaeron, they had been watching the sea at a rocky headland and Jill had called suddenly and pointed. Moving across the bay, slowly rolling in glimpses of shining black backs and tails, were five dolphins: five, they made certain, though they were not easy to count. They had shared the binoculars, watching them, until the children came down.

'Yes, I remember.'

There had been Dic's two boys and Gwen's little girl, Dawn. Gwen and her husband Alun were sharing two holiday flats with Gwyn and Jill. Dic, on regular picket duty in the coal strike, had come for only one weekend, and his wife Ellen had stayed only one day more, due back at her job in the sweet factory, which was on extra time and now their main source of income. They had asked their mother Nesta to come, but she had refused. Gwyn had said that she could come to the sea and paint, and she had said she was too tired. When Jill had then said that the sea would do her good she had given other reasons, but in the end it was clear why she was staying. She did not want to go away from Danycapel while it was being put through the wringer. That was how at last, and reluctantly, she had put it to Jill. She said nothing like this to her own children; she expected it to be understood.

But the little children had come and stayed, and Gwyn and Jill, and Gwen and Alun, who were now both teachers, gave them a good holiday. The boys were especially excited by the dolphins, though they wanted them to be sharks and kept saying that they were, the tails looking sometimes like fins. 'As clever as we are, dolphins,' Jill had said; and Gwyn had laughed and said that wouldn't be difficult. The sun had been hot on their backs as they had watched the dolphins moving and turning so easily in the glitter of the sea.

'Shall I drive?' Jill asked, as Gwyn went on sitting still.

'No. It's all right.'

'We'd better get on.'

'Yes.'

'There's still connections now. Here and now.'

He looked across at her, surprised. Then he started the car and drove on. Within a mile they were turning off into the valley towards Danycapel. The sun had broken through in the west, and the upper slopes of the mountain were suddenly bright with the red gold of bracken and the pale gold of larch. There were small white clouds above the ridge, in a patch of blue sky.

They stopped again, at the point where the road began to turn for the long descent to the valley. Halfway down, on each side, there were the fields and trees of the original country. Then the houses started, in their long close rows. The sun was throwing long shadows in the bed of the valley. Above the lines of grey houses there was a thin cloud of white smoke, from just beyond the colliery that was closed by the strike. The sun was catching the smoke and making a strange lattice of beams and arcs: insubstantial and luminous above the solid grey bed. As Gwyn watched he remembered Nesta's many paintings of rainclouds in the valley. This was different and lighter, but there was the same relationship, as now in everything that could be seen. In particular perspectives, and always in its unexpected contrasts, the valley could be seen as dramatically beautiful: 'the view from outside', he had once said to Nesta, but she had shaken her head and said it was always there to be seen; to show it to others was the problem, getting past what was already in their heads. 'But, Mam, you're not saying that really it's beautiful?' 'I'm saying what can be seen,' she had answered, reluctantly, 'but it's different what happens.'

On the western slope of the valley was the new estate, far up between Danycapel and Penybont, where Nesta now lived with Gwen and Alun and Dawn. She had kept on her own house after Bert had died and then for five more years after Dic had married Ellen and brought her to live there. Then, after their first boy, Dic and Ellen had got a house of their own and Nesta had sold the old house. With the money from that sale she had helped Gwen and Alun to buy the house on the estate. She also earned a little for herself, with drawings of children and a few watercolours of houses and farms, which she took on commission in the district. The new houses had central heating and modern bathrooms and kitchens; she had been glad of that. But the estate was stuck so far up on the mountain, and exposed to the winds, that it had got the local nickname of Fools' Paradise. Dic had often teased Gwen about being upwardly mobile. Nesta especially liked doing the drawings of children. 'There's nothing else so good to look at, though when I get them interested they do better ones of me.'

Gwyn drove down carefully, in the fading light. In Penybont there were few people about but there were cars and vans parked on both sides of the steep narrow streets, and a mist was just thickening into drizzle. Many of the shops were empty; others had large notices of Sales and Reductions pasted across their windows. After seven months of the strike there was only the smallest trickle of money. Many of the small, smartly painted terrace houses had Sale notices on posts in their tiny front gardens. They would be there a long time. As Dic had said angrily, in the summer: 'We've been designated, all of us, redundant. Only the grass will have to grow over us before we're a Tourist and Recreational Area and other buggers will buy our houses.' Yet the terraces, equally, had been there a very long time, from the first frantic building of the coal-rush which had stoked an Empire and a Navy and what was then called the British Nation. A few were now blocked up in doors and windows, but most were treasured houses, with the brightness of the paint, the variety of new doors, the decorative glass and the fine curtains in the windows. The smartness would persist for some time, in this township that seemed now under siege.

Through Penybont they turned to the wide modern road, with its abundant lighting, that climbed towards the estate. The old tip, on their left, was dark above them, but it had been grassed down to the concrete roadside wall. They climbed to the new redbrick houses, leaving behind the grey of the town. There was a multiple sign: Rowan Avenue, Walnut Grove, Spindle Lane, Oak Close, Chestnut Close. 'The new nature,' Alun had joked; 'not the trees, just the names.'

They parked under the flowering heather bank of 43 Spindle Lane. The house windows were dark. Gwyn sat for some time, with the keys in his hand, not moving. Jill got out. She went up and rang the front bell, then walked round the side and looked in at the windows.

'Nobody in,' she said, coming back.

'It's a bit early for Gwen and Alun.'

'But your Mam and Dawn?'

'I don't know.'

He was sitting looking down. He had sunk back into himself. She opened the car door and got in beside him.

'Well, I'm glad your Mam isn't here, to see you like this.'

'I don't know what you mean.'

'Gwyn, look where you are. These are people with real troubles. You can't come here brooding at them.'

'You know what the problem is,' he stirred himself to say.

'No, I don't, not compared with what they're going through.'

It was the latest exchange in a long argument over the summer. He had not really moved on from those critical days of the interview with Meele, which still burned in his mind, and then the hard dislocations of the visits to Mark, to Emma and Bill, and finally, strangely, to Pitter. The many words were all still there: the long and articulate exchanges which had appeared to make things clear but which though they ran and re-ran through his mind left only, in their outcome, a dazed uncertainty. What it came to, as it persisted, was a series of answers, clear but alternative answers, to important questions, but it would not settle as that. What seemed there, ungraspable, was some quite different question.

It had been three anxious weeks before his clearance for promotion had come through: three weeks of waiting which Jill had understood, supportively, as anxiety about the job. It was only when the tension persisted, beyond this obvious cause, that she had begun arguing with him. He had then told her, for the first time, the full substance of Pitter's revelations, carefully repeating and inserting the alternative version, from Bill and in part from Emma. It was then an interrupted, uncertain, always scrupulously qualified narrative, which in the end seemed obsessive in its continuing uncertainty. She had at first gone through it with him carefully, understanding his concern. But as he continued to rehearse it she became impatient with the repeated insertions and qualifications. He must make his mind up what was the truth, one way or the other, and if he couldn't he should forget it.

'I mean, it's their affair. It's nothing really to do with you.'

'How can you say that? I was born into it.'

'Not into these games they all played. You can't distress yourself for that.'

'I know. The flip side. If it's far enough back it was only games. Like the battle of the Jarama and the fight with the Death's Head division. Or all those boring Cold War conflicts of loyalties.'

'The fighting was serious. The rest of it isn't. They were all at it, one way or another.'

'All passing on secrets? All living a lie?'

'Not the real people, no. They had their lives to keep them busy. But the rest, you've seen them, and it's always the same. Lying and fixing, looking after their own greedy interests.'

'Is that all this was?'

'No, spying is the bit they've separated out. The bit that can most easily be seen as betrayal and stupidity. But then put in all the rest. A Labour government, there on the backs of honest people, giving a secret order to make the atom bomb, making secret agreements with the Americans for bases, lying about Korea. Living those lies to protect themselves, to stay on top in that sort of world.'

Gwyn pushed this away.

'No, Jill. That's just general politics.'

'General and particular. They were all formed by their secrets. Yes, there were these people who worked for the Russians, but there were a lot more, as time went on, working under cover for the Americans, and before long they were everywhere, in the political and commercial agencies: American, Japanese, German, the lot.'

'There's still a basic difference,' Gwyn insisted.

'Only in the way they tell it.'

'In that, of course, but it's more. The people like Braose and Pitter are in many ways worse than those others. Because they involved in their betrayal what should have been the alternative: their own working-class party, their socialism.'

'That's twisted, Gwyn. As if you wanted to write us all off.'

So, over the months, it had recurred. Whenever Gwyn had said that he must in the end go to Braose and insist on the truth, Jill had angrily opposed him.

'Even Pitter told you not to go to him.'

'Pitter! The man you called a creepy devil? That dirty rich old man?'

'All right. But haven't they all done you enough damage? And done your Mam more? What would she say if you went creeping to Braose?'

'I wouldn't go creeping.'

'You'd go sorry for yourself and expecting him to change it. But he couldn't help you if he wanted to. And he won't want to.'

'There's still an obligation to the truth.'

'Yes, but to the whole truth. You said the alternative: our own working class, our own socialism. But those are here, Gwyn, still here, whatever that damage in the past. You can't put that old trouble before your duty to be loyal now.'

There were cars arriving and lights coming on in the other houses, behind the shrubs of Spindle Lane. Jill looked across.

'Do you think perhaps they've gone down to Dic?'

'I don't know.'

'Well, we can go and see. It's no use sitting here.'

They drove back through the estate and down the new road for the turn to Danycapel. The orange streetlamps were coming on. The red of the car bonnet had changed to grey under the lights. Dic's terrace house was on the edge of the village, in an old street above the pit. It was on the opposite side of the valley from where Bert and Nesta had lived and where Gwyn had spent most of his childhood. When they found Dic's house the window was unlighted. They had knocked and waited, and were getting back in the car, when an old lady came from next door. She recognised Gwyn.

'How is she, Gwyn?'

'I'm sorry?'

'Oh, I thought you'd come from Ellen. You know they've took her to the hospital?'

'Ellen? No, I didn't.'

'Only she'd been waiting months for the operation but this morning she was took very bad and the ambulance come for her.'

Gwyn stared. Jill moved and stood closer to the worried old lady.

'Is it the hysterectomy?'

'Yes, love. It's her womb.'

'When did she go in?'

'Soon after twelve the ambulance come.'

'Where's Dic?'

'They sent him a message. He's down Port Talbot, picketing.'

'Where's his Mam, do you know?'

'Nest? Well, she's down the old Rialto. The food parcels, see, love.'

'Should we go to the hospital?' Gwyn asked, dazed.

'Let's see your Mam first.'

They drove down through the village. As he stared ahead, along the familiar narrow streets, Gwyn felt a different consciousness coming steadily through. But it was not a familiarity; it was an edge of emergency and of a need to move. As the edge came, it was as if strength began to flow back.

Under the new buildings of the pit, now locked and silent, unpicketed because of the local solidarity, several cars were parked. The yard lights showed a queue outside the old cinema building, the Rialto, which had become first a bingo hall and then a carpet warehouse and then empty. There were yellow lights inside it, and also, across the yard, in the Welfare Hall. An outside light showed the treasured bowling green, now brown with an autumn dressing of peat. The queue outside the old cinema took Gwyn back to the endless queues for filmshows there, in the Forties and early Fifties. And it was in this yard, he remembered, looking round at the new and now dark pit buildings, that he had stood holding Bert's hand on Vesting Day, in 1947, when the band had played and the flag had been raised and the speeches had said that the pits were returned to the people.

Jill had moved across to the queue. She was already shaking hands with two women near the front. Gwyn followed, at first not recognising anyone. Then he saw Jim, his uncle, Nesta's brother: not in the queue but standing at the door, as if controlling it. The slim body was still erect. The hair was a fine silver and the face – the Italian face Emma had always called it – was refined and assured. When he spoke the voice was deep and resonant.

'Come for your parcel, then, Gwyn?'

Gwyn was briefly disconcerted. The amused mockery of the question was delivered, as always, with exceptional courtesy.

'No, we come down to look for Mam.'

Jim smiled. Gwyn stared at him. In his tone and standing Jim had that assurance which Gwyn had once taken for granted, among his elders in this valley: a manner which the English, for their own reasons, had decided to call aristocratic. He was watching Gwyn carefully, with the same slight smile.

'I thought perhaps it had reached London, this little local problem of ours.'

'The food parcels, is it?'

'Aye, the sweet communal food. Like we have reversed evolution, passing from spiritual to material sustenance. Where we used to queue for Errol Flynn we now stand to for soup and potatoes.'

'Is Mam inside, then?'

'Aye, she is. And your Aunt Pattie. Feeding the five thousand as in the well-known miracle. Except, to be honest, we've grafted for most of it ourselves. We have begged door to door and in the streets.'

'You know Ellen's been taken to hospital?'

'Aye, Pattie was saying. They sent for Dic. Only Gwen and Alun have gone over, visiting her. They went from school.'

Gwyn looked along the queue. Jill was still talking there, and he now saw several faces he knew: men and women he had been to school with. He walked across and shook hands. There was a liveliness in all the voices that contradicted the patient, apparently resigned standing.

'Don't worry, boy, we've stood worse than this,' Phil Evans said to him, holding on to his hand: Phil Evans who had been the youngest boy, just started, helping to raise the flag in 1947.

'It's wicked.'

'Worse than that, boy. It's evil. But down here we are stronger than evil.'

He smiled and released Gwyn's hand. Gwyn moved away. He felt, looking round, that he had been talked to as a stranger, but there was Jill, still close, moving along with the queue, talking animatedly as if these were her own people.

He went to the old cinema door and looked inside. There was a trestle table in front of the old box-office. It was loaded with filled white-and-orange plastic bags. Nesta and Pattie were standing behind the table: Pattie handing over the bags, Nesta checking and crossing off on a list. Beyond them, on what had been the stairs to the balcony, little Dawn was sitting, in a red hooded coat, rubbing her eyes.

'Go in, mun,' Jim said.

'No, I'll wait.'

There were lively voices from the table. A middle-aged woman in a very thin, worn green coat was arguing with his aunt Pattie. The woman's hair was bleached yellow, but it was so thin and dry that he could see right through to the scalp. Pattie, beyond her, was plump and noisy and smiling.

'Only her at 47,' the woman was saying, 'there's her husband back from hospital, so that's their two, and their Ray has moved in with them, being a single man and nothing at all coming in.'

'Aye, but did she ask you to get it all for them?'

'She did. I told you. What sense I could get out of her.'

Pattie turned to Nesta, who leaned forward into the light. Her hair was now dyed black. She had put on blue eye-shadow. An intricate bright-steel necklace was tight at the collar of her close-fitting dark-blue dress.

'I can't tell from this,' Nesta said.

'What it is, see, love,' Pattie said cheerfully, 'if we give it for others to take . . .'

'Well, you did. I'm telling you. You give it my sister for her neighbour that's working.'

Nesta stared up at the woman. She was tapping her pencil on the list.

'It's all right,' she said. 'I'll find a way to mark it.'

Pattie handed over three bags. The woman clutched them and hurried out. Nesta made no mark on the list.

'It's our own discipline now,' Jim said from behind him.

'Difficult,' Gwyn said.

'No, not difficult. Because it's also our own sense of our people and their needs. Like in this district alone we've had the hundredth baby born to a mining family since the strike started. There's a special requisition form, for the different sorts of baby-food, and they come top of the list from the fund. Then the rest, the adults. I've been doing some of the buying. Like I never thought in my life I'd order a hundred tons of potatoes and a thousand dozen eggs. If I get a reduction of even a halfpenny that's a lot more families fed.'

'Is there money coming through from outside? We've been collecting.'

'Some, aye. But if the cheques say Miners on them that's it. The bank just freezes them, since the sequestration. Except what I do now, I take the cheques and discount them, never mind exactly where.'

'Can it last, Uncle?'

'While we're upright it'll last. Our own affairs, see, we've always been able to run.'

The queue was moving more quickly now. Two women, collecting their bags, leaned over the table and kissed Pattie. Jill came in, sat beside Dawn and put her arm around the little girl's shoulders. Nesta looked up and smiled across at them. She had still not looked at Gwyn.

A man in his fifties came over with his bag and stopped to speak to Jim. His face was very thin and pale, under close-cropped sandy hair. He opened the top of the bag and looked at what was inside: a tin of corned beef, a tin of tuna, a bag of rice, a pack of teabags, a packet of sugar, a carton of margarine.

'Veg is extra, Harry,' Jim said, chirpily.

'How d'you mean, mun?'

'Well, you had it the weekend. The spuds and the white cabbage.'

'Aye, good spuds.'

'Of course they were. Who do you think bought them? Because, mind you, we know about the market.'

'You reckon?'

'Always have, mun.'

Jim winked at Gwyn. Harry looked between them.

'It's being on my own, see,' Harry said. 'I don't get nothing, being a widower.'

'Aye, well, like all these young single chaps. But there's plenty of women about. Get married, that's my best advice.'

'Fat chance of me.'

'Well, it's your decision, Harry. Only watch it, mind. None of that up the mountain and cutting the throats of poor sheep.'

'Never, mun.'

'I'm telling you. A grateful government, by arrangement with the Coal Board, have given all poor colliers a free hand up the mountain.'

'You're having me on, Jim.'

'Never! You think I would? Only watch you don't go past the sheep to the ponies. The taste for horsemeat is still a bit backward down here. Up Nottingham, they reckon, them brave working miners, they can't get enough of it. It's to their taste.'

Harry closed his bag. He walked out through the wide doorway.

'Poor bugger,' Jim said. 'He seems older than me.'

'It's getting to people.'

'Not getting, boy. Got.'

The last of the queue was now at the table. Outside, the drizzle was thickening and there were big haloes of orange mist around the streetlamps. Jim and Gwyn stood watching as the table was cleared. The last people stayed to help. Everyone stood close, almost touching. Gwyn felt the physical closeness, in a shift in himself.

There were seventeen bags left. Jim was with Nesta, looking over the list. Their faces were very alike, as they bent to the stapled papers.

'I'll run this last lot round,' Jim said, and pulled away.

'Can I help?' Gwyn offered.

'No, you run your Mam and Dawn home. And this lovely wife of yours, of course. Though you can leave her with us if you like.'

Pattie came from behind the table, flushed and excited. She kissed Jill, then reached up and hugged Gwyn. He bent and she kissed his cheek. Then she took a share of the bags from Jim and they walked slowly across the yard to their car. Nesta got up, closing her eyes.

'Tired, Mam?'

She opened her eyes and looked steadily at Gwyn. She did not answer. Her face was set and assured, even proud: giving nothing away. She moved across him to Jill and Dawn and picked the little girl into her arms and kissed her. They walked out together to the car in the yard. Gwyn followed, closing the big glass door.

Jill took Dawn in the back of the car and Nesta sat beside Gwyn. He leaned across to show her the seatbelt but she quickly fastened it herself. Gwyn drove in silence. Jill and Nesta talked about Ellen. At the house Jill carried Dawn in and went through to the kitchen to make tea. Nesta sat in the front room, very upright, beside a tall white bookcase.

She said nothing until the tea was brought in, and then spoke only to Jill. Dawn, now lively again, fetched a sketchbook and showed it to Jill, who took her on her knee.

'Nan bought me special crayons.'

'I can see. They're lovely.'

'Only this was to be me as the Green Fairy. Can you see the big wings?'

'In the school play, was it?'

'Yes, but then they cancelled it. We did a different one.'

'Were you in that too?'

'Yes. I was the other end of the washing line.'

Nesta laughed, lifting her hand and covering her eyes.

'The *other* end?' Jill asked, seriously.

'Yes, Phyllis was the first end.'

Jill went on looking through the sketches. Gwyn waited. Nesta had uncovered her eyes and was watching them, smiling.

'Can we put up here, Mam?' Gwyn asked. 'Or shall we go down to Dic's?'

'Here's all right,' Nesta said, looking at him. 'We've got the pullout.'

'I'll get our bag, then.'

She raised her eyebrows but didn't answer. He went out to the car. When he came back Nesta had gone, and Jill was with Dawn in the kitchen.

'What is it?' he asked.

'What's what?' Jill said, bending over Dawn.

'Mam. She's very strange. I mean, strange with me.'

'You're imagining it, Gwyn.'

'No.'

'Go and wait for her, then, I should.'

He went back to the front room. He found the local weekly

paper and sat reading it under the lamp. Nesta came in very quietly. When he looked up she was already in the centre of the room.

'Mam,' he said, getting up.

'Don't fuss, Gwyn.'

'I'm not fussing.'

'All right. Only we're all at full stretch.'

'I know that, Mam.'

'Do you? You've got your own interests.'

He put the paper down.

'What does that mean?'

'From what I hear,' Nesta said.

Her big eyes were very bright. Her hair was shining, and there were glints of the room lights on the bright-steel necklace.

There was the sound of a horn in the street. She rushed to the window.

'Oh Dic, that's good,' she said, and hurried out to the door.

Gwyn looked out. There were two cars: one with Dic, one with Gwen and Alun. The three came in together, talking across each other to Nesta. They all stood close in the passage from the door. They had met up at the hospital. Ellen was comfortable but would have the operation tomorrow. Dic had pelted up, he said, from Port Talbot, 'faster even than scab lorries'. The others moved away, talking, Nesta with her arm round Gwen's shoulders. Dic turned and looked at Gwyn.

'You all right?' Gwyn asked.

Dic shrugged. His rough black coat was covered with white dust on the shoulders. The rain had got into his cropped dark hair. He was in some ways now very like Bert: the same height and bulk, and the heavy shoulders. The skin of the face and hands was reddened, and there was a crop of bristles around the chin.

'Been trying to stop them? The scab lorries?' Gwyn asked.

'Nobody really stops scabs. You just wait for the buggers to fall off.'

'It's disheartening, the union drivers.'

Dic flopped on to the sofa.

'You say disheartening, I say criminal.'

He looked up under his heavy eyebrows.

'It is,' Gwyn agreed.

'Only we're still,' Dic said, 'talking like kids: *Please to remember, you trade union member, If we get beat then it's your hot seat, When they finish with coal, It's you for the dole.* It isn't chanting we want. It's only the facts will break through.'

Alun brought in two tankards of beer and went back to the kitchen. Jill and Gwen were still laughing, talking to Dawn. Gwyn sat beside Dic on the sofa, brushing his coat with his shoulder.

'I agree with that, mun, but the way I see it it's the politics have gone wrong. We've taken solidarity for granted, though the whole social order has been working for years to break it up. And they've used everything, right back to the Cold War.'

'Bugger the Cold War,' Dic said, and drained his glass.

'No no. It's what's helped them. They got this story around that there were communists everywhere, all working for Russia and doing this country down. And all the rest were moderates, decent working men with their mortgages.'

Dic clenched his big fist.

'Is that our fault? Is it mine? I tell you without us communists, back to Dad's time and before, they'd be all these pussycat unions, thinking the bosses will see them all right.'

'Some of us still got it wrong, though. Getting attached elsewhere and letting them isolate us.'

Dic turned and looked hard at Gwyn. Then he got up and pulled off his heavy coat. A cloud of white dust rose around the ceiling lamp, with its fringed pink shade.

'All that don't touch us down here.'

'Yes, Dic, it is touching you. There's a whole mobilisation against you.'

Dic squared his shoulders.

'Then let the buggers come. We'll see in the end of it.'

'They don't have to come, Dic. They can do it from where they are. This is a world of paper and money. It's taken priority over coal, people, anything else that's real and alive.'

Dic compressed his lips. He sat heavily on a corduroy hassock and began unlacing his boots. Then he looked across to the doorway. Nesta was standing there gazing between them. Gwyn, following Dic's look, jumped up and turned to his mother.

'You won't go tomorrow on that picket,' Nesta said to Dic.

'Aye, five in the morning,' Dic said, roughly.

'You ought to stay to see Ellen.'

'I'll be back the afternoon, go straight up.'

'You'll have no food in the morning.'

'Aye, at home.'

Nesta put up her hand to the bright-steel necklace. Her fingers moved it around her collar.

'Gwyn will bring you some down, from here.'

'What, four in the morning? That's when I set off.'

'Gwyn will bring it. And you'll stop tonight for your supper.'

Dic eased off his boots. His heavy wool socks were matted at the heels.

'Of course I'll help,' Gwyn said, quickly.

Nesta smiled but did not look at him.

They ate in the kitchen, crowded around the table and with Gwyn and Dic perched at the modern breakfast-bar. They were all so close together that it was difficult to use their knives and forks. Gwyn and Dic kept bumping each other. The kitchen was very warm, with the heat from the cooker and the smells of bacon and baked potatoes. Dawn, perched on a stool between Gwen and Jill, did most of the talking, with a long story of the dancing practice at school and a mix-up of pumps between her and Eira. It was all to do with making a girl out of flowers, only Nan had painted the girl for them and she was called Blodeuwedd. 'A bit of the *Mabinogi Fourth Branch*,' Alun noted, but the story flowed past this until it was interrupted by Gwen's insistence that Dawn should stop talking and eat something, one of the sausages at least that Auntie Jill had cut up. Dic and Gwyn drank more beer. 'A bit like Christmas,' Dic said; 'all we want's the funny hats.'

'You should be glad to have a family around you,' Nesta said, smiling at him.

After the meal Gwyn and Alun washed up, while Gwen and Jill, with more laughing, went to give Dawn her bath and put her to bed. Dic had another beer and then went home to sleep. Nesta had gone off somewhere. Carrying up the overnight bag, Gwyn found her in the small back bedroom, making a bed on the pullout.

'Let me help you, Mam.'

'It's done.'

He stood and watched her finishing.

'What did you mean, just now, I got my own interests?'

She was folding a spare pillowcase.

'I don't want to talk about it, Gwyn.'

'About what, though? What have you been hearing?'

She looked angrily across at him. She pushed past him and shut the door. She stood with her back to it.

'Gwen told me. More than I wanted. She got it from Jill, in the summer.'

'About Braose, you mean? I should have come and told you myself.'

'Me? Why me? I've got enough of my own concerns.'

'Yes, but it goes back that far.'

'Too far.'

'Is that really what you think?'

She didn't answer. He sat on the bed.

'Mam, I've never really asked you . . .' he began, and stopped. She said nothing. She was watching him. Her eyes were bright.

'It's difficult, obviously, but I get told such different things. About him especially, and at just that time when you knew him.'

On the last words he looked at her. She smiled, encouragingly.

'I've been told that he really loved you. Is that true?'

'How should I know?' she answered.

Her face was lively and amused.

'Did you love him?'

Nesta smiled again, but did not answer. He watched her and then looked away.

'It's got nothing to do with this other,' she said, suddenly.

'No, of course not.'

'So what are you asking?'

'You know what I asked.'

She nodded. She was very firm and self-possessed, at ease with herself. Still her eyes were bright.

'I'm sorry,' Gwyn said. 'I shouldn't be bothering you. With all this hardship down here, this other's so distant. But you see it's just filled my mind. There are all the questions I can't answer. Not just questions about myself.'

She hesitated. He misjudged the moment and got up to go.

'No, wait,' she said quickly.

'I shouldn't be bothering you.'

'Me? Don't think about that. But you're a grown man, there's no need to be so frightened.'

'Am I frightened?'

'Of something. Yes, you are.'

He stood and waited.

'Come through. I've got something to show you,' she said quickly.

She put down the pillowcase and led the way along to her own room. The walls were covered with paintings; there were many more stacked against the walls, around the narrow white bed. She looked downstairs and then closed the door.

'You've been painting a lot, then,' he said.

'No. Just the years pile it up.'

She was bending over one of the stacks of paintings, against the wall by the head of her bed. She took two out, and laid them face down on the counterpane.

'Do you really want to know?' she asked, with an ironic smile.

He didn't answer. She took up the smaller painting and turned it so that she was looking down at it. Then she leaned across and propped it at the head of the bed.

Gwyn saw the colours first: sharp yellow and a surprising light blue. They seemed to jump from the cool white counterpane. He moved for a different light and then saw the head of a young man, the face turning and staring. It seemed at first that it could be reduced to startling blue eyes and loose yellow hair, but the same colours ran through the features and the shapes of the background. He went forward and looked more closely. Nesta stood beside him.

'You never showed me this, Mam. When did you do it?'

'Before you was born.'

He stepped back. He moved several paces away. He felt a rush of heat in his neck.

'I wouldn't have known him,' he said, still staring.

'No. Though Emma said it was very like.'

'Did you think so?'

She smiled.

'Well, nobody and nowhere's those colours.'

'It's happy, though, isn't it? More than happy. It's a great burst of sunlight and sky.'

'Is that what you see?'

'It's what I feel as much as see.'

'It's still the head of a young man.'

'I know.'

He sat on the edge of the bed. He kept his back to her.

'Is this the answer to my question?'

'That's for you to say, Gwyn.'

'You mean that you did love him?'

'I just tried to paint what I saw.'

'And what you felt?'

'Well, yes, I did feel it.'

He shifted and looked round at her.

'And now?' he asked.

'Now!' she said, laughing. 'I was seventeen.'

'Well, sometimes these feelings last.'

'Only this one didn't,' she said and laughed again.

'Because he didn't love you? Or because he deserted you?'

'No, before that. I just saw him one day turn ugly.'

'Something he did?'

'Something he said. He tried to make me feel bad.'

'Why?'

'How do I know why? You say did he love me? Those few days he did.'

'Then what happened?'

'It happened in him. And it killed it.'

He stood and looked across at her.

'I'm sorry, Mam.'

She turned away, touching her hair.

'No need to be sorry. I got you to remember from it. And what you have to understand, I found a much better man.'

He hesitated and then spoke again, quietly.

'Did he ever talk politics to you?'

She looked back at him, puzzled.

'They all talked politics. Except those few days, him and me.'

'Was it part of it, do you think?'

'No, of course it wasn't part of it. Haven't you looked at the picture?'

'I was wondering, that's all. Even the picture looks like some sort of brighter world.'

'Well, it was. Those few days.'

He moved, carefully.

'You still talk as if you think about them.'

'No, it's like it happened to somebody else, and with somebody else.'

'Because it's so long ago.'

'Aye, and your grey hair to remind me. But it isn't that. It was just a few days, and feelings that couldn't last. The feelings of a very young girl.'

'And of a young man?'

'Not him. He wasn't strong enough.'

'To last, you mean?'

'To be that,' Nesta said.

She moved the picture. Gwyn glanced at it again. But Nesta had leaned forward and taken up the other picture. Her eyes were narrowed as she gazed down at it.

'See this,' she said suddenly, and turned the second picture so that it stood beside the other.

Gwyn stepped back, sharply drawing his breath. He stared for some moments and then looked across at her. Her face was working in strong feelings, her mouth loose, her eyes narrowed. With an effort Gwyn looked back.

It was immediately Bert: the face was never in doubt. The oils were streaked and jabbed to the domination of the damaged eye: hard pitted lines of grey and silver and purple pulling down the staring dark socket. The whole face, under the cropped hair, was distorted around these lines which pulled from the dark hollow. Angry streaks of crimson and purple pulled beyond the hard shoulder.

Gwyn closed his eyes. He had seen and since remembered, so often, Bert's damaged face that he had supposed it could never now shock him. But this was not only worse than he had ever seen him. It was terrible beyond any likeness, as if the already damaged face was still being broken and pulled apart, as all the lines seemed to move.

He made an effort and looked again. Nesta was standing close to the picture. Her hands were tight over her mouth and she was crying silently. He walked round the bed and took her arm. From close in the thick oils seemed to disintegrate the face even further, breaking it until there were only these jabbed lines of angry colour.

'When, Mam?'

'When I'd seen him in the hospital.'

'Did he ever see it?'

'Of course not, no.'

'Why?'

She moved her hand and wiped her eyes.

'When he was dying he seemed to go back to all that. There was this tank exploding and he was shouting "Paddy!" and then "Death's Head!" I don't know what he meant. But I must have felt some of it, back in the hospital. Though Emma was there and Bert was trying to cheer me up.'

Gwyn stayed close to her. He could see her shoulders trembling.

'Thank you for showing it me, Mam.'

She didn't answer.

'It's the strongest thing you've done.'

She looked round at him, wiping her eyes.

'What do that matter?'

'Of course it matters. And with that pretty fantasy beside it . . .'

'What are you saying, Gwyn?' she burst out.

Her face was now intensely agitated.

'I'm saying that in its way this is intensely beautiful. It is a kind of—'

She grabbed at his coat. He looked down at her.

'What did you say?' she asked, in a low voice.

'I said that the painting is intensely beautiful, it is—'

Nesta screamed suddenly. He stared at her, bewildered. She pushed him hard away. He staggered slightly as he went back. Nesta screamed again.

'Mam,' he said. 'Mam, what is it?'

She was staring at him, angrily. Her face and body seemed twisted with sudden pain. He was bewildered because he had never seen her in even ordinary anger. She had been always so contained and quiet and pleasant, always younger than her age, self-possessed and slightly withdrawn.

'*It is not beautiful!*' she screamed, in a terrible high voice.

'Mam, please, I didn't mean that,' Gwyn struggled to say.

'Do you understand nothing?' she screamed. 'Do you know nothing? Have you learned nothing?'

'Mam, all I meant—'

'It is not beautiful!' she cried again. 'It's ugly. It's destroying! It's human flesh broken and pulped!'

'Yes. Yes in him. But the truth, that you saw the truth—'

'It's ugly, it's ugly!' she screamed, now past all control.

She ran towards him and began beating his chest with her fists. He stood numb and appalled.

The bedroom door was pushed open. Gwen and Jill hurried in. Gwen rushed across to her mother, putting her arm round her shoulders. Jill stared at Gwyn. He looked steadily back. Jill, turning, saw the two pictures. Her face showed her surprise.

She recovered quickly. She jerked her head, for Gwyn to go out. For some moments he could not move but then he pushed himself forward. The door closed behind him.

He stood for some time on the stairs. No one else was moving. He waited to get his breath back and then walked downstairs, still numb. The television was on in the front room. Alun was slumped in a chair, watching.

'Gwyn! Want a beer?'

'No thanks.'

He took a chair near the window. He half-watched the screen: edited highlights of rugby. As some feeling came back he tried to go over what had happened upstairs. He could still not make sense of it, and especially of that cry: 'Do you understand nothing, do you know nothing, have you learned nothing?' The figures ran and swerved on the screen. The words ran and blurred in his mind.

After what seemed a very long time – the rugby had finished and was being followed by the News – Gwen and Jill came downstairs. Gwen looked in and stared across at Gwyn. Jill sat down and began listening to the news.

'Is she all right now?' Gwyn asked.

Jill glanced at him, with irritation.

'Well, is she?'

She looked back at the screen.

'You shouldn't have disturbed her with all that,' she said.

'But I—'

'Not now.'

The News ended, and a film began. Gwen reappeared, carrying a tray of tea. She took one cup and went upstairs with it, returning almost at once. The streets of New York flowed in front of them. *Walk. Don't Walk.*

Gwyn got up and went to the kitchen. He stared out at the garden, through the rain-streaked window. Nobody else came.

Then suddenly his mother was behind him. He had not heard her come in. She was just standing, reflected in the glass. He looked round.

She went past him and washed the cup and saucer she was carrying. She put them to drain.

'I've set your alarm,' she said.

Her voice and manner were quite normal. He watched and waited.

'For three,' she said. 'And I shall be up. I want Dic to have a box and a thermos. You'll take them down.'

'Sure.'

'And Mrs Probert next door has got the two boys. I'll give you a bag you can leave on her step.'

'Right.'

'Dic's got his duty, you understand that?'

'Of course.'

'Down here we stand by each other.'

'I know, Mam. You don't have to tell me.'

She went quickly to boil a kettle. She filled a hot-water bottle.

'Good night, then,' she said, and walked quietly out.

# 5

❧ ✿ ❧

# WESTRIDGE, NOVEMBER 1984

In the deep cross-valley, under the Cotswold scarp, the trees of early November still held their dying leaves. Driving slowly along the narrow country roads, Gwyn looked at the passing trees: at the rich yellows and reds of the horse chestnuts, in leaves already hanging to fall; at the light yellows of beech and field maple and sӯcamore; at the sharper almost metallic yellow of a stand of larches; at the sudden surprising green of a line of ash which had not yet turned.

The seasons could in effect be reversed, he found himself thinking: to the reassurance of autumn, in its diversity and richness of colour, its soothing, even caring light; and to the bleak challenge of spring, in that hard light's glare and the sparseness of buds on the black and grey of old branches.

Down a sudden pitch he found the last turning: a wooden fingerpost in an overgrown, yellowing hawthorn hedge. He was very near now. He could not turn back, though he could still just drive past. Then the big white field gate was ahead of him, and the name of the house in black iron on its top bar. The gate was open. He changed down and turned in. The curving drive rose in a sharp gradient through closely planted shrubs. The shrub beds were covered with finely cut forest bark. Several laurustinus and viburnum were already bearing their first white-and-pink winter buds.

Gwyn drew up the car, short of the weathered stone porch.

He got out and looked around. On the opposite side of the valley, beyond dark cypress branches, cattle were grazing in a rich aftermath: deep green grass from the heavy autumn rains that had followed the brown drought of summer. It was very quiet. The air was damply soft. There was nobody in sight.

He walked through the porch, with its lines of rubber boots and walking sticks, and rapped the ring knocker on the big weathered oak door.

The moment had now at last come. All the hesitations of the summer, punctuated by the sudden decisions that he would on no account go, had been put behind him. Waking this morning, in the Americanised hotel, after the two-day conference in Taunton, he had suddenly known that he would be going; that the struggle to keep away had been resolved, perhaps lost. And it had then seemed necessary to go at once: without request, without notice; to go in effect as of right.

The door was not immediately answered. Then he heard the sound of the big handle being turned. He watched with words ready on his lips. As the door swung back a woman in her fifties stood looking at him: a small, stout woman, with braided black hair and dark skin.

'Sir Norman Braose?'

'He is not in the house.'

The accent was foreign, the manner indifferent.

'And you are?'

'I am housekeeper. I am Mrs Martinez.'

'You are Spanish?'

She did not answer. She waited for him to speak again.

'Is Sir Norman away?'

'No. Not away.'

'Is anyone else in the house? Could I speak to someone?'

'Lady Braose is in Chepstow with Lady Fferris. It is for racing. Only Mrs Whitlow still here.'

'Mrs Whitlow?'

A woman was coming down the stairs and turning towards the kitchen. She hesitated.

'What is it, Maria?'

'This man asks for Sir Norman.'

The woman came forward. She was carrying a tray but put it

down on a carved chair. She looked at Gwyn and stopped.

'It's . . .' she said, and smiled.

Gwyn had also recognised her: Alex, whom he had known as Alex Merritt.

'Gwyn,' Alex said. 'Gwyn Lewis.'

She came forward still smiling and holding out her hand.

'You don't remember me,' she said, as they briefly shook hands.

'Yes of course I remember. We met at Emma's.'

'And Jill. How's Jill?'

'She's fine.'

Alex turned.

'That's all right now, Maria,' she said crisply.

Mrs Martinez went through to the back of the house.

'I should have rung or something,' Gwyn said.

'Not a bit of it. Come in.'

'No, I mustn't come in. I just called on the off-chance.'

'Did you want to see Daddy?'

She looked hard at Gwyn as she spoke. In the light of the doorway he saw how much her face had hardened and reddened since that evening at Emma's. As he didn't answer she went on quickly.

'He's fine now. He had the operation and it's made him very much better. I only came down, really, because Phil's in America and I have nothing to keep me in Richmond. You did know I'd married Phil? Phil Whitlow. He works in television.'

'Yes. Mrs Martinez said Mrs Whitlow.'

'It's terrible, isn't it, how we know so little of each other.'

'Yes. Of course. We've never really been in touch.'

She again looked carefully at him, and then made her decision.

'Daddy's in his wood. His new wood, or don't you know that either? He bought it in, to protect it. He spends most of his time there.'

'Is it far?' Gwyn asked.

'No. You probably passed it. Just the other side of the road.'

'Well, perhaps I'll walk down, if you'll—'

She moved forward firmly.

'Not a bit of it. I'll take you. I shall enjoy the walk.'

'No, I mustn't—'

'I'll get on some decent boots.'

She sat in the porch and pulled on green rubber boots, then went back into the hall for a coat. As she came out she looked down at Gwyn's shoes.

'It'll be no good going like that. Pull any of these on if they fit you.'

'It's all right.'

'Gwyn, it isn't all right. Look, here's an old pair of his.'

She picked up the muddy black boots. He took them and sat and pulled them on.

'Right. Come on.'

They walked together past Gwyn's car and down the drive.

'You've been here before, of course,' she said as he walked in silence.

'No.'

She stopped. She faced him.

'Look, Gwyn, I know it's all bloody difficult. But . . .'

'I didn't want to worry you with it.'

'Or worry anybody, I hope. I mean, how long can people keep up these absurd old situations? We all know about it, for God's sake. And we're now old enough ourselves to know how these things happen.'

'Of course.'

'I mean, I don't know about your friends but I know about mine. All this secrecy, all this tension, it's Victorian, for God's sake!'

'In general of course, yes.'

'In general and in particular. I mean, look what it's done. You and I are brother and sister, half-brother and half-sister, and we're talking like strangers.'

'Because we are, Alex.'

'But that's what I'm saying, we shouldn't be. It's all right for adolescents to be guilty and furtive about their parents' sexuality, but for God's sake when we're parents, almost grandparents, ourselves . . .'

'Not Lyn just yet, I think,' Gwyn said, smiling.

'Wait and see. She won't tell you. And Jon, well . . .'

They met each other's eyes. They smiled.

'Anyway by now you must be used to it,' Alex said, walking again. 'You've got other half-brothers and sisters.'

'No, one of each.'

'Well anyway. We're all adults. We live our own lives.'

'The difference is that I grew up with them.'

'Sure you did. But when there's a split the kids have to go somewhere. It happens all the time.'

'There's one other difference. He never married my mother.'

'I know. And in their generation it would have been better if he had. But not in our generation, for God's sake!'

Gwyn didn't answer. They walked through the gate and into the road.

'Actually Mummy never talks about it,' Alex said. 'It was years before she knew. Pippa Fferris told her.'

'Pippa Fferris?'

'Yes, I think she was another of his early loves. She's a tough Tory lady. She and Mummy are great friends.'

They turned down a narrow lane beside a wood.

'This is it,' Alex said. 'There's a stile further down.'

'He bought it, you say?'

'Yes. It was going to be felled.'

They reached the stile and Alex climbed over. She turned back as he was climbing.

'Don't embarrass him with anything, Gwyn.'

He stopped, straddling the stile.

'It's not what you've been talking about,' he said; 'it's not that at all.'

'Something else?' she asked anxiously.

'Not to do with me.'

He jumped down from the stile. The ground was wet. In the overgrown wood there were patches where moss had taken over from the grass. As they stood looking into the shadows of the trees there was a sudden loud gunshot. They turned and looked at each other.

'Alex, is that him?' Gwyn asked, tensely.

'I don't know. Probably. He sometimes takes his shotgun.'

Gwyn stared into her face. She seemed to reflect his own alarm. They hurried forward, pushing through the wild undergrowth.

'More to the left,' Gwyn said breathlessly.

Alex stopped. She cupped her hands and called.

'Daddy! Cooee!'

There was no answer. Gwyn, feeling his heart racing, seemed suddenly detached from all ordinary processes. It was as if he were seeing, from outside, these two figures in the wood: half-brother and half-sister; the man in his dark office suit and raincoat, grey-haired, silent; the woman in her yellow tweed coat, with the marks of sadness and drink in her face; and beyond them, unseen, their common father, the wraith as Pitter had called him – the hidden, hiding father, with a shotgun.

Alex was pushing forward again. There was a thick undergrowth of bramble, the leaves dark green and red, old dead light-brown stalks grown through by young and self-rooting growths. Alex stopped again, and just as she did so there was the crack of another shot. It sounded much nearer, off to their right. A pigeon flapped away through the trees.

'Daddy! Cooee!'

'Here,' came a high clear voice.

They pushed through towards it.

'Ah, there you are,' Alex said, relieved.

Norman was standing with his shotgun broken open over his curved right arm. He was wearing a belted camouflage military jacket and waterproof trousers, with high green rubber boots. His head was bare, the hair thin and white. He was smiling.

'What are you shooting, for God's sake?' Alex asked.

'Rabbits.'

'I've brought Gwyn.'

'I can see.'

He came forward, still smiling, and shook Gwyn's hand.

'A little marginal destruction for a greater conservation,' he said easily. 'The prolific little buggers gnaw the bark from my saplings.'

He was still holding Gwyn's hand. Gwyn, embarrassed, drew slightly away.

'Anyway, now that I've found you,' Alex said, 'I'll get back to the house. I'm expecting a phone call.'

'Fine, darling.'

'Bring Gwyn up for lunch. I'll tell Maria.'

'Fine.'

She went back more directly through the wood. Norman turned away.

'Do you shoot?' he asked over his shoulder.

'No.'

'Then let me just show you the wood. I have exciting plans for it.'

He led the way through to a more open area, where there were fine mature beeches and a heavy litter of leaves, without undergrowth. They walked more easily until they reached a fence which had been wooden post-and-rail but was now rotten and broken in several places and had been reinforced with pig wire. Norman stopped, looking out at the adjacent field. He took two yellow cartridges from a pouch pocket, and reloaded the gun.

'I wondered if you would come,' he said, as if casually.

'I wasn't sure,' Gwyn said.

'Well, I was expecting somebody. And if anyone then preferably you.'

He turned and smiled. Gwyn noticed, as at their first meeting, the incongruity between the words and the manner.

'I don't understand,' he said, looking at the field, which was green with winter turnips, for the sheep.

'Well, Monkey passes things on,' Norman said, easily, looking along the fence and holding his gun ready.

'You mean what he told me?' Gwyn said, carefully.

'Yes, of course.'

'Is it true?'

Norman lifted the gun, still looking intently along the fence, and then lowered it. He turned and looked directly at Gwyn.

'What do you think?'

Gwyn stared at him. The skin of the fine-drawn, still handsome face was pink and clear. The expression was even and amiable.

'Monkey always tells the truth,' Norman added. 'But selectively. Precisely selected messages to precisely selected receivers. It was our common trade.'

'You mean he selected both me and his version?'

'He selected you.'

'I was afraid,' Gwyn said, 'that I'd forced his hand. After

the different accounts that I'd heard, I had no idea what to believe.'

'Nobody forces Monkey's hand,' Norman said, again tentatively raising the gun.

'It was my last resort, I suppose,' Gwyn said.

Norman turned and looked at him.

'Not here?'

'Not here.'

Norman stood very still. He reached down and broke open the gun. He put the cartridges back in his pouch.

'Nor elsewhere? Nowhere official?'

He was smiling as he spoke.

'What do you take me for?' Gwyn asked angrily.

'I don't know, Gwyn. That's rather often been the question.'

'I simply don't understand how you can live with all that you've done,' Gwyn said fiercely.

'You don't? But of course you don't. Because yours has been a much easier life.'

Gwyn turned away. On the edge of the damp wood, in his city suit and country boots, he felt out of place and disadvantaged.

'You suppose,' Norman said, 'that you inherited hardship and difficulty. In fact you didn't. Others fought and opened your road. So if you try to understand this from some bearings of your own, you may reach some rhetorical judgment but you'll never know what it has actually been.'

'Some idealism, I suppose. Some mistaken idealism and we all make mistakes. Isn't that what you'd say?'

'No, it isn't what I'd say. But look, shall we walk? It sometimes makes it clearer.'

He led the way under the big beeches. They began walking between them, on the damp litter of leaves and mast.

'It wasn't idealism,' Norman said clearly, 'that made me, from the beginning, want a more secure and more rational society. It was an intellectual judgment, to which I still hold. When I was young its name was socialism. We can be deflected by names. But the need was absolute, and is still absolute. So many dangerous and powerful forces are loose, more dangerous and more powerful than we can ever fully understand. So in intelligence and conscience we are bound to oppose them, by such means as we can find. You may think you accept this, but until you've gone through it you can't understand it. Someone like you can look back and identify this or that error, this or that disappointment or deception. But that's not really what they are or what they cost. Only we who lived them know the true cost. And a terror then comes, not so much in any danger of disgrace or punishment but in the appalling reminder that none of us, at any time, can know enough, can understand enough, to avoid getting much of it wrong.'

'Yes, perhaps. But then others, who are innocent, also carry the cost.'

'Of course. That is where we began. By trying to prevent that. By trying to get things right.'

'I don't know what you tried. I only know what you did.'

'And you reject it?'

'Absolutely. It was the worst possible thing you could have done.'

Norman stopped and poked with his foot at a large light-brown fungus cap. Then, holding his gun by the end of the double barrel, he stooped and examined the fungus more closely. Gwyn watched him, without really looking.

'You had better put your case,' Norman said, still examining the fungus.

'My case? Isn't it obvious? Any real socialism depends on an actual society. I grew up in such a society, under pressure and hardship but still with its own bonds, its own loyalties. And then no authentic act for socialism can distance itself, let alone hide, from these ties of its own people.'

Norman looked up and smiled, sadly.

'What you did,' Gwyn went on, fiercely, 'was an alien variation within the norms of your own class. You say for a more rational society, and you were convinced, I suppose, that the old men of your class were stupid and incompetent and therefore destructive. So you looked for a way of replacing them. For a means to another kind of power. And you thought you had found it with this alliance in your head. An alliance between a native working class, that you would instruct and lead, and a foreign state and social order of which you really knew nothing but which you thought would act to displace your old world.'

Norman stared up as Gwyn spoke. The faint smile had gone and he was now listening intently.

'You have been a class of betrayers,' Gwyn said angrily. 'You have always fought your internal battles by recruiting and using genuine popular interests or by lining up with some alien power. Or, as in your case, both. And then all that is new is that you damaged something authentic, something that had grown under the weight of you and in your own soil. You betrayed your own countrymen, but always and everywhere your class had been doing that, to serve its own interests. Your special betrayal was that you involved and damaged the only substance, the only hope, of our people. You involved and damaged socialism: our own kind of hope but converted by people like you to a distant and arbitrary and alien power. You say you carry the cost. A whole people is carrying the cost. And this makes it more than an error. It makes it an assault, on good people. It can never be forgiven. It will not be forgiven.'

Norman was still for some time. Then, putting his weight on the gun, he pushed himself up. He looked quickly at Gwyn as he rose. He was frowning. There were deep hard lines in the flesh between his thin eyebrows.

'Are the Communist Party exempted from this?'

'Yes, to the extent that they worked in and for their own people.'

'Bert Lewis, for example?'

'Yes, Bert Lewis. And he carried the cost. She showed me her painting: the face ravaged by fighting. What have you to put beside that?'

'He volunteered in a foreign war. For a social order of which he really knew nothing.'

'He fought beside poor people and for poor people. And then he fought the SS Death's Head. It made his face ugly. I said that it was beautiful and she couldn't bear it. She knew the fight for what it was.'

Norman hesitated. He lifted the gun to the curve of his arm.

'I respect Bert Lewis of course,' he said, firmly.

'Yes, the real fighter.'

'One of the real fighters. If still in a lost war. But what I won't

take from you is some sentimental substitution. You are not
Bert Lewis. You are not even his son.'

'I am trying to speak for him,' Gwyn said angrily.

He had felt tears start to his eyes.

'You can't, Gwyn. You have no real right. But it doesn't
matter. I know your kind of argument.'

'You can never accept it.'

'I don't want to accept it. It's a morass of illusion and rhetoric.
As what you call your own countrymen are now thoroughly
demonstrating.'

'What are they demonstrating?'

Norman's face cleared.

'Simply that what you and they call socialism, what we too
called socialism, is not in fact either practical or desired. For
that, if you will look, is the long error that has damaged so
many of our lives. There are needs and ends that are profoundly
necessary, but it was that old socialist hypothesis, that limited
short-cut, that deceived us. You abuse what you call my class
but what you are really abusing is knowledge and reason. By
the way the society is, it is here, with us, that ideas are generated.
So it has been with socialism: at once the good ideas and the
errors. Yet we have begun to correct them, and this is all that
can be done. In reason and conscience our duty now is not to
something called socialism, it is to conserving and saving the
earth. Yet nothing significant for either is generated among what
you call your fellow countrymen. Indeed that is, precisely, their
deprivation. It is also their inadequacy, and then what are
you asking of me? That I should be loyal to ignorance, to
shortsightedness, to prejudice, because these exist in my fellow
countrymen? That I should stay still and connive in the destruction of the earth because my fellow countrymen are taking part
in it? And that I should do this because of some traditional
scruple, that I am bound to inherit a common inadequacy, a
common ignorance, because its bearers speak the same tongue,
inhabit the same threatened island? What morality, really, do
you propose in that?'

'The morality of shared existence,' Gwyn said, firmly. 'Shared
existence and shared knowledge.'

Norman walked on. He stopped and looked closely at the

smooth grey bark of a beech. Around his feet were the empty husks of a heavy crop of beech nuts, still breaking in their clusters. He turned and walked back towards Gwyn, still holding the gun.

'This kind of argument isn't possible between us,' he said, stopping and smiling. 'As a son you are trying to judge me by some project of your own. But we've never shared that, have we? Never shared it as father and son. You grew up with others, and you love them, as you must. And then within that love you try to see the world in their way, though you are already in practice removed from it. So that you cling to these old and useless ideas, as a way of clinging to those people.'

Gwyn folded his arms.

'I didn't expect this of you,' he said bitterly, 'even after what Pitter had told me. I didn't expect this contempt for other people, though of course I should have known it. Not so much from your spying, though even there what you must face is that in the end you betrayed the very people you'd been working with, betrayed them in order to get out clear yourself. But it was all there before that. It was there when you used and then deserted my mother.'

'Is that how you see it?'

'Of course.'

'Is it how she sees it?'

'I don't know. I think she must. But she has put it behind her.' Norman smiled.

'Other people too must survive,' Gwyn said angrily, 'do what they can to survive. And those who have met you have learned that lesson the hard way. Whenever it was necessary, you betrayed every one of them.'

Norman stared at the litter at his feet. Without looking up he reached into a pocket and took out two red cartridges. He opened the gun and loaded it. He looked across at Gwyn.

'If I were to accept that as true . . .' he said, lightly, and stopped.

Gwyn stared at the gun.

'It would be expected, I take it,' Norman went on, 'that I should do the decent thing and blow my brains out.'

Gwyn stamped impatiently.

'I'm not staying here to listen to his.'

He turned and began walking away. Behind him he heard the sound of Norman cocking the gun.

'Gwyn,' Norman called.

Gwyn stopped but did not turn or answer.

'It's what you want, isn't it?' Norman asked in a quiet voice.

Gwyn held himself still. There was a sudden loud explosion behind him, the two barrels fired almost together. He swung round, gasping. Norman was standing with the gun pointing down at the ground. White smoke was still rising above his arms.

Gwyn stared, unbelievingly, and then walked on, in what he hoped was the direction of the stile. But he went a roundabout way. When he at last found the stile, Norman was standing beside it, holding the gun in his curved arm. Gwyn made to get over the stile, but Norman stood in his way and did not move.

'Do you now begin to understand how serious this is?' Norman said.

'I've always known that it's serious.'

'Yes, perhaps, in some general way. That you would confront me with some charge of immorality and desertion, or that you would bring out your routine arguments about class and socialism and loyalty. But none of that, I tell you, is life, and what you are now facing, or are afraid to face, is just that. Not your generalities but a life.'

Gwyn shifted impatiently.

'Let me through.'

'No. Not until we have talked.'

'We've talked enough. There's nothing left to say.'

'There's everything left to say. What you have said so far you could have said at a meeting. Or to the wind, which might pay more attention. But you came here, after all. You came to see me and to try to understand.'

'Not really that,' Gwyn said quietly. 'But it had to be said to your face.'

Norman smiled.

'To me as object, exactly. But you should have more courage. You should be prepared, for a change, to listen.'

Gwyn hesitated. Norman stood aside. Gwyn looked at him

and then climbed over the stile. Norman followed him. They walked in silence up the narrow lane.

'Let me try to put it in this way,' Norman said as they reached the road. 'Any of the means may change or deceive us, but the ends do not. Through my whole lifetime there has been a sharing of error, whatever choices we tried honestly to make. It has been a common history of errors and lies and deceptions, in which we have all in fact been guilty.'

Gwyn glanced across at him. The expression was intense and assured. They paced the road, slowly.

'One way out of that,' Norman said firmly, 'is to isolate some group, some party, some individuals even, and push all the guilt on to them. It is convenient and reassuring and self-righteous. But for some of us that isn't possible. By some accident of exposure we have to face the whole truth: not to excuse either ourselves or others but still to look for some way of redemption.'

They passed the gate to the house. Norman did not look at it but walked on. A farm truck, coming towards them, slowed. The young man who was driving it lifted his arm and waved. Norman waved cheerfully back.

'This is available to Christians,' he continued, 'indeed only to them as some organised belief. I have felt very close to them but still quite unable to share all the rest of their beliefs, which seem to me plainly impossible. Nevertheless, the emphasis is right. The only way open to any of us is a long and patient pilgrimage.'

A woman on a bicycle overtook them. Norman called good morning and she turned and smiled, returning the greeting.

'A pilgrimage to what?' Gwyn asked sharply.

'To life itself,' Norman said. 'To our shared life and all its processes. I tell you, Gwyn, in that wood I learn more in an hour than in all the labelled, alienated arguments of the world. And I put myself in relation to it, understanding reason and civilisation in quite new ways. In a hundred years none of that other part of my life will matter, but the trees I have planted will be growing, the clearings I have made will be nourishing life, and though I shall have been forgotten my one small part of the essential pilgrimage will have been accomplished, within other lives.'

Gwyn stopped. They were in the middle of the road. A lorry

came towards them, loaded high with straw. The top of the load was brushing off on the low overhanging branches. They pressed themselves into the bank. The driver blew his horn in acknowledgment. Norman waved as he passed.

Gwyn moved back to the centre of the road. He looked at Norman, who was now regarding him steadily.

'No,' Gwyn said.

Norman frowned.

'No,' Gwyn repeated. 'I don't accept this either. It's your revised version of what you once called communism. And in either version it is a frame for your ego. For your indifferent self and for its interests.'

'That's very unfair.'

'The truth can be unfair, when someone has lived as you have. What you once thought about communism, what you now think about nature, is no more than a projection of what suited you at the time. The fact that for others each belief is substantial merely enabled you to deceive them. For with them it is a bond. It imposes trust and continuity. It is that imposition which makes their choice real.'

'You think mine is not real?'

'I know it is not real. You are a master not a servant of anything. You turn your very weaknesses to an always convenient adjustment. So that now as before you are unfit to relate to others, and because of that you corrupt every belief you assume.'

Norman put his hand to his face.

'You know me well enough, you think, to make a bitter judgment like that?'

'I don't know you privately. It is enough that I know what you've done.'

'The shout of the barbarian,' Norman said, shifting his gun, 'announcing the triumph of public language, public record, public power, over each and every personal reality.'

Gwyn turned and walked back towards the gate. Norman followed him. Gwyn quickened his pace. Norman half-stumbled to keep up.

'In my world,' Gwyn said, as they turned into the steep drive, 'the personal and the political come in the same breath. We have no space to separate them.'

Norman looked down as they walked.

'Your world?' he said, quietly. 'A world I visited and left, a world you grew up in and left. It's there, yes, but not for either of us. Why don't you admit this? Why can't you be honest?'

'I am trying to be honest,' Gwyn said, angrily. 'I am trying to carry this forward. I am trying to get beyond this rejection of socialism which you and all the rest have arrived at.'

Norman stopped and faced him.

'As a fighter, would you say? For it requires that, your social-ism.'

'It isn't just an inheritance, that's all I'm saying. It isn't only an obligation. It's a position now. It's a contemporary direction. It's a way of learning our future.'

Norman hesitated.

'I'm glad you can believe that,' he said harshly, and walked on.

They moved together by the shrubs of the drive. Norman was looking closely at each shrub as they passed. They stopped by Gwyn's car. There was a difficult silence.

'Alex invited you to lunch,' Norman said.

Gwyn swung round on him. The manner had settled again. The handsome face was relaxed and assured.

'Do you think I would enter your house?' Gwyn asked, angrily.

Norman smiled. His confidence, Gwyn saw, had repossessed him. He was now easy and worldly, offering open house before the fine stone façade.

'As Birdie's son, you would be welcome,' Norman said, smil-ing.

'As *her* son? But that is a rejection.'

'Of course, Gwyn. It happened. Why can't you be honest?'

'It didn't just happen. You made it happen.'

'Yes, perhaps. What you call the personal and the political in the same breath. And then, as Monkey likes to say, I'm not asking you to accept it, I'm simply telling you what happened.'

'I know what happened. I know what happened to her. And you still can't even give her her own proper name.'

Norman smiled.

'Nesta? I know. Nesta Pritchard. Nesta Lewis. But for me,

you see, she is Birdie. She has always been Birdie. Another life I might have lived.'

'You chose not to live it.'

'I chose and was chosen. You will find that, if you look, in your socialism.'

Gwyn went to the porch. He pulled off the wet rubber boots. He relaced his shoes.

'So you won't come in?' Norman said, standing watching him.

'No.'

'There's no reason why you shouldn't. I'd have thought you might be interested. You spent the first weeks of your life in this house.'

Gwyn looked up, startled. His face had reddened, bending over to lace the shoes. He pulled his car keys from his pocket and got up quickly. Norman watched him go and then followed him to the car.

'Goodbye,' Gwyn said.

He opened the door and pushed in behind the wheel. Norman moved and stood close.

'There is still some public danger,' Gwyn said, hurriedly. 'It's still very probable that it will all come out and be published.'

Norman smiled. He grasped the car door handle.

'I am used to living with that,' he said, and made what seemed a slight bow as he bent to the door. He then slammed the door shut.

# LAST

Jon pushed his head cautiously round Allicon's door. Allicon was sprawled in a tipped-back chair, with his feet on the desk. His plump neck was creased to hold the telephone inside his open grey denim shirt. Jon made to withdraw, but Allicon pointed at him, imperiously, and then at a chair. Jon went in and sat to wait.

'Yup,' Allicon said, after a long interval. Then after another long interval, 'Yup' again.

Jon stared at the deeply indented plastic soles. There was reddish sand in the cuts.

'Right. See you,' Allicon said suddenly, and put down the phone.

He swung his legs down and let the chair fall back into place.

'Jon, comrade-in-arms,' he said, smiling.

'You got my report?'

'It's there. I haven't read it.'

'Why?'

'I rely on the spoken word. And the acted word. I am post-Gutenberg.'

'But you got my first message? That I'd failed to get Pitter in London?'

'Yes. Petra told me.'

Jon leaned forward, eagerly.

'There was only an answering machine at his apartment. It

said he was abroad and that business would be done at his New York office.'

'Which you called?'

'Yes. And that's the odd thing. On the phone I got it quite clearly. That he was there and that I could come and make an appointment. Then when I arrived they said that he was away indefinitely. And that was odd too. The receptionist said he was on the West Coast but a man I got to see said he was in the Caribbean. In either case, they agreed, unavailable.'

'Monk Pitter Futures,' Allicon said and clasped his hands. 'So?'

'So I came back. What else could I do?'

Allicon looked at him intently.

'Who authorised your trip to New York? Phil Whitlow?'

'No. Since you weren't here I went to Mackay.'

'But you see Phil Whitlow?'

'As I explained, not often.'

'He's your mother's husband. Second husband.'

'I usually see her on her own.'

'Alex? Who used to be Alex Merritt?'

'Who used to be called Alex Merritt.'

Allicon smiled and unclasped his hands.

'I ask, my dear Jon, because it seems we are suddenly in favour with Phil Whitlow.'

'That's nothing to do with me.'

'I'm glad to hear you say that. It restores my self-respect. Because he rang and said he'd had a view of the first two *Grains*. He said how impressed he was. Almost as if he was surprised.'

Jon shifted on his chair.

'I've never talked television with him. But from what my mother tells me about some of his ideas—'

'He is a good commercial man,' Allicon said, sternly.

'Right.'

Allicon got up and stretched. He went to the window and stared out at the grey brick wall.

'We'll forget Monkey Pitter,' he said, suddenly.

'Monkey? I've only heard him called Monk.'

'Monk or Monkey, we'll forget him. Don't you think?'

'If you say so.'

Allicon turned slowly.

'Did you think yourself that there was anything in it? Your report, it seemed to me, was excessively cautious.'

Jon stared back at him. The summarising words were ready in his mind, but Allicon, as before, was disconcerting.

'I wasn't sure, Jock. I worked hard on the technical stuff. I did a lot of back-reading. The difficulty is that early computing history has so many lines of development and what's been written, with any seriousness, is mostly specialist studies, leaving all sorts of gaps. Some of the stuff is still secret anyway. There's a haze, in the Fifties, around air defence systems, and then later on submarines. It would be the guidance systems that matter, but only the commercial lines are reasonably clear. Yet on what was in the dossier . . . You've got it still, by the way? I thought it would be safer here.'

'Phil Whitlow borrowed it.'

'Whitlow! But why?'

'Finish your report first.'

'Right. Okay. On what was in the dossier there was either a string of remarkable coincidences – but those happen in technology – or else there was, as suggested, some sustained espionage.'

'By Pitter?'

Jon frowned.

'Well! On either hypothesis he was in most of the right places at most of the right times.'

'On his own?'

'There's nothing on that. Apart from a list of dates, of where he was in the war, there's only the general technical material, and then the press cuttings, American cuttings, when he was dismissed from his university.'

'That's all that points to him?'

'In any definite way, yes.'

Allicon returned to his desk.

'That shows Phil Whitlow was right, then.'

'What has he to do with it?'

'Nothing. That's the point. It's all been much simpler than for a while I supposed. All that actually happened was that he saw the first two *Grains*. He liked them and he was sure he could make an American sale. But then of course he wanted to look at the third, the spies. I ran him the bits we'd got and then I told him about Pitter.'

'And he borrowed the file?'

'Right. He seemed very keen on it. But this is where it began to seem complicated. He rang a few days later and asked me to lunch. He had a project to offer me.'

'On this Pitter business?'

'No. That was hardly mentioned. In fact in the end I had to remind him, and incidentally he's still got the file. When I reminded him he just said, which had already crossed my mind, that we would only weaken *Grain Three* if we included this rather loose and unproved material. What we had already was good, hard, spectacular stuff.'

'I see.'

Allicon looked down at his hands. He seemed to be trying to control his breathing. He rubbed nervously at his thinning grey hair.

'He said one other interesting thing. He said that he'd talked about it to Sir Norman Braose.'

'What?'

Allicon smiled.

'I hadn't realised, Jon, that you were so triply well connected.'

'Triply?'

'Phil Whitlow. Alec Merritt. Sir Norman Braose.'

'He's my grandfather. My mother's father.'

'Yes. So Phil told me. A sort of three-headed silver spoon.'

Jon leaned forward again.

'No, all that surprises me,' he said quickly, 'is that Whitlow talked to my grandfather about it. It's been understood for years, in the family, that we don't bother him with that. It was his work, of course, and much of that is still secret. But it was mainly that he'd become disillusioned with it. He'd retired early and switched to his work on trees and conservation.'

'No more nasty machines?'

'It was the maths and the languages he'd worked on. But from when I was a child, and in fact getting interested in it, my mother was very firm that I shouldn't take it to him.'

'Right,' Allicon said.

He put his feet on the desk again and tipped back his chair.

'Yet Phil Whitlow, I suppose,' he said softly, 'as a more recent member of the family . . .'

'He wouldn't get anything from him.'

'Yes. That's what Phil said. Apart from a clear impression that it was all much too complicated for any amateurs to touch.'

'Yes. It probably is.'

'Though he did gather from his wife that her father and Monk Pitter had once been colleagues.'

'I didn't know that.'

Allicon stared. He searched Jon's face. Then he abruptly swung down his legs and let his weight push down the chair.

'It's very loose, very complicated and a long time ago,' he said, judicially.

Jon looked away.

'I suppose it is. Though now I've started . . .'

'You have an academic itch. Our fleeting images will eventually soothe it. But not tonight.'

'No, I didn't mean for a programme. But when I got into the material I started really thinking about it. Not just the technical case, though I'd like to understand that and I think I eventually may. But the hard questions were about that curious life, that curious time.'

'It's no use, Jon. We can't bring it back.'

'We don't have to bring it back. In fact it comes through to us. Whether we know it or not, it's been shaping some of our lives.'

'You mean because of your grandfather?'

'No, you've only just told me about that. And I've no idea what it amounts to. Though I shall ask, you can be sure of that.'

'Why, exactly? To uncover some secret?'

'That's what you asked me to do. You say now you don't want it, but I can't leave it like that. The whole thing comes too close, the pressures and then the decisions. And some of them have helped to form us. We all say we have our own lives but many of us have been formed by this kind of past.'

'It makes a difference how close it may come.'

'Of course. But still also quite generally. In what we think and say, and in what we've learned not to think and not to say.'

'Not to ask about, even? Too complicated for amateurs to touch?'

'You keep implying that about him. I'm going to find out if it's true. But not just about these particular men. I want to know what the whole shape was. The whole shape and pressure of that life. And not just what was done but its actual doing, day by day.'

'You won't get that.'

'It's what I shall ask. There's this rhetoric of the young, that we can all start afresh. What I'm saying is that we can only start at all if we really know what was done: not as error, not as scandal, though in the end it might be either, but by people in real and uncertain situations: people in that sense like ourselves, rather than figures in a history.'

'It'll take you a long way.'

'I mean it to take me a long way. Because the question I'm also putting is how someone like myself should live and act now, in as much danger and in as much uncertainty.'

'You mean you're identifying with them?'

'No, not at all. But actually identifying them, yes.'

Allicon rubbed his hand over his eyes.

'I got you into this,' he said.

'Okay.'

'You seem to be taking it hard.'

'Yes, I thought I'd explained.'

'Tommy Meurig was the same. When he heard that you were working on it, and that Phil Whitlow was involved – Phil who is married to Alex who is the daughter of Braose who was a colleague of Pitter.'

Allicon was staring into Jon's face as he spoke. Then he looked away, smiling sadly.

'Actors, Jon, I understand. I say, darling – anguish. Darling – passion, confusion, curiosity, blissful contentment. And the thing is, you see, they then do it. Can do it. Amateurs on the other hand do not. Cannot. Though doubtless they have one or another – who knows which? – of those emotions.'

'So?'

'So Tommy Meurig's face was bad rep.'

'I don't understand.'

'Right. There's a lot of it about.'

'Anyway, Meurig is working on something else.'

'Was.'

Jon waited. Allicon smiled.

'Jon, comrade-in-arms, I've been saving my only useful surprise.'

'What is it?'

'Years ago, before the wee buggers upstairs were anything like so powerful, and indeed while there were still a few of them not trying to paddle in mid-Atlantic . . .'

Jon shifted on his chair.

'. . . I had this big idea for a series. All the others were still bowing and scraping around the Tudor court. I proposed that if we wanted real intrigue, real colour, really extraordinary characters and conflicts, and none of it as costume drama, all of it connecting to ourselves, there was only one real time. The English Radicals and Romantics during the French Revolution.'

He beamed at Jon. He extended his arm and pointed a thick finger.

'A world-historical moment, and great men living through it. Wordsworth in France, and his revolutionary love-child! Young Cobbett accusing his officers of corruption! William Godwin and anarchism, Mary Wollstonecraft and feminism! Blake naked in visions and seeing the world transformed! Tom Paine in France and America! And then the children of that time. Mary Wollstonecraft Godwin going to Italy with Shelley! *Frankenstein* and *Prometheus Unbound*! Byron in Greece! Sam Coleridge sunk in opium!'

'I see the material,' Jon said, carefully.

'No, you don't see it. If you did you'd be jumping up and down. It would enlarge our screens by a quantum leap. And none of it costume. Radicals, feminists, utopians, revolutionaries, and one of the world's great events cutting across and into their lives. People said then, you know, that the English radicals were just agents of the French. They put agents to spy on them. Agents and *agents provocateurs*! They imprisoned and beat them down. So that first generation ageing, conforming, apostasising, drugged! But then suddenly a new generation: poets and rebels;

sexual freedom and political liberation! The high passions of our future!'

'It would be difficult to do,' Jon said, again carefully.

'I'm talking about a series, Jon. A dramatic series.'

'Based on those lives?'

'On the intercut of those lives. The people and the politics. The sad and muddled passions of our own time at once foreshadowed and projected in these legendary figures. At once life and larger than life.'

'Colour in distance,' Jon said.

'And whatever's wrong with that?'

'Nothing, I suppose. But our own time only *seems* smaller. Historical distance makes it too clear, too colourful. I mean, when it offers in any way to connect.'

'You'd prefer, you still think, to connect with Pitter and the others?'

'To connect anyway. Not to watch it as spectacle.'

'I know what you mean. But you can ask all the questions you like; it's still those other lives, those other people.'

'Putting questions back to us, if it really connects.'

'The bigger the people the bigger the questions,' Allicon said decisively.

He stood up.

'They employ writers,' he said scornfully, 'to address their word-processors and find interesting material. But here, in our own history, is a story running over with causes and excitements, passions and sensations, beyond anything these pallid suburbans could concoct. Phil saw the possibilities at once.'

'You mean this is the new project?'

'It is. He's lining it up. And as a big co-production. Eight, perhaps ten.'

'With actors?'

'With actors.'

'Darling, anguish? Darling, a cause?'

'You're seeing it too small, Jon. It's the sweep that matters. From conspiratorial meetings in London to revolutionary crowds in France! Gaols and hangings in England; poetry and liberation in Italy and Greece! Petra, as you can imagine, is as near frenzy as her controls allow. She's already scouring the galleries. Think of the paintings of that time for a start! It's all very extraordinary, however you look at it. It will put everything else of its kind in the shade.'

'Yes,' Jon said.

Allicon sat at his desk again.

'Phil already knew of my idea. Though when it first went in he wasn't senior enough to help. But now, having seen the *Grains* . . .'

'Was this when you met at lunch?'

'Yes. It was why he asked me.'

'When he also hardly mentioned our file on Pitter?'

'Our file? Come on. It was Tommy Meurig's file. It always meant more to him than to us.'

Jon got up.

'Okay,' he said slowly.

Allicon looked at him, surprised.

'Where are you going?' he asked sharply.

'I don't know. I supposed that since you were dropping Pitter . . .'

'That I wouldn't need you? For God's sake!'

'I don't see what else I could do, that's all. You've got your original material for the espionage programme. You remember, the boring old spies.'

'Right. But now all that really matters is this new series! The Revolution coming up!'

'I know nothing about any of that.'

Allicon looked down at his big, thick-fingered hands. He smiled.

'Phil said I could ask for anyone I wanted! For the initial research through to treatment.'

'So?'

'So I asked for Tommy Meurig.'

'Right. Okay.'

'He understands this underground politics. But he didn't want to come. He's involved in this terrorist business, half across the world.'

'So?'

'So Phil suggested a swap. You on these faraway terrorists, Tommy with me on the Revolution.'

'And?'

'It's still being talked over. He's not keen to change again. But I didn't only ask for Tommy Meurig. I asked also for you.'

'Why? I'd be no good at it.'

'With all your connections? All right, you're less experienced than Tommy. Yet I've known from the beginning that you and I could work together.'

'You mean, whatever Meurig decides?'

'Forget Meurig. You, Jon, have to decide. But I can tell you what he'll do. He thinks long term. When the relative prospects are weighed in the balance he will know, as a good professional, where his career must take him.'

'That's what you mean, I suppose, by professional loyalty?'

Allicon rubbed at his grey fringe.

'Jon, it's how things happen. It's how real things get done.'

'Yes but if these events are connected: Pitter, my grandfather, Phil Whitlow, your new series . . .'

Allicon's eyes narrowed.

'Are you saying that they're connected?'

'If they are, I don't want it. Yes, I followed the thread you gave me but it was landing somewhere else. And into quite different questions of loyalty.'

'Which may bear, Jon, if you think about it, rather closely and embarrassingly on you!'

Jon waited. He looked past Allicon to the grey wall beyond the window.

'Even so,' he said, quietly.

He went to the door and opened it. Allicon stood from his desk. He extended his arm and pointed his finger.

'As I said at the beginning,' he shouted, 'you'll cut and run.'

Jon stood holding the door. The edge of the wood was between his fingers.

'I told you. I have these questions to ask. Open questions.'